JASON JOHNSON
AND THE
FINAL
CONFRONTATION

A FATHER STRUGG~~~ SURVIVE WOR~

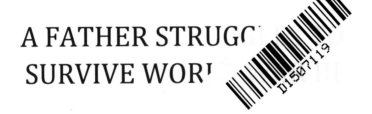

BY
JOHN BERRY

ACKNOWLEDGEMENTS

Cover Artist---Kathy Berry

Story Consultant---Kathy Berry

Editor---David Wilson

Copyright 2021, John Berry, BPMC, LLC

All rights reserved. No portion of this book may be reproduced in any form without permission from the author, except as permitted by U.S. copyright law. For permissions contact: John Berry, berry530@comcast.net, 443-690-6412.

ISBN:9798730860476

TABLE OF CONTENTS

CHAPTER ONE---SOMETIME IN THE FUTURE

Just as Dr. Jason Johnson emerges from his new e-car, the tremor hits. He quickly grabs the door frame and freezes. It's much stronger than the one yesterday--- so strong that he starts to lose his grip. He squeezes the door frame tighter, fighting to stop his swaying. Two seconds… four seconds… six seconds… eight seconds… ten seconds. They're lasting longer and coming more often now, like the pattern just before the big ones hit most of the world a month ago. Back then he wondered if that was the earth's final blow against mankind. He was wrong then, but now he's more worried than ever. Despite the severity of this new quake, it is just one of many potentially civilization-destroying phenomena at work.

The earth has also been plagued by monstrous fires, tsunamis, volcanic eruptions, mosquito-borne diseases, and crop failures. A huge but thin cloud of minute particles of volcanic ash circles the earth, creating a permanent haze. One third of the earth's population has been killed--- mostly along coastal and high-density population areas. Food shortages are the rule due to drought, pests and diseases. Starvation is rampant in the underdeveloped countries. Civilization is in trouble. Is this the beginning of the End Times?

In addition to the natural disasters, geo-political and religious tensions have never been higher, mainly because Israel has become a resource-rich country. Earthquakes in the Middle East created fissures that ran from the Saudi Arabian oil fields to caverns under Israel and off its shore. Saudi oil has drained into these caverns. Two years ago, Israel started selling this oil. Now the enraged Saudis not only want the oil back, they want the lost revenue as well. More recently, Israeli archeologists stumbled upon the largest deposit of rare-earth minerals in the world. These discoveries, along with Israel's uncanny ability to turn the desert into fertile agricultural lands, have made Israel wealthy and therefore more hated, especially by Muslims.

Islam now dominates many countries in Europe, Africa, South America, and two states in America. Germany and Sweden are under Sharia law. France is almost there. Southern Iraq, Syria, and Iran have merged into one country called Shiastan, which is controlled by Islamic militants. Democratic Kurdistan was formed from parts of Turkey, Syria, and northern Iraq. Egypt ceded the Sinai Peninsula to the Palestinians, combining it with Gaza to form a new country called Sinai. Israel facilitated the agricultural and industrial blossoming of Sinai, and most Palestinians from the west band have relocated there.

Presently, no single country dominates the world stage. Instead, some like-minded countries have formed alliances. America, Australia, New Zealand, India, Great Britain, non-Muslim Europe, Israel, South Korea, and Japan are in the Democracy Alliance. Russia, China, Turkey, and Shiastan are in another. Muslim countries in the Middle East and North Africa are in another called Allah's League, which has implemented economic and travel sanctions against Israel and Jews world-wide. Russia and China support Allah's League economically and militarily. Tensions in the Middle East are the highest in history. In an effort to prevent the outbreak of hostilities, the UN Secretary General Antonin Mora has been elected to also lead the ten members of the Democracy Alliance in an attempt to create a balance of power. On behalf of the Alliance, Mora signed a protection treaty with Israel, requiring the ten nations to come to Israel's aid in the event of a major attack.

Despite these efforts, the angry rhetoric and threats against Israel have reached an all-time high. Furthermore, the tension has now spread beyond Israel. The quest for dwindling natural resources and the thirst for world domination make a life-ending nuclear World War III a real possibility.

Against this backdrop of natural disasters and world-wide tensions, Jason will soon be pulled from a quiet existence as an engineering manager, and will be thrust into a life-threatening assignment in the defense of Israel. He has no idea that international politics, the potential destruction of the world, and threats to his family will be interwoven into an unexpected world-changing climax of good against evil.

CHAPTER TWO---JASON AND JOSHUA

Jason's once idyllic town of San Marita is slowly dying. The surrounding hills of formally waving golden grass in this small northern California town are now scarred by large swaths of fire-scorched earth. The acrid smell of burned wood still meanders through the countryside. A thin layer of volcanic dust blankets the roof tops and landscape. The town has lost 30% of its population to earthquakes, fires, and mosquito-borne diseases, but recently-developed vaccines and specialized medical treatments have brought these diseases under control--- for now.

After the quake subsides, he looks around nervously but decides to not let it spoil his plans. He is in front of a small dome-shaped home near the edge of town. The house belongs to his ex-wife Kathy. A 39-year-old software PhD of Jewish heritage on his mother's side, Johnson's job title is Vice President of Engineering for defense contractor Progressive Aviation Systems. He has also been on-call to the CIA for the past three months.

He removes his rumpled hat, revealing a slightly high forehead with faint strands of grey in his wavy dark brown hair. His nose is caved-in a little at the bridge from an old football injury when an opponent's foot somehow wedged through his face mask. He was a tinkerer as a child, preferring to work with things instead of cultivating relationships. Naturally, this led him to become a brilliant and creative engineer, quickly advancing up the corporate ladder. He married Kathy in his mid-20s, and they had a son early-on. They have been divorced for six years. Two months ago, he would have been extremely anxious about being around Kathy, but they have recently forgiven each other for the hurt and trauma of their bitter divorce. Now he feels more relaxed in her presence and can actually be friendly towards her for the benefit of their son. He takes a deep breath and raises his eyebrows.

'Well, here goes,' he says to himself as he steps onto the home's walkway, still just a little nervous about seeing his ex-wife again.

Jason feels sympathy for his ex-wife--- living there alone raising a young boy, but he has no romantic interest in her. Their marriage was filled with immaturity, anger, and misunderstandings. Both were holding unresolved issues from their childhoods that hampered their relationship. He said things he shouldn't have. Kathy did, too. They would argue, and then patch things up. The cycle would repeat. As the conflicts accumulated, their marriage became like a broken china plate--- glued back together but never the same again. Eventually the conflicts became intolerable, and their son suffered. Kathy hasn't re-married, nor is she romantically involved.

After his divorce, Jason had a few dates, but his heart wasn't in it. The divorce was long and ugly, and he just didn't feel like jumping into another relationship. His life was consumed with his work plus a couple of good friends and Sunday morning handball. He often worked late. After a couple of years living and eating alone in an unremarkable condo, he realized he missed stimulating female companionship. Then he met Liezel. They married three years ago.

Although he's spent many weekends with his son since the divorce, for some reason there's something apprehensive about this day. He wonders if seeing his ex again is the issue, or is it something else--- maybe the earthquake. As Jason continues his approach to the house, his wrist comm chimes-in. A holographic image pops-up. It's his CIA contact Christian Christopher. It must be something urgent for him to call on a Saturday. "Chris, hi," Jason says. "What's up?"

"Sorry to bother you on a weekend, Johnson, but things have apparently heated up in Israel. They want you and Willis there early next week. They need your help with the drones."

"Already? I thought they wouldn't be ready for us until next month. What gives?"

"I can't tell you, yet. Everything's hushed-up right now, but there's a new serious development. You're booked on a plane Tuesday. The flight info is on your comm. You'll be there for at least three weeks, so pack accordingly. Sorry again to interrupt your Saturday, but at least you'll have the whole weekend. Have a safe trip."

"Will do, Chris. Bye."

Jason frowns. His puzzlement turns to worry. *'This isn't normal,'* he says to himself. *'Why are the Israelis advancing the schedule? I have a bad feeling about this.'* Suddenly, a young boy flies out of the front door, sending it crashing against the front of the house. The windage from the door creates a puff of volcanic ash that drifts along the front of the house. The boy is Jason's son Joshua. He quickly spins around and yells to his mother, "Dad's here, Mom. I'll see you later." Joshua is a gangly, dark-haired fifteen-year-old. As he awkwardly runs down the walkway toward his father, he stumbles a bit in excited anticipation of the outing he and his father have planned. "Hi, Dad. Did you bring it?"

"Yes, Son, it's in the car."

"Great! I was hoping that tremor wouldn't stop you from coming."

They smile at each other. "Of course not," Jason replied. "You didn't really think something like that would keep me from seeing my favorite son, did you?" Jason winks.

Joshua's mother pops her head out of the front door, a large strand of unkept hair dangling across one eye. She's grasping the front of a drab and frayed old robe, holding it closed near her neck. She's not wearing any make-up. "Have him home before dark please, Jay." Kathy can't help noticing that Jason is still the tall, handsome, well-built man she was attracted to years ago, despite his slight mid-life bulge above his belt. But as they both painfully learned, physical attraction cannot overcome major sources of conflict in a marriage.

"Don't worry, Kathy. Just track us if we're not back by six."

Jason and Joshua hug. "Let's see it, Dad," he blurts excitedly. Jason opens the car door to reveal a large multi-colored box on the front seat. Joshua leans-in with eyes wide open in excitement, and yanks the cover off to reveal a high-tech drone. "Wow, Dad, this looks super! Let's go!"

They climb into their seats. Passenger restraints automatically nestle against their bodies and the sides of their heads. Jason presses a couple of buttons on the dashboard, and says, "Destination: Brown's field." The wedge-shaped car takes-off with a faint whine.

"Wait a minute," Joshua says in a puzzled voice, "This is a new car, isn't it? When did ya' get it, Dad? It looks cool!"

"I've only had it a week. It's an FSE 300--- powered by hydrogen fuel cells, a solar panel, and solid-state batteries. So far, I haven't had to re-fuel the fuel cells, and it's easy to drive. It knows my voice, and only responds to me unless I over-ride the voice recognition. I can tell it to lock the doors, open the trunk, go to a destination, and other things. It has Artificial Intelligence, so it keeps going even if I fall asleep in it. And I don't even have to touch the steering bar if I don't want to. Check-out the holographic trip screen."

They drive past whole neighborhoods where vacant or burned-down houses have been demolished by the state--- a sad reminder of the pleasant days of San Marita before the natural disasters cursed the earth. So many people died that an over-supply of abandoned homes developed. Joshua and Kathy, for example, were living with her brother and his wife until both of them were killed in an earthquake while at work. Without their income, the home became unaffordable by Joshua's mother alone. She's fortunate that a small less expensive recently-built home was available. After a pause, Jason inquires, "So anyway, what do you think of your new house?"

"It's okay, I guess. It looks funny, though--- kinda like an upside-down bowl. The whole neighborhood's like that."

"That style's been around for a little while now, Josh. It's a pretty cost efficient and energy efficient. That's why all new houses look like that these days. It's been the law for a couple of years now."

"Well that law sucks," Joshua complains. "The windows are so small you can hardly see out. And after dark only a couple of lights are allowed on. You can only watch the comm screen for an hour!"

"Gee, what a shame. That means you have plenty of time to do your homework," Jason grins back.

"Yeah, just what I look forward to every night!"

"Just be glad you don't have to live in one of those multi-family towers," Jason replies. "I don't see how those people can stand that kind of confined life--- small rooms, curfews, and arguments between neighbors. Each building has to have a cop living there just to keep a lid on things."

As they near the end of the demolished area, Jason pulls the car over and stops. "Why are we stopping, Dad?" Joshua inquires.

Jason's eyes start to glisten as he wistfully scans the former home sites. "My parents used to live here. It's a shame you never knew them. You would have loved them. I know they would have loved you."

Josh replies, "Yeah, I'm sure I would've. I remember several years ago you told me they died on vacation, but I can't remember anything more. So, what exactly happened?"

"I guess you're old enough now to know the details," Jason replies as the car moves-on. "They were in Rome on vacation--- a couple of years before you were born. Their tour group was in one of the old churches when a Muslim terrorist group broke-in and took the group and a priest hostage. They threatened to kill everyone unless one of their leaders was released from prison. City negotiators arranged for the release of all the hostages and the priest, except for Mom and Dad. Eventually, the police stormed the church. All the terrorists were killed, but so were Mom and Dad. There's more to the story, but I don't feel like talking about it anymore--- maybe some other time."

"Gosh, Dad," Josh says, "you must have felt terrible. I can't even imagine how I would feel if you or Mom died, especially that way."

"I'll never forget that day. It was devastating. I flew to Rome to bring them home, but I'll never go back there again."

Farther along the road they pass several people on solar-battery e-bikes, many of whom are blocking the road. As Josh and Jason pass them--- maybe a little too close--- some of the riders give the pair an irritated glare. "There are lots of e-bikes out today, aren't there?" Jason points-out. "Liezel had a bike like that red one over there. They found it on this road somewhere." Jason drifts into a sad silence.

After a long awkward pause, Joshua asks, "You still miss her, don't-cha, Dad? How long has it been?"

Jason takes a deep breath and responds with a slight quiver in his voice. "Yes, Son, I sure do. It's been over a year, now."

Sensing his father's grief, Joshua doesn't know quite what to do or say. Finally, he asks, "Any word from the cops lately?"

"Nope. I've pretty much given-up. The cops think she ran away because she left her wrist comm at home. You can't communicate or buy anything without it so the cops think she must have left it there on purpose. I don't think she ran away, though. We loved each other too much. I think she was kidnapped. The cops don't agree, because there wasn't any ransom request. They say without a ransom request, she either ran away or was killed. Either way, they say the chance of finding a missing person diminishes as time goes by."

"Sorry, Dad. I liked her a lot. I hope she turns-up someday."

"Thanks, Son--- me, too, but I'm not very hopeful. She loved you, you know," he replies somberly.

"Yeah, I could tell. She always had a smile for me, and she seemed interested in what I was doin'. She even played catch with me one time when you were out of town." Joshua is starting to grieve, as well, so he stops talking.

Several minutes pass. Jason looks over at Joshua, admiring his son like he hasn't done so in quite some time. Although Joshua is lanky, his shoulders are developing noticeable muscles. "Say, what's that med-cap on your shoulder---vaccination?"

"Yep," Joshua replies. "Got it yesterday. Didn't hurt as much as the last one."

"Great," Jason says in a relieved tone. "I'd hate to lose you. The newer vaccines seem to be working, but so many people I know have died--- very sad. We're very fortunate to have dodged these plagues so far."

"Yeah, last month my best friend Charlie and his family caught it. They didn't make it."

"Sorry to hear that, son. Are you okay? Want to talk about it?"

"No...I'm good."

"For whatever it's worth, I know how you must feel. I lost my best friend when I was about your age, too. His name was Kevin, and he lived next door. We did everything together. He spent a lot of

13

time at our house--- like he was almost a member of the family. We didn't know it at the time, but there was a problem at his house--- his parents and older brother. It turned-out they were heavy pot smokers. It was legal back then, and a lot of people used it. I remember how stinky Kevin's clothes were. Then one day Kevin came over, and his breath smelled like his clothes. After that, our friendship started to deteriorate. He became irritable, and he skipped school at lot. He started hanging-out with the wrong kind of friends. Then both his parents lost their jobs, and they had to move away. I would still see him at school sometimes, but he always seemed angry at everything and everyone. He dropped-out half-way through our senior year, and I never saw him again."

Jason continued somberly, "The next I heard about him was just after I graduated from college. Another friend of mine told me that Kevin and both his parents had died. They robbed a store and were killed in a police shoot-out. Marijuana was found in their systems. About a year after that, reports starting coming-out showing images of how heavy use of marijuana damages the brain. It turned-out there were all sorts of studies and reports from decades ago documenting how brains were damaged from chronic marijuana use, but the reports were squelched for years by the marijuana industry and by politicians who wanted the sales tax revenue. It was a huge scandal, and a lot of people went to jail. It was then made illegal again. Penalties for dealing and using were extremely harsh. All hell broke loose, of course, but after a year or so the crime rate dropped and so did the number of unemployed. Then the anti-addiction vaccines came out. School attendance and performance picked-up noticeably. Kevin's story was very sad. That's why I've been so insistent that you stay away from any illegal drugs and the people that use them."

"I get it, Dad. Don't worry. I know which way to go."

"I know, son. I trust you. But I just don't trust any of your friends that might pressure you or deceive you. It's evil. I can't stand evil people. There are too many of them running around today trying to control things and tempt good people. So, bring me up to date some more. I know you're doing better in school. Are there any teachers you particularly like? And (winking) is there anyone else you particularly like?" Joshua suddenly looks nervous, and his face gets a little red. "So, what's her name?" Jason says with a grin.

Joshua looks away and mumbles, "Err, it's Sherri," he says embarrassingly, "Sherri Frederick." He hasn't had a conversation with his dad about girls before, so he feels awkward.

"Sherri, huh. So, tell me about her," Jason says. Then Jason realizes that he hasn't had "The Talk" with Joshua. Suddenly his little boy is becoming a young man. Jason makes a mental note to have "The Talk" when he returns from his trip. He gets a little nervous at the prospect.

Joshua slowly responds to Jason's question. "Well...she's cute... brown hair... and she plays volleyball. She's a little taller than me."

"And...?" Jason prods. Getting information from Joshua is like pulling teeth, but Jason understands because his father had the same difficulty with him at that age.

"She's pretty smart. We're science class partners."

"Anything more?"

"Not really...Well, she goes to church. I've even gone to her Bible study a few times."

"Really?" Jason says. "So, what have you learned there?"

"I learned about God and Jesus, and about the prophets. Do you believe in God and Jesus, Dad?"

"Actually, I really don't know what to think anymore. I guess I believe in God. I can't see how everything in the world and universe happened accidentally, but if there is a God, it certainly doesn't look like He's doing anything about what's happening in the world today. I don't know about Jesus, though. I must admit that I haven't practiced my Jewish faith in a long time. I can't remember the last time I went to synagogue--- probably before Mom and Dad died. I think the way they died sort of disillusioned me about God and religion. I figured if Mom and Dad were in trouble in a church, God should have rescued them. I was angry at God. That's probably why I stopped going to synagogue. Liezel was a practicing Christian, 'though. She tried to get me to come to church, but my heart wasn't in it. But I'm glad you're getting some exposure. You're old enough to make your own decisions about that."

After a while, their mood lightens-up. They travel through an unpopulated area characterized by large flat grassy fields with rolling hills in the distance. A few scraggly trees dot the roadside. Josh perks-up and points ahead to the foothills.

"Dad, look. See those big tanks and the solar farm and wind turbines?"

"Oh, over there. Now I do. I recognize the solar panels and wind turbines, son, but I've never seen tanks like those before."

Then Josh boasts, "I know what they are because we just finished studying them in school. I got an A on our science quiz."

Jason grins as his pride in his son starts showing. "Of course you did. So what are they?"

"It's a solar and wind farm that generates electricity during the day. Most of it goes to the electric grid, and the rest goes to a hydrolysis system that separates the hydrogen and oxygen in the water that's stored in those shorter tanks. The hydrogen is compressed and stored in the tall tanks. Then at night the hydrogen is burned in turbine-generators to generate electricity. It's pretty neat because the exhaust gas is water vapor--- no carbon. Some of the oxygen is sold for industrial uses, but the rest is just vented into the air. As a result, the oxygen content of the air is increased so people nearby breathe healthier air."

"Wow," Jason exclaims, "that sounds like a win-win situation. I didn't know you knew so much. Have you thought about a career in this sort of thing?"

"Umm, maybe."

Jason says, "I heard this type of storage system was being tried somewhere in California, but I didn't know it was here so close to home. It's well-timed because the earth is running-out of battery metals. I don't know what will happen with e-cars and bikes then. I hope we don't need to go back to fossil fuels."

The car passes a metal gate which bars access to a small dirt road that appears to lead into the hills. A sign on the gate reads "WARNING. ELECTRIFIED GATE. KEEP OUT."

"What's that up there, Dad? See those reflections?"

"I'm not sure," Jason replies with a puzzled look on his face, "Maybe solar mirrors? But they don't look like a solar farm--- too small and spread-out. That gate we just passed might be for the road up there. That's funny--- the reflections just disappeared."

"Can we check it out, Dad?"

"Better not, Son. That gate is telling us no one up there wants to be disturbed."

Suddenly, a large, noisy military van bounds over the hill towards them, crossing the dividing line in the middle of the road. "Watch-out!" Jason yells. The e-car automatically swerves at the last second, avoiding a collision that would have crushed it and both of them in it. The car skids off the road and screeches to a stop.

"Wow, Dad. We almost got killed! That guy must be crazy!" an out-of-breath Joshua exclaims. "Where's *he* goin' in such a hurry?"

"Don't know, son. I'm just glad he didn't hit us. We would've been goners for sure. Hey, I think this new car just saved our lives! Are you okay?" Joshua silently nods his head affirmatively. "I'm going to slow down in case there's another one like that on the road ahead." They gather themselves together and pull back onto the road again.

Minutes later, they turn off onto a small gravel road leading onto a large grassy field surrounded by tall eucalyptus trees. The dusty gray leaves flutter in a gentle breeze, releasing their refreshing signature aroma. It's a beautiful clear day--- perfect for drone flying. They get out of the car with the drone box and walk toward the middle of the field. As they pass the end of the tree line, two large conical metal-framed towers come into view. A short antenna peeks out of the top of each tower, pointing to the other.

"Look, Dad, what are those?" Josh inquires.

"That's an old ozone generator," Jason says. "There's a bunch of them all over the world, but I don't think they operate anymore. There's a layer of atmospheric ozone at the earth's poles that shields the earth from certain harmful rays from the sun. Decades ago, this layer became damaged by airborne chemicals, and the sun's damaging rays started to get through. So these generators were built to replenish the ozone layers. Over many years the ozone was re-established, so the generators weren't needed anymore." After a pause, Jason says, "That's odd, there's a truck by the building at the bottom of the towers. I wonder what someone's doing there--- probably just a maintenance check."

Joshua can't wait to open the box. "What's this, Dad?" He asks as he picks-up a glove-like device.

"It's the controller, Son. Just slip it over your hand--- like a glove. See those wires and electronic nodules on the surface? Hold your hand like you have a play finger gun. All you have to do is point your finger at the drone and lead it where you want it to go. Open and close your thumb to control the speed. Pretty slick, huh?"

"Yeah, Dad. How do you start it up?"

"Just hit this button here on the glove. Go ahead. Don't worry about keeping it steady. It has an automatic stabilizing feature."

Just as Joshua launches the drone, a small flock of geese fly by. The drone causes them to veer toward the towers. Suddenly, an alarm horn sounds at the towers. Seconds later, a bolt of lightning strikes with a loud bang between the tips of the towers just as the geese are flying through. Some of them tumble to the ground. The remaining geese scatter away in a confused panic, honking as they go. The lightning bolt continues buzzing in a loud, erratic fashion. Startled, Jason and Joshua instinctively drop to a crouch, covering their heads with their hands. Josh's control finger now points behind him, far away from the drone. The drone continues on a straight line in the direction it was going before they ducked--- right towards the towers. Realizing what's happening, Jason quickly grabs Josh's hand and points it in the direction of the drone.

Jason screams in a panic, "Josh! It's headed towards the towers!" Josh recovers and establishes contact with the drone just in time to divert it away. "Whew," they both sigh together. "Nice job, Son," Jason says proudly. "Sorry to yell."

As Joshua continues to fly the drone, they walk farther away from the towers. After thirty minutes or so, Josh starts to complain about the hot sun. "Boy the sun is hot today. I'm ready for snow any day now. I haven't even had a chance to use that new sled you bought me a few years ago. You're a scientist, Dad. Can't you make it snow this year?"

Smiling, Jason replies, "Sometimes weather scientists can make it snow by seeding the clouds with chemical particles, but the conditions have to be just right--- big dark clouds on a cold day. That's not going to happen anytime soon. Winters have been getting warmer here for a long time now."

"How come, Dad? Is the sun getting hotter?"

"Actually, it is. You see, the sun's radiation varies from time-to-time, mostly due to sunspot cycles over several years. It's this fluctuation in the sun's radiation that affects the earth's temperature the most. Back near the beginning of this century the earth warmed a little, and then it cooled-off a little. Now it's been warming-up for the last ten years or so. When the earth started warming at the beginning of this century, governments around the world passed laws to try to stop the warming. They limited the use of fuels that generate carbon dioxide when they're burned. You might know from your science class that carbon dioxide in the atmosphere can cause the air to warm. But despite those laws, the air kept warming due to increased solar radiation and because water vapor in the atmosphere also causes warming--- and there's much more water vapor than carbon dioxide. So, although those laws greatly reduced man-made carbon dioxide levels, the warming continued due to these other factors. So, it turns-out the sun is the real problem, but we can't do anything about it. Eventually the earth will cool again when sun spot activity changes. Unfortunately, the carbon-limiting laws were very costly to implement, and the alternatives to burning carbon-based fuels are very expensive. That's why electricity costs so much, and that's why you can't watch more than an hour of comm screen at night, and it's why so many people use e-bikes now. If it weren't for the ash clouds, the reduction in carbon would normally make our air much cleaner."

"So, can't they change back to the old fuels so we can use more electricity?"

"Not really--- at least not for electricity generation, but most of the less developed nations still use gasoline and natural gas for cars and trucks. Of course, oil and gas are still used to make plastics. The old fuels are now harder and more expensive to find and process. Besides, the United Nations is in control of that right now, and it's too hard to change back. The UN leader is especially stubborn, and he seems to have an uncanny influence over everything. What's worse, the earth is running-out of the rare earth metals that are needed for solar and wind systems, as well as for other important electronics and batteries. Israel has the last major mining operation left, so things are going to get even more expensive. I don't know what we're going to do twenty or thirty years from now."

After an hour or so, Joshua is ready to go home. He brings the drone in for a rough landing, and one of the wheels breaks. Jason says patiently, "Don't worry, Josh. I'll take it home and print a new one. Maybe we can try again tomorrow, but in a different field!"

"That'd be cool, Dad. This was a lotta fun. Thanks for the drone. It's really neat--- the best present ever! And thanks for saving it from being hit when that ozone thing cranked-up!"

Driving home, they hear faint explosions, and see smoke in the mountains. They pass the electric gate again and stop. This time the gate is open, and the frame has been badly bent. They hear weapons fire, and see military hovercrafts buzzing around near the smoke. "What's going-on, Dad?" Joshua says excitedly.

"I'm not sure, Son, but it looks like the area where we saw those reflections is being attacked." Just then an armored vehicle speeds down from the mountain road in a cloud of dust. A heavily armed officer in a light grey uniform pops-out. His shoulder has an emblem on it--- a black dragon on a red background. He jogs menacingly towards the car, and sternly tells Jason to move along. Nodding, Jason drives away.

Soon, they pull-in to a UN food store. Jason picks-up three packages of vegetables, half a head of lettuce, two jugs of water, and a family-pack of chicken. He pays for them by placing his wrist comm under a scanner. Expressing dismay at his bill, he presses a button to summon the store officer. Others in line behind them start frowning and become fidgety. "What are you doing?" one of them says with a scowl. "You're going to get us all in trouble!"

The officer arrives. She's frowning and pressing her lips tightly together, obviously resenting being bothered. She's wearing a plain dark grey uniform with a familiar black dragon emblem on her shoulder. Jason squints at the officer's name badge. "Officer... Brown, there must be something wrong with the scanning system. The total here is way more than it should be."

"Costs have gone up," she gruffly barks, clearly irritated. "Volcanic dusts, disease, pests, and drought have hit the northern agricultural areas. You're lucky you found what you wanted. Now leave the store with them or without them. You're holding things up. Give me any trouble, and I'll revoke your food privileges." Jason and Josh shrink-back and walk quickly out of the store.

"Boy, she was kinda mean," Joshua says. "Can she really keep you from buying food?"

"I'm afraid so. The UN controls food distribution now because so many countries can't grow enough for their own people. Haven't you noticed that there aren't many over-weight people anywhere these days? America is fortunate that we still have decent agricultural areas--- until now, that is. Many people think more food could be produced if the UN didn't regulate farms so much. The farmers really don't have much incentive to maximize production anymore."

About a mile from Josh's home, the car starts veering. Along the road, trees start swaying and small rocks roll down the hillside onto the road. Jason shouts, "It's an earthquake, and it's a bad one! Hold on." With a loud rumble, a crevasse opens-up across the road ahead. The pavement drops about two feet on the far side of the crevasse. More rocks roll onto the road as the car automatically brakes, but it can't stop in time. It skids over the edge of the crevasse and slams down onto the road below, leaving the rear wheels of the car on the high side of the crevasse. All is quiet. Jason and Josh are blinking their eyes--- obviously dazed. Josh's right eye is turning red, and he starts to whimper. "Are you okay, Son?"

"I think so, Dad, but the drone box hit me in the eye, and my knee hurts a little. Are you okay?"

"I'm a little shaken-up, too. My knee hurts, too, but I'm going to try to get us out of here. Just sit tight. I'm going to try to open the doors." Jason commands his restraint to release, but it only partially does. Fortunately, he's able to force it the rest of the way. He pushes his door open as it laboriously grinds and squeaks. He looks down to find his footing. The crevasse is about three feet wide, and he's directly over it. Fortunately, the door pivots upwards, allowing him to stretch and find solid footing. He painfully maneuvers himself down to the ground, and limps around the front of the car. The front wheels are dangling in mid-air, and the crushed front of the car is the only thing keeping it from falling into the crevasse. Jason slowly makes it to Josh's side of the car. The door is jammed. He limps back to his side again, and calls out, "Josh, can you crawl over the console so I can pull you out?"

Josh weakly responds, "I'll try, Dad, but my knee is starting to hurt more." Jason commands Josh's restraint to release. To his relief it does, and Josh starts to crawl slowly over the console, his sun-burned face grimacing in pain.

There's a brief after-shock. "Whoa, son. Don't move!" Jason exclaims, freezing his position.

As Josh looks desperately at this dad's face, his eyes glance to the side and widen in fear. "Look-out, Dad!" he screams. Jason jerks around just in time to see a boulder rumbling down the hill towards the car. He quickly jumps to his left as the boulder crashes into the rear of the car, pushing it sideways a few feet. One of the rear wheels slides over the crevasse, and the car tips down and starts to rock. Now three wheels dangle over the void. The car is in real danger of falling-in.

23

Panicking, and with a lump in his throat, Jason quickly turns back to Josh. "Are you okay?" he yells.

"Yeah, but I just wanna go home," he sobs.

Jason drops his head in relief, and loudly exhales. "Whew, he puffs--- thank God you yelled in time. That was way too close! Just sit tight. I'll pull you out, but don't make any sudden moves--- the car could tip over any time. Jason grabs Josh under the arm pits. The car rocks again, and Jason freezes. Little by little, Jason gingerly pulls Josh out of the car. As his front foot finally touches the pavement, Josh slips a little but catches himself by tugging at his father's shirt. This sudden movement causes Jason to lose his balance. He has to thrust his foot half-way over the edge of the crevasse to stabilize himself, and he barely avoids falling-in. The car rocks again. Jason slowly shuffles both of them to safety. Still whimpering, Josh hugs his father. They stand still for a moment. Then Jason brings his wrist comm to his lips, "Kathy?...Kathy?...Damn, my comm isn't working. I don't see any other cars or bikes around. We'll just have to walk home. It's not far." They start limping down the road.

"Wait, Dad. What about the drone?"

"You're more important than the drone, Son. I'll come back for it later. Same for the food. Right now, we have to get to your mother's house before dark. That quake was pretty strong. I hope your mother's alright." Jason tries to use his wrist comm again, but it's still not working. They continue on. Josh's knee is really bothering him now, so Jason carries him on his back. After 20 minutes Jason stops and lets Joshua slowly down to the road.

"What's the matter, Dad?" Joshua asks.

"Sorry, Son, I'm not as strong as I used to be. You can lean on me, but you'll have to walk from here."

"I get it, Dad. It's okay. I'm impressed that you carried me this far. Thanks for that much. You know, I was thinking... that quake was pretty scarry. Things seem to be getting so much worse in many ways. I'm kinda worried. What do you think?"

"Well, I'm worried, too, Son. I think we should all be prepared for more of the same--- maybe even worse. I have to leave town for a few weeks, so you and your mom should stock up on food and water. Make sure you have enough fuel for the generator. I'm trying not to scare you too much, but there are other things about to happen in the world that I can't tell you about, so just be prepared. And take care of your mother."

It's dark when they limp-up Kathy's walkway. She sees them, and runs outside to meet them. "Oh my God," she cries. "I was so worried when that quake hit and I couldn't raise you on your comm. What happened?" Obviously tired and in pain, Josh turns to his mom and hugs her. He tells his mom that they're banged-up but not too seriously. Jason begins to tell her their story as she takes them inside to tend to their injuries.

Obviously concerned, especially for her son, Kathy says, "You look in bad shape, boys. I think you both need to go to the Med Center right away."

"I'm sure they're over-run by now," Jason says. "If you can rustle-up some ice packs and anti-inflammation pills, I think we'll make it. That was a pretty bad quake. How did you and your house hold-up? You don't look hurt."

"I'm fine, and the house is fine. These domes are pretty strong. A couple of pictures fell down. No big deal. I don't know why I keep re-hanging them."

Jason finishes filling-in Kathy on everything that happened, and then asks, "Have you heard from anyone? What kind of damage is being reported?"

"Amazingly, the comm screen is still working," Kathy says. "I haven't been able to reach Christina, yet. Tony and Mary stopped-by, and they're okay. The news outlets are reporting more earthquakes all over the world. They seem to have all hit around the same time--- quite a bit of damage. A lot of people have been killed. Lots of fires, too. And to top it all off, the Statue of Liberty finally came down."

"What? Nooo! But she was the symbol of America!" Jason's head drops, and he lets out a sigh. Shrugging his shoulders and raising his hands he sadly says, "Well, that's it then. This country's been falling for a long time now, so I guess it's fitting that our national symbol should fall as well. We might as well get used to it--- the America we knew as kids is finally gone."

"I guess you're right," Kathy laments. "Gosh, between the plagues, food shortages, and the earthquakes, I sometimes wonder if the human race is going to survive. They just interviewed the United Nations Secretary General--- what's his name---"

"Antonin Mora," Jason interrupts.

"Yes, that's it. He said the UN relief organizations are overwhelmed, so all countries are on their own. He also announced that the UN headquarters has just moved to Strasbourg, France since New York had been battered by that big quake and tsunami last month."

"I don't trust that guy," says Jason. "He emerged on the world stage from nowhere, and he's taking over everything without objection. Now he wins the Nobel Peace Prize and the Nobel Prize in Economics. I don't know how he pulled it off, but he orchestrated the elimination of almost all major debts among the nations. It's like a biblical debt jubilee. And he's not even Jewish! He's also the one who organized the production and distribution of food in the world--- except it's not working! I almost got in a fight with one of his stupid officers at the UN store today. Miraculous accomplishments, granted, but I still don't trust him. There's just something about him. Just look what he's done. These wrist comms are now required for everyone over the age of

15. They're great for communication and information, but everyone's location can be tracked. And all banking must be done electronically through them, and no one can purchase or sell anything except through the comms. I can't prove it, but it wouldn't surprise me if he were behind the dissolution of the EU. Now he's got the new head of the United Religions Counsel, Domenic Precora, at his side which gives Mora influence in all major religions of the world. I'm telling you, he's dangerous."

Just then, Jason gets a call on his comm. "Hey, it's working now," He says in surprise. "I have to take this." Jason walks into another room for some privacy. He returns shortly. "Sorry, Sport," he says to Josh, "but I have to fly to Washington tomorrow instead of Tuesday. You're in no condition for an outing tomorrow, anyway. And I'll need time to do something about my car, as well."

"But you're in no condition to travel, either," Kathy says. "Maybe you should spend the night here. I'll even fix breakfast in the morning--- maybe one of those omelets you always liked."

Jason defensively stiffens at Kathy's uncharacteristic hospitality. Does she have an ulterior motive? He diverts the conversation. "I'll be alright. I'm a lot better-off than my car!" he says sarcastically. He then pushes-up Josh's pant leg to expose his sore knee. "It's swollen a bit, but it doesn't look broken--- just bruised. The dash probably hit it when the front of the car got crushed. Where's your med scanner, Kathy?" Kathy pulls the scanner out of a nearby drawer, and hands it to Jason. He turns it on and lightly presses it on Josh's shoulder next to the implanted biochip. "It doesn't show anything worrisome. Keep his knee on ice for the next couple of days. If it gets worse, call the Med Center. I'll stay here for a little while, and then I'll have to call an auto-cab. I have an early flight tomorrow."

He finds a much-needed chair, drops into it with a sigh, tilts his head back, and closes his eyes. Unfortunately, his heart is still racing, preventing him from relaxing. After a few minutes he gives-up the effort to calm-down, and says to Kathy, "Boy, I could sure use a beer. Do you have any?" He starts to rise, but his painful knee quickly pulls him back into the chair. As she returns from the kitchen, Jason notices that Kathy has fixed her hair and has applied make-up since this morning. He then looks at the bottle label and says, "Thanks, Kathy. Hmm… interesting, it's from Strasbourg. Mora probably owns the brewery there, too! By the way, I'm so glad we buried the hatchet a couple of months ago. The tension between us seems to have melted away, and I've noticed a big difference in Josh's demeanor and in his schoolwork. I wish we would have cleared the air a long time ago."

"Yeah, I agree completely," Kathy replies. "Josh is much happier now. So am I. I didn't realize what the lingering bitterness was doing to all three of us. You know, it just sort of invisibly sat there and worked on us without us realizing it." After a short pause, she nervously continues. "Since things seem to be better now, and since Liezel is gone, I was wondering…" She stops herself and looks away. Jason realizes what she's getting at, but he doesn't respond. He needs to go.

The auto-cab arrives. Jason thanks Kathy, kisses his son on the top of his head, and limps down the walkway to the cab. On the cab ride home, Jason wonders why his trip has been moved up to tomorrow instead of Tuesday, and now he's going to Washington, D.C. first. Have things gone from urgent to critical? He hates getting incomplete information.

Then his thoughts turn to his missing wife Liezel. He's been so busy with projects at work that he hasn't focused on her disappearance lately. When this trip is over, he vows to prod the police again. If they haven't made any progress, he will pursue the case himself. He starts to nod-off, but perks-up when the cab's brakes engage. The cab's headlights illuminate three people in the distance walking briskly along the road, their backs toward the cab. One of them turns around, and then they all dart off into the woods. As the cab gets closer, Jason squints into the woods and barely makes-out the back of a red and brown jacket as the trio disappears into the darkness. *'What's that all about?'* Jason wonders. He doesn't realize it now, but this seemingly insignificant event will turn out to be not so insignificant after all.

CHAPTER THREE---THE LAST ASSIGNMENT

Early the next morning Jason woke-up in pain. His body still ached from the previous day's trauma, so he swallowed a pain pill and some anti-inflammation pills. Grimacing, he managed to catch a monorail to the Portland airport. Normally he would have flown out of San Francisco, but the earthquake damaged the monorail line on that route. As the pills kick-in during the ride, his thoughts drift back to the time he met Liezel.

The night he met her was magical. Carl Wilson (probably his best friend) thought it was time Jason started dating again after his divorce, so he dragged Jason to a country-western night club one evening where dance lessons were given. Jason was a novice, of course, but Carl was a good dancer. Jason struggled with the two-step, but finally reached the point where he wasn't embarrassing himself too much. He had a couple of partners during the lesson, but they really didn't click with him. When the lesson was over, the two men went to the bar. Soon the club started to fill-up with what appeared to be regulars--- mostly women. One of them caught Jason's eye immediately. She had long dark wavy hair, bright blue eyes, and a stunning figure. It was Liezel. She wore a white blouse with cowboy hats embroidered on the collar. Her blue jeans were tight, but not too tight--- tasteful. Her boots were red. She walked-in quickly, smiling and talking with a girlfriend. The two women dropped their purses with the bartender and skipped onto the dance floor for a line dance. Jason was mesmerized. He couldn't take his eyes off her. She never stopped smiling, and at one-point Jason caught her glancing at him. Jason asked Carl if he knew her. Carl said yes and told Jason her name. Carl didn't know much about her, except that she was very popular--- never lacked for a dance partner. Carl prodded Jason to ask her to dance, but Jason balked, fearing he would make a fool out of himself. Jason anguished as cowboy after cowboy danced with her.

Gradually, the two men migrated closer to where Liezel and her girlfriend were parked when they weren't dancing. After some more of Carl's prodding, Jason finally found the courage to approach her. Her back was turned when suddenly the two women darted-off. They retrieved their purses from the bar and left. Jason was heartbroken. He felt as if someone just played a cruel trick on him, depriving him of a chance at something special. Crushed, he and Carl returned to the bar. Having missed his chance, Jason didn't feel like there was any point in staying, so he and Carl finished their beers and headed for the door. When they reached the door, Jason's heart jumped. Liezel and her girlfriend were coming back in! Apparently, they had only gone to the ladies' room. She and Jason almost ran into each other. They both said "Sorry" at the same time. Then Liezel gave Jason a smile that could melt steel. Jason was speechless, but he wasn't going to let this opportunity slip away. He followed her to the bar. When she and her girlfriend turned around, Jason was there. Liezel acted surprised but gave Jason that steel-melting smile again. "Hi, again," she said. When Jason didn't respond, her smile morphed into a look of concern, wondering what might be wrong with this handsome man.

After an agonizing pause, Jason finally utters, "Hi, err, I just learned the two-step tonight, and I was hoping I could talk you into practicing it with me." He never felt so inadequate before. His nervousness was obvious, but in such a boyish sort of way that Liezel was disarmed.

"Sure." she said, "Don't worry. I'll help you through it." Jason couldn't believe that someone so beautiful and charming would be kind enough to endure the stumbling that was sure to come. Jason was both apprehensive and thrilled. Liezel counted-out the steps while Jason's eyes darted back and forth from her face to his feet. He wanted to talk to her, but every time he tried, he screwed-up his steps and stepped on her feet. Liezel was amazingly patient, and just kept smiling. After the dance, Jason apologized profusely, but Liezel laughed it off, saying that she struggled the first time, as well. They talked and smiled. She said she grew-up on her father's horse ranch ten miles from San Marita. Her mother died of cancer when Liezel was six. Her father never re-married. She loved the outdoors, especially horses, and she was an accomplished rider. Living in a remote area where bobcats and even bears sometimes turn-up, she also knew how to handle a rifle. Fishing bored her. She liked to catch fish but spending half the day just feeding the fish was not her idea of fun. Jason said a couple of things that made her chuckle. He was hooked. She wouldn't give Jason her comm number, but she said she would be back next Friday. The rest is history. She became the best thing that ever happened to him.

Jason's eyes tear-up a bit as he recalls his amazing life with Liezel, as heartbreakingly short as it was. He didn't deserve her, and he missed her so much. But time has a way of diminishing feelings, and his hopes of finding Liezel had all but evaporated. As the monorail arrives at the airport, he gets a call from Carl who is dealing with Jason's car. He tells Jason that the car has been transported to a repair shop, and it's repairable. As Jason expected, the drone and all the food are gone. Jason is understandably irritated, but he thinks the bonus he'll get from this new assignment will cover the deductible. He wonders if the car will ever be the same.

He breezes through airport security, checks-in without any hassle, and pre-boards the plane. At least something is going right today. He sits down next to two elderly men with unkempt shoulder-length grey hair and long scraggly beards. They look disheveled, but there is an air of peace about them. One of them has an eye that is half-closed. Jason can't help looking at it. The man nods.

Jason nods back. Due to yesterday's trauma and injury, Jason did not get much sleep the night before, so he takes a sleeping pill to try to catch-up. As the plane takes-off, Jason's eyes become heavy, and he drifts off to sleep. He's awakened by the jostling of the plane as it touches-down. He blinks and looks around, momentarily confused. The man with the half-closed eye is smiling at him. "Have a nice snooze?" The man says.

Groggily, Jason mumbles back, "Yeah, I guess so. Are we here already?"

"We are. Don't forget your briefcase."

"Right. Thanks," Jason replies. There's a line of passengers already in the aisle, preventing Jason from getting up. Awkwardly rising, he pulls his briefcase from under the seat in front of him and looks forward along the aisle. No one is moving. After ten minutes, the air in the plane is starting to get a little gamey. Still no movement. 'Great,' he thinks, 'the fastest plane in the world, and we have to wait forever to get off.' He looks down at the two men. They're smiling at him like they know something or know something about him. He does a quick, half-smile back, trying unsuccessfully to avoid looking at the man's half-closed eye. Finally, the line starts moving. A break in the line appears, and Jason jumps into the aisle. He turns and nods to the two men who are still smiling at him. Hastening down the aisle, he wonders what those two are all about. He collects his checked bag and proceeds to the auto-cab island outside the terminal. His leg is a little less painful than it was yesterday. On the way to the pick-up island he pauses to watch a comm screen broadcast of smoking rubble and fires from earthquakes in major cities around the world. A huge tsunami struck the Korean peninsula, Russia, Japan, and parts of China. Over three million people are dead or missing.

During the auto-cab ride to CIA headquarters in Langley, Virginia Jason sees plumes of smoke rising from multiple areas ahead. The cab comes to a slow stop at the end of a long line of vehicles. He sees a police car ahead with its lights flashing. A cop is there, directing all traffic to exit the highway. As the cab finally makes the turn off the highway, Jason looks back and sees that the overpass just beyond the police car had collapsed. The cab crawls along behind other cars. After twenty minutes or so, the cab turns the corner into a chaotic scene. Emergency vehicles are everywhere. An earthquake has struck this area, too. Disaster workers are frantically scurrying about. Scores of people are lying in the street. Many have white sheets covering their bodies. Others, dusty and in pain, are sitting down on benches, holding bandages on their wounds. Many windows have fallen onto the street, and firemen are hosing-down a fire at the corner of a building. He peers down the blocked street to see other buildings damaged and on fire. One of them has fallen across the street and has crashed into a building on the other side. The air is filled with choking smoke and dust. He is struck by the magnitude and extent of the damage, and he wonders if more earthquakes are coming. He also wonders if there is some undiscovered explanation for all the disasters that have struck in the last few years. The frequency and severity of these disasters is definitely increasing. Concluding that there is nothing he can do to help, and realizing he will be late for his meeting, he commands the cab to find another route to Langley.

The cab pulls-up to the main gate at Langley, and Jason shows the guard his I.D. The guard waves it under his portable scanner. He hands the I.D. back to Jason, and then asks him to pull the cab into a scanning tunnel. The guard returns to the gate house to check the screen. He quickly speaks into his wrist comm, and then leaps out of the gate house. Pointing his side arm at Jason, he yells excitedly, "Sir, get out of the car slowly with your hands in the air!" Jason is understandably bewildered and scared. Jason obeys the guard. Both men remain motionless for several minutes. Soon, two other vehicles arrive, and six heavily-armed soldiers spring out of their vehicles. They spread-out, also pointing their weapons at Jason. He is so scared he opens his mouth, but the words don't come-out. A bead of sweat starts to meander down his temple. He pees a little in his pants.

Finally, he utters, "Wha', what have I done, officer?" The first guard returns from the gate house with a portable scanner. Just then another car pulls-up.

"Johnson, what's the problem?" a familiar voice barks. "Put your weapons down, men." Relieved, Jason turns slowly around to see his main contact at the CIA, Christian Christopher. Christopher is in his late 60's, short and bald. He tries to appear polished by wearing an expensive suit, but instead it just makes him look sloppy because he's over-weight. His wrinkled shirt and loosened tie complete the untidy picture. "This man's okay," Christopher says. "What's the problem?"

"The scan alarm went-off, Sir," the first guard says. "A possible explosive substance is indicated under the front seat of the cab. I was just going to check it out when you pulled-up."

"Well go ahead then, but be careful," Christopher says with a worried look. Everyone backs-up.

The guard carefully crouches next to the car seat, and waves the scanner near the rear of the seat. The scanner emits a muffled high-pitched tone. The guard looks at his scanner screen with a puzzled expression. Timidly, he peeks under the seat with a flashlight. He then reaches behind himself to pull-out a glove from his pants pocket. He nervously gropes under the seat and pulls something out. "Hey, it's just a can of Play-Goo," he announces triumphantly. "My son has one of these." He removes the lid, checks the contents, and nods that it's okay. Everyone, especially Jason, sighs in relief.

Christopher slowly shakes his head, and chuckles. "Okay, fellas, the show's over. Johnson, get in my car. You're late." The car speeds down the road, and then parks in a no parking zone in front of the main building.

Jason is escorted quickly up the steps, and he follows Christopher into a large conference room with about twenty-five people there. Twelve of them are sitting at the table. All but one is uniformed military. Other military and civilian CIA personnel are seated around the room against the walls. Christopher introduces Jason to the group, noting to Jason that Secretary of Defense Dr. Chelsea Devon is sitting at the head of the table. The joint chiefs of staff are also there. "Sorry I'm late, gentlemen," apologizes Jason, "but I was held-up by an earthquake and some Play-Goo." No one laughs. Jason sheepishly sits down on one of the wall chairs, clutching his briefcase to his chest as if it's some sort of protection. He nods to a thin, blonde, geeky-looking man next to him--- Rick Willis. Willis returns the nod. Willis was Jason's chief engineer on a key defense project that Jason led at Progressive Aviation Systems. Jason notices that Willis has grown a lop-sided mustache since he saw him last. His blonde hair is a little long and unruly. A few strands of it dangle over his right eyebrow. Willis is a bit of a character--- smart but a little odd in a likable sort of way. He fancies himself a lady's man, but he hasn't been able to make a relationship last.

Christopher turns-on a holographic screen at one end of the room showing the Middle East, Africa and the Indian Ocean. In a shaky voice he explains that the surveillance satellites covering Russia, China, the Middle East and Northern Africa went dark yesterday. On-the-ground intelligence from the U.S. and its allies have identified massive armies in the Middle East headed toward Israel. A Chinese combat flotilla is now off the coast of West Africa, heading north, and a smaller one in the Indian Ocean has been heading west. President DeAngelis has tried to contact the Chinese and Russian premiers, but he has been unsuccessful. Their embassies here and in our allied countries have been mysteriously abandoned, as have the embassies of Turkey and several Middle Eastern countries. The consensus is that Israel will be attacked. Secretary Devon announces that the President and key congressional leaders have agreed to aid Israel, with or without the UN. The U.S. Air Force, Space Force, and Navy are mobilizing. India and Australia will assist, as well.

Christopher then informs the group that Israel has requested assistance in readying millions of military drones that Israel secretly purchased from the U.S. over the last few years. The drones were manufactured by Progressive Aviation Systems. Jason and Willis were the leads on these programs. They will leave for Israel immediately after the meeting. They will be joined by Captains Wilson and Agnew and Major Huie. After a brief discussion around the table, Secretary Devon dismisses the meeting.

Christopher summons the five men to follow him into his office. On the way there, Jason reflects on what his life has meant and what may lie ahead. Since Liezel disappeared, his focus has been his technical work--- challenging, but not meaningful to mankind. He has a son who he loves greatly, but who he only sees every other weekend. He has not practiced his Jewish faith and feels disconnected from God. He lives alone--- no pets. He fears Liezel is gone forever, but he has not felt like dating since she disappeared. The assignment before him is both dangerous and critical to the future of Israel and possibly the world. Perhaps it will provide the meaning to his life that he has been missing. In addition, he has always wanted to visit Israel, and this could be the adventure of a lifetime. He's apprehensive, but despite the danger he's ready for the challenge.

Christopher motions the men into his office, and shuts the door. He hangs-up his suit jacket, revealing wet arm pit stains on his wrinkled white shirt. Christopher introduces the team members to each other, and then says somberly, "You all realize, of course, that what you are about to undertake is undoubtedly the most important and dangerous mission of your lives. Johnson, Willis, as civilians I can't force you to go, but technically you are quasi-CIA agents, and you agreed to our conditions of service when you signed-up. However, if you have doubts about going, now's the time to tell me. The world may never be the same after this battle. Certainly, the fate of Israel--- and maybe the world--- will be in your hands. Since the Russians and the Chinese are involved, we may also be on the verge of World War III. You're Jewish, aren't you Johnson?"

Jason straightens-up, raises his chin and boldly replies, "I am, Sir. And you can count me in."

Willis strokes his brown unbalanced mustache for a moment, deep in thought. His girlfriend has just moved-out. He's never been married, and he doesn't have any children, at least not that he knows-of. Although he likes his job, it's not particularly fulfilling. He's never been to Israel, either. What the heck. He agrees to the assignment.

"Very well, then." Christopher says.

"What about our manuals? We're going to need them and the interface plugs," Jason queries.

"Don't worry. They're all in your transport. Everything will be taken care of---clothes, transportation, contacts, and so forth. Here are your info-pods so you can familiarize yourselves with Israel's defense systems and weaponry. I think you'll find the Israelis are more advanced than anyone outside of the intelligence community realizes. After you've reviewed the material, give the pods to your driver. One more thing--- enemy spies monitor everyone in and out of this facility, so to disguise your mission, you and Willis will be stopping in Strasbourg, France. You'll be joined there by our UN Ambassador R.J. Harper. You'll be his guests at the ceremony honoring UN Secretary General Antonin Mora with the Nobel Peace Prize and the Nobel Prize in Economics. Afterwards, you, Willis, and Harper will meet with Mora privately. Apparently, Mora has a message he wants to convey to the U.S. in person." Jason bristles at the thought of meeting this powerful yet untrustworthy man. Christopher notices.

"What's the matter, Johnson? You look like someone just slapped you in the face with a wet rag."

"Sorry, Sir. It's nothing. Just surprised is all."

"Is there an issue with Mora?"

"Not really. I just don't think he's the savior that he appears to be."

"I can't say that I disagree, but you need to put that aside. You have a mission to accomplish. Is there going to be a problem here?"

"No, Sir. I'm good."

"Okay then. After the meeting with Mora, you and Willis will fly to Israel separately from the other three, since they won't be going to Strasbourg. Thank you all for doing this, gentlemen. May God go with you." The five men leave the office, feeling the weight of what they are about to undertake.

On the way to the airport, Jason makes a quick call to Joshua to see how he's feeling. He still hurts a bit, but he's planning to go to school tomorrow. Jason and Willis also use the time to plan their drone readiness activities and to review the top-secret information on the info-pods. There are three types of drones they will deploy--- small airborne types, small under water types, and larger land-based types. All have A.I. (artificial intelligence) capability. The airborne types are the most numerous. They are about the size of a food platter and have small but powerful explosives attached. They will be released in large groups called swarms and will communicate with each other to organize themselves into an efficient offensive or defensive pattern. In the defensive mode, their tactic is to form a large tightly spaced stationary curtain or cloud in front of incoming missiles or planes, exploding when the enemy flies into them. Offensively, they can form clouds or lines to attack specific targets. Each drone has a small rocket booster that propels it to the confrontation point quickly. The underwater types are torpedo-shaped, 24 inches long, and can be used to infiltrate water intakes on ships and submarines. They also carry explosives. The strategy behind the swarms is to overwhelm enemy defenses with sheer numbers, guaranteeing that most targets will be hit. Their cost is inexpensive relative to other types of missiles or aircraft because both the U.S. and Israel have developed unique 3D metal printing technology which has produced millions of these weapons. The land-based drones are about the size of a medium-sized bicycle. They're also made by 3D printers. They are fast all-terrain vehicles and carry anti-personnel cannons and armor-penetrating laser-guided rockets. They also utilize A.I. technology to coordinate with each other. In addition to the U.S. supplied drones, Israel has an arsenal of hypersonic missiles (some with conventional warheads, and some with mini-nuclear warheads) which can travel at twenty times the speed of sound. They also have a compliment of heavily armed piloted aircraft and large airborne attack drones. Thousands of small ground-to-ground missiles are poised to meet attacks from any direction. Finally, a small number of nuclear-tipped ICBMs (intercontinental ballistic missiles) with heavy payloads are hidden in fortified underground silos. Jason and Willis will prepare the swarms for deployment and integrate them with the rest of the Israeli defense system. After reviewing this new information, they now realize the magnitude of the assignment and the obstacles involved. They wonder if they can pull it off. They hope the three other officers know their way around these systems, because Jason and Willis know they can't do it by themselves. The ride to the airport is a very quiet one.

CHAPTER FOUR---STRASBOURG

Still apprehensive about their new assignment, Jason and Willis collapse into their seats on the plane. For a few moments they just stare ahead in silence. Just before the doors close, two elderly men slowly make their way down the aisle, searching for their seats. They smile as they focus on Jason and the two empty seats next to him. "It's you again!" one of them cheerfully says to Jason. "What a coincidence! Are you going to Strasbourg, too?" Jason blinks back into reality and instantly recognizes them as his seatmates on the flight to Washington.

Jason tries to act aloof. "Yes, I remember you," he says. "Nice to see you again." The two men struggle to place their small carry-on bags in the overhead compartment, and then collapse into their seats with a slight grunt.

Trying not to attract the attention of the two men, Willis leans toward Jason and whispers, "Jay, I know who these men are. They're some kind of evangelists, and they've been in the news for warning people about Antonin Mora. I don't know their names, but I remember them because one had a droopy eye, and the other one looks like Abraham Lincoln, only without that creepy wart on his face. We should try to avoid giving anyone the impression that we're associated with them."

"Got it. Good idea," Jason whispers back. As the plane takes-off, Jason and Willis get reacquainted since they have been working on separate assignments since the Swarm Drone Project. Willis has just been dumped by his girlfriend of six months, so he's licking his wounds and looking for a new conquest. He keeps picking women that remind him of his mother, with whom he has a broken relationship. He took-up golf for a while, but he couldn't get the hang of it. Besides, none of his geeky friends played. Like

Jason, his main focus is his work. Jason tells Willis about the successful mending he and Kathy achieved through dialogue and mutual forgiveness, but Willis doesn't think it will work with his mother. Apparently, she's pretty stubborn. Jason brings Willis up to date on the earthquake back home, the police action on the hill side, and the car wreck. Willis didn't feel the earthquake because he was visiting his sister in North Carolina at the time. When the conversation hits a flat spot, they pick-up their reading pods and catch-up on some technical journals. The flight is uneventful. Jason reads and responds briefly to occasional inquiries from the droopy-eyed man. He tries not to engage him too much, but he lets it slip that he and Willis are going to the Nobel ceremony. He mentally kicks himself for the mistake.

Much to Willis' disappointment, meals and beverages are served by droids instead of by the attractive flight attendant he saw when he entered the plane. Jason and Willis both select the least offensive-looking meal--- allegedly sliced beef in a mystery sauce. Jason has coffee while Willis orders a beer. The two strangers have the special meal. Jason has trouble finishing his dinner, but Willis seems to actually enjoy his. Willis looks over at Jason's tray, and says, "Uh, Jay, are you done with that?"

"Yeah, I guess I wasn't that hungry. Why, do you want it?"

"Only if you're done," Willis says. In wide-eyed anticipation, Willis quickly switches trays. Jason watches him make fast work of the remaining food, and he notices a trail of mystery sauce on the front of Willis' shirt. He doesn't say anything about it. Jason then orders a scotch and soda to flush-out the meal's after-taste. It's dark now, and their two seat-mates doze-off. Jason and Willis watch different action-adventure movies. Eventually they fall asleep, too. Later all are awakened by an announcement that the plane is descending to land. "Well that was quick," Willis says, blinking his eyes. Jason slowly comes to life as well, and glances at Willis' shirt again to discover that the trail of mystery sauce has morphed into a large smear.

The plane lands, and the four men wrestle with their belongings, preparing to de-plane. The elderly men rise awkwardly and manage to squeeze into the aisle. One of them looks down at Jason and Willis, and says softly, "Don't stay too long with Mora. He might sense that you're going to Israel."

Jason and Willis look at each other in amazement, and then they turn back to the old man. "What gave you the idea we're going to Israel?" Jason replies.

"I thought you said something about it," the man says with a slight grin.

"I'm sure I didn't," Jason says.

The man shrugs his shoulders. "My mistake," he says as he subtly winks. "Enjoy your visit here." The two elderly men follow the slowly moving line. Jason and Willis make it into the aisle moments later. As Jason looks ahead in the line leaving the plane, he catches a glimpse of the back of a red and brown jacket on one of the elderly men. It looks familiar, but he can't place it. When Jason and Willis enter the main part of the terminal, they look around. Curiously, the elderly men have vanished.

Jason and Willis collect their luggage and emerge from the terminal. They are met by Jill O'Toole, a representative from the U.S. embassy. She is a slim, attractive blonde in her mid-thirties with long curvy hair and piercing blue eyes. She looks more like a model than an ambassador's assistant. Jason surprises himself at being intrigued. Is Liezel's presence in his mind fading, finally allowing him to be attracted to someone else? She shakes Jason's and Willis' hands like she wants them to know she's definitely not available romantically. Jason notices that she's not wearing a wedding ring. So does Willis. Jill has an auto-car with a security officer waiting at the curb. They all get in and drive-off. Still groggy from the flight, Willis makes a pathetic attempt at small talk with Jill. She picks-up that he's hitting on her, and she brushes him aside. In a strictly business tone, she explains that she's aware the visitors are on another (unknown to her) mission. She coaches them to remain quietly in the background during the meeting with Antonin Mora. He has an uncanny way of seeing-through people.

The car drives through an impressive iron gate into the U.S. embassy compound. As Jason steps out of the car he glances back to see a darkly dressed man across the street, leaning against a building and staring at him over a holographic reading pod. Jason turns forward to climb the steps into the embassy. At the top, he turns back again. The man is still staring at him.

Jill escorts the two men into Ambassador Harper's office where she makes the introductions. Harper is tall, partially bald, and surprisingly thin for a man in his 50's. His hair looks like he had an expensive shampoo and blow-dry just minutes ago. Jason speculates he's had a chemical peel or two. He is impeccably dressed and extremely gracious--- the perfect ambassador. He briefs the men on what to expect the following day. After the ceremony the three will meet with Mora and Domenic Precora, the President of the United Religions Counsel. Mora has something important to convey to Harper, but the meeting will be short. Echoing Jill's counsel, he advises Jason and Willis to be silent at the meeting unless they are spoken-to. Harper then says, "Gentlemen, I'm sure you're tired from your flight. Jill will take you to your hotel now. I suggest you don't wander-off. Some tourists were mugged near there last night. The food there is very good anyway. Get a good night's sleep. I'll meet you in the restaurant next to the lobby at 8am tomorrow morning for breakfast. We have a private room arranged. The ceremony is at 10 o'clock, so that will give us time to talk during breakfast. After the ceremony we will meet with Mora at 12 noon. Any questions?"

"Yes, actually," Jason says. "So why is Precora attending the meeting?"

"I'm not sure," says Harper. But in the last few months he seems to follow Mora around everywhere. He keeps singing Mora's praise, like he's his right-hand man or something. And Mora appears to have a lot of influence with the Counsel. I've made some inquiries about their relationship, but no one has been able to shed any light on it. Anything more?...Very well then. Have a good evening."

On the ride to the hotel the atmosphere in the car is awkwardly quiet. Since Jill previously bruised Willis' ego, he has given-up trying to crack her armor--- at least for now. The men check into their hotel as darkness falls. They're tired and not very hungry, so they decide to put their luggage in their room, grab a light snack and a beer at the bar, and then hit the sack. At the bar, Jason goes for the Strasbourg beer again and some Frenchy foo-foo sandwich. Willis echoes the order. "So, what do you make of Jill?" Willis says as he gives Jason an elbow.

"She's pretty--- a little untouchable though," Jason replies, trying to mask his interest in her.

"I'm trying to decide whether or not to take another crack at her," Willis says. "What do you think?"

"If you do, I think you'd better do something about your crooked mustache, first. Maybe shave it off completely. Somehow your blonde hair and brown mustache don't really work together for you."

"Gee, thanks for giving it to me gently," Willis responds sarcastically. "So, do you think she'll join us for breakfast?"

"I have no idea. But if she does, I bet her meal matches her attitude--- dry toast and black coffee."

"I'll take that bet," Willis confidently replies. "She seems more like a grapefruit and yogurt woman to me." Jason and Willis argue some more about what Jill will have for breakfast until they both realize that jet lag and the lack of good quality sleep are making them sound stupid. They finish their beers, but Jason could only choke-down half his sandwich. Willis inhaled his, plus Jason's half. As they head for the elevator, Jason notices out of the corner of his eye the same darkly dressed man leaning against one of the lobby support columns. The two men walk into the elevator. As the doors close, Jason looks-out at the mysterious man who is staring back at him.

Both Jason and Willis have trouble sleeping due to jet lag. About 1am they hear sirens--- distant at first, then stopping right outside the hotel. Rays of flashing red lights poke through the gaps in their window curtains. Jason turns in his bed to take notice, and then rolls-over and closes his eyes again. Willis is more curious. He gets-up and pulls the curtains aside to see what's going-on. He can't see much--- just an ambulance and a couple of police cars. Policemen are hovered around something in the street. A little frustrated that he can't see what the fuss is all about, Willis returns to bed.

The next day in the private breakfast room, Willis opens the morning paper while waiting for Harper to show. His eyes pop, and he slaps Jason's arm to get his attention. "Check this out, Jay," he exclaims. "Those two guys on the plane with us were found beheaded last night! Their bodies were discovered right in front of the church across the street from our hotel. That's what all the commotion was about last night!"

As Willis and Jason plow through the paper to learn more, Harper shows-up. Jill is with him, and she joins them for breakfast. Willis has shaved-off his mustache. Jason clues-in the new arrivals about the two murdered men, and how he ran into them twice before. He also relates the mysterious nature of the men, and how they apparently knew things that they shouldn't have known. Neither Harper nor Jill can add anything new about the men. Jason also mentions the mysterious man he noticed yesterday and again in the hotel last night. Harper trivializes the encounters, remarking that intrigue is the name of the game in this town. They chat a bit more about Mora and Precora, and Harper tells a few entertaining ambassador stories. Jason caught Jill looking at him a couple of times, but he quickly glanced away. Both he and Willis noticed that she devoured a three-egg omelet with two croissants and a pot of tea with lots of sugar.

CHAPTER FIVE---ANTONIN MORA

The Nobel ceremony is boring, so Jason and Willis yawn a bit. Jason struggles to keep his eyes open. Sitting next to Jason, Jill nudges him to keep him awake, grinning as she does so. Jason perks-up and gives her a quick smile. He revives just in time to hear the host introduce Antonin Mora. The host recites Mora's history, starting with his time as mayor of Rome. The host specifically praises Mora for successfully negotiating with terrorists for the release of a priest and tourists as they were held hostage in a church. Jason quickly puts the pieces together and realizes that Mora is the man who left his parents in the church where they were killed. He is the one who was responsible for his parent's death! The muscles in his jaw ripple and he clenches his teeth and mumbles, "You bastard!"

Jill notices Jason's strange behavior, and whispers, "What's the matter?"

He leans toward her and whispers, "I'll tell you later."

After the ceremony, Jill drops the three men at the former E.U. Parliament building. A security detail in another car has joined them. Both cars wait at the curb. Jason is still upset. His heart is pounding, and he is increasingly apprehensive at the thought of soon being face-to-face with Mora.

"Jay, are you okay," Willis asks. "You look a little pale."

"I'm fine," Jason replies. "Just a little tired."

The building is a strange-looking structure--- circular and truncated at the top. It's supposedly patterned after the Tower of Babel. A statue of the pagan goddess Europa riding a bull adorns the patio area in front of the main doors. As they walk inside, they immediately see a large golden statue in the middle of the lobby. Jason asks, "Ambassador Harper, is that Mora?"

"Please, call me R.J. I believe it is. This is new!" Harper says, surprised. "Mora sure didn't waste any time erecting an idol of himself." They notice that most people give it a slight bow as they pass-by. The three men do not. The ones that bow are all wearing dark grey uniforms with a patch on the shoulder of a black dragon on a red background. They also notice a large painting on the lobby wall depicting the Tower of Babel.

Soon, an exceptionally tall (about 6'2") and stocky woman named Madam Derofski approaches and introduces herself as a representative from Mora's office. She coldly welcomes them. She's wearing a black uniform with a dragon patch on her shoulder, as well. She looks to be in her mid-40s. Her shiny jet-black hair is tied-back so tightly it appears to pull the skin back from her black beady eyes. She has a very pale complexion, thin lips, and no lipstick. Her countenance is unfriendly at best. The room suddenly feels chilly. She escorts the men to the top floor. After a brief walk down the hallway, she stops at an ominous large bronze double door with twin dragons embossed on it. A uniformed guard opens the door, and they walk-in.

Derofski leads them into a dimly lit parlor. The walls are made of heavy ornate dark wood paneling. Gaudy plush red chairs line the walls. A large wood desk faces the door they came through. Behind the desk is a high-back leather chair in front of a tall stained-glass window. The image on the window is of the goddess Europa riding a bull. On the front of the desk is a name plate reading 'Madam Eve L. Derofski'. The room has a faint smokey odor. "Wait here," she says in a crisp tone. After about five minutes she returns and says, "The Secretary will see you now."

Derofski turns to the men, and points her arm towards an opened door which leads to another room. "This way, gentlemen," she says. They proceed through the doorway and immediately see

Antonin Mora and Domenic Precora. Mora is an imposing figure--- about six and a half feet tall--- larger than he appeared on the stage at the ceremony. His grey shoulder-length hair is tied in a short ponytail, and he has a matching neatly groomed beard. Reportedly in his early 60s, he looks ten years younger. He's wearing a dark grey suit and a red tie. Jason's anxiety peaks as he instantly senses something powerful yet disturbing about this man. Anger, fear, and nervousness well-up within Jason, and he begins to perspire. Can he contain himself, or will his anger get the best of him and ruin the meeting with an outburst?

Precora is smaller in stature, with a ruddy complexion. He's dressed in a magnificent neatly pressed white robe with a red satin sash and a matching cap. His sash has the dragon's emblem, as does Mora's tie. Derofski makes the introductions, and they all shake hands. Precora's handshake is dry and limp. Mora's is strong and cold. Jason's hand is trembling a little as he squeezes Mora's hand a little too hard, and glares into Mora's eyes. Mora takes note and gazes back with a slight frown. Jason feels a chill.

"Have we met before, Dr. Johnson?" Mora asks of Jason.

"I don't believe so," Jason replies, "but my parents were in Rome when you were the Mayor." Jason fights to hold-back any further comment, but starts contemplating how he might take revenge for his parent's death at Mora's hand.

"I see. I trust they enjoyed their visit." Jason grits his teeth in silence. Mora's face appears puzzled when he doesn't get a reply. "Well then," Mora says with a half-smile, "it's an honor to meet you and your staff, Mr. Ambassador. Please sit down. Would you care for some tea, coffee, or another beverage?"

"Hot tea would be nice. Thank you." Harper turns to his companions, "Jason, Rick?"

"No thank you. I'm fine," Jason replies. Willis shakes his head 'no' and waves it off. As they all settle-in, Jason glances at Precora, wondering if this meek-looking man is the priest that Mora rescued from the terrorists many years ago.

"Mr. Secretary," Harper begins, "I want to add my personal congratulations on your Nobel Prizes. I believe you are the first to win two, certainly two in one year, and in different categories at that. I'm sure it was an extremely difficult task to get enough countries to agree to re-distribute the world's food resources. As if that weren't enough, you also nearly eliminated the sovereign debts which were crushing the world's economies and impeding international commerce. How did you manage these unbelievable accomplishments?

"Thank you, Mr. Ambassador," Mora nods graciously. "It was difficult, but most countries eventually recognized the serious nature of these food shortages. Many nations were, and still are, in decline. It took some time, but apparently I was persuasive enough. To begin with, minimum production quotas were negotiated with the producing countries. As to the organizational aspect of it, I pulled together the best management minds in the world, and sequestered them for two months until they had a workable plan. The plan is in its infancy, but I have high hopes. Actually, that's the subject I want to discuss with you today. As you may be aware, food production levels are dropping further in the less healthy countries. With that in mind, we need America to increase its food production by at least 15%, 20% if possible."

Harper falls back in his chair, startled. "My word, 15% is a tall order, Mr. Secretary. With the rash of earthquakes and the new droughts, I don't see how we can do it. If you'll allow me, those nations which continue to decline are socialist dictatorships or oligarchies backed by military force. There isn't any incentive to maximize the production of anything. The key to success, as we've proven in America, is a combination of democracy and economic liberty."

Mora glances at Derofski, showing restrained anger at Harper's push-back. He squints his eyes, and glares at Harper. Then his face relaxes. "With respect, Mr. Ambassador, America is the exception due to your abundance of mineral and agricultural resources. Other countries are not so fortunate. That's why central control is necessary to equitably distribute those resources. For example, as you surely know I have recently appointed four Czars to manage world efforts to tackle the most pressing issues of our day, namely deadly plagues, pestilence, famine and impending wars. And I believe progress is being made on all four fronts."

Putting-on his most diplomatic persona, Harper takes a deep breath and replies, "Likewise with respect, Mr. Secretary, while some may agree with your last statement, I'm sure you are aware that others do not. In fact, there are many who feel that since those four Czars took office, the situations they control have only worsened."

Mora's steely-eyed squint returns. "Well, then, Mr. Ambassador, we will just have to agree to disagree. Time will tell, Mr. Ambassador. Time will tell. Just take my request back to your government… please," he demands, drumming his fingertips on the desk. After a tense pause, he says, "To answer your other question, the sovereign debt issue was actually simpler to facilitate. To make it simple, let's say country A owes country B, and country B owes country C, and country C owes country A. When their stubbornness was overcome, they realized that their intertwined debts could be neutralized by merely agreeing to do so. The key was to move private ownership of foreign debt into their own country's sovereign ownership. That involved tax credits and other adjustments. Therefore, almost all countries became both foreign creditor and foreign debtor nations. We then had to adjust for the differences in debt from country to country. That was handled by negotiating the free transfer of goods and services from one country to the other to compensate for any debt inequality. Of course, this arrangement only addressed debts and credits *among* countries. It did not address any country's remaining debts owed to its own residents."

"Amazing," Harper says admiringly. "How's it working?"

"The first part has been accomplished," Mora proudly boasts. "Most debts have been canceled or greatly reduced. The transfer of free goods and services has begun. I believe it will work-out, but there's a major complication. I'm sure you're aware of the escalating tension between the Arab world and Israel, and it's causing a problem. It stems from the severe earthquakes that hit the region two years ago. As you know, the quakes caused large horizontal fissures under the Saudi oil fields that drained the oil into Israel's underground caverns. Israel has been exporting that oil for a couple of years now. The Saudis are naturally furious about this, and now they want their oil back. And they want monetary compensation for the oil that Israel has already sold. I fear that Israel may be attacked not only for the oil but for their rare-earth mineral mines and their highly productive agricultural land. Since Russia's and Shiastan's oil has all but dried-up, Israel is the most oil-rich nation in that part of the world. So you can see why these developments make Israel a target. It's getting worse day-by-day."

"Of course," Harper says in a somber voice. "That jibes with our intelligence assessments as well. Can you see any way to defuse the situation?"

"Presently, the only deterrent is the Israel Protection Treaty I signed with Israel on behalf of the UN 10-nation bloc that America is a part of. This has kept the lid on things for now, but I'm not sure how long the forces of war can be kept at bay. The Treaty has angered not only the Muslim countries in the Middle East, Africa and Asia, but also the Muslims here in Europe, as well. Military conflict is now a distinct probability. Since America is the most powerful of the ten nations supporting the Treaty, can I rely on your continued political and military support?"

"Of course," Harper replies sharply. "The treaty was ratified by both houses of Congress and signed by President DeAngelis, so our commitment can be relied upon."

"Excellent! I will put in a call to him to make sure that our efforts are coordinated. Now to the other pressing issue--- the long-term survival of our civilization. It should be obvious by now that the depletion of natural resources, the loss of millions of people to starvation and disease, the on-going natural disasters, various agricultural issues, and the geo-political tensions I just mentioned have brought the world to the brink of collapse. Countries acting alone or even in small groups or alliances cannot provide the solutions we desperately need. We therefore need a single organization to coordinate efforts to maximize our chances of survival. The four Czars that I have recently appointed are a good start, but we need to go farther--- and quickly. I will shortly propose to the nations of the world that the UN be that organization. I am pre-announcing my proposal to the United States through you today so that I can have your support in advance. I certainly don't expect an answer from you today, but will you take our conversation back to President DeAngelis and congressional leaders for their consideration?"

Stunned at Mora's power grab attempt, Harper falls back in his chair again. He gathers himself, trying to formulate another diplomatic response. "Mr. Secretary, I certainly agree with your description of the dire condition of the world. And I will take your proposal back to our leaders, but what you are proposing is for America and the other countries in the world to surrender their remaining sovereignty to the UN, and really to you. Do I understand you correctly?"

"You do, Mr. Ambassador. I don't see another option at this point, do you?"

"That's not for me to determine, Mr. Secretary. Is there anything else?"

"No, I believe that's it. Thank you for your time today, and for your nice compliments. Madam Derofski will show you out. I enjoyed finally meeting you, Mr. Ambassador." All rise from their chairs as Harper's tea arrives. "Oh, I'm so sorry you didn't have a chance to enjoy the tea," Mora superficially laments. As they're walking out of the office, Mora looks at Jason and Willis, and quietly says with a sly smile, "Gentlemen, have a safe trip to Israel." Jason and Willis try unsuccessfully to hide their puzzled expressions.

All is quiet on the elevator ride to the ground floor. Jason successfully hides his nervousness and anger at meeting the man responsible for his parent's death. All three men are frowning as they descend, and they can't wait to leave the building. Derofski walks them down to the sidewalk and glares at them as they drive away with the security detail.

Safely in the car, the three of them simultaneously blurt, "How did he know we/you were going to Israel?"

"I have no idea," Harper says in a bewildered tone. "Your mission was top secret. Not even Jill here knew about it." Jill looks in the rear-view mirror from the front seat, but knows to keep quiet. She now knows the mission, but she had guessed it anyway.

Harper continues, "Do you believe what we heard today? Mora wants to be king of the world! Incredible! I think we've surrendered too much to the UN already, but this is a bridge too far. I'll have to take this back to Washington, of course, but there isn't a snowball's chance that the U.S. will consider it seriously. We'll have to appear to do so, of course."

Jason is still upset at meeting Mora, but he covers it by chiming-in, "Well, I certainly hope his proposal is a non-starter. I don't know about either of you, but I kept getting these cold, uncomfortable feelings about Mora, Precora, Derofski, the building--- everything, especially Derofski. She was the spookiest of them all." Harper and Willis agree. "The sooner we're on that plane the better,"

Jason says. Jill looks in the rear-view mirror at Jason. Jason looks back.

Suddenly, they hear deafening explosions behind them. Debris hit the trunk of the car and the rear wind shield. Instinctively, they all duck. Jill grabs the steering bar and quickly swerves the car around the corner, following the security detail to safety. The security officers leap out of their car and crouch next to the Ambassador's car, weapons drawn. The lead officer yells at the Ambassador to stay in the car. He then yells into his wrist comm for help and instructions. A cloud of papers and dust billows into view from the main street. Sirens faintly sound in the distance, then get louder. Dust-covered people are fearfully running away from the explosion, covering their mouths. Soon two more security details arrive at the Ambassador's car. After a brief discussion, the four cars speed away. Instead of returning to the hotel or the embassy, the cars drive to a safe house. The lead security car drives into a large open garage, followed by the Ambassador's car. The two other cars park on the street. The garage door closes, and the security team and the four from the Ambassador's car scurry into the house. Once inside, three security officers peek through the blinds of the windows in time to see emergency vehicles race-by, sirens blazing. Everyone is jittery.

"Let's turn on the comm screen," Jill finally says. They are all trans-fixed on the screen, still shocked and wondering if there will be a follow-up attack. Jason and Willis can't understand the language--- some German, some French. Harper finally explains to the two Americans that the E.U. parliament building has been blown-up. It has totally collapsed. There are no signs of life except the emergency crews frantically plowing through the rubble. After gluing themselves to the comm screen for two hours, the group starts to relax. A security officer brings out some snacks and beverages. Harper, Jill, Jason and Willis share a bottle of red wine at the kitchen table. The security officers drink sodas.

"That has to be deliberate," Harper says. "We don't know if the bomb was meant for us or for Mora, or for the U.N. for that matter." Harper asks one of the security officers who is monitoring the news, "Anything new to report, Jeff? Any speculation as to the cause?"

"Not much change, sir. A few bodies have been recovered, but no one has been found alive, yet. They're interviewing a dust-covered woman who was just outside the building when it blew." The group returns to the screen.

"Look," Jason exclaims, "It's Derofski!" Wouldn't you know that *she* would survive. I wonder if she had anything to do with it."

It's well past sunset now. After they watch the comm screen a little more, the group decides to turn-in for the night. Everyone is emotionally exhausted. There are only 4 bedrooms for 12 people. Jill gets a room to herself. Jason and Willis share a room. Harper and one of the security officers share a room. Three officers sit in chairs outside each of the three bedrooms. Two officers peer out of the windows. The remaining two officers are in the fourth bedroom. The officers rotate duties during the night.

Hours pass, but Jason can't sleep. Willis is snoring, oblivious to the trauma of the day. Jason wanders down to the kitchen, hoping to find some sleep-inducing milk. As he opens the refrigerator door, he sees a partially open carton. He pulls it out and takes a sniff. "Ugh!" he says with a scrunched-up face.

Just then he's startled by a soft voice from behind. "You, too, huh?" It's Jill.

Jason is overwhelmed by feelings of surprise and embarrassment, because he's just wearing boxers, a tee shirt, and black socks--- a real fashion statement. "Yeah," he says, "Willis' snoring kept me awake. I came down here hoping I'd find some milk."

"I see you've found some," Jill points-out. "Is there enough for me?"

57

"You can have it all if you like sour milk," he says sarcastically. "There's a bottle of sparkling water in here, though. Do you want to share it?"

"Sure," she says. She's wearing an oversized man's robe she found in a closet. Her blonde hair is pulled-back in a ponytail, and she's without lipstick. She looks a lot less like a model, but her natural beauty is not lost on Jason.

They sit at the kitchen table for a while, making small talk. Adjusting her robe, she chuckles at something Jason says. He shares some of his life's story with her. She reciprocates with her story. She's a widow--- her husband was killed rescuing hostages in Shiastan. No children, but she has a pet cat named Sadie. She has a law degree and worked for the FBI for a few years. Her father knows Harper from college, which is how she managed to get the job interview. Feeling more comfortable with her, Jason then describes his parent's tragic death, but there's more to the story than the abbreviated one he told his son Josh.

Jason continues, "As you heard in Mora's introduction, he was the Mayor of Rome who negotiated with terrorists for the release of hostages. During the negotiations, the Mayor learned that my mother was Jewish. He then informed the terrorists that one of the hostages was Jewish, and he would tell them who it is if the terrorists released all the other hostages. Since the terrorist were Muslims, and they hated Jews, they agreed. Naturally, my father wouldn't leave my mother, so he stayed behind as the others were let go. When the police stormed the church, the terrorists used Mom and Dad as human shields, and they died in the shoot-out." Jill is deeply moved, and fumbles for the right words of sympathy. She now understands Jason's puzzling reaction at the Nobel ceremony.

An awkward moment of silence follows as Jason briefly relives the heartache and anger of his parents' violent death. Watery-eyed, he then looks-up at the ceiling, and takes a deep breath, trying to regain his composure. "Sorry," he says, "but sometimes it's hard to accept that they're really gone."

Jill's sad eyes tell Jason she is genuinely sympathetic. "Of course it is," she responds. "What you're feeling is completely normal. It must have been infuriating to suddenly realize that Mora was responsible, and yet there he was, ironically accepting these accolades with you in the audience--- and then you meet him in person! I can't imagine what that must have been like. I'm so sorry you had to go through that." She gently places her hand on Jason's arm. "Did he have any idea who you really were?"

"I don't think so, although I did give him a clue. Thanks for your understanding. No need to dwell on it. What's done is done."

They continue their conversation, looking back and forth between their glasses of water and each other, but mostly at their glasses. Jason's heart is racing a bit--- a sensation he hasn't felt since Liezel's disappearance. He's captivated by Jill, and he's not sure what to do about these new feelings. She seems to be interested in him, but there isn't any opportunity to see where this could go since Jason and Willis will be leaving for the airport soon. Their conversation lasts a couple of hours, but it only seems like a few minutes have passed. Then the room starts getting lighter. The sun is coming-up. "Well," Jason says regrettably, "I guess we had better return to our rooms. Everyone else will be getting up soon, and I have a plane to catch at noon today."

"I guess we'd better," Jill says. "I didn't realize we had been talking so long." As they leave the kitchen and pass through the living room, one of the security officers at the window looks at them with an impish grin. They nod back and say 'good morning'.

Later, one-by-one everyone drifts into the living room and kitchen. They share morning greetings. One of the officers turns on the comm screen. After a few minutes, more information about the explosion is revealed. There were no survivors of the blast. Mora's and Precora's lifeless bodies were found badly mangled, and they were taken to the morgue. Derofski accompanied them in the van. A combination of relief, satisfaction and justice passes through Jason at Mora's demise. Jason is surprised at how good justice feels. Although he wishes he had a hand in it, he now has his revenge. Jill turns toward Jason and gives him a nod. She's glad for Jason, hoping that he will now be at peace. There is still no word on the cause of the explosion, but the lead investigator speculates there were several massive bombs planted at key points in the structure. The perpetrators must have had unfettered access to the building, probably through the delivery area. The security cameras were destroyed by the blast, but the recordings were transmitted to police headquarters in a nearby building.

Harper has much to do, so he directs Jill to drive Jason and Willis to their hotel to get their belongings, and then leave for the airport. One security team accompanies them. The other two teams leave with Harper. During the drive to the airport Jason catches Jill looking back at him from time to time in the rear-view mirror. Jill drops them off at the airport, and she and Jason share a lingering handshake. Their eyes send silent messages to each other of affection and regret that they will not see each other again. They slowly separate and say good-bye. A security officer walks them into the airport. Jason looks back at Jill as he goes through the doors. She gives Jason a diminutive wave and manages a sad smile.

As the trio make their way to the gate, they pass through facial recognition detectors and scanners that are designed to detect suspicious items. At one point they stop to check one of the many comm screens for the latest news. Incredibly, Mora and Precora are alive! By the time their van arrived at the morgue, they had miraculously revived. Jason's feelings of anxiety and hatred return. "Rick!" Jason shouts, "are you seeing this? What is it with this guy? No one could have survived that collapse. Mora has not only survived but has apparently come back from the dead! Or perhaps he didn't die in the first place. I thought justice had been served, but obviously not." Jason glares at the screen. "Maybe I'll have to handle this myself some day."

"Jason," Rick replies, "I've never seen you so angry. You've got to cool down. That kind of talk can only lead to bad things for you, and it will eat you up from the inside. Believe me, I know. I remember feeling angry and revengeful when my ex-fiancee dumped me. That went on for almost a year. It only made me miserable, and it didn't hurt her a bit. Finally, a good friend of mine gave me some really good advice to forgive her and move on. I was a lot happier after that. Anyway, what can you really do about Mora? He's in France, and we'll be in Israel. Your paths will never cross again."

"You're probably right, Rick, but I can't just turn-off my feelings like that." Suddenly, Jason points to the comm screen. "Shhh, look, there's Mora."

On the comm broadcast, Mora's wounds are being dressed as the attending physician is being interviewed. The physician describes their recovery as a miracle, especially since they were the only survivors of the blast. Mora's face is bloody and bruised. His ponytail is unraveled and full of dust. He angrily vows to find the perpetrators and bring them to justice. Jason and Willis now realize there is something scary and supernatural about this man. The pair board the plane. Once they're settled-in, the two men silently look at each other, knowing what the other is thinking: *'If Strasbourg was this dangerous, what lies ahead, and what will Mora do next?'*

CHAPTER SIX---TENSIONS MOUNT

The flight from Strasbourg stops in Rome to discharge and take-on passengers. Anger wells-up in Jason once again as he looks out of the window at the city where his parents were killed. After an hour, the plane continues on to Tel-Aviv. The flight is uneventful, and there's nothing to look at out the window due to the pervasive volcanic dust cloud, so Jason and Willis manage to snooze a little. On the approach to the Tel-Aviv airport, an alarm in the cabin suddenly shocks them awake. The plane banks hard to the right. Anti-missile flares and decoys deploy. Now wide awake, Willis peers-out of his window in time to see a barrage of small rockets racing toward the plane. Most of the rockets hit the decoys or follow the flares. However, a couple of them get through the plane's defenses, glancing harmlessly off the side of the plane without exploding. Another rocket succeeds, and blows-off the back half of the port engine. The plane shakes. The passengers scream. Amazingly, the pilot manages to regain control of the plane. Willis looks out of his window again to see a large piece of engine housing whipping around under the wing, barely attached. The engine is on fire.

The plane vibrates violently as it swerves back and forth on its final approach. Jason and Willis don't wait for the 'assume the position' announcement. They quickly bend forward, heads resting in their arms. The plane vibrates wildly. The men look at each other. Fear grips their faces. For the first time in years, Jason starts to pray. Just before touch-down, the plane tilts. The wheels on the low side slam onto the runway, and the dangling engine piece scrapes the pavement in a shower of sparks. It quickly flies-off. The plane then bounces and tilts the other way. Finally, the plane starts to settle down. The nose wheels briefly touch-down, bounce, and then stay down. Since the blown engine doesn't have its reverse thruster anymore, the pilot pumps the wheel brakes hard. They start squealing and smoking. Hearing and seeing the "high brake temperature" alarm, the pilot decides to ease-off the brakes. The end of the runway looms rapidly ahead. His only recourse is to engage the reverse thruster on the starboard engine. When he does so he simultaneously hits the brakes again, and the plane lurches to the starboard side. The pilot and co-pilot fight to steer the plane back, but they can't hold it, and the plane veers off the runway. The nose gear collapses, and the front of the fuselage slams to the ground. The plane finally skids to a halt, carving a huge gash in the ground. Emergency vehicles swarm around the plane, sirens blazing. Smoke billows from the damaged engine, and fire crews flood it with clouds of extinguishing foam.

Buses quickly arrive, and the passengers start to deplane via the inflatable chutes. As Jason and Willis shuffle to the front egress, the cock pit door opens. A sweaty and weary Capt. Ron Ben-Zvi steps into the doorway. Still shaking, Jason and Willis can only mutter a weak "Thank you," and then they slide down the emergency chute. Airport personnel quickly assess the passengers' condition, and provide water and aid where necessary. No one is injured, but everyone is emotionally spent. Some are in shock. All are bussed to the terminal.

On the ride to the terminal Jason leans toward a frowning Willis who is staring straight ahead. "You know," Jason says, "I had a bad feeling about this assignment, and now it's come to pass. I wish I had just said 'no', but it's obviously too late to turn back now. Wouldn't it have been ironic if we had bought it before we even got to the dangerous part?... Rick?... Rick?"

"Huh?" Willis perks-up. "Sorry, I guess I was just re-living my past. Dangerous part, yeah, dangerous part. Can't wait."

Jason and Willis stagger into the terminal, still shaken by their ordeal. They are soon met by their contact agent and a uniformed security detail from the Israeli Defense Force (IDF). The agent is Lt. Anah Kunkel. She looks to be in her early 30's with heavy black-frame glasses that match her large dark eyebrows. Like Jill, Anah has piercing blue eyes. A military cap is slightly tilted over her short black wavy hair, and her uniform is smartly-pressed, covering a modestly muscular build. Her handshake is stiff and firm--- very military. She's not wearing make-up or lipstick, but she doesn't need to--- she's naturally attractive. Despite his shaken condition, Jason perks-up when he sees her, and he instinctively tries to comb his unruly hair with his fingers. Of course, she wants to know if they're all right, and she is relieved when they tell her they are.

"That was quite a welcome for you," she says. "We normally don't get this fancy." Her attempt at humor is lost on the two men. She informs them that similar attacks have occasionally occurred in the past, but with only one or two rockets. Obviously, the attacks are becoming more alarming. "I'm sorry to be so abrupt," she continues, "but we have no time to lose. The situation here has become critical." Anah informs the pair that Antonin Mora has now accused Israel of being responsible for the Strasbourg explosion. He has terminated the Israel Protection Treaty, and is seeking revenge. Israeli intelligence sources, however, have concluded that the explosion was planned and carried-out by one or more members of the UN ten-nation bloc that Mora leads. Apparently, these nations were gravely worried about his abuse of power and about how he was leading the world on a destructive path. "Were either of you aware of America's involvement in the incident?" She asks.

Jason replies, "I'm not aware, nor would I have been aware of any American involvement. Rick and I and Ambassador Harper met with Mora prior to coming here, so I can see why someone would want him out of the way. He's power hungry. There was definitely something sinister about him and his weird assistant Madam Derofski. Actually, I think she was more in control of things. It would be an understatement to say she made us all feel very uncomfortable. And another thing--- Mora knew we were coming here. Only a few people had that information. I can't imagine there was a leak from our side. Is it possible that the leak was from your side?"

Anah snaps-back angrily, "Look, Dr. Johnson, we've been constantly attacked since the 1940's. We sleep with one eye open--- in a constant state of fear. Any leak from our side would be self-destructive and totally idiotic. You obviously don't know anything about the Israeli people. I'm insulted you would even entertain such a thought!"

Jason stops walking and defensively holds-up both hands. "Whoa, Lieutenant. I didn't mean to accuse you or Israel of anything. I just asked the question. The leak came from somewhere." Suddenly, Anah did not seem so attractive anymore. "I'll tell you what," Jason continues, "I'm going to contact my boss and tell him what happened. If there's a leak on our side, he'll find it. I apologize for insulting you. I certainly didn't mean to."

"Apology accepted," Anah says in a softer tone. "I'm sorry I snapped at you. I'm a little on-edge right now. Just to make sure, I'll have the leak checked-out on my end as well." Jason sees her in an attractive light once again. Anah informs the men that the remaining three members of their team will be arriving in a couple of hours. They will be picked-up separately, because Jason and Willis are needed in the IDF Command Center immediately.

As they walk through the airport, Jason and Willis notice armed IDF soldiers on patrol. Anah explains that the entire country is on heightened alert. The military is mobilizing, and civilians are preparing for the worst. On their way out of the airport they pass through body scanners. Anah is waved-through, but Jason and Willis are stopped by a security officer. Two other armed guards instantly appear, hands on their weapons. "Excuse me, gentlemen," the first officer says in a stern but polite voice, "I'll have to ask you to please remove those devices from your breast pockets--- slowly." Jason and Willis nervously comply.

"These are special comm units so my partner and I can communicate without being hacked." Jason says. The officer examines them and shows them to the other guards.

"I've seen these before," the older guard says. "I used to work in a unit that uses them, too. They're okay." The guard waves his hand in front of the other guard and says in an artificially low voice, "These are not the droids we're looking for. Let them go." The guards smile and chuckle, but Jason, Willis and Anah look at each other with clueless frowns. They're in a hurry, so they don't ask the guards for an explanation. They exit the terminal and pile into a transport. Another transport with an armed security detail is parked ahead of them.

The transports drive east toward the mountains near Jerusalem. They observe frantic activity everywhere--- driverless military vehicles moving supplies; armed soldiers at street corners; people impatiently lined-up at stores. The roads are clogged with vehicles heading for the mountains. Clearly, panic is in the air. As they pass into agricultural areas, the traffic congestion clears. Jason marvels at the seemingly unending acres of beautiful bright green crops and fruit trees--- amazingly abundant in what used to be a barren desert. He points–out the scene to Willis. Surprisingly, Willis knows how the desert miracle was accomplished. "Decades ago," he explains, "Israel constructed desalinization plants which processed sea water into potable water. The water was then used for domestic consumption as well as for agricultural purposes. In addition, wastewater was extensively treated and recycled for agricultural use. Irrigation systems were constructed to supply water to the desert. Finally, compost was generated from domestic bio-degradable waste, and it was applied to the land. Evaporation-inhibiting films were developed. Crops were scientifically selected and genetically developed for the conditions in the region, and monitoring and regulating systems were installed to improve watering and composting efficiencies. The desert was therefore transformed into an enviable agricultural miracle."

Jason is amazed at Willis' knowledge. "So how do you know all this, Rick?"

"I'm not just a pretty face, you know," he quips. Anah is likewise impressed, and compliments Willis to his pleasant surprise.

To discourage anyone from following the vehicles, they turn-off the main road and enter a small town. While Jason and Willis enjoy the ride, the driver keeps glancing worriedly into the rear-view camera screen. "Lieutenant, I think we're being followed," he finally says. "I'll alert the detail in the other transport." Jason, Willis, and Anah turn around to see an old e-car with two shadowy figures inside.

"I'll check their plates," Anah says sharply. Grabbing a comm from the driver, she navigates to a vehicle registration data base. "It's a fake tag," she says loudly. "Pretend like we didn't make him. I'll call for support." After the call she says, "Combat drones are on the way."

A few minutes later, the front transport suddenly explodes. It catapults through a cloud of smoke straight towards Anah's vehicle. The driver veers sharply to the right, but it's too late. The flying vehicle smashes the front corner of the transport where Anah is sitting. She instinctively ducks and covers her head. The crushing blow thrusts a sharp metal strip towards her, knocking her cap off and ripping a 4" gash in the back of her hand. Blood oozes down her arm. She grabs her hand and squeezes the wound. She then leans toward the driver to keep away from the metal that pokes menacingly at her. Suddenly, bullets ping across the right side of the transport and the bullet-proof windows. Everyone quickly turns to see a dusty beat-up truck racing at the transport from a side road. The truck gives chase with an armed man hanging out one of the side windows. He fires a burst from his weapon, but the bullets merely bounce off the transport. People on the sidewalks scream and scramble for cover. Anah's driver turns sharply around a corner, scraping a light pole. As the pursuing truck speeds around the corner it also heads toward the pole. Wide-eyed, the gunman at the window tries to duck back into the truck. He's too late. The pole tears-off his head and one arm. The truck continues the chase with the gunman's remaining arm and bloody torso hanging out of the window. Suddenly the truck explodes, flinging debris into the nearby buildings. Jason and Willis pop their heads up to see the flaming truck roll over and over and crash into a building. The combat drones have arrived. In an instant the attack is over. Everyone in the transport struggles to catch their breath. "Oh my God!" Jason finally speaks-up. "Is everyone okay? Lieutenant?"

"I have a nasty cut on my hand, but I'll live," Anah replies in a shaky voice. "Corporal," she says to the driver, "you were amazing. Thank you. Where did you learn to drive like that?"

"I'm not just a pretty face, Lieutenant," he says as he turns and winks.

Willis chimes-in, "So who were they, and why us?"

"Yeah," Jason interrupts, "we've been attacked twice now in the last couple of hours. If it is Mora, he's not wasting much time."

Anah replies, "I suppose it's possible, but more likely it's the remnants of Hezbollah or one of the other militant groups."

"But I thought they were pretty much side-lined after Sinai was established," Jason says.

"True," Anah replies, "their support evaporated when the Palestinians gained a country of their own, but the fighters didn't just disappear. Most of them found legitimate employment, but the hard-liners had nowhere else to go, so they just kept fighting, regardless of how weak their cause was. The Communists didn't disappear when the Soviet Union was dissolved, did they? They just put on a different face. But we have other enemies, too, some of them very powerful. I'm sure you know who I mean. They have eyes and ears everywhere, even inside our fortified walls. I don't know how, but they must have known you were coming, and what you came here to do. The forces against Israel are so full of hate they didn't care who was on your plane when they attacked it. They even sacrifice their own people. Unfortunately, the violence seems to be escalating. I hope your comrades make it here safely."

Anah calls headquarters to report-in. She wants to go back to the other transport, but she's directed to continue-on because Jason and Willis are desperately needed at the Command Center. Medical and military vehicles are on their way to the other transport anyway. Jason and Willis sit back in their seats, solemnly looking at each other, contemplating the gravity of the situation. This is a lot more dangerous than they expected. Their thoughts quickly turn to their families back home, wondering if they will see them again. Fearing a follow-up attack, Anah's driver takes an erratic routing to their destination. The drones shadow them for the remainder of the trip.

CHAPTER SEVEN---A DAUNTING TASK

Their journey continues until they reach the historic Petra foothills south of Jerusalem. The transport enters an imposing labyrinth of vehicle barriers in front of a heavily guarded gate. They are obviously about to enter a well-fortified compound surrounded by high concrete walls. Battle stations protrude from the tops of the walls. They drive through the compound on an inclined roadway toward a large concrete bunker near the top of the mountain. Jason turns back to see an awesome view of the valley below--- green trees, lush farmland, and clean white-washed cities. The air is clear, and he can see for miles. He focuses on the old city of Jerusalem, the Wailing Wall, the Dome of the Rock, and the recently constructed Temple. The Temple stands-out from its surroundings with its towering columns, stark white features, and gold trim. It gleams in the late afternoon sunlight. He mentally compares this marvelous sight with the backwardness and squalor found in the surrounding countries. Israel has been truly blessed.

Huge steel doors in the bunker slide open, and the transport enters. Instead of stopping, it proceeds into a long well-lit tunnel. It passes another transport going in the opposite direction. The drivers give a subdued wave to each other. Anah tells Jason and Willis that the fortress they entered outside the tunnel is a decoy. The operational bunker is a half-mile ahead. As they drive along, Anah points-out four escape tunnels in case the main entrance is blocked or compromised. At the end of the main tunnel, Jason and Willis are greeted by two Israeli officers and a plain-clothed official. After introductions, they are quickly ushered into a large Command Center plastered with comm screens, computerized control stations, and several large holographic screens, one of which displays the entire Middle East. The room is buzzing with activity. Jason looks up to a mezzanine lined with drone operator stations. Still clutching her bleeding hand, Anah tells Jason and

Willis that there are two more areas of those. The room is quite long, and there are small camouflaged windows at each end so each side of the mountain can be observed in case the exterior cameras fail.

They make their way across the room towards a group of high-ranking military officers. One man is noticeably taller than the rest. He is Abraham Dayan, the Commanding General of the IDF. He is statuesque--- snow white silky hair, strikingly green eyes, and a well-trimmed white beard and mustache. He looks to be exceptionally fit for a man of his age and rank. He exudes confidence and competence, and he appears paradoxically calm in the face of the escalating crisis. Dayan's grip is both firm and comforting. "Welcome to Petra, gentlemen," he says in a deep commanding voice. "As I'm sure you know, we are facing a dire situation here, and we need your help immediately. Several key surveillance satellites have been disabled or destroyed by, we think, the Russians and Chinese. Fortunately, we have deployed high altitude stealth drones to give us eyes again. They have observed massive armies from Russia and Northern Shiastan converging in Jordan and moving toward Israel from the north east. Convoys from Saudi Arabia and Southern Shiastan are also converging in Jordan and moving from the south east. Since we have heavily fortified the Golan Heights, I believe that the armies will cross the Jordan River at the most fordable spots north and south of the Dead Sea where our defenses are weaker. As if that weren't alarming enough, a Chinese flotilla is headed toward the Persian Gulf, and another one is off the West African coast, headed toward the Mediterranean Sea. We have mobilized our defenses, and America is mobilizing theirs to come to our aid. Of course, the UN is now against us, and none of the other countries want to be involved.

This is shaping-up to be the defining battle between good and evil. Israel must not only survive, but we must completely vanquish these evil forces knocking at our door. If we prevail, the

71

world can be at peace for a long time. If we don't, the world will enter a new dark age. We *must* prevail. We *will* prevail. So we must do all we can to 'keep the wolves at bay' while we wait for help from America. That's where your team comes-in. We have a sizable inventory of airborne and underwater swarm drones and a number of large land-based drones which we purchased from America. In addition, we have secretly made thousands of all these drone types on our 3D printers. Also, we have developed miniaturized high-powered explosives to replace the weaker ones furnished with your drones. I understand you gentlemen developed the latest applications of this swarm drone technology, so we need you to upgrade these systems to our current needs. We also need to coordinate our drones with yours, and all the drones with our other defenses. Our survival depends on it. Can we count on you, and what do you need?"

"That's why we're here, Sir," Jason replies. "We have our manuals and plug-ins to program and integrate the systems. Just show us the interface stations, and we'll get to work. We'll also need one of each type of your drones to examine and test. Then the new instructions can be downloaded to all your systems." Jason wonders how Dayan can project such confidence in the face of these overwhelming forces. The task ahead is daunting, and the chances of surviving are dim at best. If the Americans don't get here in time, he fears Israel will surely be destroyed, and he could be captured or killed. He may never see his son again.

"Very well," Dayan says. "Lt. Kunkel will make sure you have everything you need--- technical support, food, coffee. No booze." He offers a tight-lipped smile, trying to lighten the atmosphere a little. "Our staff here will help you with the details of our strategy. We only have two or three days at the most before the attack begins. Will we be ready?"

"We'll do our best, Sir," Jason says hesitantly, trying to conceal his lack of confidence.

"We'll need better than your best," Dayan replies. "The fate of the world is at stake, not just Israel's. You have two days to integrate and test everything."

Just then a message comes-in. The plane carrying Jason's other three team members was hit by rockets on its approach to Tel-Aviv. The plane exploded and crashed into the Mediterranean Sea. No survivors have been spotted yet. Jason and Willis look at each other. Their faces turn pale as they try to conceal their panic. They only met the three men briefly, but their apparent death of course saddens them. Furthermore, without the other team members, the time allowed for their work is grossly inadequate. The task seems impossible. They must get to work immediately. Anah expresses her condolences and then escorts the men to their workstations. She seems a little cold and unsympathetic to the loss of the three men. Jason rationalizes that she has probably seen many of her friends and countrymen die, so he cuts her some slack. She makes more introductions to the nearby techs and operators. Jason and Willis unpack their bags and get ready to work. As Anah leans over the workstation to help them access the IDF systems, her arm brushes against Jason's shoulder. They both instinctively flinch and say "Sorry" at the same time. However, Jason didn't really mind the accidental touch. Neither did Anah.

Jason takes the lead since the new application of swarm technology was his creation. Willis was the chief engineer on the project. After three hours of work, the sad news of the lost team members has taken a back seat to the urgency and pressure of their task. Willis leans-back in his chair to rest his eyes a little, and he whispers to Jason, "Did you notice that there's an unusual number of women in here?"

"The fate of Israel is in our hands, and you're concerned with women?" Jason replies rhetorically. After a pause he says, "Yeah, that's the way it is here. Since Israel is such a small country, the military needs to utilize all the able-bodied people they can. Both men and women are required to join a defense organization for at least four years. They used to require a shorter term, but they had to increase it a few years ago due to the heightened threats in the region. Don't look now--- and I even hate to mention it--- but there's a young woman to your right that keeps looking at you." Willis turns. "I said *don't* look," Jason whispers back, frowning in frustration.

"She's not bad," Willis says. "But she looks like she could be my sister. Thanks for suggesting I shave-off my mustache."

Jason sneaks another peek at the woman. Willis is right--- she's thin, has short blonde hair, and looks kind of geeky, but she's prettier than Willis. "Forget it," Jason urges Willis. "We've got serious work to do. Maybe you could stroll over there when we take a break, *if* we get a break."

The first break comes along about 6pm. When Jason pushes his chair back and announces the break, Willis turns to the 'woman of interest,' but she's gone. After a quick snack and coffee, the work continues into the night. About 10pm Jason and Anah grab a sandwich in the cafeteria. Willis continues to work because he snuck a quick sandwich two hours ago, and another one is on his desk.

"How's your hand?" Jason asks.

"It still stings, but I've felt worse," she replies, trying to mask the pain. Jason sees-through her masquerade, but he's impressed by her grit. He then notices Anah's necklace. The pendant is a Cross laid on the Star of David. "That's an unusual necklace," he remarks.

"I'm a Jewish Christian, also called a Messianic Jew," she replies. "It means I'm culturally Jewish, but I also believe Jesus is the Messiah. We observe all the Jewish customs and traditions, but we celebrate Christmas and Easter, as well. Jesus was a Jew, you know."

74

"Well of course he was," Jason replies. "I'm afraid I haven't been the most pious Jew," he laments. "It seems like I always have other things to do instead of attending synagogue. Mostly, I'm either working or spending time with my son." Jason fills-in Anah on his son, his divorce, his town, career, and his wife's mysterious disappearance. He also relates the tragic story of his parent's death at the hands of Antonin Mora. Anah was aware of Mora's apparent death and miraculous recovery. Jason is surprisingly forthcoming with someone he just met. Anah explains more of her background. She's single--- never been married. Her parents and older brother emigrated from Germany, but she was born in Israel. She's very patriotic and dedicated to defending her country. As they periodically make eye contact, Jason notices how beautiful she is, especially her bright blue eyes. He senses a mutual attraction. He also remarks that she isn't wearing a wrist comm. She explains that they can be tracked or monitored, and not just by the proper agencies. All IDF personnel on bunker duty were ordered to discard them. Jason wonders how she functions without one, so she explains that she lives in a self-sufficient enclave about 5 miles away from the Command Center. She eats most of her meals here, but when she needs to buy something outside the enclave, she uses a trusted friend. In order to pull this off, she had to 'drop-off the radar', so to speak. Not even her family knows exactly where she is.

Jason realizes he's still wearing **his** wrist comm. When he points that out to Anah she jumps-up in a panic, and makes him take it off immediately. She then runs back into the main room and gets Willis' as well. She rummages around and finds a hammer, and then smashes the two wrist comms into pieces. The loud bangs of the hammer smashing on the metal desk makes the personnel in the room jump. Some instinctively crouch. A senior officer quickly comes over. Anah sheepishly explains that in the heightened stress of the day, neither she nor the security personnel thought to check the two guests for wrist comms. The officer glares at Anah, but lets her off the hook. Realizing that the security personnel are more to blame, he struts-off to give them a reaming-out.

As the night wears-on, Jason and Willis start losing efficiency, and they make a couple of mistakes. It's time to get some much-needed rest. Anah agrees, and she shows the two men to their quarters. She says good night. As she closes the door, she lingers a bit and looks back at Jason. He makes eye contact with her. Jason wonders why she never married. Maybe she has a boyfriend she didn't tell him about. He also wonders why he has been attracted to two different women in the space of just a few of days, whereas he hasn't found any women of interest back home in San Marita. Perhaps he's now ready to let go of Liezel and move-on. Then it dawns on him--- both Jill and Anah have blue eyes, just like Liezel's. He looks down at his wedding ring, and slowly spins it around his finger with his other hand. After several moments of contemplation, he finally concludes he will never see Liezel again. He slowly slides the ring off and puts it in is pants pocket.

Fresh from a short but decent night's sleep, Jason and Willis make fast progress the following morning. By 11am they have completed their programming and check-out. By 4pm they have integrated their systems into the IDF systems. It takes another four hours to test and re-test the integration. Amazingly, everything seems to be ready, but technology is famous for throwing curve balls. Only time will tell.

The two men are exhausted. They return to their quarters and flop down on their beds. It's now 8:30pm, and it's dark. Willis starts snoring already. Jason closes his eyes, but can't fall asleep. Minutes later there's a soft knock on the door. Jason gets-up and opens it. It's Anah, and she has two cups of chamomile tea. Jason invites her in as he gingerly grabs the hot cup. Seeing no chairs in the dimly lit room, they sit on the edge of his bed. Anah congratulates him and thanks him for his successful hard work. He thanks her for her help, too. She tells him that the approaching armies and flotillas will be close enough to engage by noon tomorrow. The two men will be needed in the command room in case of problems or last-minute adjustments. Tactics will undoubtedly change as the battle unfolds, and the systems will need to adapt. The two engage in some nervous small talk. The teas get cold. They cease talking for a moment as their eyes dart back and forth into each other's eyes. Anah starts to lean very slightly toward Jason, but then pulls back. She realizes that this is not the time, and she breaks the mutual gaze. She takes his cup, saying he really needs a good night's sleep, for tomorrow the fate of Israel will be decided. She quietly leaves the room.

CHAPTER EIGHT---THE FINAL BATTLE

About 4am the following morning, Jason and Willis are rudely awakened by a loud pounding on the door. An IDF officer barges-in. They are needed in the command center immediately. Groggy and rubbing their eyes, the men slowly get up. Neither man was able to sleep much--- thinking about the life-threatening conflict that lay ahead. As they quickly dress, the officer informs the men that during the night hostile submarines launched nuclear-tipped hypersonic missiles that hit key U.S. air and naval bases in America, Europe, Japan, and Guam. America's strategic bombers never made it off their runways. 70% of America's air and sea capabilities were destroyed, including all the aircraft carriers in the open sea on their way to Israel. The Strategic Air and Space Command headquarters in the Colorado mountains was severely damaged. Command and control systems were disabled, but some information got out. EMPs (Electro-Magnetic Pulse) nuclear missiles detonated high in the air, and have disabled most non-military electronic equipment, vehicles and communications in America. Electricity, energy, and food production have been crippled in most areas by a massive cyber-attack. Concentrating on rural areas, sleeper cells were activated to bomb grocery stores, poison water supplies and murder as many Americans as possible. As in 1941, Pearl Harbor is again an underwater graveyard. But also as in 1941, the sleeping giant has been awakened.

From hidden bunkers; from strategically placed submarines; and from stealth space-based platforms, America retaliated with an onslaught of nuclear hypersonic missiles and ICBMs of their own. Russian and Chinese air and naval bases and key cities in those countries were reduced to radioactive rubble, as was Tehran and military targets in Iran. However, before the American missiles hit their targets, China and Russia launched a second wave of ground-based hypersonic ICBMs. The key cities of Washington, D.C.., New York City, Los Angeles, Chicago, Houston, and San Francisco have been flattened and forever contaminated with radiation. The oil refineries on the Gulf coast and the storage facilities in Cushing, Oklahoma were also destroyed. World War III started and ended in one day. All missiles on all sides have been spent, and a nuclear winter will surely follow, threatening the survival of all life on earth.

Obviously, America is now too weak to come to Israel's aid. A feeling of impending doom washes over the two Americans. Jason and Willis voice their nearly paralyzing fear to each other about their families back home. They realize there will be no way of communicating with them because the infrastructure in the U.S. is gone. Jason speculates that San Marita is probably far enough away from key targets, but he's still worried. He knows Kathy will be too paralyzed to do what needs to be done. Joshua will have to step-up. Will he be able? Then there's the real probability that radiation or an errant missile has... Jason forces himself to stop thinking the worst. Willis has family near San Francisco and Los Angeles, so he's frantic and he breaks-down. In all the years they've worked together, Jason has never seen Willis so emotional and vulnerable. Jason tries to console him. "It's out of our control, Rick. All we can do now is hope for the best. If we survive this thing there must be some way of getting information from back home. I'll try to contact Chris Christopher, if he's alive. If anyone can help, he can. In any event, this looks like it's going to be our last assignment, so we'll just have to pull ourselves together and give it our best. We don't want to be responsible for the defeat of Israel because we couldn't rise to the occasion."

"I guess you're right, Jay," Willis sighs as he slowly pulls his hands from his face. Jason places his hand on Willis' shoulder. They raise their heads, and take a deep breath. Willis says with fire in his eyes and a clenched jaw, "Alright then, let's send these bastards to hell!" Jason now sees Willis in a completely new light. The crooked-mustached, stained-shirt, uninspired goof has been transformed into a driven let-me-at-'em go-getter. Both men are charged-up, and they hustle into the Command Center with new vigor. Anah is there with two cups of coffee for them. She briefs them on the local situation: Israeli surveillance drones revealed that the invading armies are almost near enough to begin the attack. But instead of attacking, the armies have stopped well beyond Israeli defensive missile and artillery range. Jason silently wonders why Israel was spared from the nuclear attack. He will get his answer later.

Anah continues, "I know you've been briefed on the nuclear exchange that happened over-night. Do you have friends or family near the bomb sites?" Both men painfully nod. "I hope they're alright. You must be very worried. Many in this room have been in your shoes, as well, including me. We should keep getting surveillance drone images as the day unfolds. We also have some stealth surveillance satellites over America, so I'll let you know if any information comes through. Right now, you're needed at your work stations. I'll bring you something to eat."

Back in San Marita, the attack came in the early evening when Josh and Kathy were eating dinner. They were interrupted by multiple flashes of light, followed by muffled thunder-like claps. Naturally curious, they walked outside and looked with horror to see the mushroom clouds over San Francisco and the naval base at Bremerton, Washington. Kathy grabbed Josh and they ran back into the house just as the pressure waves hit. Fortunately, San Marita is far enough from the blasts so that the waves were fairly weak by the time they reached Kathy's house. Still, the house shook, startling Kathy and Josh. Kathy rushed Josh into the bathroom, and they laid down in the bathtub, gripped with fear.

After thirty minutes or so, they timidly emerged from the bathroom. All comms were down. Kathy fought-back fear and panic, trying to be brave for her son. Josh saw through her facade. "Don't worry, Mom," Josh said with a quiver in his voice. "I know what to do. We talked about things like this in school. First we need to fill-up the bathtub before the radiation contaminates the water source." Kathy plugged the tub drain and started filling the tub with water. "I'll check the solar and wind turbine systems," Josh said, his confidence growing. "Can you take stock of our food and other supplies?"

Kathy was so frightened that she had trouble focusing. She was both surprised and relieved that Josh was taking charge. He was filling the void left by his father's departure. At fifteen years old, Josh's voice was deeper, and some muscles were appearing on his lanky frame. He, too, was frightened, but as the 'man of the house,' Josh had developed a sense of responsibility. Now he was rising above his fears. He loves his mother, and feels a strong need to protect her.

The solar panels and wind turbine should provide enough electricity if they managed things carefully. The fuel for the generator could last for a couple of weeks if it was used sparingly. Kathy guessed they had enough food to last about a month if they rationed it. There were several jugs of drinking water on hand, but not enough to last as long as the food. Boiling the bathtub water would have to do. But how to keep radioactive fall-out from seeping into the house? "Come-on, Mom," Josh urged. "Help me shut all the windows and doors tightly. "I'll tape over all the joints and seams." With the house this air-tight, fresh air would be a concern. A bountiful collection of indoor plants could provide some oxygen, but who knows for how long. The plants would need precious water, but they're not going to get it.

Kathy had an old shot gun her father gave her. If marauders showed-up, there would be nowhere to hide, so she would have to confront them. She knew she would be so afraid that she didn't think she could pull it off. She rummaged through her bedroom closet, and brought it into the living room where Josh was finishing his taping job. "Gosh, Mom," Josh exclaimed, "where'd that come from?"

"Dad gave it to me just before he died," she replied. "I never thought I would need it. But desperate people do desperate things, and someone needing food or money or something else might try to break-in here. There could even be gangs of looters out there--- or worse. I wish your father were here. We don't even know where he is or if he's even alive. If San Francisco was bombed, Washington D.C. surely was, too." Then it hit Josh--- his dad went to Washington, and, yes, as the nation's capital it must have been bombed--- probably worse than San Francisco. Josh's lower lip started quivering, and his eyes began to water. He dropped to his knees. His hands quickly covered his face. The thought of his father being incinerated in a nuclear attack was too horrible to bear. He burst into tears.

After a few minutes he looked up and saw a sense of hopelessness creep onto his mother's face. He knew he had to step-up. He finally took a deep breath and rose to his feet. "You know, Mom, Dad might have been on his way home when the attack came. Or maybe they sent him somewhere else. He could be in town already, but we just don't know since the comms are down. Let's not assume the worst until we get some information. He might just show up here any time now. As for the shot gun, don't worry, Mom. I got this. Last year, Dad taught me how to shoot his rifle. I knew you wouldn't approve, so we kept it a secret." Josh was lying. His father never had a rifle. "So, where's the ammo?"

Kathy looked down in despair, and solemnly shook her head. "There isn't any."

Josh's confidence left him, and he swallowed with an audible gulp. "No ammo? Okay then, we'll just have to fake-it."

Josh didn't know how, but he knew he would have to grow-up quickly. At least for now, Kathy and Josh were safe. They could survive for a time, but the prospects for long-term survival were slim.

The atmosphere in the command center is understandably tense. Beads of sweat form on the foreheads of the techs and operators as they focus on their comm screens and communication systems. As daylight breaks, it becomes evident how massive the enemy forces are--- an estimated two million men and vehicles. During the last few days the water level in the Jordan River has uncharacteristically dropped, exposing the muddy bottom in some areas. Taking advantage of this development, the armies aligned themselves into two main columns which are pointed toward shallow crossing points in the river north and south of the Dead Sea--- just as Dayan predicted. Two more hours pass. Then Dayan gets word that Antonin Mora has negotiated with the Russians and Arabs to let the residents of Jerusalem evacuate before the attack. Also, the Temple Mount will be protected. The residents have twenty-four hours to complete the evacuation. The news lifts the spirits a little in the command center, since many of the personnel have family in the area. As the evacuation proceeds, the command center personnel rotate rest shifts so that everyone will be more alert when the battle begins.

The next morning, surveillance drone transmissions show Arabs moving into Jerusalem with cheers and celebratory weapons fire. Soon, a small convoy of black vehicles drives-up to the Temple. The sides of the vehicles have the emblem of a black dragon on a red background. Mora, Precora, Derofski, and their entourage emerge from the vehicles. They climb the steps and enter the Temple. Cameras inside the Temple broadcast the scene of Mora approaching the Ark of the Covenant, and defiantly sitting down on it as if it were a throne. Jaws drop in the command center. No one speaks, but tempers boil at this blasphemous and insulting spectacle.

Jason bristles at the sight of his seemingly invincible nemesis. Willis notices that Jason is transfixed at one of the screens, his jaw muscles rippling as his teeth grind in anger.

"Jay," Rick says, "what's the matter?"

Maintaining his motionless glare at the screen, Jason quietly mumbles, "It's Mora--- that bastard Mora."

Microphones in the Temple pick-up Mora's voice as he announces that he is anointing himself with the new title: "Savior of the World", and Jerusalem is now his headquarters. Precora and the entourage kneel at Mora's feet. Derofski stands behind him.

Everyone in the command center now realizes why Israel was spared from the devastating nuclear attack--- Mora wants to rule the world from Israel, and he can't do it if Israel is totally destroyed. It's now clear that Mora conspired with the invading countries and double-crossed Israel. These countries are so desperate to plunder Israel's riches, that in return for Mora's deceitful cooperation they will allow him to assume more control over world affairs. Word comes to the command center that a group of the highest-ranking Israeli leaders, including the Prime Minister, are on their way to the Temple to see if Mora can persuade the invaders to stop their attack. Dayan delays attacking the enemy, hoping the Prime Minister can succeed in gaining Mora's help to avoid the battle. Dayan suspects Israel will have to give away their oil, minerals, and possibly land in exchange for peace--- a peace he knows won't last long. But at least millions of Israeli lives will be saved.

Suddenly, alarms sound in the command center. Surveillance drones and ground-based scanners have picked-up images of missiles coming from hundreds of miles east of the armies. Immediately, Dayan directs Jason and Rick to spring into action.

They release thousands of swarm drones that pour out of their bunkers like angry bees from a hive. They form clusters in front of the missiles, waiting for impact. The sky fills with orange flashes and smoke as the missiles detonate pre-maturely when they hit the drones. However, several missiles get through. Another wave of missiles approaches and meets the same fate from another wave of drones. The missiles that survived the swarm rain down on Jerusalem and other major cities, killing Arabs and Jews alike. Fortunately, the missiles are not nuclear-tipped.

Most of Israel's population centers are hit, and all but two Israeli air bases are rendered useless. At least three hundred thousand Israelis are killed, including the Prime Minister and the entire leadership delegation. More Israelis would have been killed if it weren't for bunkers constructed in homes and businesses. The detonations are non-nuclear, presumably so the nearby enemy armies would not be affected by radioactive fall-out. Amazingly, the Temple Mount is unscathed. Temple comms transmit a new angry image of Mora. He stands and defiantly shakes his fist. With fire in his eyes he shouts, "The conquest of Israel will now begin!" His ambition to rule the world is becoming a reality. Jason feels helpless to stop him. He and Willis look at each other, realizing the extent of the evil forces now at work.

Surprisingly, the Arab and Russian armies remain in place. Dayan speculates that extreme factions in Iranian Shiastan went rogue and launched the missiles pre-maturely. In their bitter hatred of Israel, they couldn't wait any longer to pull the trigger. A new weather report informs Dayan that the prevailing winds from the west will soon reverse. He now fears that the enemy will be using nuclear and/or chemical weapons, and they have so far hesitated to commence the attack fearing the winds would blow the fallout over their own armies. With the changing wind direction, Dayan cannot afford to wait any longer. He must attack now.

Since the Chinese Mediterranean fleet is almost in position to commence their attack, Dayan orders an immediate pre-emptive strike. However, the Chinese fleet in the Indian Ocean is still too far away to be reached. Each Chinese fleet consists of carriers, submarines, stealth missile ships, and swaths. (A swath is a flat platform several feet above the water. Thin connecting structures on each side of the platform extend below the water to torpedo-like propulsion pods. With this design, swaths can cut through high seas without being tossed about.) The Chinese swaths are carrying troops and land drones for beach assaults.

From hidden coastal locations, Israel launches pilotless high-speed stealth boats. Doors open to underwater cargo holds in the boats, and thousands of underwater swarm drones are released. They're too small for the enemy's sensors to detect. Like intelligent schools of hungry fish, the drones communicate with each other and coordinate their routing so all enemy ships are effectively attacked. They explode at the water intakes of the Chinese ships and subs, taking-out their protective intake grills. Right behind the first swarm, another wave of drones immediately races into the vulnerable intakes, penetrating into the ships' interiors before exploding. The strike took the fleet completely by surprise. Almost simultaneously, thousands of airborne swarm drones are released from stealth cargo-type aircraft launched from the two remaining Israeli air bases. The sheer number of drones overwhelms the enemy fleet's defenses. These drones form themselves into nearly invisible ribbons that fan-out from each aircraft toward the ships. Most drones get through, and they explode at the communication towers and bridges of the Chinese ships. On the heels of the airborne drones, Israel launches land-based hypersonic missiles which crash into the fleet. The sea appears to be on fire. Thick smoke drifts over the water's surface, obscuring most of the fleet. The Chinese fleet is heavily damaged and dead in the water. Most ships are sinking, but those remaining afloat can still mount a limited attack. Chinese pilots and airborne drones muster on the flight decks of two of the crippled but operational carriers. Other ships manage to launch a few missiles, but it's almost too late. Another wave of Israeli swarm drones destroys most of the missiles, but some get through to hit military targets. A few explode on and near the Petra decoy bunker. A second wave of Israeli missiles strikes their targets to finish-off the fleet. The Chinese planes and drones never get airborne. Cheers erupt in the Israeli Command Center.

The Chinese Indian Ocean fleet is now on high alert but not quite in attack position. As the fleet prepares to enter the Persian Gulf, the ships are suddenly hit with underwater explosions followed by hypersonic missiles and stealth torpedoes. When the mysterious attack ends, a few of the ships are still afloat, but all the carriers and missile ships are sinking. None of the surviving ships can move. This exciting development goes unnoticed in the Israeli command center because most personnel are focused on the success in the Mediterranean and on the enemy armies to the east. Jason's eyes glance across the screen monitoring the surveillance drone above the Indian Ocean fleet. He sees what just happened, and begins shouting excitedly. The cheering in the room drowns-out his shouting, so he grabs one of the officers and thrusts him at the screen. They both yell and announce the amazingly good news. "Rick," Jason shouts, "put this image on one of the big screens." Operators turn to the screen and start cheering again. Then the cheering is interrupted by a loud whistle.

"Who ordered that attack?" Dayan shouts.

Everyone looks around. No one responds. Then another operator barges-in and yells, "Hey, listen to this, everyone." He puts a voice transmission on the speakers. It's from the Admiral of an American submarine armada. They were following the Chinese fleet from the time the fleet left China and other Southeast Asia ports. The Admiral had received word of the World War III attacks from a coded transmission from U.S. Central Command before the signal went dead, but since the Admiral couldn't communicate with Washington., he acted on his own. He suspected what the Chinese were up to and launched a surveillance drone from a clandestine base in India. The drone flew ahead of the projected route of the Chinese fleet until the enemy armies were spotted in Shiastan and Saudi Arabia. He then asked Australia and India to join the Americans, which they did. The Admiral couldn't risk trying to communicate with Israel since he knew the Chinese would be monitoring Israeli communications, so he decided to attack before the fleet entered the Gulf. Australian submarines joined the American armada while India launched the hypersonic missiles.

Elated, Dayan thanks the Admiral profusely, and asks if his armada can proceed up the Gulf to assist Israel in the land battle. The Admiral balks at the request because Shiastan controls the Strait of Hormuz at the entrance to the Gulf, and the allied subs would be sitting ducks if they tried to pass. He also says that the subs' weapons inventories are depleted. "May God be with you," he concludes.

The wind from the west diminishes and seems ready to shift as predicted. All those in the command center fear the carnage that's about to descend. Instead, a new weather situation develops. The wind picks-up again, but curiously resumes blowing from the west, only stronger. Then an unusually massive dark cloud rapidly forms over the entire invading armies. Dayan is about to commence his attack on the enemy armies, but he holds-off to see the effect of this new weather development.

Suddenly, alarms sound in the command center again. Forty missiles are racing toward Israel--- this time from the south. Once again, Jason and Willis release bursts of swarm drones out of their bunkers to meet the enemy missiles. Most missiles explode when they hit the drones, and the pieces fall harmlessly into the Gulf. However, a few missiles get through, and they explode north and south of Jerusalem and on Tel-Aviv. Command center personnel stare at their screens in horror as their worst fears become reality. Mushroom clouds dot the landscape. The explosions are small-scale thermonuclear detonations. Some detonate in the air as EMPs. Some hit the ground. Fortunately, Israel has developed

EMP shields for their military communication systems, vehicles, and equipment, so the EMPs have no effect on the IDF. The missiles that hit the ground, however, are devastating. Large areas are flattened and are consumed with fire and smoke. Of those Israelis that aren't killed by the blasts, many will later die from radiation poisoning. An Israeli surveillance drone over the Gulf identifies the missile exhaust trails as from a submarine-launched attack. Judging by the limited number of missiles, Dayan speculates that they're from a couple of subs from Shiastan, or from Chinese subs that survived the American attack. In any case, there is no follow-up wave. While the missiles take their toll on Israel, again the Temple Mount is spared.

Before the Israeli Command Center can assess the damage from this new attack, high altitude drone-based scanners indicate thousands of planes over Shiastan and Saudi Arabia--- all headed for Israel. The scanners also indicate that Russian fighters and drones are among them. Evidently, the Russian aircraft were flown out of harm's way before the U.S. retaliated with their nukes. Israel responds quickly by launching hundreds of thousands of swarm drones into the attacking aircraft, taking-out more than half of them. Larger IDF interceptor drones are launched in tandem with fighters from the two remaining operational air bases. Each Israeli interceptor fighter has a pilot and a weapons officer who can control as many as five drones. The weapons officers use holographic screens and controller gloves to direct the drones. The pilots have holographic wind shield displays for navigation and for targeting the plane's laser-guided rockets and nose cannons. Vastly outnumbered, the crews understand they are on a suicide mission.

Captain Anita Issa is one of the more seasoned Israeli pilots. Her weapons officer, Lt. Robert Ben-Zvi (brother of airline Capt. Ron Ben-Zvi) is also well-trained and experienced. Along with seventy-five interceptor drones, Issa takes her squadron of fifteen interceptor fighters south to confront the Saudi air force. The drones are expendable and much more maneuverable than the fighters, so they lead the charge. They take-out many enemy aircraft with their laser-guided rockets, and after exhausting their ammo, they crash into others. After the drones have done all they can do, Capt. Issa orders her squadron to directly engage the enemy. Most Israeli rockets hit their mark. Her squadron then hurls itself into the enemy formation. Chaos erupts in the sky as planes dodge and fire at each other. Plane after plane on both sides are hit, and the sky fills with smoke. The sky is so smoky and congested that some planes inadvertently collide. The Israeli pilots' superior training and advanced technology overcome the enemy's numerical advantage, and the battle turns Israel's way. After twenty minutes, all Issa's rockets have been fired. She then opens fire with her nose cannons. One more Saudi aircraft bursts into flames and tumbles down from the sky.

Soon, only four planes are left. Capt. Issa and one other Israeli plane are dueling with two enemy planes. These particular Saudi pilots are more capable than the others, as they have so far eluded the fate of their fellow countrymen. The four planes dive and loop. No one is getting a good bead on the other, and Issa is running out of fuel. Then one of the Saudi fighters disengages from the dog fight. Issa thinks he's retreating, but quickly realizes that he's heading for Israel. She radios her wing man to stay in the fight while she chases the other plane. Shortly, Ben-Zvi informs her that his rear scanner has picked-up two explosions behind them. Both remaining planes have shot each other simultaneously, and are spiraling downwards, leaving trails of smoke behind.

Issa quickly gains on the Saudi as he heads toward Jerusalem. She sends a warning to the Command Center, but the IDF has nothing available to take-out the incoming fighter in time. She fires her cannon but misses. The enemy now descends, apparently on a kamikaze mission. Issa is right on the Saudi's tail. She fires again with the last of her ammo, but he swerves. A small trail of smoke bursts from his wing, but he remains on his path. With the Temple now in sight, Issa has only one choice. She kicks-in her after-burner, and hits the Saudi under his wing with the nose of her plane, knocking him off-course. They barely miss the Temple. Instead, Issa's aircraft rips into the adjacent Al-Aqsa Mosque and the Saudi buries his plane into the golden Dome of the Rock. Both Muslim shrines are destroyed, but Issa has saved the Temple.

The Russian and Shiastan air forces are more successful. They take heavy losses but wipe-out the outnumbered Israeli air force. The surviving Russian aircraft release their bombs over Israel. They then head back to Russia, not knowing if their homes are still standing, or if they will even be able to land. The Shiastan pilots defiantly crash their planes into Israeli population centers.

Back in the Command Center, observers report that the radioactive fall-out from the Chinese submarine attack is now drifting over the enemy forces, halting their advance while they don their radiation suits. Cheers resume in the room. There hasn't been much more for Jason and Willis to do, as all systems have performed magnificently. Willis stares at the holographic image of the mysterious dark cloud above the enemy armies. He gets an idea. Wide-eyed with excitement, he taps Jason on the shoulder and suggests that if the new dark cloud were induced to rain or snow, more of the nuclear fall-out would wash down on the enemy. Jason agrees and persuades Dayan to try to make it happen. The plan is to change warheads on several Israeli ground-to-air missiles, and seed the cloud. As the enemy armies start advancing again, the seed missiles explode in the cloud. Jason and Willis anxiously wait and watch while other operators stand-by to deploy heavily-armed land drones. Soon, the air under the cloud turns white. Basketball-sized hail starts pounding the enemy troops. Chaos erupts in the armies. Since most of the enemy soldiers were transported in open trucks and trailers, the hail bombards the exposed troops in vast numbers. The dense ice balls seem to explode as they crash onto men and equipment. Some of the soldiers manage to hide under the vehicles, but several hundred thousand are killed. The wounded survivors are trapped in snow and ice five feet deep. Most of the enemy's land drones and light vehicles are heavily damaged and buried.

Spirits are once again lifted in the Command Center. Everyone realizes that Israel could have been completely destroyed by now. However, the good news is dampened by the death and destruction inflicted on the Israeli military and population centers. The sun soon emerges through the dissipating cloud, and the hail starts to melt. The silence on the battlefield breaks as engine after engine revs-up again. Like maggots wriggling out from a rotting carcass, soldiers begin to crawl out of the icy tomb. After a couple of hours, the enemy armies gather themselves. Tanks and other tracked vehicles drive through the ice and over their dead and wounded comrades. The trapped wounded soldiers scream as they are crushed by the heavy equipment. The armies re-group.

Just as the sight of the re-grouping armies brings discouragement to the Command Center, the weather smiles on Israel again. A dense fog descends on the confused enemy armies. Dayan seizes the opportunity. He decides to launch Israel's land drones. The drones are housed in hidden bunkers scattered across the eastern Israeli hills. Dayan directs Jason and Willis to program the drones according to the following battle plan: once launched, the drones are to form two single-file lines. One will set-up in the fog within a quarter mile or so of the northern army, and the other will set-up within a quarter mile of the southern army. Once the drones cross the Jordan River, all the bridges will be blown-up. When the lead drones reach the rear of both armies, the northern line of drones will open fire on the southern army, and the southern line of drones will open fire on the northern army.

Master Sargent Babyde is the station chief in one of the drone bunkers. He and his crew have been readying their drone squadron all day, and they are fully loaded with ammo. Babyde scrambles the mechanics and technicians to their posts to start the final check-out. They launch in fifteen minutes.

Each drone is about the size of a short bicycle, with computer-controlled independent floating drive tracks on each side. Each drone has a battery of laser-guided rockets that are initially targeted by operators in the bunker. Once the battle begins, the targeting switches to A.I. so each drone selects the subsequent targets.

The programming has been completed and double-checked. Babyde gives the order to start the electric engines. They all start flawlessly, except one. Babyde spots the laggard immediately. Fortunately, it's at the end of one of the rows, so it's easy to get-to. He marches over to it and kicks it. No response. He shifts his stance and kicks a different spot. The stubborn engine revs-up with a whine.

Babyde is in his early 50's--- single and bald with an unmilitary-like protruding stomach. He's not handsome or personable, and he's never had a girlfriend. He has few friends, even among the military. The military is his life, but he's tired of it, and he knows he will never advance beyond his current rank. He never knew his biological parents, so he was raised in a group home. He views his future as unpromising, so this is the exciting moment he has waited for. It's as if the drones were his children. He has conscientiously prepared and maintained them, and he's now sending them out to do their best in the world. He proudly surveys the group, wiping a little smudge off of one of the lead drones. Then the "ready" alarm sounds. The bunker door slowly opens. Babyde looks around at the drones, and then looks back at his crew at the rear of the bunker. He sticks a cigar in his mouth, and starts moving it from side to side like he's searching for the perfect spot for it. The "launch" alarm sounds. As the lead drone starts to move, he surprises everyone by hopping onto it. He turns back to his crew, and salutes as the drone disappears over the slope of the hill toward the battlefield.

Other lines of drones emerge from their bunkers, as well. As programmed, they form two single-file lines and they cross the Jordan River bridges. They then head toward the enemy armies. With the dense fog concealing the columns, the lead drones--- and the one with Sgt. Babyde on it--- reach the ends of the fog-blinded armies. In a stern but calm voice, Dayan gives the order, "Fire." Nothing happens. "Fire, I said!" Panic fills the room. "Johnson!" Dayan yells, "get on it!"

Jason back-hands Willis in the arm. Frantically, they start punching their keyboards and scouring their screens for the glitch. Two minutes go by. Still nothing. His calm demeanor evaporated, Dayan nervously paces the floor, glaring at the two Americans. "Johnson?" Dayan says, straining to maintain control of himself.

"One more thing to check, sir," Jason replies.

"Come on, Johnson. The fog is about to lift. If we don't fire now, the enemy will see our drones. They'll be annihilated!"

Jason's hands are shaking. His face is flush, and trails of sweat are slowly running down his forehead. "Rick, what are we missing?"

"I don't know. I can't see it. Everything checks-out here."

Jason slowly turns towards a scowling Dayan. He opens his trembling mouth to say 'sorry' when Willis blurts, "Hey, there's a lock-out in the Fire Control station! We'd better get up there fast!"

"General," Jason yells in a commanding voice, "have a security team follow us to the mezzanine!" The pair dashes up a nearby stairway, followed by three security guards. The Fire Control operator's seat is empty. "Where is he?" Jason yells, spinning around to reach the other operators. "Where is he?" The other operators scour the area, but no one answers.

Then one of them says, "I think he went to the lav over there." Jason drops into the operator's seat as the security detail rushes into the lav. Jason finds the lock-out, but he can't clear it. Only the operator can. Just then the security team drags the hand-cuffed operator out of the lav, guns pointed at his head.

"Don't shoot!" the operator pleads. "They made me do it. They have my family. I didn't know what else to do!"

With fire in his eyes Jason shouts, "Remove this lock-out *now* or none of us will make it out of here alive--- including your family. And you'll be the first one to go!" One of the security guards lifts his weapon to the operator's forehead. "Come on, son," Jason continues, trying his best to be consoling, "you know this is the right thing to do. If this works, Israel will be spared and you will save millions of lives. We'll try to find your family when this is all over."

The operator's face turns pale as he realizes what he's done. "Okay, okay," he weakly responds, let me sit down." His lower lip quivering, he quickly types-in the override key and holds his finger over the launch button. He can't bring himself to hit the button. Seeing how the operator is paralyzed by his dilemma, Jason thrusts his hand on top of the operator's finger and pushes it down hard. The operator then collapses back into his seat and drops his head. Tears form in his eyes as thoughts of his family consume him.

All in the room turn silently to the big screen. Suddenly, the drones open fire. Cheers erupt. Rockets light-up the fog and rain down on the enemy vehicles and troops. While the explosions are relatively small, there are thousands of them, and they have the desired effect.

With zero visibility in the fog, and with their communications knocked-out, the two enemy armies mistakenly return fire on each other, believing the other is the Israeli army. Explosions illuminate the fog like orange strobe lights. The noise is deafening. Israel then launches several waves of ground-to-ground missiles into the battlefield. After what seemed like an eternity, but only lasting about five minutes, the explosions and weapons-fire gradually cease. Soon the fog slowly lifts. Air surveillance drones transmit images of victory for Israel. The enemy armies suffer huge losses--- three quarters of their men have been killed or wounded, and most of their vehicles have been destroyed. Smoke and fires blanket the landscape. All the Israeli land drones lie scattered in barely recognizable pieces. Sgt. Babyde's bloody corpse rests peacefully in the mud beneath his drone.

Jason can't believe what has happened. The plan worked perfectly. Everyone starts celebrating with cheers, hugs and high-fives. Anah embraces Jason, and then Willis. "I can't tell you how grateful I am--- how grateful *we* are," as she beams with joy. "God bless you. Thank you, thank you, thank you!" Anah's and Jason's eyes meet again. They start to embrace again, but a loud whistle abruptly stops them.

It's Dayan. "I understand your elation," he says in a somber voice, "but this battle is not over. There are still thousands of surviving enemy troops and equipment out there. Unless I miss my guess, they will conclude that they have nothing to lose by continuing the attack. Remember, they hate us, and they will be seeking revenge. Our air force has been destroyed, and our army has been crippled, so we cannot mount a counterattack. We don't yet know what kind of fighting assets we still have, but they can't be much." The celebratory atmosphere in the room gives-way to worry again. All personnel return to their stations. "It's going to take some time to reconstitute their forces, and it will be dark soon," Dayan continues, "so we'll return to our shift schedule with a third crew on each eight-hour shift. You all need some well-deserved rest and food. Thank you all for your magnificent work, but we still have work to do. Our night vision drones will monitor the enemy, so be prepared for a night attack just in case. I want my senior staff to meet me in the planning room--- now."

Darkness descends on the region. Surveillance drones scout the Israeli countryside and transmit horrific images of destruction and dead bodies. The few undamaged emergency vehicles are scattered around in the areas where radiation risks are negligible. Residents and emergency personnel plow through the debris using flashlights and portable flood lights, desperately searching for survivors. Over 50% of the Israeli army has been killed or wounded. Smoke drifts over the country, and thousands of large and small fires glow throughout the night. Amazingly, the lights are on in the unaffected Temple.

Drone images from over the enemy territory reveal an even more destructive scene of carnage and fires. As dawn spreads over what's left of the enemy armies, a bizarre scene unfolds. Thousands of birds are feasting on the dead bodies. The sunrise casts a red pall over the area--- a combination of blood and the sun's reddish rays.

As the day progresses, drone images indicate scattered movements in the enemy armies. The outer edges of each army have survived. Their capabilities and numbers have been greatly diminished, but they are re-forming into two long columns to strike a final blow at Israel. Fortunately for the IDF, the enemy thinks the Petra bunker was destroyed, so they didn't fire additional missiles into the mountain. Dayan believes the enemy also thinks Israel's aircraft and missile arsenals were destroyed, and that most of Israel's army has been destroyed or critically weakened. Israeli fighting vehicles are few, and most ammo facilities have been depleted or destroyed. The disheartening incoming reports turn the mood in the command bunker from exhausted relief to discouraging panic as the personnel realize that Israel cannot defend itself against the newly mobilizing enemy force. A few missiles, five batteries of artillery, and a couple hundred swarm drones are all that's left at Israel's disposal. Command Center communication with the scattered Israeli army is difficult. No one outside the Command Center seems to be in charge. Somehow Dayan is able to organize the remainder of his army, and he pulls them back to a line along the foothills of the Petra mountains. He decides to wait to release the last of his fighting assets until the two lines of enemy armies cross the shallow beds of the Jordan River.

Late in the day, the two enemy columns blow-up the border walls and cross into Israel. The decimated Israeli forces stiffen-up as they prepare to open fire with all their remaining assets. Jason, Willis and all in the Command Center understand that the enemy's superior forces mean this will be a futile fight to the death for them. Jason and Willis slowly shake hands in a solemn good-bye. "It's been great working with you, Jay," Willis says.

"Same here, Rick. At least we're going-out doing something noble. I'm not sure I even want to live in what's left of the world anyway." His thoughts drift to visions of Joshua, Liezel, and Kathy. Out of the corner of his eye Jason sees the General. He appears much too calm for the grave situation. Why? Does he know something we don't? The General returns Jason's glance. They hold eye contact with each other for a brief moment. The General winks.

Suddenly, the ground starts shaking--- mildly at first, then much more violently. Rocks and dirt roll down the Petra mountains, striking some of the scattered Israeli forces. The earth begins to crack open in front of the enemy lines, forming two huge crevasses that race toward the advancing armies, getting wider and deeper, undermining the helpless enemy. Screaming men and equipment cascade like a rumbling waterfall into the darkness below. After a few seconds of disbelief, spontaneous joy erupts in the Command Center. Most personnel pump their fists in the air yelling, "go, go, go!" until the last vehicle has disappeared into the abyss. Brown clouds of dust billow from the crevasses. It's over in 5 minutes. Jason and Willis are stunned. They jump from their chairs, cheering and hugging each other. They will not die today.

Another crevasse opens at the Temple. Mora, Precora, Derofski and their staff emerge from the temple onto the steps. Wide-eyed, their faces fill with fear as they and the Temple slowly slide into the abyss. Smoke and flames spew from the crevasse amidst their screams. For a moment, Jason allows himself to get excited at seeing Mora tumble to his death. But then doubt sets-in.

Everyone in the command center glues their eyes to the screens in amazement. The celebration continues with more hugs, high-fives, and tears of joy. When the amplitude of the ebullience diminishes, Dayan calls for quiet. He congratulates everyone, but he calls attention to the supernatural events that saved their lives and their country. It's time to pray. They drop to their knees and give thanks to the God that has kept his covenant with Israel. Jason and Willis join them. For the first time, Jason is convinced that the God he ignored and even hated for years is with them today. Nothing else could explain the supernatural events that just occurred. It's an awesome moment for him. He feels shame for his previous lack of faith, but also joy at his new spiritual re-connection. These conflicting emotions bring tears to his eyes. As everyone else rises, he lingers on his knees, continuing to give thanks and praise. He asks God for forgiveness--- forgiveness for rejecting God in the past. A warm sensation flows over him, and he knows that God has indeed forgiven him. From behind, he feels a comforting hand on his shoulder. He quickly looks around, but no one is there.

With a renewed sense of joy and gratitude, Jason slowly rises and sees Anah knifing her way through the ebullient crowd towards him. They embrace. Their faces drift closer, but something keeps Jason from kissing her. Willis finds his sister-look-alike, and they embrace as well. As the celebrating continues, Jason turns his attention to the screen showing the crevasse where the Temple used to be. He's cautiously elated at the apparent demise of Mora, but wonders if he will return from the dead once again. Only time will tell, but as of now justice has been served.

Dayan directs the personnel in the room to take inventory on the remaining military assets--- both personnel and weapons--- and then perform diagnostics on the remaining defense systems, just in case. The surveillance drones will remain active. Putting Colonel David in charge, Dayan says he's going to personally speak to the troops on the hillside where the earthquake caused some injuries. Everyone in the room snaps to attention as he passes. He grabs his driver, and looks around the room with pride as he leaves.

A few minutes later, a single explosion somewhere outside startles the personnel in the Command Center. The Colonel sends a small detail out to investigate. Ten minutes later they report back. They found the General's white Bronco at the mouth of an escape tunnel. Several tons of dirt, rocks, and a large slab of concrete fell on the Bronco and completely crushed it. All that the men can see is the rear bumper and tag. It's definitely the General's transport. Although they can't see him or the driver, there's no way the two men could have survived the cave-in. When the Colonel announces the grave news, a dark wave of silent sadness descends on the Command Center. There will be no more celebrating tonight.

CHAPTER NINE---THE AFTERMATH

Yawning and rubbing his eyes, Jason emerges from his quarters the following morning. Willis is still snoring. Only a few operators and Colonel David are in the command center. "Colonel," Jason says in a subdued one-word greeting as he tries to balance the elation of victory with the loss of a great leader.

"Good morning sir," the Colonel replies in a surprisingly cheery tone. "I have some good news for you--- General Dayan is alive! Right now, he's on top of the Wailing Wall in Jerusalem. There he is on the first comm screen."

"What? How's that possible?" a suddenly upbeat Jason asks.

The Colonel fills him-in. "The General's Bronco was almost at the exit of the escape tunnel, but the passage was partially blocked by debris from a landslide. So he and the driver left the transport, and stepped over the debris. Apparently, an unexploded enemy warhead finally detonated in the tunnel, causing the cave-in. The blast knocked-out the General and his driver, so they couldn't tell us what happened until they regained consciousness. Pretty amazing, huh?"

"Amazing isn't the word--- more like a miracle! There have been a lot of those lately," Jason replies. "Is he okay? And what's the latest on damage and casualties?"

"He and the driver are fine--- just a little headache and some lacerations. As to the damages, reports are still coming-in, but the news is pretty devastating," the Colonel says as his face turns somber. "Over two million Israelis are dead or wounded. More will die from their wounds or radiation poisoning. Thousands of buildings and much of our infrastructure have been destroyed or heavily damaged. Our army and air force were the main targets, and they have been decimated. As you know, our weapons and munitions are spent."

"So sorry, Colonel," Jason says as his face turns sympathetically somber as well, "I can't imagine what you and all of Israel must be going through. Have you heard from your family?"

"Nothing yet, sir, but thanks," he says.

"Well, I hope you get good news about them soon. You know, you and your staff here did an amazing job. General Dayan was certainly the right man at the right place at the right time, wasn't he? He's an outstanding leader."

"He certainly is, sir," the Colonel answers admiringly. "I'd follow that man anywhere."

"So what's his background?" Jason inquires. "I try to keep up with news from Israel, but I've never heard of him."

"I really couldn't say," the Colonel replies. "He's only been here a couple of months. He just sort of appeared on the scene one day. I heard his father was an Italian Jew, and his mother was native Israeli. And I believe he was born in a small town just south of Jerusalem. I don't believe he's ever been married. I do know he commanded an air base before coming here. I can tell you that no one rises from Base Commander to Commanding General of the IDF that quickly without extraordinary ability, and he certainly has that. I've never known a military officer with such an unusual combination of leadership, kindness, and almost supernatural vision. Every decision he makes always turns-out to be the right one, even when it doesn't make sense at the time. When he first arrived here he said some pretty controversial things, so he made some enemies. But he was always proven right. With all our politicians dead, I guess he'll be our leader until a new Knesset is formed. By the way, you and Mr. Willis did a bang-up job, too. Your systems performed brilliantly. The coordination was perfect, and there weren't any electronic failures that I saw. There was one squadron of land drones that didn't respond, but the bunker crew eventually got them going. All Israel thanks you for your contribution."

Feeling a genuine sense of humility, Jason states, "Thanks, but I'm just glad to be a part of this. Looking at the size of those armies, I couldn't see how we were going to make it. But I think we had some extra help, don't you?"

"I think we did, sir. I think we did."

"By the way, Colonel, have you seen Anah this morning?"

"I haven't seen her today, sir."

The Colonel fills-in Jason on other details: no one in the enemy armies has survived. The earth just swallowed them up. While Israel needs major rebuilding, there are millions of survivors. Some of the friendly countries that escaped the nuclear devastation will soon be sending aid. The Colonel also informs Jason that heavy rains fell during the night all over the northern hemisphere of the earth. The rains are lifesaving, because they're washing the radioactive particles out of the sky. The earth's radioactive dead zones will therefore be limited to the areas around the detonations. Furthermore, many of the footprints of the detonations were somewhat small due to the necessarily small size of the hypersonic missiles. (Excessive air resistance prevents larger missiles from flying at hypersonic speeds.) Prior to the battle for Israel, over 1.5 billion people were killed in America, China, Russia, and Shiastan. Life will be difficult for the survivors, and many will eventually die from radiation, starvation, and lack of medical care, but the world will be spared from a nuclear winter. Jason's hopes rise with the possibility, although remote, that Joshua, Kathy, and his friends in San Marita will be okay.

Jason approaches the comm screen that's monitoring Dayan and his staff. The group is dressed in white radiation suits, but they have removed their head gear because the area is not contaminated. Jason spots Anah in the group around Dayan. Then his heart stops. He squints at the screen. His eyes pop. "Colonel, how can I get down to the General?" he frantically asks. "I need to get there as fast as possible!"

"Bischoff," the Colonel barks at an operator in the break area, "Take my Bronco and run Dr. Johnson down to the General."

"Thanks, Colonel," Jason gratefully replies. He can't get into the transport fast enough. 'Where is Bischoff?' he frets. Bischoff finally shows-up.

"Sorry, sir," Bischoff apologizes, "But I can't find the fob."

"It's right here on the dash, Corporal!" Jason screams. "Let's go!" The Bronco bounces down the mountain at a risky speed considering the debris that's scattered on the road. On the way down the mountain, they hear celebratory trumpets blaring throughout Israel.

By the time Jason makes it to the Wailing Wall, some of Dayan's group has moved down to the bottom of it. Dayan and several others remain at the top. He's standing next to his replacement Bronco, barely visible through a light haze that just moved into the city. Jason's Bronco has to stop about thirty yards from Dayan's group due to impassible rubble in the road. Jason bolts out of the transport, and hops and trips his way to the group. As he approaches, the General calls-down to Jason, but Jason doesn't hear him because his focus is elsewhere. His eyes eagerly flit from person to person. Then he sees Anah.

"Anah," he shouts in an anxious voice, "Is there a woman here named Liezel?"

"Why, yes," Anah replies. "I believe she's over there." She points to another group bending over some wreckage. "How do you know her?"

Anah never gets an answer. Jason darts away, stumbling over pieces of concrete and steel. He scampers up to the group, losing his balance and almost stepping into a small fire along the way. He reaches a woman who's crouched at the ground. Her back is to him, and it reminded him of the first time he approached Liezel the night they met. He pauses, out of breath. Barely managing to speak for fear he will be disappointed, he timidly utters her name---"Liezel?"

The woman spins around. Her jaw drops and her eyes widen in joyful surprise. "Jason!" She exclaims. She jumps-up and slams into him with a tight embrace. They kiss passionately. They separate, looking-over each other to make sure they're imaginations are not playing tricks. "How? What?" She can't find the words.

Jason gently caresses her cheeks, and runs his fingers through her dusty hair. She gives him that steel-melting smile of hers. Finally, Jason manages to say, "I...I can't believe it's you! I thought you were dead."

Liezel acts puzzled. "Dead? But didn't you get my letter?"

"No, what letter?"

Frowning, she replies, "Why, I gave my friend Belinda a letter for you. She said she would give it to you on her way to Nevada. You mean you never got it? I don't understand. Oh my God. I'm so sorry. No wonder you thought I was dead. I'm so, so sorry. I don't know what could have gone wrong."

"Look, honey, I don't know and I don't care." Jason replies, "The important thing is that we're finally together again." They embrace again as their expressions reflect the thrill of their reunion. "So what really happened to you?"

"It's sort of a long story," she says. "I had to get away without telling anyone. If you knew anything about what I was involved with or where I was going, your life would have been in danger. It all started when my friend Susie at work began talking me about what was really going-on with Antonin Mora and the UN--- how they were persecuting Believers and planning to rule the world. Then one time when you were out of town for a few days, she took me to an enclave in the hills. We had to leave our wrist comms at home so we couldn't be tracked. The people there were followers of Jesus. They were working to expose Mora, and they showed me all the proof I needed to convince me he had to be stopped. Since they were in danger, their location had to be hidden. The compound was fairly self-sufficient, so they avoided discovery for several months. Susie said she would be permanently joining them soon, and she invited me to join as well. But of course I said I couldn't. When I went to work the next day, armed UN goons dragged Susie away. When I looked out of the window, I saw her break away from them. Then they just shot her--- in broad daylight. Right in the back! I was afraid they would come for me next. That's why I had to leave immediately. I couldn't risk calling you, so I took-off my wrist comm, and rode my bike toward the enclave as far as I could until the bike died. Then I hiked up the rest of the way. I missed you terribly all this time, but I couldn't go back or get in touch with you. I thought if I waited a while the danger would pass. I waited for over a year, but things only got worse." She pauses to catch her breath. Jason's eyes widen in anticipation. She continues. "At one point, I finally had enough. I missed you too much. So despite the risks I decided to leave the enclave, but before I could, we were attacked."

"Wait a second--- that must have been the police action Joshua and I saw in the hills," Jason says. "So how did you survive the attack?"

"It wasn't the police. It was the UN. Anyway, I was saved by two men I never saw before. They huddled over me until the attack was over. Then they hid me in the woods next to the compound. Everyone else was slaughtered. I was scared to death, and I didn't know what to do next, so I went with them through the woods to a safe house in town. The Believers there gave me a fake wrist comm and helped me catch a plane for Israel where they thought I would be safe. Before I left I wrote you a letter and gave it to Belinda. The two men arranged contact with Anah over there so I could stay in an IDF barracks near these mountains. Even with their help I almost didn't make it here. On the approach to the Tel-Aviv airport we were hit by rockets. The plane barely made an emergency landing."

"Hold-on," Jason says, his voice filled again with excitement. "Did your flight come through Rome five days ago? And did the rockets hit one of the engines?"

"Why, yes. How did you know?" She asks.

"Because I was on that plane, too! I don't believe we were that close and we didn't see each other! Wait, the two men who helped you--- were they elderly and sort of poorly dressed--- grey hair and beards? I think one of them called the other Mo."

"Yes! Morris and Mordecai. Do you know them?" She queries.

"I think I did," he says sadly. "I sat next to them on two flights. I'm beginning to think that was more than a coincidence. Unfortunately, they're dead--- beheaded on the streets of Strasbourg. No clues."

"Mora! I'll bet it was him," Liezel replies as she grits her teeth.

"It wouldn't surprise me if it was, but we won't have to worry about him anymore. He's at the bottom of that fiery crevasse over there--- the one that swallowed the Temple."

"Thank God," Liezel replies. "I don't think there's been a more evil person on earth." They clutch each other, determined to never be separated again.

Then Jason's face turns from elation to puzzlement. "So why didn't you call me when you knew you were safe here?" He asks.

"I'm so sorry, Jason, I couldn't. None of my contacts had working wrist comms, and foreign communications were restricted. Then all hell broke loose with the bombing here. I asked someone else to call, but the comm systems were down. I was frantic when I heard about San Francisco being bombed. I was so afraid for your life. It's a miracle that we're both safe and wound-up here together!"

"Yes, honey, a wonderful miracle!" He continues, "You know, I wasn't sure God even existed, but all the supernatural things that happened here are undeniable. And to make things even more incredible, I think I was literally touched by Him in the command center. Suddenly, I felt forgiven and full of joy. I left Him once, but I'll never do it again. I feel like a new person."

Liezel looks-up at Jason, and gives him one of her sweet steel-melting smiles of understanding and admiration. He had almost forgotten how wonderful those smiles were. "Jason," she says, "ever since I fell in love with you I have been hoping and praying that you would re-discover God again. And now that you have, I am so happy for you. In spite of all the death and destruction around us today, I feel we are truly blessed."

They kiss again, and then pivot toward Dayan to watch his Bronco coming down through the haze from the top of the Wailing Wall. He's followed by the rest of his group. It's a gray overcast day filled with smoke, but a bright golden ray of sunshine has bored its way through the clouds to envelope Dayan. He reaches the bottom of the hill, and climbs-up on the hood of his Bronco. "Dr. Johnson, we couldn't have survived without your and Willis' help. You have our immense gratitude." He then pauses and, with a sad sigh, slowly scans over his ravaged country. He turns toward Jason, and announces with conviction, "We will rebuild, but we can't do it alone. Will you and Willis stay here for a while and help us?"

Jason looks at Liezel. She nods her approval. Jason starts to respond affirmatively to the General, but catches himself as his thoughts quickly turn to Joshua. Indecision takes-over. He **must** find-out if Joshua is alright. But how can he, knowing that communications are surely down in the U.S. Finally, Jason speaks. "General, my son lives in California, and he may be in trouble or worse. If I can't get in touch with him soon I'll have to return home to find him. In the meantime, I'll do what I can here. I can't speak for Willis, sir, but I'll ask him as soon as he wakes-up."

Liezel franticly tugs at Jason's arm, pulling him around to face her. "Jason," she says, "we're safe here. We have food, water, and other resources. Israel can recover, but the U.S. has been destroyed. There's nothing to return-to. And how are we going to get there, anyway? Let's think this through."

Jason's elation at finding Liezel now turns to frustration that she doesn't share his feelings. "Honey, can't you understand? He's my son. I can't just forget about him. I have to find him. We must find a way."

Liezel is not convinced. "Okay then, I understand. I love Joshua, too. So, can we see if we can get in touch with him first? Then we'll decide what to do." Jason is resigned to Liezel's sensible plan, and nods in agreement.

"All right," he says, "we'll try it your way."

Just then, Anah comes over and embraces Jason and Liezel. The trio then look-up admiringly at Dayan as he encourages the people around him. Although most of Israel was heavily damaged, and all-too-many Israelis were killed or wounded, Israel will survive and re-build. Knowing that Israel's enemies have been completely vanquished, Dayan looks-up and declares, "Thanks be to God. We are finally at peace." The clouds slowly part, casting a golden hue over the city.

CHAPTER TEN---A COSTLY VICTORY

Still elated with his reunion with Liezel, Jason can't help noticing the first responders and soldiers searching through the rubble from the recent battle. Behind him two men in white radiation suits and face masks finish freeing a bleeding dust-covered woman from a would-be tomb of rubble. Smoke and dust float through the air, some of which have stuck to the beads of sweat on Jason's forehead. His chiseled jaw line and three-day growth of whiskers convey rugged masculinity, but his face reflects the understandable fatigue and stress that he and all of Israel have just been through. His arms are wrapped tightly around his wife Liezel. She hugs him and leans her head against his chest. Their smiles and tears reflect their joy at being reunited.

General Dayan is standing in front of the Wailing Wall on his white Bronco transport. All are inspired by his confidence and leadership. He led Israel in the battle, and he now must lead the country to recovery. Over the top of the Wall, heavy smoke and dust billow from the huge crevasse that swallowed the newly built Temple along with Mora, Derofski, and Precora.

Jason focuses on Dayan and notices something odd about him. He rode the Bronco down from the top of the wall through the dust, smoke and mist, yet his white radiation suit is not only unblemished, but it appears to shimmer, bathed in a narrow beam of sunlight that has somehow penetrated the smoke and clouds. Dayan's silky white hair and clean smooth face are radiant. His kind eyes meet Jason's. In that moment, Jason understands that Dayan somehow knew Israel would be victorious. Likewise, Jason is now convinced that Dayan will succeed in the recovery, as well. Jason wonders, *'Just who is this man, anyway?'*

Jason and Liezel continue their incredible reunion. He looks down at her bright blue eyes, and lovingly runs his fingers through her dusty black hair. For the first time, he notices the beginnings of crow's feet at the dusty corners of her eyes, but she's still as beautiful as he remembers--- she could pass for Elizabeth Taylor's sister. "I still can't believe I found you, Honey, and here in Israel of all places," he says. "I can't tell you how much I missed you."

"I missed you, too, Jay--- more than I can put into words. You don't know how many times I almost called you or left the enclave where I was hiding, but I couldn't risk putting us both in danger. I'm just so sorry you never got my letter explaining why I disappeared. Belinda is so reliable. I don't understand why she never gave it to you. After she left town, I never heard from her again, so I have to believe something must have happened to her before she could give it to you. You must have been so hurt and confused. Can you ever forgive me?"

"Why of course I can, Honey. It obviously wasn't your fault. But I have to tell you I was frantic with worry. I couldn't sleep or work. I hardly ate anything for a long time. It's been over a year, you know. After all that time, I had all but given up hope. The police said you probably ran away, but I didn't believe it. We had too much going for us. And I knew you weren't kidnapped, because there wasn't any ransom request. Eventually, I came to believe you were dead, but that's all behind us now."

"Thank God for that," Liezel replies. "It's a miracle the way everything happened here--- the cloud, the hail, the crevasses, you and me showing-up here, and this impossible victory. Surely there must have been some divine intervention. I keep shaking my head in disbelief. Yet here we are." Giddy with happiness, she bounces on her toes a little and squeezes him again and again. "Let's promise each other that we'll never be separated again, okay?"

"Absolutely," Jason says. "I promise I'll never let you go."

"And I promise I'll never let *you* go," Liezel replies.

Jason wraps his arms around her tightly, oblivious to the commotion and destruction around them. Tears run down their cheeks, creating white trails through the smoky dust that had settled on their faces.

After a moment of silence, Liezel lifts her head up and says, "Okay, Honey, so what do we do now?" Turning towards Anah, she says, "Anah, Jason can live with me in the barracks, can't he?"

Anah responds, "Of course. I'm sure the others will be okay with it, as well. The bunk beds aren't ideal for a couple, but I'm sure you'll manage. Thanks to our preparedness program, we should have enough food and water there for a few weeks until the distribution systems are re-established. If I know the General, he'll get critical things like that operational in no time."

"Great," both Jason and Liezel say in unison. "Thank you." Although Anah is talking to both of them, Liezel notices that Anah has been looking at Jason almost the entire time. Not that Liezel blames her--- despite being dusty and needing a shave, he's still the well-built attractive man she remembers.

Israel survived the invasion, but destruction is wide-spread, and recovery is in doubt. Fires from the attack dot the landscape, and thick acrid smoke fills the sky like a giant blanket. Periodically, the sun manages to peek through, but it does little to brighten Israel's spirits. Two and a half million Israelis have died. Many more will later die from their wounds and from radiation poisoning. As it did during the battle, the weather continues to smile on Israel. A strong westerly wind blows the radioactive fallout into Jordan, sparing Israel from further harm.

Initial reports indicate the agricultural areas and water resources are mostly intact, but one of the two refineries was destroyed. The remaining refinery sustained only minor damage and will be able to produce a limited amount of petrol. Half of Israel's industrial capacity was lost. It will be incredibly challenging to scrape together enough materials and skilled labor to re-build key roads, bridges, and the distribution networks for food, water, and other necessities. If these things are not re-built quickly, many more could die from starvation and disease.

The recovery task in Israel seems daunting, and Jason isn't sure what he could do or how helpful he could be. But he promised General Dayan he'll stay for a while. Liezel definitely wants to stay, believing Israel will be safer than the nuclear wasteland of America. As soon as he agreed to stay, however, Jason began regretting his decision. His heart tugs at him to return to San Marita to find his son Joshua, who Jason is convinced is still alive. He and Liezel agreed that after a couple of months without any word or communication with Joshua, they will return home to San Marita to search for him.

With their immediate needs secured, Jason's attention turns to his nemesis Antonin Mora. "Liez," he says quietly, "I need to go up to the Temple crevasse. I need to make sure Mora is really dead. Ever since I realized Mora was responsible for my parents' death, my gut has been in turmoil, and I've had nightmares about him. Meeting him in person made it even worse, so I desperately need closure."

Liezel is both shocked and puzzled. "Wait a minute," she says, "Mora was responsible for your parent's death?"

"He was. I just learned this myself when I saw him in Strasbourg. When he was the Mayor of Rome years ago, a group of Muslim terrorists captured the tour group my parents were in and held them in the church they were visiting. Mora learned that my parents were Jewish, so he offered to tell the terrorists who they were in exchange for releasing the other captives. The terrorists agreed. Later, the police stormed the church, and my parents were killed in the attack.

Liezel's expression turns to sorrow. "Oh my God, Jay, I'm so sorry. What a horrible way to go. I remember how unsatisfied you were with the explanation the authorities gave you about how they died. Now I understand why seeing Mora's body is so important to you. But do you really think he could have survived the fall and the fire and the Temple crashing down on him?"

"Yes, It's possible. He cheated death before. He was in the U.N. headquarters when it blew-up and collapsed. They even pronounced him dead at the scene. Either he wasn't really dead, or his spooky assistant Madam Derofski resurrected him somehow. That's why I have to be sure he's really dead this time. The footing up there might be dangerous, so I don't want you to go with me. Just stay here with Anah. I shouldn't be too long."

"No way!" Liezel snaps-back. "We just *found* each other. You're not going anywhere without me! Remember what you just promised me?"

"Don't worry. I'll be fine. It's not that far. If I'm not back in thirty minutes, you can come look for me."

Liezel sees the worried look on Jason's face, and realizes how much he needs to confirm Mora's death. Despite a feeling of apprehension that has just swept over her, she relents. "Okay, Jay," she says with a loving smile. "Just be careful. I'm timing you starting right now." He glances down at her wrists and gives her a sweet kiss, smirking a little because he knows she doesn't have a wrist comm or anything else that can tell time.

He hikes to the top of the Wailing Wall. His emotions are churning--- a paradoxical combination of hope that Mora is really dead, coupled with a torturous doubt that he isn't. The footing is indeed difficult, and the path is steep. He steps on some loose stones, and they roll under his foot, causing him to stumble to the ground. The sharp edge of a partially buried piece of shrapnel rips through his pant leg and slices a long deep gash in his shin. Other rocks lacerate the palms of his hands as he tries to catch himself

114

when he falls to the ground. Then the pain hits him. He opens the rip in his pant leg to get a better look. The leg is more wounded than he first thought. A loose strip of flesh dangles from the wound, exposing bare bone. A steady stream of blood flows down his leg and onto his boot. The bloody stain on his pant leg is expanding rapidly. *'I'll need to get back quickly,'* he says to himself. *'But I must see into the crevasse first. I have to know'.* As Jason limps near the top of the Wall, he sees flames and black smoke billowing over the ridge. The heat is intense, so he walks farther along the edge where there aren't any flames. He is awed by the size and depth of the chasm. The smoke wafts back and forth, stinging his eyes and periodically obstructing his view. He rubs his eyes, but it brings no relief. His eyes start to water.

He steps closer to the edge for a better look. Through the smoke and flames he sees nothing but blackened rocks and dirt at the bottom of the one-hundred-foot-deep chasm. Then when the smoke drifts to one side he sees it--- the very top of the Temple, with half the Star of David exposed on the gable. The rest of it is completely buried in charred rocks and dirt. No one could have survived that fall, let alone the fire or the suffocating dirt. He wishes he could see Mora's body, but he's convinced that it will never be found. On a fearful hunch, he peers across the crevasse to the other side. A small landslide falls into the crevasse from the far edge. Then there is bare ground all the way to the rubble that once was the Rock of the Dome. When he sees no sign of Mora anywhere, he yells down into the crevasse, "Stay dead, you bastard!" Then relief sets-in. His parents' death is avenged. He can finally be at peace.

After a moment of giving thanks, he realizes that Liezel might be worried, and his wound needs immediate attention. He'd better head back. He spins around, but the pain forces his leg to involuntarily buckle. He thrusts his hands forward to catch his fall, but he's too close to the edge. The dirt gives way under one of his hands, and it slips over the edge. His head and body follow. No one hears his scream.

Liezel is starting to worry. She's sure it's been well over a half-hour. Anah is worried, as well. "Anah, I don't like this. He should have been back by now. I think something's wrong."

Anah looks into Liezel's worried eyes and shares her concern. "He's probably fine, but if he's not back in another five minutes or so, I'll go with you to get him."

"No," Liezel barks, "I'm going now. Are you with me?"

"Right behind you," Anah replies. They head-off.

The going is tough, but they arrive at the ridge without incident. As they peer down into the fiery abyss, they are momentarily frozen by the scope and fury of the scene. When they gather themselves again, they start yelling Jason's name, but the flames are too noisy for their voices to carry far. They decide to move farther along the edge. They yell again. Suddenly, they hear a muffled, "Over here! Over here!" They jog to where they thought they heard the cry, but no one's there. Then Liezel looks down and hears Jason's cry once more. Her heart pounding, she lies on her stomach and scoots herself forward so she can see over the edge.

"Jay!" she exclaims. She's frantic. "Are you alright? Are you hurt?"

"Liezel! Thank God! I cut my leg, and I took a nasty bump on the head. I can't crawl back up." The face of the cliff where Jason went-over is not as steep as elsewhere, so his fall was more of a tumble and slide. He's about thirty feet down, clinging to a large rock that juts out from the face of the cliff. His legs are straddling the trunk of a small tree that also sticks-out from the face. "Get some help--- and a rope. Hurry. I don't know if this tree is going to hold." His words are weak, and full of panic.

Liezel thrusts her arm over the edge toward Jason in a symbolic attempt to reach him. "Hang-on, Honey. I'm not going to leave you. Anah's going for help now."

Fifteen minutes later, a military Bronco pulls-up from the other direction. Three IDF soldiers and Anah jump-out. They quickly unravel the cable on the front winch of the vehicle and start feeding it down to Jason. "Hang-in there, sir," one of them yells. "Can you wrap the cable around your back and under your arm pits?"

"Yeah, I think so," Jason weakly utters. Fright gives way to relief, but he's starting to feel light-headed from the loss of blood. He struggles a bit with the cable, but finally gets it looped around and hooked. Slowly the winch starts turning, pulling him up the slope. The rock he was holding onto painfully grinds into his chest as he's pulled over it. Liezel and two of the soldiers help Jason to his feet. He's dirty, shaking, and bleeding from the swollen bump on his forehead. His hair is full of dust, and he feels woozy. Before anyone can get the cable removed, Liezel immediately embraces him.

"Thank God you're safe. I was afraid I lost you again!" Liezel says. "What happened?"

Jason welcomes her embrace, but he winces. His ribs hurt, and he's losing feeling in his wounded leg. Then he tells his story. Liezel backs away and notices his pant leg, now saturated with blood and mud. A bloody puddle has formed on the ground next to his boot.

"Jay," she cries, "look at this! We need to get you to a medic--- quick!" One of the soldiers removes the cable. Then Jason wraps his arms around the necks of the two soldiers, and they drag him to the Bronco. They scoot him across one of the seats. One of the soldiers takes his undershirt off and wraps it around the bleeding wound. He then takes his belt off and wraps it around the shirt. Liezel cinches the belt to keep it tight. They all hop in the Bronco.

As the Bronco starts down the slope, Jason looks back to take-in the fire and smoke emanating from Mora's tomb. Still dizzy and in a lot of pain, he rests his head on Liezel's shoulder and closes his dusty watery eyes.

The nearest intact medical facility is back at the IDF Command Center hidden deep inside the Petra mountains. The main entrance was destroyed in the missile bombardment, so the Bronco takes an unassuming dirt road to one of the emergency escape tunnels. The tunnel is dark and confining. The headlights of the transport create eerie shadows on the walls and ceiling. Two security guards check them in, but Liezel doesn't have the proper I.D. because she's a civilian whose never been there before. Anah explains the need for Liezel to accompany her husband, so the guards let everyone through. After all, there's no longer such a need for tight military security.

The two soldiers pull Jason out of the Bronco. Liezel, Anah, and the driver are told to wait outside the medical facility doors. Anah thanks the driver and lets him go. Anah then suggests that she and Liezel wait in the Command Center mess hall. She'll check on Jason's status from there.

One of the soldiers carrying Jason kicks one of the large metal doors. It flies open, but not all the way because it hits a wounded patient sitting on the floor. The patient screams. The soldier says, "Sorry, buddy," as they hustle Jason through. The facility is packed. Chairs and stretchers are crammed together. Some of the wounded are sitting on boxes. Many are leaning against walls or sitting on the floor. Blood-soaked bandages and clothing are strewn about. Men and women in blood-stained white coats scurry from patient to patient. The air is filled with the pungent smell of alcohol. Medical personnel are yelling and pointing, drowning-out the muffled groans of the wounded. The lucky ones are those who are able to hold their heads up.

As Jason is dragged to the intake desk, he notices a military nurse replacing a bloody towel on a woman's head as she lies motionless on a stretcher. There is one soldier ahead of Jason at the desk. An orderly is steadying the wounded soldier by holding him under his arm. The soldier is holding a blood-soaked shirt against his face. "Hurry, please hurry," he moans in a muffled voice. The intake nurse looks concerned, but she's obviously tired. She's seen too much of this in the last 24 hours. She points to an area of the room, and the orderly pivots the man around. As he does so, Jason's arm and the wounded man's arm collide. The man's hand and shirt are accidentally yanked from his face, revealing a bloody crater where his nose used to be and an empty and bleeding eyeball socket. The soldier screams. Jason faints.

Later, Jason opens his eyes and realizes he's lying on the floor against a wall. There's a folded piece of clothing under his head as a make-shift pillow. He blinks a few times, and then looks around. His hand gingerly probes his forehead. There's a bandage on it. Most of his right pant leg has been cut-off, and a medic is just finishing wrapping Jason's knee. "Good, you're awake," the medic says in an unemotional tone. He's obviously hurried. "My name is Benyamin. You're all set. I had to put a lot of stitches in your leg, but you fared much better than most in here. How do you feel?"

Jason lifts his head, then promptly lays it back down. "Uh, actually, I have a splitting headache, my leg is killing me, and the room is spinning. Oh, and because of the way I fell on that tree, I won't be making love anytime soon. I think that's about it."

"I really can't feel sorry for you, fella," Benyamin replies unsympathetically. His tone is cold and he's obviously tired and annoyed. "People are dying in here. Many are missing body parts." Benyamin pulls-out a scan and places it against Jason's shoulder at the implanted biochip. He then checks Jason's eyes with a light probe. "You have a concussion," he says. "Just rest here for a while. I'll come back when you can leave. Do you have anyone who can take care of you?"

119

"Yeah, my wife, but I don't know where she is."

Looking at Jason's wrist tag, Benyamin says, "I see your name is Johnson. That's hardly a Jewish name. Are you a Jew?"

"I am on my mother's side," Jason replies.

"Hmm," Benyamin says. He stands up. "Look, I'd ask you what you're doing here in Israel, but I've got to go. I'll find out where your wife is, and I'll fill her in. Don't sit-up. Just lie there and try to stay awake."

Jason nods, and then stares at the ceiling. A moment later he slowly turns his head and glances around the room. He doesn't recognize it. Other patients are lying on the floor. Most are resting like he is. There are others in chairs, many with their eyes closed. Some have crutches. Most have large bandages. This is not the intake room or even a place where patients are being treated. The room is quiet. As he looks at the others in the room who are in far worse shape than he is, he begins to feel embarrassed that his relatively minor injuries have taken-up precious time from those who need it more. Embarrassment turns to guilt. So many have died, and others will be handicapped for the rest of their lives. He mentally kicks himself for being so careless at the crevasse. Thinking of the others in the room, he closes his eyes as a small tear runs down the side of his face. He closes his eyes and tilts his head upwards. "Father, please take care of them," he murmurs.

While Jason is being treated, Anah and Liezel eventually find a spot in the mess hall to sit. Despite the victory, the air in the Command Center is tense. Soldiers scurry around, trying to assess the extent of the severe damage to their homeland. Water and food will have to be rationed until the distribution networks are restored, but Anah decides it's okay to share a glass of water. After a brief silence, Anah says, "You know, I had no idea you were Jay's wife. He told me about you, and you told me about him, but neither of you mentioned names, so I never put two-and-two together. Considering all that both of you went through, it's a miracle that you found each other."

"I know. It's unbelievable. I keep pinching myself to make sure it isn't a dream--- except for Jay's tumble. *That* I wish *was* a dream!". Anah nods with a quick half-smile. Picking-up on what Anah just said about she and Jason sharing personal information, Liezel looks hard at Anah for the first time. When Anah takes off her glasses to clean them, Liezel sees her in a new light. Although Anah is dusty and tired and not wearing make-up, she is naturally beautiful, with dark unplucked eyebrows and blue doe-like eyes. Liezel begins to wonder, so she asks Anah, "So how is it that you and Jay got so personal? You couldn't have known each other very long."

Anah is suddenly nervous. "Well, I guess it comes from working so closely together in a very tense and pressure-packed situation. He told me a lot about himself--- mostly during our meal breaks."

"I suppose," Liezel says. "So, exactly what did *you* share with *him*?"

"Oh, nothing much," Anah replies, trying to hide her discomfort with the conversation. Her muscular-looking hands start fidgeting on the table. When she realizes how revealing that must look, she quickly pulls them onto her lap. "I just told him a little about my background and family. That's all." From Liezel's tone and piercing look, Anah now knows that Liezel suspects something.

The awkward conversation is interrupted by an announcement requesting Liezel come to the room where Jason is recovering. When Liezel and Anah enter the room, she asks a medic about Jason. Benyamin overhears her, and he brings them to Jason. He instructs Liezel to keep Jason quiet without a lot of visual stimuli. He should be fine in a few days, and he can resume normal activities when his headache stops, but he shouldn't run or make sudden movements. He also needs to drink plenty of water to help replenish the blood he lost. Benyamin helps Jason up, and then darts-off to another patient. Jason doesn't get a chance to say thank you or good-bye. The two women steady Jason as they make their way out.

Several Broncos and drivers are waiting just outside the medical facility, ready to take patients home. Anah summons one of them. "Can you give us a hand with this man, Corporal?" she says. "We live about five Ks from here. I'll show you the way, but we need to avoid jarring this man on rough roads. He has a concussion."

"Yes, Lieutenant," he replies. "I'll be careful." They drive-off. From this high vantage point in the mountains, it's easier to see the devastation. Pockets of fire, smoke and rubble surround the craters where missiles and bombs landed. Rescue workers and residents crawl over the piles of rubble, frantically searching for buried survivors. Most civilian vehicles do not have protective EMP (Electro-Magnetic Pulse) shields, so the only vehicles operating are military--- Broncos, front-end loaders, and an occasional ambulance. Farther down the road, they approach a cliff where the safety rail has been torn away. A crushed Bronco burns at the foot of the cliff while three blackened bodies lie a few feet away, face-down. Two men in white radiation suits approach the bodies.

Anah barks at the driver, "Stop the car!" She gets out. "Do you need help?" she yells down. The men in the white suits look up and shake their heads as they frantically motion her to move away quickly. Then she scans the scene more closely. She sees a flattened and burned landscape and a bomb crater about two hundred yards away. Beyond that, a Bronco with a yellow and black emblem on the side tells her that the area is radioactive. She quickly jumps back in their Bronco, and they continue their drive.

As they progress down the mountain, they veer-off onto a non-descript gravel road and arrive at Anah's barracks. It's a group of three small camouflaged bungalows with metal roofs and small circular windows. They're tucked behind some trees and brush so they can't be seen from the main road. The bungalows are not damaged. No other vehicles are parked at the barracks when the Bronco arrives, so Anah knows the others are either working, wounded, or dead. Each bungalow houses four people. One houses two couples. Another houses four single men. Anah's unit houses her, two men and Liezel. They all worked in the Command Center, except Liezel, of course. The scene is much the same as when Liezel first arrived there, and her thoughts drift back to that more peaceful time.

One week before the battle, Liezel arrived at the barracks as arranged by her California rescuers Mordecai and Morris. There wasn't much for her to do, but she was so grateful for her new safe situation she felt she had to do something to show her appreciation. That's the way she was raised--- serving others and carrying her own weight. So shortly after her arrival she tended to the yard and cleaned her bungalow inside and out. After caring for her father and working on his ranch, she wasn't afraid of hard work. She's a bit of a neatnik, so it took her a couple of days to take care of the dust and mess that Anah and the two men were living in.

Anah's bathroom was bearable, but it needed a good scrubbing to measure up to Liezel's high standards. However, the men's bathroom was disgusting. At first glance, Liezel couldn't tell if the shower walls were dirty or moldy. It turned-out they were both. A bar of slimy soap sat near the drain. She initially thought the fixtures were brushed nickel, but they were actually chrome with a filthy haze on the finish. The sink was stainless steel that was paradoxically--- stained. An electric razor lay near one of the sink knobs. A toothbrush and a tube of capless toothpaste rested near the other with some of the paste oozing-out onto the sink top. There were patches of what looked like powder in the sink that turned out to be whiskers from shaving. The cabinet mirror was the easiest part of the room to clean, and the cabinet interior was a pleasant surprise--- a bottle of pain killers, a can of shaving cream, a straight razor, a bottle of eye drops, another toothbrush and paste, and a box of prophylactics. Then she noticed what was missing--- deodorant. The rug on the floor was so hopelessly stained she threw it out. She didn't have the courage to tackle the toilet until the next day. Unable to find any cleaning gloves, she grabbed a rag and, with a scrunched-up face, slowly opened the lid of the toilet. Peeking apprehensively inside, she immediately pulled her hand away, and let the lid slam shut. Her face still distorted from the disgusting site, she jumped upright, flapping her hands in front of her face like a baby bird trying to fly. When she finally composed herself, she gingerly flushed the toilet with one finger. Despite feeling nauseous, she held her breath and finished the cleaning job. Apparently, the men's interests were in their assignments rather than in maintaining clean pleasant surroundings. Maybe they thought if they waited long enough some elves would magically take care of everything. In any event, Liezel's work was greatly appreciated by her three new friends, but in a motherly tone she insisted that everyone keep things clean from then on.

Liezel and Anah help Jason into his spartanly furnished new home, and they ease him onto Liezel's neatly made bed. He grimaces as they straighten his legs. Looking at his filthy clothes and torn-off pant leg, Anah says, "You're quite a mess, Jay. I think we have some spare clothes that might fit you. I'll be right back."

Liezel sits down on the edge of the bed. She lovingly looks into Jason's sad and tired eyes. She reads his mind. Before he apologizes, she says, "Now don't say anything, Honey. The important thing is that you're alright now." With a sweet smile, she reaches down and gently runs her fingertips through his wavy dark brown hair. "Just rest. I'll take care of you." She pauses, then looks into his eyes and says softly, "You know, I thought about you every day while I was in hiding."

"Same here, Honey." He gazes into Liezel's bright blue eyes. His eyes then drift down to her lips. Although devoid of lipstick, they're still inviting. He then follows the outline of her face. Although her hair is tangled and dusty, he fondly remembers how exotically dark and silky it really is. "I love you so much," he says. "I really don't deserve you." He manages a half-smile. The pain meds finally kick-in, and his eye lids slowly close.

Anah noisily re-enters the room, unintentionally waking Jason from his half-sleep. "I think these should fit you," she says. "Mordecai left them here. I guess he was in a hurry."

"Mordecai?" Jason and Liezel exclaim together.

"Yes," Anah says, surprised at their joint response. "Does that name mean something to you?"

"Maybe," Liezel replies. "Did he have long grey hair and a half-closed eye? And did he have a friend named Morris?"

"Yes, that's him. Morris was here, too. Why, did you know them?"

"We both did," Liezel responds. "They're the ones I told you about--- you know, the ones who saved me in California, and they helped me get here. Coincidentally, Jay ran into them on two plane flights. Now he tells me they were both be-headed in Strasbourg. I'll bet anything it was Mora's doing because they were trying to expose him as an evil fraud."

"And for good reason," Jason pipes-in. "He *is* an evil man. I think I told you that Mora was responsible for my parents' death many years ago."

"Yes, I remember you sharing that with me," Anah says.

'*Hmmm.*' Liezel thinks to herself, '*I wonder what else they shared.*'

CHAPTER ELEVEN---ISRAEL RECOVERS

No sooner had Jason bedded down than another miracle rescued Israel and the rest of the world from the nuclear winter everyone feared. The rains came, and came they did--- for four straight days. They washed the radioactive dust from the air, thereby stopping the spreading plumes and limiting the size of the dead zones. Although the size of the dead zones were restricted, the radioactive run-off water began migrating to the rivers--- headed for the oceans to create a new threat to the earth's survival.

For the next three days Jason just rested. Liezel cleaned his wounds and changed his bandages daily. Finally, his headache subsided, but he could only hobble around the house stiff-legged. Anah introduced Jason to the other residents of the barracks. The two couples in one bungalow are Micah and Naomi, and Joel and Esther. The four men in the other are Zeke, Jonah, Dani, and Josh. Jason remarked that he had a son named Josh, and that his son and Israeli Josh had similar builds--- thin but muscular. The men in Anah's bungalow are Jacob and Nathan. The demands of the recovery work meant that the residents of each bungalow pretty much stayed in their own circles instead of socializing with those in the other bungalows. Since the invasion, everyone worked 12 to 16 hours, 6 or even 7 days per week. By the morning of day five Jason was still in pain, but he needed to contribute. Anah drove him to the Command Center where he teamed-up with Rick Willis, his former teammate at Progressive Aviation Systems. Willis and other Israeli operators had already begun trying to restore military and public communications.

Jason arrives at the Command Center. He still has to keep his wounded leg straight until the stitches come out, so he must swing his leg out to the side in a sweeping motion to step forward. The personnel in the Command Center take notice of Jason's return and start applauding. He feels he just did his part--- nothing heroic--- but he appreciates the gesture. He nods and smiles and tries to move-on to get out of the spotlight. General Dayan is nearby, and he walks over with his hand extended. "Welcome back, Dr. Johnson," he says. "I'm glad you felt like coming in today. How are you feeling?"

"My leg's a little sore, sir, but I'll be fine in fast order. My pride was hurt more than my body. So, how is everyone else? Did we lose anyone here?"

"Not in this Center, but some of the family members of the operators here didn't make it. Naturally, they have some time off. Willis and his team have made some good progress already towards restoring communications in the country. I'm sure he'll be glad to see you again. He's over there. Please give me a status report at the end of the day."

"Will do, General. Thanks." Jason hobbles over to Willis' workstation.

"Nice of you to show-up, boss," Willis says sarcastically. "You trying to do an imitation of Chester Goode?"

Jason acts confused. "Chester Goode?"

"Yeah, you know, from the old "Gunsmoke" series on the comm screen."

"Gunsmoke?"

"Never mind. I'm just pulling your leg--- no pun intended. Really, I'm glad you're back. How do you feel?"

"I wish people would quit asking me that. I really don't deserve any sympathy. This isn't a war wound. I cut myself on some shrapnel and then fell into the crevasse. It was all my fault. Just stupid. Anyway, I'm here to work. So, what have you accomplished so far?"

"I'll start from the beginning. The General decided to integrate the IDF comm systems with the public, since we really don't need heavily secure defense comm systems anymore. Because the few remaining military facilities had protected their communication systems from EMPs, they're viable and can act as communication hubs. Information can flow from the Command Center to the hubs and back; and then from newly constructed towers at the hubs to the public. The difficult part is to connect to the non-military residents. The residents all had wrist comms, but they were rendered inoperable by the EMPs. Fortunately, a couple electronics companies were spared from EMP damage because they were housed in metal buildings, so they're still able to manufacture replacement chips and components for wrist comms. Production is ramping up into high-gear--- 24 hours per day. Bit by bit, the populace will get plugged in."

"Great. Then I assume you're writing the software to facilitate all this."

"Roger that," Rick replies. "I've got four operators working on the IDF-to-hub interfaces. They're about twenty percent complete. Can you help me and my guys tackle the hub-to-public ones?"

"Sure, let me see what you've got so far. I hope we can get this up and running quickly so I can try to contact my son as soon as possible. Let's get going. The General wants a status report at the end of the day."

"Sure thing. By the way, have you noticed how nice the women here are looking this morning?"

"Focus, Rick, focus."

The day wears-on, and more progress is made. The men take a lunch break about 2pm. Anah brings them each a sandwich, and they split a soda. She lingers a little beside Jason. She can't take her eyes off him. Jason notices she's wearing an intoxicating perfume.

Willis is denied his customary three sandwiches due to rationing, and he's having a tough time dealing with it. He eyes Jason's plate next to his workstation. There are maybe two good-sized bites left. "You finished?" he says to Jason.

"Sure, Rick, go ahead," Jason says with a smile. "I see you haven't lost your famous appetite."

"Some men need more nutrition than others. Besides, I have to keep up my stamina," Willis says, winking. "Thanks."

"I see," Jason says. "So, you and Mariam are an item now, huh?"

Willis gives Jason another wink. The rest of the sandwich is gone in one gulp. Some of the sauce drips down on Willis' shirt. Jason shakes his head with a smirk and thinks, *some people never change!*

With Jason going back to work, Liezel decided she wanted to work, too. Israel needed all the help available. Since Liezel was mechanically gifted from working on her father's ranch, she found work converting vehicles to run without electronic components. (The enemy EMPs wiped-out all unshielded items that had electronics--- vehicles, computers, communications, appliances, medical and industrial equipment, even toys). Liezel was on one of thirty teams of mechanics. Farm equipment were prioritized so food distribution could proceed. Then construction equipment were converted so rubble-clearing and road repair could progress beyond what the military was doing. Finally, police vehicles were the next to be converted so order could be maintained. Eventually, newly-manufactured electronic components were installed by the teams.

Her first day on the job was exhausting. The shop was a mess--- greasy parts, tools, and dirty rags were scattered on top of the work benches. The floor was covered with oil-absorbent granules.

The only thing missing was the obligatory pin-up calendar. Being the only woman on her team (and an attractive one at that) she was the subject of much staring from the men. She reacted by making sure her top button was always buttoned. She also went without lipstick. Despite their interest in her, the men didn't cut her any slack. In fact, she out-worked two of the men trying to prove herself. She even found time to clean the place up a bit. That's how she was--- independent and an over-achiever. She had trouble communicating with one of them, because she didn't know Hebrew and he didn't speak English. Another one named Ivan was always scowling and was kind of spooky. There was something about him that she just didn't trust.

She was quite a sight by the end of the day. The overalls they gave her were too big, and they looked more like a clown's costume. But she rolled-up her sleeves and cuffs and made it work. Her knees and forearms were stained with dirt and grease, and her hair was so straggly she asked one of the men to tie it back in a ponytail. Two others tussled for the privilege. Gloves were not an option due to the meticulous work, so her hands and fingernails were caked with dirt and grease. There was a smudge of something across her forehead. When she looked in the mirror during clean-up, she scared herself. She welcomed the end of the day and rode her e-bike back to the barracks. After a few more days, the men's attitude changed from skepticism to admiration. They would even argue about who would drive her home and pick her up in the morning. Sometimes she even accepted the offers, especially in poor weather.

When she drove up to the barracks, she noticed Anah's Bronco in the yard. 'Wonderful,' she thought to herself, 'Jay's home.' But when she entered the small bungalow, Jason was nowhere to be found. "Hi, Anah. Jay's not here?"

"No, he's working late again. He'll get a ride home from someone. Jake and Nate are working late, too. I was lucky. I only had a ten-hour day." She sounded somewhat cold. "I decided to treat myself to the beer that's been sitting in the fridge forever. Grab one and join me."

"Don't mind if I do. I'm parched, and I had a long first day being a grease monkey. Is it cold?"

"Absolutely. EMPs don't affect solar panels, so the fridge still works."

Liezel grabs a beer (now a real delicacy) and she plops down into a chair at the table, slouching back with her feet stretched out. After taking a huge gulp, she leans her head back and lets out a sigh. "This really hits the spot," she says. "Any idea when he'll be home?"

"Not really--- probably not for a while, yet. Since it's just us girls here, why don't you tell me something about yourself. We really haven't talked much since things got crazy right after you got here."

"Sure, why not. I'm a country girl--- raised on my father's ranch in California. I went to college, but I dropped-out when Mom died so I could help Dad on the ranch. College didn't do much for me anyway. I loved working with animals, especially horses. I probably should've been a veterinarian. My dad was a great man. He taught me a lot about fixing things around the ranch. I guess I could have been a mechanic, too, but I liked animals better."

"So, you still have the ranch?"

"No, no. Dad developed early dementia. I took care of him for a while until I just couldn't give him the care he needed. Then he went into a nursing home, and I had to sell the ranch to pay for it. He died six years ago."

"Sorry, Liezel. I know how you feel 'though," Anah says sympathetically. "I lost both my parents in a rocket attack 12 years ago. After that, I wanted to help protect other families from the same pain. That's why I joined the IDF."

131

"I'm sorry for your loss, as well. I guess we have something in common after all."

After a moment of painful reminiscing, Anah returns to her line of questioning. "So, is Jason your first husband?"

"He is. I dated a few men before, but nothing seemed to click. After a while I sort of gave-up on men, and I just concentrated on work and country western dancing. Then I met Jay."

You know, you're very lucky. He's quite a catch. So, how exactly did you two meet?"

Liezel takes another gulp of her beer. "I guess it was about four years ago. We literally bumped into each other at a country western dance club. It was his first time dancing, and he stepped all over my feet. I laughed it off. He was really nervous, but in a charming sort of way." Liezel smiled and looked up at the ceiling to better visualize the occasion. "I remember being surprised at my immediate interest in him. That wasn't like me. I'm usually more cautious. His good looks played a factor, for sure. I especially remember being attracted to that dimple in his chin because it reminded me of Kirk Douglas."

"Who?" Anah asks.

"Kirk Douglas. He was an American actor from decades ago. I got hooked on a bunch of his old movies. He always played these rugged, masculine characters. I sort of developed a crush on him, even though he's long gone. Anyway, there was just something about Jason's personality--- sort of shy but at the same time masculine. Looking back, my love for animals might have been a factor, too. I think his ineptitude on the dance floor triggered a rescue-the-lost-puppy response in me."

Anah sees an opening. "Some women can't resist the temptation to "fix" a lost man, but that isn't a good foundation for a lasting relationship is it?"

"Well, you're absolutely right, but after I got to know him better, I saw other qualities in him that I really liked and respected. He has a huge heart and there's an air of competence about him. He sort-of reminds me of my father."

"Well, he is good looking," Anah agrees with a sigh. "I wish there were more like him around here." She wonders if their marriage has a chance of cracking due to their long time away from each other and their disagreement about returning to America. Taking a risk, she decides to see how strong their marriage is. "So, did he ever tell you he tried to kiss me?"

"WHAT?" Liezel explodes out of her chair.

Just then Jason pops through the door. "Hi, Honey, Anah. What's up?"

Liezel wheels around, obviously furious. "What's up? I'll tell you what's up. You tried to kiss Anah?"

"Whoa, easy Honey. Anah, what did you say to her? No, I mean we got a little, er, close one time, but I never really made a move on her. Besides, I thought you were dead."

Liezel spins back at Anah. "So, did he or didn't he, Anah?"

Anah can't find the words right away. Feeling a little sheepish, she realizes everything is back-firing, and her tactic was a big mistake. Now their friendship is compromised. "Well," she says, "I *thought* he was interested. I guess I might have exaggerated a little. I did flirt with him, but he resisted. I'm sorry I even mentioned it."

"I thought so," Liezel fires back. "I suspected you had a thing for my husband all along. Well you can forget about it. He's mine!" Still furious, but not at Jason, she puts one hand on his chest and pushes him backwards through their bedroom door, unbuttoning the two top buttons of her overalls with the other hand. The door slams shut. Anah's hopes sink as she hears the lock click.

Aid from the countries that escaped the nuclear holocaust was minimal. Most of it went to America, China, and Russia. The rest of the world didn't seem to care very much about Israel, but that was nothing new. As the days turned into weeks, the desalinization plants and water distribution systems were restored, but not fully. Water rationing was lifted anyway, since there were two million fewer residents to service. Farms were back in business, but not at full production. A limited amount of food came in from other countries, but imports were well below normal. Vehicle fuel production ramped-up. National electricity service was only partially re-established, but most buildings had their own solar panels and wind turbines. The speed of the progress in most areas was impressive. But then almost everything Israel ever did was impressive. It was like they had an invisible hand helping them.

Jason's leg healed to the point where he walked with barely a limp, but he was not quite ready to run or even jog. The scars on his forehead and leg would be a permanent reminder of his near-death experience at the Temple crevasse. But he is not a stranger to near-death. In San Marita, he and his son Joshua survived an earthquake that almost sent his car into a crevasse; he narrowly missed being killed in Strasbourg when the U.N. headquarters exploded; his airplane was hit by a rocket as it approached Tel-Aviv, and finally his ground transport was attacked by terrorists on the way to the Command Center. These experiences toughened him up and bolstered his confidence. He became convinced that he could handle any obstacles that might pop-up on their way to California. He would later be humbled by new threats lurking ahead.

It's now two months into the recovery, and Israel has turned the corner faster than anyone expected. They're going to make it. Jason and Willis have nearly wrapped-up their work at the Command Center, and final testing of the national communication system is underway. Nationwide communications should be launched in three days. Willis decided to let his crooked mustache grow back in. Despite how goofy he looked with it, he somehow convinced Mariam to be more than friends. Jason just smiled every time he saw them flirting at work. He hadn't seen Willis this happy in years.

The whole world saw Israel's amazing recovery, and they were awed and envious. The phrase "The Chosen People" was being tossed about again. Recognizing General Dayan's leadership role in the battle and in the recovery, Israelis and many others all over the world began referring to him as "The Lion of Judah."

As his assignment came closer and closer to concluding, Jason's thoughts of his son Joshua became more intense. Was he hurt? Was he even alive? Despite Jason's futile attempts to reach anyone in America, he couldn't bring himself to believe that Joshua was dead. The kid was just too scrappy and resourceful. Although Liezel continued to be reluctant and apprehensive, she and Jason started making plans to leave.

Word came to the Command Center that Muslim leaders were requesting a meeting with General Dayan, who is still the default leader of Israel until a new Knesset is elected--- a few months off. The subject of the meeting is detente with the Muslim world and establishing effective communications with them to ensure the peace. Knowing Jason's expertise in communications, the General asked Jason to join the delegation. The General insisted on meeting in a plain masonry building with large windows where one of the crevasses that swallowed the Arab army could be easily seen.

The meeting participants arrive with little fanfare. Besides the General and Jason, Israel has Anah, Col. David and Major Weiss from the Command Center, and Ira Gold and his assistant Rachel from the Foreign Ministry. The other government officials that would normally be in such a meeting were either killed or seriously wounded in the attack. The Muslim delegation includes two factions--- Prince Khuruf from Saudi Arabia representing the Sunnis, and Ayatollah Karakul from Shiastan representing the Shiites. Rachel has provided the General with bios on the two Muslims. They both are devout believers and former military commanders who lost sons in the battle. Ira Gold informs the General that coincidently their names in Arabic and Farsi mean "sheep or lamb." They are wearing traditional Arab and Persian attire. Both men are in their sixties, with full beards streaked with gray and black. They're very humble and respectful, appropriately reflecting the severe thrashing their forces suffered in the battle. Their military had been annihilated, and now they are defenseless. In contrast to the Muslim's demure posture, General Dayan exudes confidence and power. His silky white hair, neatly trimmed beard, and six-foot four frame force the shorter Muslims look up subserviently to him.

Out of consideration for Middle Eastern seating customs, the room is arrayed with carpets and pillows along the walls. Dayan motions for the guests to make themselves comfortable. The Israeli contingent semi-reclines as well, although somewhat awkwardly. Pleasantries are exchanged for a few minutes, and tea is served. Jason wonders what the Muslim's angle is. The Muslims nervously look down at their tea, avoiding eye contact with the General. The awkward silence is broken when Karakul's shaky hand causes his cup to rattle against the saucer as he puts the cup down. Everyone immediately glances his way. He retreats against his pillow in a futile attempt to hide. Finally, it's Khuruf who clears his throat to speak. Jason leans forward in anticipation. "General Dayan," he began, "We--- that is, the Islamic leadership--- have just come from a meeting with prominent Imams and leaders from most of the Muslim world. Your amazing victory was so supernatural and so complete that we concluded that it was a sign that Allah was involved. We believe that Allah punished us for being blinded by our hate and for following the wrong path in jihad. These events have also caused us to re-examine some of the key passages in the Quran regarding the 12th Imam and the way he will bring peace to the world. In the light of this re-examination, we believe your victory here is now consistent with the teachings of the Quran, and we have therefore arrived at an inescapable conclusion. We now recognize that the long-awaited 12th Imam who will bring peace to the world has arrived... and that man is you."

Dead silence. Jason and the team members can't believe what they just heard. As Jason searches the other team member's faces for reactions, they all seem equally shocked except the General. Instead of raising his eyebrows in surprise, he squints, deep in thought. After a long pause, the General speaks. "So, if you believe that I am who you say I am, does that mean that you believe Allah and the God of Israel are one and the same?"

The Muslims are caught flat-footed. They look at each other, hoping someone has an answer. Finally, Khuruf speaks. "There are many gods, but Allah is the one true God, and Mohammed is his prophet, praise be upon him."

The General chooses his words carefully, "The answer to that question is immaterial at this point. The question is: will the Muslim world now accept Israel and *all* non-Islamic religions and nations, and will *all* hostilities cease, or will there need to be more punishment?"

"We will have to take this back to the Islamic Council, but I believe the answer will be that we will choose peace for all nations."

The General responds. "I know your definition of peace is that peace is only possible when the world submits to Islamic rule. Our definition of peace is the cessation of hostilities and the onset of cooperation. So, which definition of peace do you mean?"

After a tense hesitation, Khuruf looks down and softly replies, "Your definition, General." Karakul scowls in silence.

"We will await your official answer in the form of a treaty," the General replies. "In the meantime, we have prepared a meal for us. Would you care for more tea?"

Jason's heart is pounding with excitement. After centuries of wars and conflict, the peace that has eluded the Middle East appears to be happening. With the demise of the super-powers of America, Russia, and China, world peace may finally be here as well. It's finally time to go home.

During the post-meeting lunch, some personal chit-chat occurs, but the atmosphere is still tense and, in Jason's view, quite weird. Dayan asks the Muslims about the details of what the 12th Imam would actually do upon his return, and if their view has now been altered.

Prince Khuruf replies. "Well, he was to bring peace by defeating the infidels and unifying the world under Islamic rule. As for the alteration of our view, your victory has of course changed everything. Again, General, the Islamic Council will be making a definitive statement, but we are obligated to respect the words of the 12th Imam and follow his guidance. I will be supporting that position."

Jason is still having difficulty absorbing the gigantic implications of what he's hearing. As Khuruf gives his reply to the General, Jason focuses on Ayatollah Karakul. His tight lips and beady eyes tell Jason that Karakul is not fully on-board with the way things are going.

The meeting breaks-up. Everyone is cordial, but no one smiles. Time will tell if the words actually become reality. The Muslims bow toward the General. As he leaves, Karakul momentarily stops and glares out of the window in sadness and frustration at the smoking crevasse that destroyed his entire army. He puts the palm of his hand on the glass as if he's reaching out to the dead.

On the drive back, Jason and Dayan have a chance to get better acquainted. "General--- or should I call you something else? --- do you really believe they believe you are the 12th Imam?"

"Do *you*, Dr. Johnson?" the General asks with a smirk.

Jason is starting to enjoy this little cat-and-mouse game Dayan's been playing with the Muslims, and now with Jason. Jason plays along. "Whether you're the 12th Imam or the Messiah or someone else, it doesn't matter what I believe, Sir, it only matters what they believe."

"We'll see soon enough," Dayan replies.

Jason digs-in some more, looking for more clues. "So, General, I'm fascinated by the way you guided Israel to victory. Your strategies were unorthodox but brilliant. Can you tell me something about yourself--- what your background is, and how you came to lead the IDF?"

"You flatter me, Dr. Johnson. There's not a lot to tell, really. I was born in a mostly Muslim town just south of Jerusalem. My parents immigrated there from Italy. They're both deceased now. My father was a Jew, but my mother was not. Interestingly, the doctors told my parents that my mother couldn't conceive, but nine months later I was born. I joined the IDF relatively late in life, at thirty-three. Prior to that I was working as an architect, but after a few years I felt a calling to serve. I had some very good mentors and I moved through the ranks quickly. I was fortunate."

"You're too modest, Sir. I think you were in the right place at the right time. And now you're leading the country into recovery. Your military organization skills are exactly what this country needs right now, not the people-pleasing caution of a politician."

"Again, you flatter me, Dr. Johnson. Are you trying to butter me up for some reason?"

"Why, no, Sir." Jason is surprised at the General's perception--- but he shouldn't be. "But I do need to talk to you about something. Willis and I have been working our butts off trying to get Israel's communication system working again, and we're almost there. Final testing should conclude tomorrow, so I'm not sure what further use we will be. You may not remember, but I have a son in California that I haven't been able to contact. I'm awfully worried about him. I don't even know if he's alive. Right now, communication within America is impossible since the entire country's infrastructure has been destroyed. So, I'm hoping to leave as soon as possible. Can I count on your help to help me find my son?"

"I can do more than that, Jason. I'm not sure we could have achieved victory without your and Willis' help. I'll have Anah make some arrangements. One of our oil tankers should be able to get you to the terminal in Lavera, France. If you can make it from there to our consulate in Strasbourg, we'll alert them to have the necessary travel certificates waiting for you so you can get to England and from there to America."

"Travel certificates, Sir?" asks Jason.

"Yes. Since the War, inter-country travel is very restricted. The certificate chips are something new. They load into your wrist comms. Anyway, I have no idea if American dollars are worth anything anymore, so we'll load some Unicoin in your wrist comms. We'll also give you some Krugerrands just in case. Having said that, the journey you and your wife are planning will be a real test of your survival skills. Our reports from Canada and Mexico paint a very discouraging and dangerous picture of conditions in America--- starvation, fighting, even cannibalism. Are you sure you don't want to reconsider?"

"We're sure, Sir. Our hometown isn't near the cities that were attacked, so I hope things there won't be as bad there as in other parts of the country. I can't thank you enough, sir. But why

Strasbourg? I thought you have an embassy in Paris. Why not send us there?"

"We had to abandon it. The Muslim dominance of the city and the accompanying threats and violence gave us no choice. As you may know, many parts of France are under Sharia Law. By the way, I understand your wife is here, and she's staying with Anah. Frankly, I'm surprised you brought her along on such a dangerous assignment."

"Oh, I didn't bring her, Sir. It's an amazing story. She had disappeared without a trace over a year ago, but two old men rescued her and sent her here where she would be safe. Safe--- ironic, isn't it? Even more ironic, I met the two men on an airplane. Unfortunately, they were later beheaded by Antonin Mora in Strasbourg."

Strangely, Dayan doesn't seem surprised at the bizarre tale. "That's quite a story, Jason. Well, I'm glad you and your wife are reunited again."

Jason's eyes drift towards the window of the transport. "Me, too, Sir. Me, too."

Then the General says, "We'll hate to see you go, but when you're ready to leave, be sure to stop-by my office. I have something to give you."

CHAPTER TWELVE---SAN MARITA STRUGGLES

Inside a small domed house in San Marita, California, Jason's ex-wife Kathy and their 14-year-old son Joshua are fearfully hunkering-down following the nuclear attack. San Francisco and the naval base at Bremerton, Washington were flattened, and they will be radioactive dead zones for centuries. Fortunately, those areas are far enough away from San Marita so that radiation is not a direct threat. Furthermore, the rains washed the fallout from the skies, limiting the dead zones' size. National communications were destroyed, but some regional communications infrastructures survived where the EMP detonations were far enough away to spare the local electronics. Kathy had wisely accumulated some long-term storage food. Between the water jugs and the full bathtub, there might be enough water for perhaps three or four weeks if they really conserved. Since San Marita is surrounded by agricultural and livestock areas, there is hope that food distribution could be restored. Even then, food choices would be limited since so much of it came from other areas and countries.

The local comm screen broadcasts said radioactivity should not be a concern since San Marita was well north of any plume drifting west with the prevailing winds from San Francisco, and it was well south of Bremerton. The national electric grid was knocked-out, but with proper energy rationing, local solar, wind, and the local hydrogen gas turbine plant should provide power, albeit inconsistently.

Then there's the money problem. Since the Federal government was destroyed, the flow of money came to a halt. No Social Security checks. No government payroll checks. No government payments to contractors and suppliers. More than half of the people in the country depended directly or indirectly on government expenditures.

After a couple of weeks, the value of money skyrocketed, but so did the cost of goods. Local banks were inundated with requests for credit and withdrawals, but the money wasn't there. Some depositors were so angry they turned violent. Gun fights ensued. People were killed. The system collapsed.

Then bartering became the norm. Those who spent all their money or had nothing to barter with became desperate. Some women turned to prostitution. Young children became a liability. Although the earthquakes, floods, pestilence, and other calamities mysteriously ceased, people started dying from otherwise treatable sicknesses and starvation. The U.N. food distribution system collapsed. Local lakes and streams were fished-out. Water supplies dwindled because the filtering and distribution systems failed from lack of spare parts. Desperation turned to panic. Crops, ranches and citrus groves were raided and stripped bare, whether ripe or not. Livestock were shot and butchered where they fell in barns and pastures. Farmers and ranchers were murdered if they tried to protect their property. Some ranchers let their animals loose to save their lives. Law enforcement became impossible. Police officers were shot. Armed gangs were now in control of San Marita. Stores were looted for everything useful.

Jason's ex-wife Kathy and their son Joshua huddle in the front room of their house. With the conditions as they are, Kathy has understandably let herself go. Beauty salons are a thing of the past. She has been wearing the same bulky sweatshirt and over-sized jogging pants almost every day. Her hair is straggly and greasy. Joshua has patches of thin whiskers trying unsuccessfully to become a beard and mustache. Although Joshua is thin, he's muscular and strong for a boy his age.

The City water system stopped functioning, so Josh sneaks down to a small stagnant pond every few nights for bathing water so he and Kathy can merely wipe themselves down. When it occasionally rains, they catch some water in pans and jars and pour it into the bathtub. The only time their clothes get washed is when it rains. For the first few days after the bombing they nervously glued themselves to the comm screen. Report after report made it clear that chaos had set in. Then the screen went blank. Since then, their situation has become more dangerous.

Looking up at his mother through the reddish-brown hair dangling in front of his eyes, Joshua says, "Gosh, Mom, it's been days since we've had any information about what's goin' on. What do you think we should do?"

"I don't know, Josh. I'm beginning to get scared. I had hoped the food and water distribution networks would have been re-established by now, but it looks like things have only deteriorated."

Joshua's lightly freckled face reflects his worried mother's concern. "So how much food and water do we have left?"

"Not enough, I'm afraid. We'll have to trim down to one meal a day until we find another way. I don't know what to do. I haven't been able to reach any of our friends or family since the wrist comms went down. And I'm afraid to go far from the house. There are violent gangs out there just waiting to hurt us and take what we have here. That's why we need to keep pretending that no one lives here."

Josh senses the desperation in his mother's voice. "But I'm hungry *now*, Mom. There must be somethin' we can do. Why don't we wait for nightfall? I can try to reach Uncle David and Aunt Mary then."

"Oh no you don't! You're not leaving this house. If something happened to you, I'd never forgive myself. Whatever we do, we do it together. Besides, they live where all the riots and shootings were. If they could, they would have been here by now. They might not have made it."

"I hope you're wrong, Mom, but we'd better think of somethin' soon. I sure wish we had somethin' more than kitchen knives and tools to protect ourselves with. I'm gonna bring the shovel in the house just in case. Hey, wait a minute. Don't we still have that old shotgun Grandpa gave you years ago?"

"We do, Son. It's on the shelf in my closet, but it's not going to help."

"How come?"

Kathy sighs and slowly shakes her head. "I never got any bullets for it."

Joshua's heart sinks. "Well maybe we can find some bullets for it somewhere."

They retire for the night, but Joshua's hunger pangs keep him awake. Suddenly, his attention shifts. Through his bedroom window he sees a flickering light coming from the front yard. Then the light gets brighter, and he hears muffled voices. The front doorknob jiggles. Someone's trying to get in! Quietly, he tiptoes into his mother's room and wakes her. "Shhh," he whispers. "Someone's trying to open the front door. Stay here. I'll get the shotgun."

"Be careful, Josh. They're probably not our friends."

"Right, Mom. I sure wish we had some bullets. If they're bad guys I'm not sure I can bluff 'em." Josh silently retrieves the shotgun and ventures out into the living room to confront the intruders. Suddenly, the door bursts open with a loud bang! Josh flinches and squints as he's blinded by two strong flashlights. He then hears the clicks of two guns cocking. He starts quivering.

A deep voice pierces the awkward silence. "Hold-it, kid. Don't do anythin' stupid. All we want is food and money. Just show us where it is, and we'll be on our way. Otherwise, we'll drop ya where ya stand. You alone here?"

Still hopelessly squinting, Josh musters all the fake confidence he can. "Yeah, I'm here by myself, but I'm not backin' down. If you don't get out now, I'm gonna start firin'. You might get me, but I'll get at least one of you."

A gruff, booming new voice breaks the stand-off. "Put yer guns down, boys. He ain't gonna shoot no one, are ya, kid?" The flashlights move out of Josh's eyes, and he sees a silhouette at the front door of the biggest man he's ever seen. He's so big his shoulders brush against the narrow door frame as he lumbers through. Josh can feel the vibrations in the floor from the man's footsteps. He can't quite make-out the man's entire face, except to see that he has shoulder length mangey hair and a foot-long scraggly beard. His eyebrows are dark and bushy. As scared as Josh is, he has the feeling that this monster of a man is in total control of the situation, and unless Josh does something stupid no one will be shot tonight.

"Hey, Bubba," one of the men says. "So, what do ya wanna do with this scrappy kid?"

Just then, Kathy bursts into the room, quickly wrapping her motherly arms around Joshua and pulling him towards her. "Leave my son alone!" she commands.

"Well, well," Bubba says. "What do we have here? Seems like the kid's been holdin' out on us. There's bound to be some food here, otherwise they wouldn't be here. See if the lights work, then start lookin' around." One of the marauders finds a light switch and turns it on. The battery storage system kicks-in, and a dim light comes on. Josh sweeps the shotgun back and forth, from one man to another. They still aren't positive he won't shoot.

"Hey, I found some cans of food in here," the man in the kitchen says triumphantly."

"Okay, okay," Kathy says. "Now take the food and get out."

Bubba walks over to Josh and Kathy. He slowly reaches down and wraps his massive hand around the barrel of the shotgun. "Let-go, son," he growls, "You ain't gonna pull the trigger, are ya boy?" Josh is powerless as he lets the gun slowly slip from his trembling hands. His head drops--- defeated. Kathy is too tired and weak from hunger to do anything. She, too, drops her head and starts to sob. Bubba opens the shotgun's breech. "Just as I thought," he says in a confident swagger, "no shells."

"That's what we like to see," says one man, "cooperation. Now we need to take something else besides food and water." He moves toward Kathy with a big grin and a gleam in his eyes. He has a grubby-looking beard, long greasy hair, and brown teeth. His tee shirt has a large hole near the collar, and it looks like it hasn't been washed in several weeks. The shirt has the words "BORN TO DIE" on top of a skeleton. As his head moves within a foot of Kathy's, she pulls her head back and wrinkles her nose. The man stinks out loud.

Josh now realizes what's going to happen. His fear vanishes, and with fire in his eyes he screams, "You leave my mother alone, you jerk!" He tears loose from his mother's grip and kicks the stinky man between the legs. The man jack-knifes forward, grabbing himself with both hands. He falls to the floor and rolls-over in excruciating pain.

Bubba and the other men can't control their laughter. As the laughter subsides, one of the men says, "Hey, Shorty, havin' some trouble over there? Need someone smaller to pick-on?" More laughter. Then Josh sees what no one else sees. When Shorty hit the floor, his gun popped-out of his pants. Josh seizes the opportunity and dives for the gun. He grabs it, rolls onto his back and points it at Shorty's head. He cocks the hammer. The other men are shocked, and they swiftly point their guns at Josh.

"Well," Bubba says, "looks like we have a stand-off here. I'll say one thing, son, you gotta lotta grit. Tell ya what--- you give Shorty back his gun, and we'll let you and your Mom go."

"No way," Josh fires-back. Then he points the gun at Bubba. "We're goin' out the back door. Don't follow us. I'll shoot anyone that does. He points to the man at the kitchen door with the cans of food in his hands. "You!" he barks, "give those cans to my Mom."

"Stand yer ground, Gordy," Bubba says. His voice now sounds meaner and more irritated.

Josh realizes he's pushed too far. "Okay then, give us two cans. You can have the rest."

Then Kathy tugs at Josh's arm. "Josh, what are you doing! That's all the food we have left. Where will we go anyway? This is our home!"

"We can't stay here, Mom. They know about us now. Even if they leave tonight, they'll be back. We'll never be safe."

"Better listen to 'im, lady. We're gonna get what we want, whether it's tonight or tomorrow. Gordy, give 'em the two cans."

"Don't worry, Mom. I have an idea." Then he says to Gordy, "Leave the two cans on the floor, and back-off." His voice is quivering. The pressure is getting to him. "Let's go, Mom." Gordy moves aside. Kathy picks-up the cans, and they start to back up slowly towards the rear door. Josh holds the gun with both hands, training it on Bubba. The gun is starting to shake.

"You ain't leaving here with that gun, boy," Bubba growls back, really irritated now. He's making a fist in both hands and gritting his teeth. The tension in the room intensifies.

Josh's eyes dart back and forth. He's searching for an answer---something Bubba will accept. All the men in the room are scowling now. Josh can tell they're getting impatient. If he doesn't think of something fast, he's afraid the men might start shooting. Seconds tick by. Then he perks-up. He has an idea. "Okay, listen, we're goin' out the back door. When we do, I'm gonna count. If I don't see anyone come out of the house by the time I reach twenty, I'll lay the gun down on the ground."

Bubba takes a step toward them, but he stays silent. Josh thrusts the gun at him, and Bubba stops. Josh and Kathy start slowly backing up again, and they leave the house. So far, the plan is working. "Head for the woods, Mom. I'll catch up to you in a second." As Kathy takes-off running, Josh lays the gun down and runs after her. When they get about twenty-five feet into the woods they duck behind a large tree and peek back.

Three men barge out of the house and scour the ground with their flashlights. "Here it is!" one says triumphantly. "Good, now let's get those bitches." One of the men turns his flashlight toward the woods. Josh and Kathy jerk their heads behind the tree. The flashlight beam sweeps across the tree, and then back to the yard.

Then Bubba squeezes out of the house. "Nah," he says. "Let 'em go. We got the gun and some food. I don't feel like stumblin' around in the dark trying to find 'em. We'll run into 'em another day. Then you guys can have yer fun."

Joshua and Kathy breathe a sigh of relief. They hug each other in silence. Finally, Kathy speaks. "Josh, you saved our lives. We would have been killed if it weren't for your courage and quick thinking."

"I really don't know what happened, Mom. I was just reactin' on instinct and adrenalin. My heart was poundin' so hard I thought it would pop out of my chest. I have an idea where we might stay, but these two cans aren't going to last us very long. We'll have to figure somethin' out soon."

"So where were you thinking we could go? I don't want to stay here in the woods."

"Me neither. There's a place Dad and I saw the day before he left. It's in the hills about three miles from here. We should get goin' while it's still dark so no one'll see us."

They set-off, sticking to the shoulder of the road so they can jump back into the woods if necessary. There's a quarter moon in the sky, so they can see where they're going, but it's not so bright that they'll be easy to spot. Then a cloud covers the moon. The only sounds are the crunching of gravel and sticks beneath their feet. Then the "hoot" of an owl startles them. "I hope that's just an owl," Kathy says.

"Shh," Josh whispers. "You never know who might be around."

The night is quiet again. They're tired, hungry, helpless and hopeless. But their feet keep plodding along almost robotically, one foot after the other, only vaguely aware of their surroundings. Their eyes are half-closed. The cloud that has covered the moon until now has just pulled away, revealing a new danger. Josh perks-up just in time to see what the dim moonlight has just revealed. It's a crevasse--- the one that suddenly opened-up in front of his dad's car when they were returning from their drone-flying outing. He abruptly stops, but Kathy takes another step.

"Hold it, Mom!" he yells, as he thrusts his arm in front of her.

Kathy perks-up, too. "Huh, what's the matter?"

"Don't move. Look down." He whispers.

"Woah!" Kathy exclaims. Her foot is at the edge of the crevasse. "I'm glad you saw this in time, because I sure didn't. You saved me again, Josh. So, now what?"

"I remember this. This is the one Dad and I told you about---the one where we almost bought it. It's not very wide--- only about five feet, but it's deep and it's long. The other side is a couple feet higher. Do you think you can jump it?"

"No, I don't think so, Josh. Maybe we can find a log and make a bridge?"

"Okay, let's scout around."

After twenty minutes of frustration, the only suitable log they found was a large fallen tree. But it's too big and heavy for them to move.

"Let's go back, Mom. I have an idea."

They find the best spot for a crossing. "Okay, Mom, I'm gonna jump across. When I tell you, stand at the edge, hold your hands up high, and just let yourself fall towards me. Keep your feet on the ground and stay as stiff as a board."

"What? I can't do that. I'll fall-in!

"No, you won't, Mom. I'll catch you and pull you up."

"I just can't do that, Son. I'm too scared."

Jason takes a running jump across. He lands on his stomach, scraping his hands and bare arms on the pavement. His lower legs dangle over the edge. He hoists a leg up and scrambles to his feet. Then he turns to his mom and says, "There, now we can do this. Trust me, Mom. Just close your eyes and do it. I know you can. Just keep your arms extended. Don't try to catch my hands. I'll catch yours."

Kathy raises her arms hesitantly, then her arms collapse to her sides. She drops her head in discouragement. "I'm sorry, son. I just can't."

"We can't stay here, Mom. If you're not gonna do this, I'll have to go on by myself." Josh turns and starts to walk away.

"Wait. You're not really going to leave me here, are you?" Josh doesn't say anything. He just keeps on walking. Deep in her heart she knows Josh is just bluffing, but then there's that tiny bit of doubt.

"Okay, okay, I'll do it." Kathy finally caves, but she's scared--- so scared. She gingerly shuffles forward, eases her toes over the edge, and raises her arms. She looks down. Fear takes over and she balks.

"Don't look down, Mom. Look at me, then close your eyes and just let yourself fall forward. I'll catch you. I *promise* I will."

Kathy concludes that she really has nothing to lose. The way things are going they may not survive anyway, so why not take a chance. After another pause, she takes a deep breath and closes her eyes. She lets herself go. Time slows down for her as she pivots forward. It seems like she's floating when suddenly she feels Joshua's hands clamp down on her wrists. Her feet slide off the edge. Then her knees and chest slam into the other side of the crevasse, knocking the wind out of her. For a moment she's relieved, but then she realizes Joshua isn't pulling her up. Her wrists start to slip through his hands. His knees buckle, and she slides down the face of the crevasse a few inches. Joshua tightens his grip. She looks up to see Josh grimace as he strains to save her. He throws his head back and slowly straightens his legs. She's coming up! Josh is now standing up straight, but Kathy's stomach is not quite to the edge. She's still not safe. He starts backing up, one small step at a time. The edge of the crevasse scrapes Kathy's stomach.

"Come-on, Mom. Get your knee over the top. Hurry, I can't hold on much longer!" Josh is really straining hard now, so it's difficult to get the words out. He didn't realize that going so long with less than his normal amount of food not only caused him to lose weight, but it sapped his strength as well. Kathy tries to get one knee up, but she can't quite reach the top. Her weight pulls Josh forward, and she slides farther down.

Kathy turns her head and looks down into what seems like a bottomless abyss. "Don't let go, Josh! Don't let go!" she frantically screams.

Josh puts his back into it, but his forearms and fingers are aching. Suddenly his feet slip out from under him and his butt hits the ground. Now he has no leverage, and he's bent forward. Kathy's weight drags Josh's feet and lower legs over the edge. When his knees reach the edge, he realizes they're both about to cascade to their death. A few small pieces of road asphalt crumble at the edge and bounce off Kathy's head. Her feet start scrambling like she's trying to run up the face of the crevasse. Then fortune intervenes--- her right foot finds a large protruding rock for support.

"Josh, I've found a foot-hold." She can barely utter the words. "I think I can push myself up a little."

Josh is now completely bent over, and his hands are over the edge. "Mom, can you grab my pant legs and start pullin' yourself up? I'll keep holdin' onto your wrists and guide your hands."

The side of Kathy's face rests against the face of the crevasse. Her lips touch the dirt, and she spits a couple of times. "I'll try," she says, spitting again. She takes a deep breath and summons all her strength. One by one her hands advance up Josh's legs. Now she's where Josh can let go of one of her hands, and he grabs the back of her right upper arm, then the left. Now he leans back with everything he's got. Kathy grabs his shirt and pulls, as well. Finally, she gets a knee up. With one last push she falls on top of Josh. They both groan from exhaustion. She's safe.

For a few moments, Kathy just rests her head on Josh's chest. Neither one can move. Finally, she rolls-off onto her back. They both lie there for a while until their breathing calms down a little.

"Sorry, Mom," Josh gasps. "That was a lot harder than I thought. I guess I'm a lot weaker than I used to be, but I don't know what else we could've done."

"That's okay, Son. The point is we're safe. We should keep going."

"Right," Josh says. They start walking again.

It's the middle of the night, and they haven't seen anyone--- no lights, no noise, nothing. As dire as the situation is, the night sky is beautiful. Without city lights and clouds to impair his view, Josh marvels at the thousands of stars he's never seen before. Suddenly, he glimpses a small flying creature swooping down within a few feet of their heads. It's a bat. He watches it dance in the dim moonlight for a couple of seconds. Then it disappears. He starts envying the wild animals. Their food chain is intact. Their lives go on, unaffected by the catastrophe and chaos that has befallen mankind. America is dying, but wildlife will survive and rule once again. He closes his eyes, robotically putting one foot in front of the other.

He doesn't know how much time passed, but he faintly hears something down the road. It's a whirring sound, and it's quickly getting louder. He lifts his head to see what it is. It's an e-bike, and it's about to run them over. At the last second the bike veers away, skids off the road, and crashes into a ditch. The rider is thrown-off, tumbling onto the ground. Kathy and Josh run over to the rider. Josh realizes from the rider's small frame and long blonde hair that she's a woman. She's face-down and pushing herself up.

"You alright, miss?" Josh says.

Stumbling to her feet and brushing herself off, she responds, "I'm fine, you idiot. What are you doing in the middle of the road?"

Then she turns to face him. Josh recognizes her immediately. She's Sherri Frederick from his school--- the girl he's sweet on. She's the one in his science class that he told his father about, and the one who brought him to church a few times. She's tall, smart, and very pretty--- although her hair is messier than Josh remembers it. A small patch of light-colored freckles adorns her nose and the areas just below her eyes. She reminds him of photos of his mother when she was much younger.

"Sherri?" Josh asks excitedly.

"Joshua! Thank God it's you." Her anger softens. "Sorry I almost ran you over, and I'm sorry I called you an idiot. I guess I was just upset. I suppose it was really my fault for not having my lights on."

"No problem. You don't want to have the lights on anyway. So, what are you doin' way out here by yourself?" Josh inquires. "Don't you know how dangerous it is?"

"Yeah, I know, but I didn't have a choice. You know it's been just me and my dad since my mom died a couple of years ago. Well, now he's gone, too. Two weeks ago, he went to the Rutland Store to see if there was any food left. He never came back. I was so scared. So, the next day I rode my e-bike down there to try to find him. When I got to the store, it was burned to the ground. I picked my way through the smoldering ruins and found three bodies. They were pretty unrecognizable, but I think one of them was Dad. I was so shaken-up I didn't know what to do. No one was around, so I went back home."

"I'm so sorry, Sherri. This is my Mom, by the way." They both offer a short "Hi" to each other.

Then Sherri asks, "So, what are you and your mom doing out here in the middle of the night, anyway?"

"A gang of bad guys just took-over our house. Took our food, too. We barely made it out alive. Now we have no place to go. Say, can we stay with you?"

"No way. A gang took-over our home, too. I'm lucky to have escaped out the back door before they knew I was there. I was headed into town to get the police when I almost ran over you."

"The police won't help. There aren't any anymore. They're either dead or they joined a gang, or they left town. If you show up, I can only guess what'll happen to you. Besides, a crevasse opened-up down the road, and you can't get past."

Hopelessness sets in on Sherri's face. Dejected, she softly utters, "Great. So, what am I supposed to do now? Hey, where are you going?"

Then Josh explains the idea he had earlier in the woods with Kathy. "I know of a place that's out of the way. Hopefully, no one's found it yet. But we'll have to hurry. It'll be gettin' light soon, and I don't want anyone to see us. Wait, I just remembered. I left two cans of food on the road back there. You and Mom hide here in the woods 'til I get back. I'll take your bike, if that's okay?" Josh checks the bike. The front wheel is bent a little, but it's ridable. The women watch him take-off and wobble down the road. Ten minutes later he returns with the cans. Since the bike is made for only one rider, the youngsters insist Kathy gets on. They disappear into the darkness.

CHAPTER THIRTEEN---THE NEW JUDAH

The moonlight is dim, so Josh almost misses the gate he's looking for. It's hardly recognizable because it's over-grown with vines and brush, and a tree has fallen over it, blocking the dirt road leading into the hills. It doesn't look like anyone's been through there in a long time. He explains to Sherri and Kathy that this is where he and his dad saw police action in the hills. There were explosions and weapons fire from hovercraft. He also remembers seeing solar reflectors there, so he figures there must be some sort of settlement or compound. He has no idea if anyone's there now, or if food and water might be there, but he doesn't know where else to go. They carefully push aside some of the brush and put it back after they pass, concealing their passage.

It's a bit of a hike up the hill. The dirt road is over-grown with weeds and grasses. Josh hopes that the tall brush on both sides of the road will hide it from anyone on the main road below. Suddenly, something darts across their path about fifty yards ahead. Neither Josh nor Kathy see it, but Sherri does.

"What was that?" Sherri gasps.

"What was what?" Josh queries.

"Something just ran across the road. Didn't you see it?"

"No, what was it?"

"I don't know, but it was bigger than a dog."

"I don't see anything." He's starting to doubt her. "It probably *was* a dog, or maybe a cayote."

"Can we wait a minute?" Sherri asks in a trembling voice.

"Sure. Here, stay close to the bike and give me the cans. They're the only thing we have to defend ourselves with."

Carefully and quietly they continue up the hill, nervously glancing from side to side in case whatever it was decides to come back. A faint orange glow appears above the horizon, signaling the approach of dawn. Finally, they pass around a line of trees and see three domed cabins, overgrown with vines. The scene reminds Joshua of a small Hobbit village, except two of the cabins have been partially destroyed by explosions. The third has burn marks on one side, but it seems intact. All are heavily scarred with black pot marks from laser weapons. There's a small demolished shed and a broken solar panel on a mast lying on the ground. Two shallow bomb craters lie just ahead. Three more craters lie farther on. Several dead and broken trees lie on the ground nearby. Pieces of an e-bike lie next to one of the demolished cabins, and there's a fire pit with a broken grill.

Shocked by the destruction before them, Kathy puts both hands to her cheeks and exclaims, "Oh my gosh. What happened here?"

"Like I said, Mom, the police attacked this place. Don't know why. Maybe they had a bunch of guns up here and were causing trouble."

Half the front window to the intact cabin is missing, and the door is ajar. They peek through the window, but they can't see much. It appears abandoned, so with great apprehension they slowly creep in.

Sunrise is upon the trio now, so the cabin is illuminated enough to see the details of the interior. The main room is a combination kitchen, dining area and living room. There are two open doors on the left wall and two on the right. The furniture is a hodge-podge collection. Along with pieces of shattered window glass, a couple of used cups and a few empty plastic bottles lie scattered on the floor. A kitchen knife covered in dried blood lies near the door. There's a pile of old books in the corner. The ones on the top have many missing pages. On the floor next to the books are some bloody handprints and a streak of dried blood that runs all the way to the front door. A sofa is on its end, leaning against the window as if to shield the occupants. Laser weapon marks dot the interior walls along with what appears to be splattered blood. The kitchen counter has some food-encrusted dishes on it, and there are some more in the sink, along with a couple of glasses and some tableware. Flies are buzzing around, and the place smells of garbage. There's also a bucket on the counter that's half-filled with stale water. Clearly, people were living here until the attack. Something scurries across the floor and into one of the other rooms. Josh and the two women turn toward the noise, but whatever it was is now out of sight. The two women quickly duck behind Josh.

"What was that?" the startled women exclaim in unison.

"Prob'bly just a mouse or rat. Nothin' to worry about. They won't hurt you," Josh confidently replies.

"That's what you say," Sherri whimpers. "I'm staying right here."

"Me, too," says Kathy.

"Okay," says Josh. "I'll go over and shut the door." As he closes the door, he peeks in. "It's a bedroom. Let's check-out the other rooms."

Kathy and Sherri stay by the front door as Josh disappears into the first room. Suddenly the door slams shut, startling the women again.

"Josh?... Josh?" Kathy says timidly. No reply. Seconds tick by.

The door slowly opens part way. More silence. Kathy and Sherri back up and clutch each other. Then Josh pops his head out. "Boo!" he laughs. Sherri picks up an empty plastic bottle and throws it at him.

The trio discover that the side rooms are all bedrooms. The rooms are small and contain bunk beds. There's a lamp and a chest of drawers, but no closet--- pretty spartan. They leave the "rat" room door closed. They also discover that there isn't any bathroom. Josh looks around outside while the women check-out the inside. He finds one outdoor shower for the entire compound, but it doesn't work. There's no sign of an outhouse. *'Where did they "go"--- in the woods?'* he wonders. The trio will have to use the woods and the pages from the old books unless there's a special facility around that he hasn't found yet. He hopes there's a shovel around somewhere.

Josh figures that to supply water for the shower, there must be a well and a pump. He's quite sure water isn't piped-up here from the city. He sees another bucket under a spigot near the bottom of the shower pipe. *'That must be where all the drinking water and household water come from.'* He notices two pipes running to the top of the dome, so he backs-up and sees a solar water heater up there. Behind the cabin he finds broken pieces of two solar panels. The panels and the surrounding ground were obviously damaged by laser fire. The other cabins are so damaged they will be totally useless. Then he finds the only solar panel that seems to be intact. He thinks he can move it to the spot behind their cabin to give the cabin and the water pump the electricity they need, but he'll need tools to do it. Before he does anything more, he pulls some siding off the damaged shed and props it up against the front of the cabin to cover the hole in the window. If he can find some tools, he'll cut and fasten the panel to the window frame.

Next, he scouts around the area up the hill, and he finds some wild berry bushes. He picks a couple--- delicious! He eats several more and picks a double handful for the women. Everyone is starving at this point, but he knows not to strip the bushes bare. They will need to stretch the supply. During his exploration he looks back at the valley they came from. It's a beautiful view--- tall tan grasses slowly waving in the breeze. Oak trees dot the hillside. *'Oak trees! Maybe they'll be acorns there!'* Farther away and to the left he sees large swaths of scorched earth from last year's fires. Farther still, he sees the ozone towers and the field where he and his father flew the new drone just before he left. His thoughts quickly turn to his father. *'Where is he? Is he still alive? Is he coming back, and if he is, how will he find us?'* He's not sure he and the women can survive alone. Off to the right he sees the crevasse and the outskirts of San Marita. A faint column of smoke slowly rises from the town. His eyes start to water as sadness overcomes him. Things will never be the same. He's scared.

He's not far from the top of the hill, so he decides to see what's up there. He lays the berries down and starts up the hill. Soon the climb steepens, so he traverses the grassy hill at an angle. He comes upon a narrow trail and follows it upward toward the top. As he clears the ridge, a large flock of startled birds flutter-off. Several geese waddle away. Then his jaw drops, his eyes pop, and he breaks into a huge smile. He can't believe what lies in front of him--- a field of crops! He runs up to it. There's corn, soybeans, peas, squash, and tomatoes. Other plants have nothing on them, but there might be something below the soil, so he drops down and digs around with his hands. Yes, potatoes! He sits back as relief overwhelms him. Then he looks to the sky. "Thank you, Lord, thank you," he says softly.

Josh can't wait to tell the women the unbelievable news. He charges back down the hill along the trail. He's so excited he loses his footing and falls, tumbling down the trail for several yards. Dusting himself off, he continues-on more carefully.

As he approaches the cabin, he hears a scream from inside. He's almost to the door when the women rush past him yelling, "Snake, snake! There's a snake in there! Do something!"

Josh gives a half-smile. "Okay, okay, let me check it out. It's probably not poisonous--- just there for the mice. Where is it?"

Kathy waves her hand like she's trying to shoosh something away. "It's in the bottom cupboard next to the sink. Hurry!"

Josh creeps into the cabin. The cupboard door is open, and he sees the snake. It's black without any markings. *'Prob'ly a black snake,'* he thinks. Looking around the room, he eyes the broom the women were using. He picks it up and slowly sneaks toward the snake. The snake isn't moving, and it's coiled-up in a protective position. Trying not to startle the snake, he slowly thrusts the handle end of the broom into the middle of the coiled snake. It suddenly wraps itself around the handle, causing Josh to flinch. He carefully pulls it out of the cupboard and heads toward the rat room. He throws the broom in there and quickly shuts the door. "All clear, ladies," he yells proudly. He tells them where he put it, but they're still squeamish.

"Are you sure it won't come out?" Kathy says, trembling a bit.

"I'm sure," Josh replies. "It'll take care of the rodent problem, too. After a couple of weeks, I'll check it out. It'll either be dead or it'll have found his way out through the window."

With the excitement over, Josh tells the women about his life-saving discovery. They don't believe him. They think it's another practical joke, so he begs them to see for themselves. He's so insistent that they decide to play along and go with him. When the women reach the field, they can't believe it either. They start roaming through the rows of plants in amazement. They run their hands over the tops of the leaves and gently touch the life-sustaining produce. Kathy grabs an ear of corn, and she peels some of its husk. Her joy turns to a frown--- worms and rot. She checks another ear--- same thing, only not quite as bad.

"Oh no," Kathy says, "this corn is no good. Check the other plants."

The trio frantically spot-check the rest of the crops. It's obvious the plants have not been attended to. They all show signs of attack by insects, rabbits and deer. Some are salvageable, some are not. Most of the tomatoes are rotting on the vines. Thanks to northern California's continuous growing season and plentiful rain, the field appears to have been planted in stages so new crops would mature every month or so. Since the field was probably meant to feed more people, they conclude that if they conserve and plan correctly, they should make it, even if some of the current crop isn't fit to eat. Josh then tells the women about the berries and the possible acorns. The tall grasses have grains that might be edible, as well. Their spirits lift.

Since none of them have eaten since last night, they're starving. Their basic instincts take over and they tear into the crops trying to find something edible. "Aren't you going to say grace, first?" Sherri jokes, half serious.

Kathy and Josh say, "Thank you, Lord" in unison, then they plow ahead. They all eat enough to satisfy themselves for now. Concluding that there seems to be plenty of harvestable crops left, they gather as much of the remaining edible food as they need for their next meal, and they head down the hill. When Josh goes after the pile of berries he left behind, they're gone! Worried, he looks around, but he doesn't say anything about it. He doesn't want the women to wonder who or what took the berries. He grabs a few berries off one of the bushes just to show the women. When they go back to the cabin, he locks the door behind them.

As Josh puts his armful of food on the kitchen counter, he notices that the place has been cleaned-up. He compliments the women.

"Thanks for noticing, Josh," Sherri says, smiling. "Check-out the refrigerator."

Josh opens the door in anticipation. "Ugh!" he shouts as he's thrown back. It's full of mold and unidentifiable whatever, and it stinks beyond belief--- like rotten eggs and meat. He quickly slams the door, and he turns to see Kathy and Sherri laughing hysterically.

"So how does it feel, Josh, now that the shoe is on the other foot?" Sherri says, still chuckling. She and Kathy give each other a high five. Josh can't help smiling, too. Unfortunately, the stench is now all over the room, so they open a small window in the kitchen. Josh tells the women what he's found outside, saying he thinks he can use the remaining solar panel to get the water pump working. Recognizing that the home was operated by two panels, he hopes the one panel can at least work the pump. With water and a supply of food, no matter how meager, a glimmer of hope rises in all of them.

Josh finds the tools he needs in the demolished shed, and he moves the solar panel behind the cabin and connects it to the main circuit breaker. He also finds a battery bank in a large box outside the rear wall. From his science class he knows that solar panels produce dc voltage, but normal lights and appliances run on ac. He finds a charge controller in the box to keep the batteries from over-charging, but he doesn't see an inverter to convert the voltage, so he's stymied. Discouraged, he heads back into the cabin.

When Josh explains the apparent dead end with the electricity feed, Sherri pipes-up, "Hey, when we were cleaning up, we found some small electronic boxes on the cords to the lamps and refrigerator. What do you think they might be?"

Josh perks-up and checks-out one of the lamps. He doesn't dare go near the refrigerator. "Nice find, Sherri," he says. "I think these are small inverters. I'm gonna flip the main circuit breaker. There's plenty of sun now, so let's see if this works." Josh flips the breaker and runs back into the cabin. He turns on a lamp. Nothing. Everyone frowns. Josh gives a disheartened sigh. Then he hears a faint hum. "It's the refrigerator!" he exclaims triumphantly. "It's workin'! The bulb in the lamp must've burned-out." Without opening the refrigerator door, he puts his ear to it to be sure. He gives the women a thumbs-up.

He hustles outside to check for water flow. When he opens the spigot, nothing happens. Then he hears the sound of air rushing out. He starts jumping up and down in jubilation--- water, precious water squirts-out! He lets it run for a few moments. He cautiously smells it. Then he tastes it. It's cool and pure--- much better than he had hoped. He rushes back inside to announce the good news. They do a group hug and bounce. For the first time since the bombing they feel they have a real chance of surviving. The cabin becomes a home.

Later in the day, Josh decides to explore some more. He follows a small trail to a clearing where he finds two sawhorses with two boards on top. Under the board is a trench. There's a shovel on the ground. "It's a latrine!" he exclaims. "I knew there had to be one here." He looks to one side and sees evidence of a former trench that's been covered with soil. Farther-on, some young tomato plants have popped-up. "Terrific," he says, "now we have a source of fertilizer."

He decides to go back to the field to take crop inventory while Kathy and Sherri start preparing dinner. When he reaches the top of the hill, he scares more birds away. Then he gets a lump in his throat. The birds are eating their food! Panic sets in. He'll have to come up with a way to keep them away. Then he gets excited when he realizes that they could actually be a source of food themselves, especially the geese. Meat, real meat!

He goes through the rows, mentally keeping track of each type of plant and their stages of maturity. Since he doesn't have any paper or a pencil, he makes marks in the dirt at the end of each row. The tally is encouraging, but what to do about the birds? *'A large net would be perfect,'* he thinks. *'How about a scare crow or two? Loud noises?'* Nothing seems practical. He places his hands on his hips in discouragement. He **must** think of something. After reviewing the tallies at the ends of the rows, he heads back down the hill.

On the way down, he sees a plume of smoke rising from the enclave. "Oh, no!" he shouts. He scampers down the trail. Soon, he sees where it's coming from. It's from the fire pit. Somehow Kathy and Sherri used their ingenuity to put the grill together, and they've started a fire with a magnifying glass. He runs into camp yelling, "Put it out! Put it out!" The women are puzzled. Then they see the fear on his face. They back-off as Josh kicks at the burning wood to separate it. Then he starts throwing dirt on the fire to put it out. Gradually, the smoke dissipates. Out of breath, he calms down and explains that the smoke can be seen for miles--- seen by the gangs. Fortunately, the fire had just started, so they're all hoping no one saw it. Only raw vegetables are on the menu for tonight.

While it's not the finest meal they ever had, it fills the void. The trio welcomes water the most, for without it they would be doomed within days. Since the women prepared dinner, it's up to Josh to clean-up. He does the best he can without soap, and he sets the dinner bowls to dry on the counter. As he finishes up, he hears the women mumbling. Sherri is running her finger on the table like she's trying to draw something. "So, what's going-on?" he asks.

Sherri responds, "Well, your mom and I were talking about what a shame it is to not be able to cook. Then I remembered our science project last year. We learned how to make a solar oven. I don't think you were in that class, were you?"

"Yeah, I was there. You just didn't notice me then. I sat in the back of the room."

"Oh. Sorry, Josh. I had no idea."

"I don't blame you. I was pretty much of a wall flower back then. But I sure noticed you." Sherri blushes a little. Kathy smiles.

"So, do you think we could build one, Josh?"

"Maybe. It's almost dark now, but tomorrow I'll scout around for the materials. Between the solar panels and windows from the other houses, there might be enough glass. It'll be more of a challenge to figure-out the framing and reflectors."

With all the walking and climbing and lack of sleep the night before, they're all exhausted. And with some food in their bellies, they're ready to hit the sack. Josh locks the front door, and they adjourn to separate rooms. The two women fall asleep almost instantly, but Josh lies in bed with his eyes open. He's worried. The smoke from the fire; the gangs; the fleeting animal on the dirt road; and the mysterious disappearance of the berries--- there's plenty to worry about. Despite the worries, his eyes eventually close.

In the middle of the night, a moon beam pokes its way through Josh's window and slowly finds its way to his face. He unconsciously rubs his nose. Moments pass. He rubs his nose again, then he rolls on his side. He's disturbed, but not fully awake. The quiet night is interrupted by the sound of a stick crunching outside the house, then some shuffling about. Josh's eyes spring open. His heart starts pounding. He listens--- nothing. His ears strain to pick up anything more. Five minutes pass. Then ten. Still nothing. He gets up and cautiously peeks out of his window, exposing just his eyes and forehead. The moon is dim, but it's bright enough for Josh to see clearly. A gentle breeze rustles the tree leaves, but nothing else is moving. He calms down, but he'll get no more sleep tonight.

The morning arrives. Josh is the first one up. As he dresses, he wonders if they're all going to have to wear the same clothes forever. He opens the top drawer in the chest to find women's underwear and a hairbrush. The next drawer has a pair of jeans and a sweatshirt. He pulls out the jeans and holds them against the front of his waist. Even with his slim build, it's not going to fit.

They're way too short. *'Well at least **somebody's** gonna get a change of clothes,'* he says to himself. *'Maybe the other rooms will have some men's clothes.'*

He decides to check around outside before the women get up. It's a cool, beautiful morning. Birds are chirping. A hawk soars high in a bright blue sky, faintly screeching. The air is fresh and clean. It's as if the dire situation his world is in doesn't exist. Venturing further, he explores an area where the tall grasses are pushed over. His fears are realized. He spots the paw prints of a bear! From the size of the prints, it doesn't look like it's a large one, but it's a bear, nonetheless. He looks around but sees nothing but the beautiful morning. He quietly follows the prints for fifty feet or so as they head down the hill. That's far enough. He wonders how he's going to tell the women without freaking them out. Moreover, how do they protect themselves against the bear's return? He breaks-off a leafy tree branch and covers-up the tracks so the women won't see them and ask worried questions.

He returns to the cabin and looks through the window. No one else is up yet, so he rummages through the remains of the other bombed-out cabins trying to find materials for a solar oven. He finds a hunting knife and some twine. He also salvages a piece of glass from a window, but he can't find anything else that will really work. Besides the glass, he needs reflecting panels to form a box. Frustrated, he's about to leave one of the cabins when he sees it. "Of course," he exclaims, "the refrigerator." It's a box, and it has insulation--- a bonus. Now he just needs reflecting panels. He pulls the refrigerator away from the wall and checks the back of it--- a shiny metal plate. "Great," he says. Full of hope, he walks briskly to the other cabin and finds another refrigerator. *"I think I can do this,"* he says to himself. He drags the two refrigerators out into the open.

The women are up by now, and hearing all the ruckus, they come out to see what's going on. "What the heck are you doing, Josh?" Sherri asks.

"I'm making a solar oven, can't you tell? Hey, can you grab that screwdriver I used yesterday... and the hammer?"

With Sherri's help, he removes the back panel. As he does so, he catches a glimpse of the shiny inside surfaces of the metal side panels--- more reflectors! Including the top and bottom panels, they now have five metal panels. They're not super shiny, but they'll do.

Kathy looks-on with admiration and curiosity. It's hard for her to realize that this gangly hair-in-his-eyes young son of hers has become such a competent leader. She can't imagine where she would be without him. As the morning wears-on, she's getting hungry. "Say, Josh, where did you say those berries were? I think I'll pick some for breakfast."

Alarmed, Josh shoots back, "Don't go up there alone, Mom. Neither of you should go anywhere without me from now on. Grab a couple of pots. We'll all go." Frowning, Kathy and Sherri look at each other wondering why Josh is so worried.

"What's the big deal, Josh?" Sherri asks.

"Nothing, I just think we should stick together. That's all."

The solar oven project is put on hold while the trio march-off to gather some berries. Josh takes the hammer with him.

After their return from berry picking, Josh and Sherri resume work on the oven. Fortunately, the metal plates are thin enough, so they are bent to fit the sides, bottom and door of the refrigerator. Josh dives back into the other cabins to find some way of fastening the panels. He comes up short. Then Sherri has an idea. "I'll be right back," she says, dashing off to one of the other cabins. She returns with a handful of tableware. "Look, Josh," she says, I think we can bend these into U-shaped clamps and slide them over the edges of the panels."

169

"Good thinking, Sherri! What a combination--- beauty *and* brains." Sherrie smiles and looks approvingly at Josh.

As they work together to form and install the clamps, their heads get closer. Sensing the closeness, they both look-up into each other's eyes. For a couple of seconds, the work stops. Then they snap back into reality and continue the work in nervous silence. Kathy observes this from the doorway, and smiles. "Hey you two, breakfast's ready."

After their short breakfast, they finish the new oven. Sherri brings a small pot of water to test their creative invention. Josh tilts the oven toward the sun and props it up with sticks. Sherri puts the pot inside and puts the lid on it. Josh places the glass over the mouth of the oven and holds it in place with more clamps. They anxiously wait--- fifteen minutes, then twenty. Josh can't wait any longer. He opens the oven up and pokes his finger in the water. "Hey! That's really hot!" He sticks his finger in his mouth to cool it off, smiling as he does so. Kathy and Sherri proudly pat him on the back. Sherri kisses him on the cheek and gives him a big smile.

With the basics provided for, Josh turns his attention to protecting the crops from the birds. They're attacking almost half of everything that's ripe. Josh and the women decide that they're okay with eating food that the birds have picked at, so they'll have more food available for consumption. He tries draping some of the bed sheets from the other cabins over the portion of the crops that are ripening---those which are most subject to attack. He ties the corners of the sheets to branches he's hammered into the ground, and cuts flaps in the sheets so the wind doesn't blow them away. He stands back and admires his creation when it all seems to work.

Josh is starting to impress himself with his new-found abilities. He removes the door of the cannibalized refrigerator and drags the box up the hill to the field. He breaks-off a stout stick and props the fridge up with the opening facing down. He then ties some twine around the stick and places some soybeans under the box. He unravels the twine and crouches behind a bush, waiting for a goose to be tempted. The geese aren't cooperating. Then he realizes why--- there's too much food on the ground around the plants for them to be bothered with the bait. Josh spends the hour picking-up the free bird food in the field. The sun is setting. He's tired and dirty, and decides a cool shower and dinner are too inviting. He gives-up and goes home. Much was accomplished today.

Kathy and Sherri prepared an expanded menu of beans, squash and potatoes--- all cooked. The potatoes were somewhat under-done, so the women decide to cut them into smaller pieces next time. "So, how did the great hunter do today?" Kathy asks.

"Geese 1, Josh 0," he sheepishly replies. The ladies chuckle. "But I'll get one tomorrow," he says with confidence.

Although the water is quite cool, the shower feels like a royal treat. He just wishes he had some soap. When he's dried-off, he wraps the towel around his waist and scampers back to his room. To his welcomed surprise he finds a set of men's clothes lying on his bed.

Sleep still eludes Josh despite the tiring day. Thoughts of the goose trap, the oven, the bear, the gangs, and his father flow in and out of his mind. Then he gets a disturbing feeling. The feeling grows, eventually causing him to go to the window. It's a beautiful night. The moon is brighter than last night, but he can still see millions of stars. Then something grabs his attention. On the other side of the trees at the entrance to the enclave, moonlight reflects off of two large eyes. After a second or two, they disappear into the night. The sighting rattles him. The bear, or something else? He gets-up and checks the front door again. He doesn't sleep for the rest of the night.

The days drift along, and a routine develops--- two meals per day; showers every three days; read old books before the pages get used at the latrine. Josh finally traps his goose, and the trio eat meat for the first time. Most of their time focuses on meals---trapping, gathering, prepping, and cooking. Josh sleeps better, and he dreams about Sherri. The trio operate as a highly efficient team, so their situation seems more like camping than surviving. They decide to name their enclave "The New Judah" in consideration of Josh's dad's Jewish heritage.

One day while Josh is trying to trap another goose, he hears motorcycles on the road below. Moments later he hears two crashes. He crawls over to a spot where he can see but not be seen. Whoever they are, they found the crevasse. He sees one bike wedged in the crevasse. The other is lying on the road, its front wheel bent beyond repair. The two riders are on the ground on the other side, along with what looks like fuel cans that apparently flew-off the bikes when they crashed. One of the downed bikers is sitting up and holding his arm like it's in an imaginary sling. The other is lying flat on his back. Four other bikes and riders managed to stop in time, and they're standing at the crevasse's edge talking to the men on the other side. He's tempted to go down and try to help, but fearing the worst, he stays-put. The bikers don't look friendly. At this point he and the women are much safer remaining out of sight. After a few minutes, the downed bikers retrieve the gas cans. They then use the wedged bike as a bridge and crawl over to join their buddies. In the process, one of the cans slips out of the biker's grasp and falls into the crevasse. The riders double-up on the undamaged bikes, turn around, and head back up the road.

As more days pass, Josh and Sherri spend a lot of time together---whether harvesting, exploring, or just enjoying where they are compared to where they could be. They smile and laugh more than someone in survival mode should. Josh was smitten a long time ago, but his fear of rejection holds him back from making what he perceives will be a fumbling advance towards her. Over time, he and Sherri draw closer. One night, Kathy retires early, leaving the two youngsters sitting on the couch beside a dimly lit lamp. They don't say much, and they're both nervous. Joshua's knee is bouncing up and down rapidly. Sherri is twirling her hair with her finger.

Sherri breaks the awkward silence. "So, do you want to go outside for a walk, Josh?"

He really wants to, but he fears how dangerous that might be. To protect them from extra worry, he hasn't yet told the women about the bear or the two glowing eyes. "Actually, I think we'd better stay here," he says. "You never know what might be out there."

Sherri's puzzled at Josh's serious response. "Really? What are you trying to say? Do you know something I don't?" Josh delays his answer, trying to formulate the right words. Sherri doesn't wait. "Josh?" Sherri says in an even more serious tone. Now she knows something's not right.

Resigned to be truthful, Josh gives-in and tells her about his sightings. Sherri quickly squeezes Josh's forearm with both hands and blurts-out, "Yikes! So, what do we do? Wait, that's why you don't want us going anywhere alone, and that's why you carry that hammer with you all the time, isn't it? And you shouldered that fear by yourself so we wouldn't worry." She peers deeply into his eyes. "You know Josh, you're more of a man than you should be at your age. You're certainly not the boy I didn't notice last year. And another thing, I think you're amazing for fixing the solar panel, and building the oven, and trapping the goose. I could go on and on, but I won't. Come here."

With that she grabs Josh behind the neck with both hands and pulls him forward until their lips touch. Josh's eyes pop wide open in surprise. Then he relaxes, wraps his arms around her, and closes his eyes. It was the most wonderful experience of his life.

After breakfast the next day, the trio decide to gather more acorns. It's been three weeks since the last successful outing, so there should be more on the ground now. They use an old trail they previously found, because it leads right to a large stand of oak trees. This time Kathy leads the way. Josh whistles a western tune, but it's hard to recognize it. He and Sherri keep smiling at each other. With Kathy in the lead, she can't see Josh and Sherri holding hands.

Arriving at their destination, they startle a squirrel who darts away with cheeks full of acorns. Since the stand of trees can be easily seen from the road, Kathy watches for anyone approaching, while Josh and Sherri scrounge for acorns. Fortunately, word of the nasty crevasse has apparently reached the few remaining people in the area, so the road is pretty much abandoned. Kathy gets bored, so she looks around the hillside. Something catches her eye. It's a large flat boulder she's seen before, but there's something black covering the top of it. It's about fifty yards away. Curiosity gets the best of her, so she plows her way through the tall grass to get a better look. When she's almost there, Josh notices that she's missing. Panic sets-in. He spots her and starts to yell at her, but he catches himself. He doesn't want his voice to carry too far in case someone else might hear, so he drops his bucket and runs after her. Sherri follows him. Kathy hears Josh's approach, and she turns toward him.

Just then, they both hear a loud "hiss". A mountain lion has just bounded-up on top of the boulder! Everyone freezes. The lion hisses again, showing its threatening teeth. Josh slowly creeps forward. "Shh," he says to his mom. Adrenalin pumps through his body. His protective instincts overwhelm the urge to run. For a moment, it's a stand-off, but it doesn't last long. The lion drops to a crouch and hisses again. Then it springs. Kathy throws-up her hands in self-defense as the cat pounces onto her. She screams as the cat's claws slash into her shoulders. Instinctively, Kathy covers her head as the lion's fangs clamp-down on her arm. They both hit the ground with a thud. Helpless, she pulls her knees up into a fetal position. As she does this, she hears Josh yelling, "Get off my mom, you bitch!" His yell is quickly followed by a hammer blow to the cat's head. It howls in pain and quickly rolls-off her, paws in the air. Josh delivers another blow. This one crushes the cat's skull. Disoriented and in intense pain, it tries to crawl away, but Josh pursues it. Blood splatters on Kathy's face and arms as Josh delivers the final strike. With fire in his eyes, he screams and delivers another blow to the lifeless cat. He raises the hammer again.

Sherri has now arrived on the horrific scene. "Josh!" Sherri shouts, "stop, stop! It's dead."

Josh drops to his knees, gasping for air. Blood is all over his face, hair and clothes. Sherri is struck by this violent side of Joshua she's never seen before. She's incredibly proud of him, but at the same time his violent attack scares her. Josh collapses onto his back, releasing the hammer. He stares up at the sky, still breathing heavily. He barely knew what he was doing because his heroic action was all instinct. Gradually, he comes to his senses and looks for his mom. Sherri has pulled-off her tee shirt and is wrapping Kathy's badly bleeding arm with it. Kathy's contorted face and moaning tell the story of her pain. They need to get her back to the cabin immediately. Sherri and Josh help her up, but her legs buckle as she discovers a new pain--- the lion's rear paws had ripped through her jeans and slashed her legs, as well. She can barely walk, so Josh and Sherri prop her up under her arms, and they eventually make it back to the cabin.

They gently lay Kathy on the sofa. Then Josh runs into his bedroom and snatches one of the sheets. Sherri starts ripping the sheet into strips for bandages while Josh fills a large pot of warm water from the shower and pours it into the solar oven. They're both moving as fast as they can while Kathy's moaning becomes louder. Sherri puts pressure on Kathy's wounds to try to stop the bleeding, but she can't keep the blood from dripping onto the sofa. Josh grows impatient with the solar oven. *'This is gonna take too long,'* he thinks. *'Fire. Fire will be much faster.'* He quickly builds the makings of a fire, and then runs back into the cabin for newspaper and the magnifying glass.

Sherri immediately realizes what he's going to do. With panic in her voice, she shouts, "What are you doing, Josh? You can't. You'll give us away!"

"I have to," Josh shouts back. "She's gonna bleed to death!"

"No, look, the bleeding's slowing down. See?"

Josh pauses for a moment to check-out his mom's wounds. It's true. Her leg wounds are not that bad, and Sherri's nursing skills are proving affective on the claw marks on her shoulders. However, Kathy's arm is a different story. The tee shirt around the wound is soaked red with blood, and it's starting to drip. The cat's fangs must have hit a larger blood vessel there. Sherri throws the bloody shirt onto the floor and wraps a strip of sheet around the punctures. Wrapping another strip around Kathy's upper arm, she uses a kitchen knife to twist the sheet tight to form a tourniquet. Josh holds-off on the fire. Instead, he puts the remaining bandages in the oven. Thirty minutes go by, with Josh impatiently testing the water's temperature every five minutes. He remembers from his science class that most bacteria are killed at 125 degrees, so the water doesn't have to boil. When the water's almost too hot to touch, it's time. He tilts the refrigerator to pour the water out, and some of the bandages fall onto the dirt. "Shit!" he uncharacteristically shouts. He grabs the clean ones and runs to the sink to squeeze-out the water. His hands feel like they're on fire from the hot water. As Sherri pulls-off Kathy's jeans to better treat her leg wounds, Kathy winces in pain as the jeans slide over the gashes.

Sherri continues nursing Kathy while Josh rinses-out the dirty bandages and starts the oven again. Between Sherri's nursing and Josh's bandage prep, Kathy is stabilized. She spends the night on the sofa, but the pain doesn't let her sleep. Sherri unselfishly sits beside Kathy all night, periodically releasing then tightening the tourniquet. Sometime during the night, the claw wounds stop bleeding and become more of an ooze. The arm punctures take another three days.

Seeing that his mom appears to be on the mend, Josh feels confident enough to leave her with Sherri so he can re-visit the scene of the lion attack. From a distance, he notices several buzzards circling above. As he walks closer, he comes upon squawking buzzards blanketing the lion's carcass and also the top of the boulder. Several buzzards are hopping around, squeezing between their friends and fighting for a share of the meat. The stench is repulsive. Josh waves his hands and softly yells. A possum with a blood-stained head darts-off from behind the lion. Most of the birds scatter and fly-off, but the brave ones hop around nearby, waiting to dive-in again. Josh has to hold his nose, but he's curious about the dark and furry thing on top of the boulder. As he comes around to the other side of the boulder, the mystery is solved--- it's a dead bear! *'Is this the bear that walked through the enclave that one night?'* he says to himself. It's not a large bear, so it certainly could be the same one. Bears and mountain lions have large territories, so he hopes there aren't any more around. Despite the stench, Josh is glad he came back. The women will feel relieved when he makes his report.

The scattered vultures fill the sky, so Josh becomes worried that someone will notice and come up to investigate. He must bury the carcasses. He briefly thought about carving-out some bear and lion meat to take back, but he ultimately rejected the idea. The animals have been rotting in the sun for too long. He goes back to the cabin and returns with a shovel. The digging is tough going. The first foot or so is easy, but he soon runs into clay and rocks. Two hours later the graves are ready. He's thirsty, sweaty and exhausted, and he wished he had brought some water. A cool shower is going to feel great. Fearful of getting a disease from the beasts, he hooks the lion with the heel of the shovel and drags it into the hole. Next, he tackles the bear.

The shovel scrapes against the boulder, causing a fingernails-on-chalkboard sound. He shivers at the irritating noise. Then he hears a faint cry--- like a kitten meowing. He stops and listens. There it is again. Holding his shovel like a weapon, he cautiously creeps around to the other end of the boulder. There's a large hole under the boulder--- like a cave. He peers into it. His jaw drops and he jerks back at what he sees. It's a small lion cub--- about the size of a house cat! The cub meows again. When he moves closer, the cub backs-up further into the den, revealing another cub on the ground. It looks dead. Josh doesn't know quite what to do. The cub cries again. Without his mother to care for it, the cub will surely die. Josh's heart melts with compassion. He reaches into the cave and extracts the cub. The cub squirms and harmlessly digs its tiny claws into Josh's arm. Josh drops the shovel and starts stroking the cub's head and back. The cat continues meowing, but releases its grip on Josh's arms, apparently comforted by the affection. "Wait 'til Mom and Sherri see you," he says. He sets the cub down and finishes burying the animals.

Back at the cabin, Josh enters the living area. His mom is asleep on the sofa, and Sherri is preparing the afternoon meal--- goose and corn. "Look what I found," he proudly announces. Sherri turns around, setting her knife down.

"What in the world?" she exclaims. "Where did *that* come from?"

"She was in a den under the boulder where Mom was attacked. I think her mother was just protecting this little one."

Sherri starts stroking the new arrival. The cat claws at Sherri's hand and starts licking it, probably for the salt. Sherri reaches-out and bravely takes the cat from Josh. She caresses the cub against her chest and continues to stroke her, but the cat keeps meowing. "Oh, she's so cute. Can we keep her, Josh? Can we?" Sherri begs.

"Maybe," Josh replies. "She'll die unless we do, but we don't have any milk to feed her with. She can't survive on vegetables, and she's too young for meat."

Sherri ponders. "Maybe, maybe not. How about goose juice? It's got protein."

"Okay, let's try it," Josh says. "We got nothin' to lose. After three days without her mother, she's gotta be pretty hungry."

Amazingly, the cat laps-up the juice and sniffs for more. She even swallows a few small pieces of goose meat.

Two months have now gone by since the bombing. The earthquakes, fires, and floods that plagued the earth for the last few years have strangely ceased. Kathy's wounds have healed, but the scars will always be a daily reminder. The ordeal caused a streak of her hair to turn white. It's a small price to pay, considering she's lucky to be alive.

The playful nature of their new pet brought a welcomed relief to the routine, and the cat has more than tripled her size. They unimaginatively named her "Cat". The goose trap was too slow for squirrels and rabbits, so Josh built a different snare to catch them. He used the furry rodents to teach Cat to hunt. Sometimes Cat would be gone for a couple of days, but she always came back, sometimes with a rodent of some sort in her mouth as a present for her new family. As Cat grew, Kathy became more apprehensive of her. She reminded Kathy too much of Cat's mother. Sometimes Cat would briefly stop and stare into Kathy's eyes, giving her the willies.

Josh and Sherri did everything together--- harvesting, maintaining the area, fetching water. They grew more in love, and their make-out sessions lasted dangerously longer. Hands began to roam.

The population in San Marita declined rapidly. Muslim and Communist sleeper cells showed-up and set fire to several buildings. They shot dozens of residents, but the gangs eventually took care of them. Most of the people died of starvation, relying in vain for the government to bring supplies. Those who left town generally headed for the coast for an unknown and equally bleak future. The remaining survivors lived off of long-term storage food and water they had acquired for catastrophes such as this, but their supplies are depleting. They tried to hide from the predatory gangs, but the gangs found many of them. When they did, the people were killed, and the food and water were taken. Eventually even the gangs succumbed to the diminishing resources.

Since there wasn't any reason for anyone to come to San Marita, the road below the enclave was quiet. Occasionally an e-bike would appear, but it would turn around at the crevasse. Once, a small group of people emerged from the woods at the crevasse. Josh and Sherri happened to notice them while gathering acorns. They crouched out of sight and watched intently through the trees as the group proceeded away from town and toward the camouflaged gate. When they reached the area of the gate, one of the members of the group pointed to something on the side of the road, and they all stopped and looked. For the first time, Josh and Sherri feared being discovered. They held their breaths. To the couple's relief, the group moved-on. Then one day, everything changed.

CHAPTER FOURTEEN --THE RETURN HOME

Back at the Command Center, Jason and Willis fall back into their chairs with relief. Their work on Israel's communications system is finally complete, but they wonder what's next. Everything is working as hoped--- Israel has internal and foreign communications once again. All those in the Command Center give each other slaps and high fives. Someone breaks-out two bottles of champagne. Everyone takes one sip. Although subdued, the celebration continues into the early evening. Having completed Jason's and Liezel's trip arrangements, Anah starts to leave without having any champagne. Without saying a word, she gives Jason a brief cold hug, looking to the side as she does so. She then walks quickly toward the door, blotting her watery eyes.

With his work complete, Jason says good-bye to his comrades in the Command Center. He has mixed emotions. He's excited about the possibility of finding his son, but sad to leave the people he's come to know and respect. And then there's the scary leap into the dangerous trip that lies ahead. After he makes the rounds, he turns to Willis who has his arm around his conquest Mariam. The two men smile and hug.

"I'll miss you, boss," Willis says with a lump in his throat.

"I'll miss you, too, Rick. What are you going to do since I won't be around to pilfer sandwiches from anymore?" They both laugh. "If you ever get back to San Marita, look me up."

"Count on it, boss. Let me know if, I mean *when* you find your son."

Jason balks at the word 'if.' He turns and walks away, reminded of the long odds against finding Joshua. He also doubts that he'll ever see Willis again.

In the emotion and commotion of the moment, Jason forgets to say good-bye to the General. Dayan stands in his office and looks through the interior window with an all-knowing smile as he watches Jason leave for the last time.

Corporal Bischoff drives Jason back to the barracks. They're almost there when Jason realizes he forgot to say good-bye to the General. "Oh, no," Jason exclaims, "I forgot to say good-bye to the General. We've got to go back."

"He's left the Command Center by now, Sir. No worries, he gave me this envelope for you." It's too dark to read it now so Jason puts it in his backpack.

As they pull into the barracks, the Bronco's headlights shine upon an abnormal scene. Something's amiss. The doors to all three bungalows are open, and there aren't any lights on inside. All the other transports are parked there, but the place seems strangely deserted. Jason says to Bischoff, "Corporal, draw your side-arm and follow me." They reach the door of Jason's bungalow, and he slowly pushes the door open. It hits something and stops. Now more apprehensive, Jason gropes for the light switch. When the lights come on, he instantly sees what blocked the door--- it's a body. Jason steps back with a gasp. Then he notices he's standing in a puddle of fresh blood. He retreats again, heart pounding.

Panic sets-in. He quickly checks-out the body. It's one of the male residents. He's not sure who, because his throat has been cut and his face is smeared with blood. "Liezel!... Liezel!" he shouts. "Quick, search the place!" he shouts at Bischoff. Jason bolts to his bedroom--- empty. Then he checks Anah's room--- also empty.

Bischoff calls-out from the other rooms. "Nothing in here, but there's another man's body by the couch. His throat's been cut, too. Let's check the other bungalows."

They're just about to leave when Jason spots two legs under a collapsed kitchen table. He rushes over. It's a woman, lying face down in a puddle of blood. "Please, God, please," he mutters. His lower lip starts quivering in fear as he turns the woman over. It's Anah. He sighs and drops his head in relief. Then grief sets-in. *'Why, he wonders--- what's going-on?'* He slowly rises and starts to back out of the scene. Then he stops. Removing a jacket from the nearby coat rack, he gently places it over Anah's face. After pausing for a moment to give a final good-bye to Anah, he snaps back into the search for Liezel. "This can't be happening. I can't lose her again!" he mumbles. His heart is really pounding now. The men run back outside. "Corporal! Quick, check that bungalow over there. I'll check the other one." The men find the same grizzly scenes, but Liezel isn't one of the bodies. *'Where could she be?'* Jason wonders. "The shop!" he shouts. "We've got to get to her shop!"

Earlier, Liezel's last day in the shop is filled with mixed emotions. She actually enjoyed getting her hands dirty and she felt like she was one of the "boys". She accomplished a lot, and she liked the other men in the shop--- all except a moody one named Ivan. The men were somber as she gave them all good-bye pecks on their cheeks. They silently watched her go until the door closed behind her. Liezel's mood was somber as well. Although she looks forward to spending more time on a new adventure with her husband, trading the relative security of Israel for the dangers of a dystopian America was not a decision she would have made. Now that the time of departure is upon them, her level of anxiety has increased. The trip will be fraught with danger--- maybe even death. She's starting to have second thoughts, but she loves Jason dearly and understands his need to find Joshua. They are as prepared as possible, and she will make the best of it.

Half-way to the barracks, Liezel realizes she left her other shoes at the shop--- shoes she will definitely need on the trip. The men should have gone home by now, but the iris scanner will still allow her to open the door. She reaches the shop at dusk. A light is on

183

inside, but that's not surprising. What **is** surprising is that the door is not locked. She doesn't see anyone around, so she opens the door slowly and quietly. As she walks over to the cupboard where her shoes are, Ivan (the spooky mechanic she didn't trust) barges into the shop from the office. Liezel is so startled she slaps her hand to her chest and gasps, "Oh!... Ivan... you scared the hell out of me." (She normally doesn't cuss, but being with men mechanics every day, some of their language rubbed-off on her.)

"What are you doing here?" Ivan yells, obviously surprised and irritated. "You're supposed to be home."

"I... I forgot my shoes. What are you doing here so late?"

"I'm just finishing-up on a couple of things. I was just about to leave. Here, I'll walk you out."

Liezel senses that something's not right. Ivan is behaving strangely--- nervous and agitated. She grabs her shoes, and she quickly heads toward the door. Ivan follows her. As she approaches the door, she sees Ivan's reflection in the door glass. He has a large knife, and he's raising it to attack her! Instinctively, she wheels around and kicks him in the groin before he can react. The knife flies out of his hand and he doubles-over, yelling something in a foreign language. Liezel follows-up with a swift heel kick to his face. His head jerks to the side, and blood flies out of his mouth. As he falls back his head hits a large vise on the work bench behind him. His body immediately goes limp and he collapses. His head hits the floor with a thud. He's out cold. Fearing he will regain consciousness soon, she fumbles around in his pockets and finds his e-car fob. Then she smashes his wrist comm and the office comm. Checking him one more time, she sees that he's coming around. She grabs a huge wrench off a nearby shelf and drives her knee into his chest. With her other hand on his throat, she raises the wrench, about to strike him.

"Why, Ivan, why?"

With his eyes half-closed, dazed and spitting blood, he mumbles the words, "Mora's orders. You can't escape. You'll see." His head drops back onto the floor, losing consciousness again.

Liezel drops the wrench and bolts out of the door. She purposefully drives over her e-bike on the way out so he can't use it. On her way to the barracks, Liezel re-plays Ivan's strange behavior in her head. *'He said, "You were supposed to be home. You were supposed to be home."'* It's like she spoiled his plans. But what were his plans? She speeds-up.

Back at the barracks, Bischoff quickly reports the massacre to the Command Center, then the men jump into the Bronco. Bischoff hits the throttle hard. The spinning tires spray dirt and gravel around as the Bronco roars away. Almost immediately, another pair of headlights speeds around a corner. Both vehicles slam on the brakes, but it's too late. They skid towards each other, and the bumpers crash together, snapping everyone forward.

Jason shakes the cobwebs out of his brain. Blinded by the headlights, he yells, "Hey over there. Are you okay? Who are you?" to the other driver.

"Jay? It's me!"

"Liezel! Thank God!"

Jason and Liezel jump out of their vehicles, rush toward each other and crash together in a tight embrace. Holding her head against his chest, Jason kisses the top of her head several times. "Thank God it's you," he finally says. "Are you okay? Where have you been?"

Breathing hard, she says, "Yes, I'm fine. I went back to the shop to get a pair of shoes I forgot. Ivan was still there, and he attacked me. It turns out he's a terrorist--- Chechen, I'm guessing. He was also one of Mora's men. He said so."

"Mora?" Jason exclaimed, "You mean that bastard still has a reach even after he's dead? So how did you get away?"

"Thank God I still remembered my Karate. He'll have a huge headache when he wakes-up. He hinted that the others here were in danger, so I raced back here to warn them. Is everyone okay?"

Jason hangs his head and replies sullenly, "Sorry, Honey. They're all dead… Anah, too."

"Oh, no," she cries-out, dropping her forehead onto Jason's chest. "So that's why he was surprised to see me. I was supposed to be killed like the others. If only I could have been here sooner I might have warned them."

He strokes the back of her head, trying to comfort her. "No, Honey, thank God you weren't. Then it might have been you lying on the floor in there. Corporal, can we make it back to the Command Center?" Jason asks.

"I think so, Sir. It looks like the bumpers absorbed the brunt of the crash. It doesn't look serious. The tires are okay, and the engine's still running. I'm ready when you are."

Jason and Liezel spend the night in the Command Center. Just after dawn the following morning they say their good-byes again to the few operators still on duty, and they head for the terminal with Corporal Bischoff. On the way, Bischoff informs them that Ivan and his terrorist buddies are indeed Chechen. How they managed to fool Israel's immigration security gauntlet is a mystery. The good news is that during the night Mossad captured the perpetrators already and they have traced their origins to some of Mora's former staff in Strasbourg, France. A team has been dispatched there to round them up.

The drive to the terminal is quiet and uneventful, but both Jason and Liezel keep looking around for signs of trouble. They'll feel more at ease once they're on board the tanker. Thinking about yesterday's events, Jason turns to Liezel, "You know, Liez, after such a convincing victory, you would think Mora's remaining forces would just throw-in the towel. Afterall, aren't we now supposed to have a thousand years of peace?"

"That's after the second coming, Honey. We're not there yet."

"But maybe we are. You weren't at our meeting with the Arabs, but they think General Dayan is their 12th Imam. So, maybe things won't happen exactly as the Bible or the Quran say. I'm really confused. But based on what happened to you and our friends at the barracks yesterday, I certainly agree that it doesn't look like the thousand years has begun yet."

"I get it, Honey," Liezel replies. "Biblical scholars have debated things like that for centuries. No one really knows for sure. To make things even more confusing, some Muslims speculate that the 12th Imam could even be Jesus, and he will be on their side. And, as you well know, Jews have been looking for the Messiah for centuries. He and the 12th Imam could even be one in the same. The way I look at it, it will be what it will be. So, don't trouble your brilliant mind about it. We have more than enough to worry about right now."

The oil terminal is a plumber's nightmare of pipes and storage tanks. The smells of petroleum and ocean fill the air. As they approach the terminal, the Bronco disturbs a flock of sea gulls resting on the pavement. They lazily start waddling out of the way, then as they see they're not moving fast enough, they scatter into the air and squawk, obviously irritated. One of them leaves a parting gift on the windshield. After the Bronco passes, they defiantly settle back down in the same place--- it's their spot. The travelers check-in at the main gate, then go on to the first of three piers. Each pier is 200 yards long and wide enough to accommodate two lanes of vehicles. Two huge pipes straddle the sides of the piers on their way to the oil loading gantries. Jason and Liezel say good-bye to Corporal Bischoff and thank him for his help, then take an elevator to the ship and come aboard. A crew member greets them and takes them to their quarters.

Their quarters are less than small. A large closet would be more spacious. Liezel frowns, but she doesn't say anything out loud for fear of insulting the crewman. *'Bunk beds and steel lockers,'* she laments to herself. *'I had hoped for something a little more romantic for a sea cruise.'* Their escort tells them that someone will fetch them later to take them to meet Captain Rumsey. He points-out·the head, which is the first door down the corridor. The shower is the second door. All alone now, Jason breaks out a big smile. "Isn't this great, Honey? This could be our second honeymoon!"

Liezel is still frowning. "Fine, since you like our quarters so much, you can have the top bunk."

Jason grabs her shoulders with both arms and kisses her passionately. She melts. "Maybe you'd like our quarters better if I didn't spend much time up there," he says with a boyish grin.

Two hours later the ship finally gets under way. Jason and Liezel get antsy, so they decide to explore. They keep climbing stairs until they find themselves on the bridge. The bridge is occupied by a thirty something helmsman, a young seaman, and a petite middle-aged red-haired woman. Surprised, the three of them turn toward the intruders.

"Who are you, and what are you doing on the bridge?" the woman barks.

Jason and Liezel are blown back, thrown off-guard by such a commanding voice coming from this small woman. "Sorry, mam," Jason sheepishly says. "We're looking for Captain Rumsey. We didn't realize we had found the bridge. Do you know where we could find him."

"I'm Rumsey" the woman snarls. "Are you the passengers the IDF sent over?"

"Oh, sorry Mam. Yes, we are. I'm Jason Johnson and this is my wife Liezel. We're trying to get to…"

Rumsey sharply cuts him off. "I know where you're going. You should have been told to stay in your quarters until I sent for you," Rumsey coldly replies.

"Yes, I know. The crewman did tell us. I apologize again, Captain. We'll go back there and wait."

"Hold on," Rumsey says in a softer tone. "It's almost lunch time. I don't want you to go stumbling about the ship. It can be hazardous if you don't know where you're going. Remain here, but just stay out of the way. We'll go down to the galley in a few minutes."

Jason and Liezel feel like they've just been scolded by their elementary school principal. After they shake-off their embarrassment, they gaze out the window at a beautiful sight. It's a sunny day with a bright blue sky. Scattered white clouds drift peacefully by. Four sea gulls flank the ship on the port side, hoping the churning water forces some fish to the surface. After a few more minutes, they give up and disappear. The ship's bow creates a spray of fresh salty ocean air. The rolling waves gently rock the ship back and forth…back and forth…back and forth. Jason is starting to get a little nauseated. Soon, he bolts out of the door and out of sight. He returns after a few minutes, looking a little pale.

"You alright, Jay?" Liezel asks rhetorically.

"Fine, Honey. Just fine." Liezel grins a little. Quickly changing the subject, Jason whispers to Liezel, "Boy, the Captain's a bit feisty, isn't she?"

Liezel whispers back, "Yeah, I'd hate to tangle with her. Her personality is just like her hair--- fiery red."

At lunch, Captain Rumsey tersely explains that the trip should take two days, weather permitting. Jason and Liezel are to confine themselves to certain areas of the ship--- mainly the decks below the bridge and to the stern top deck. Rumsey never said anything more, and she never smiled. The lunch consists of chili and a mixed green salad. Jason looks at the grease floating on the top of the chili, and he hustles out of the galley. Rumsey finally loosens-up and smirks.

Two days later, just as Jason gets his sea legs and he's finally able to hold some food down, the terminal at Lavera comes into view. It's the usual sterile collection of tanks, pipes, and gantries. However, next to the port is the town of Lavera--- a more interesting set of quaint brightly colored homes, stores, and restaurants. There's a marina with dozens of large very expensive-looking yachts. Jason and Liezel are on the stern deck leaning over the railing quietly enjoying the view. This leg of their trip has been easy, almost like a vacation--- at least for Liezel. Except for the first lunch, the food has been surprisingly good, and the fresh sea air has been invigorating. But now that this part of their journey is concluding, disturbing feelings of apprehension creep into their minds.

On a whim, Liezel decides to jump up onto the mid rail of the railing and hold her arms out a la the movie "Titanic" to get a last feel of the wind and the sweet salty sea air that seems to cleanse her lungs. The quickness of her move catches Jason by surprise, and he begs her to come down. Neither of them notices a small boat racing toward the ship. The boat is very fast, and it's not stopping. At the last second, Liezel sees the speedy boat right below her. Then a huge explosion knocks her overboard and into the fireball. Instinctively, Jason leaps over the railing to save her. They both flail about in slow-motion summersaults, and then slam into the chilly water. The force of hitting the water from a fall of 50 feet blasts water up their noses and other places, and they're flipped upside down.

Liezel recovers first. She somehow makes her way upwards. She breaks the surface, gasping for air. When she wipes the stinging salt water from her eyes, her heart stops. A body is floating face-down in front of her! "Jason!" she yells. She quickly grabs him and tries to flip him over, but she only pushes him under the water. She must get his mouth out of the water quickly or he'll drown. With adrenalin pumping through her, she finally flips him over. It's not Jason. The man must have been one of those from the attack boat. Now in a heightened panic, she spins around, desperately searching the surface of the water.

Moments earlier when Jason hit the water, his head hit hard. Dazed, disoriented, and with closed eyes, Jason starts swimming downward by mistake. He feels a hand grab his shirt, pulling him upwards towards daylight. He breaks the surface, gasping for air. He immediately finds Liezel just a few feet away. They lunge toward each other and grasp hands.

Oil seeps out of the wounded tanker and spreads towards them. Fortunately, the fireball quickly exhausted itself before the oil started leaking-out. A cloud of black acrid smoke billows from a gaping hole in the hull. They're lucky to be alive. If they hit the water in any other way, they could have been knocked-out or their necks could have been snapped.

As the crippled ship continues on its course, Jason and Liezel yell and wave franticly, but they get no response. Two seamen emerge onto the deck and run toward the stern. Then they run back, obviously focusing on the immediate crisis. Jason's and Liezel's attempts to draw their attention go unnoticed. Dejected, they drop their arms and cease yelling. The ship slides farther away, leaving a river of smelly oil in its wake. As they desperately tread water, Jason reaches out and gently moves Liezel's drenched matted hair away from her eyes. He's never seen her with such a worried look before, and she's having trouble breathing. Apparently, the fall took the starch out of her. They gag and cough from water in their noses and throats, and they're bodies ache from the impact with the sea. The oil slick has now reached them. As they bob in the oily water, a small wave slaps Liezel in the face. She swallows some of it and starts coughing and spitting. Jason tries unsuccessfully to wipe the oil from Liezel's face and lips. She starts to whimper. The port is at least 2 miles away. Liezel shakes her head in discouragement. "I... I don't think I can make it, Jay."

Then Jason sees a piece of debris floating nearby. "Wait, Liez, that debris might keep us afloat." He pulls it in, but it sinks under his weight. Discouraged, he says, "No good. It's too small." Then he notices a partial emblem on the piece. It's the remains of a black dragon on a red background--- the emblem of Antonin Mora's cadre within the U.N. "Mora!" Jason exclaims.

"Here... take my hand," a voice from behind them says. It's two fishermen in a small boat. Jason can't believe it. They just came out of nowhere. He tries to push Liezel up, but he just pushes himself under water. When he pops back up again he sees Liezel half-way in the boat. Then the fishermen pull Jason in. The water-soaked pair collapse in the bottom of the boat, eyes closed. Jason's and Liezel's hands blindly grope for each other and finally clasp. They rapidly blink their eyes open, but they're blinded by the sun. All they see of the two fishermen are silhouettes bending over them. "Just rest," one of the men says in a thick French accent. "We will be in port in ten minutes. A medic will meet us at the dock. You're going to be okay." Jason and Liezel close their eyes again. No one speaks until they arrive at the marina.

A medic and two others help the bedraggled pair off the boat. The medic says something in French to the fishermen, but all Jason and Liezel can make out is that one of them is named Mordy. When they have both feet on the dock, they turn to thank the fishermen. Their saviors are in their late twenties, but their short red beards and overly tanned and weathered features make them appear ten years older. One of them has a strangely familiar droopy eye lid. The "thank you" is a brief one as the rescued pair are whisked away for treatment.

The medic checks them out quickly. Liezel's ribs are sore from the impact with the sea, but they don't appear to be broken. They spend a lot of time in a hot shower scrubbing each other. The oily slick on their skins and in their hair is tough to get out, and the odor will likely last for a few days. The saltwater in their noses and stomachs finally gets to them, and they rush to the toilets and heave. Jason looks over at his battered wife and says jokingly, "So, did you enjoy our second honeymoon, Honey?"

"Sure, Jay, let's do it again sometime," she sarcastically replies, wiping her mouth. They both manage a chuckle.

Jason spits in the toilet again. "You know, ever since I drew this damned assignment I feel like I've been cursed. Things really started spiraling downhill since I met Mora. It's been like a dark cloud following me wherever I go, even after Mora died--- or maybe he didn't. I don't know. Now I've gotten you involved, too."

"Don't worry about it, Honey. I'm just thankful we found each other. Speaking of thanks, thank God those fishermen were there. They saved our lives, and we never really had a chance to thank them properly."

"I know. Maybe we can find them after we get out of her. You know, you saved my life, too, Liez. Thinking back on it, I must have been swimming down instead of up. If you hadn't grabbed me, I probably would have drowned."

"What are you talking about?" Liezel says in a puzzled tone. "I didn't grab you."

"Sure you did--- by my shirt. You pulled me up."

"I'm telling you, Jason, I didn't. I was too busy fighting for my own life out there. I didn't even know where you were." They both frown, deep in thought. The trauma of the event must have played tricks on their individual recollections. What other explanation could there be?

After drying-off, they notice someone has kindly left two pairs of overalls and some flip flops for them. Liezel's outfit is a little too big, but she's grateful for anything to wear right now, because their own clothes are beyond salvaging. They check their wrist comms. The comms are working here, so their identities are verifiable, and they can communicate, at least here in Europe. Josh tries anxiously to get some sort of signal from America, but to no avail. Without the ability to communicate with American banks, they can't get American credit. Therefore, they must rely on the Unicoin the Israelis loaded into their wrist comms, and on the emergency Krugerrands. Jason and Liezel express their gratitude to the medic and his helpers. They head into town to by some clothes and purchase hyper-train tickets to Strasbourg.

Once outside, they look around for their rescuers, but their boat is gone. Liezel says to Jason, "Honey, did you get a good look at the fishermen that saved us?"

"Sort of. Did you catch their names?"

"Someone on the dock called one of them Mordy. I don't know about his buddy."

Jason is now deep in thought. "Right... Mordy. Could that be short for Mordecai?

"Maybe," Liezel replies, now deep in thought herself. "Wouldn't it be something if they're related to Mordecai and Morris, the ones who saved me in California, and the ones you met on the plane? Maybe their sons or grandsons?"

"That would be way too much of a coincidence, although one of the men on the plane did have a droopy eye lid like Mordy's. But our rescuers seem too young to be their sons, and too old to be grandsons. If we ever run into them again, we'll have to ask. You know, there's something else I just thought of--- there wasn't any fishing gear on their boat. Strange. I wonder what they were doing out there. I didn't even notice them until they were right on top of us."

The walk into town is actually quite pleasant, although they struggle a little with their sea legs. The first store they enter has an adequate selection of clothes, shoes and backpacks. As Jason checks-out his new pack, it dawns on him that he forgot about the unopened letter General Dayan gave him that's in his old pack on the ship. *'What could it have said?'* he wonders. *'Probably just thank you and good-bye.'* After purchasing clothes and backpacks, their stomachs had settled down enough so they feel like getting something to eat.

They find a sunny open-air café on the waterfront. Jason orders lunch in broken French, trying to recall some of what he learned in high school. When the food arrives, they discover that he has been mostly successful in ordering some traditional Mediterranean food and two glasses of wine. However, a side dish contains a gelatinous mess of mystery meat. He first pretends it's what he thought it would be. But when Liezel scowls at it and gives Jason a questioning look, he slowly pushes the plate aside. They both chuckle. A violinist is playing some sappy but pleasant music as he strolls around. He dwells at the couple's table, then he smiles and moves on. After a cramped nauseous cruise, it's beginning to seem like a real second honeymoon after all.

Jason reaches out and caresses Liezel's hand with both of his. "Liezel, Honey, now that we can actually relax and enjoy each other's company, I have to tell you how proud of you I am. These past two months have shown me an amazingly different side of you. You defeated an attacker, you worked hard on dirty vehicles, you survived an explosion and a nasty fall into the sea, you rescued me from the crevasse, and although you disagreed with me, you supported me in my decision to return to America. All that, yet you never gave up and you never complained. I think I love you more now than ever before."

Liezel's eyes get a little watery. She takes her free hand and squeezes the top of Jason's hand. "You know, Jay, I could say the same sort of things about you. You were a quiet engineer in California, just minding your own business. Then you volunteered for a potentially suicidal assignment to help Israel. And you always protected me. You gave me the reassurance and confidence to do everything that we've been through, knowing you would always be at my side. I'm sure I love you more, too." They lean across the table and kiss. The violinist returns with a bigger smile.

The hyper-train speeds into Strasbourg in two hours. As the afternoon wanes, they get directions to the Israeli Consulate, and they start walking. They pass the former American Embassy. The gate is padlocked, and vegetation has creeped up the building to the first-floor windows. The two travelers stop at the rusting gate. Jason grabs two of the gate's bars, and he gets a little wispy as he's reminded of the demise of the greatest country in the history of the world. They move-on, passing the site of the destroyed U.N. headquarters. The rubble has been removed, but there's no sign of any attempt to rebuild. "It's just as well," Jason says to Liezel. "This is where I met Mora. Everything about that building gave me the creeps anyway. It just felt evil. You know, its shape was supposed to resemble the Tower of Babel--- crazy. I hope this spot stays empty forever." He tells Liezel about his intimidating meeting with Mora and Mora's nefarious assistant Madam Derofski and the priest Precora. It was here in Strasbourg that Jason learned that Mora was the one who gave the order that led to the death of Jason's parents.

As they pass a small alley. Suddenly two men pop-out, one ahead of them and one behind. They quickly display large knives. The one in front presses his knife against Jason's side, while the other grabs Liezel from behind and holds a knife to her throat. They look nervously around and start barking in French. Neither Jason nor Liezel can understand them, but their meaning is clear--- they want anything valuable. The men force the couple down the alley. After surviving all the life-threatening experiences he's had, Jason is desensitized to danger, so he remains unusually calm with this new threat. The thieves point to the backpacks and bark some more non-understandable orders. The two victims hand their packs over. One man angrily spits on Jason, then they both run away.

Their hearts pounding, Liezel buries herself in Jason's chest. "Are you all right, Liez?" Jason asks.

"Yeah, I'm fine--- I can't decide if I'm more scared or mad. I tried to figure-out a karate move, but since there were two of them, and one had a knife to your side, I decided not to."

"I think you made the right call, Honey. They were pretty intimidating, and it just wasn't worth risking our lives over some clothes. Fortunately, those idiots didn't check my pockets where the Krugerrands were. I guess they figured since no one uses hard currency anymore, they didn't think I had anything valuable there. We should report this to the police as soon as possible. Someone in that café across the street should be able to help. And I don't know about you, but I could sure use a drink anyway."

Liezel agrees. Suddenly, the skies open up with a loud clap of thunder. It starts to pour. Dashing across the street, they open the door to a narrow dimly lit room. The place smells of cigarette smoke, wine and old wood. Jazzy metallic music is playing. A long bar on the right is filled with loud jovial patrons, mostly older men. One of them is leaning over the bar, apparently trying to make time with the woman bartender. She's smiling, acknowledging his effort, but goes about her business as she draws a beer. There are two tables at the front windows and another row of tables trailing to the rear of the café. Most of the tables are filled with men and women. Some are laughing and talking loudly. Two couples at one table are quiet and unemotional, looking like they can't wait to leave. Heavy wood panels with thick ornate moldings adorn the walls, and the bar has several mirrors behind shelves full of brightly colored bottles. Plain globe lights hang from sculptured medallions against a black plastered ceiling. Two of the lights have burned-out, and several white spots on the ceiling indicate places where some chunks of plaster have fallen-off. The wood floor is unevenly worn. The place is obviously old, perhaps 200 years or more.

As Jason and Liezel step into the café, two men at the corner of the bar turn to look. One man at a front table looks up and focuses on Liezel. The woman next to him scowls and back-hands him on the arm. The wet and scraggly new arrivals just stand there and look around for a server or host. Seeing none, they find an empty table. No sooner had they seated themselves, a server emerges out of the smoky fog. She welcomes them in French, but, obviously over-worked, she doesn't make eye contact. A long strand of blonde hair dangles in front of her face. She tosses her head and blows the hair aside, ready to write their order.

Jason looks-up in surprise. "Jill? Jill O'toole?"

She quickly looks down over her dark-rimmed glasses. Her mouth drops open. "Jason?" she replies, wide-eyed. "Jason Johnson?"

"Yes, it's me." He quickly jumps-up, and they hug. Liezel folds her arms and frowns.

"I can't believe it's you!" Jill says. "What are you doing here. I thought you were in Israel."

"I was, but after the battle I stayed and helped Israel rebuild. Now we're on our way back to America. So, what are you doing here?"

"Well, when Washington was destroyed, R.J. and the whole Embassy staff were basically out of work. The Embassy was closed because we had no funding or purpose, so I had to find work."

"And what about R.J.? How is he?"

"He's fine. He's the day manager here. He's going to be so excited to see you again," she says smiling. "We were both wondering what happened to you over there. Thank God you survived."

Liezel sees what's going on between them, and loudly clears her throat. Jason embarrassingly recognizes his rudeness. "Oh my gosh. I'm so sorry. Honey, this is Jill O'toole. She was Ambassador R.J. Harper's assistant when I came through here on my way to Israel. This is my wife Liezel."

"Wife!" Jill replies, shocked. "You mean you found someone in Israel and married her already? You're a fast worker. It's only been a couple of months since you were here!"

"No, no, we've been married for over three years. She's the one who disappeared. She turned-up in Israel of all places."

Her eyebrows still raised in amazement, Jill says, "You can't be serious. This is a story I have to hear!"

Jason invites Jill to sit down, and he brings her up to date on all that's transpired since she and Jason had that lingering good-bye hug at the airport. Although a bit over-worked at the moment, Jill still has that model-like attractiveness and, like Liezel, she has strikingly beautiful blue eyes. Jill and Jason smile at each other as he tells his story. Liezel notices and thinks to herself, 'So, is this another one I have to worry about?'

Jill brings the couple something to eat and drink and she tells Jason how to report the robbery to the police. She leaves them alone for most of the evening, but she invites them to stay with Harper and her in the former safe house where they all stayed after the U.N. headquarters blew-up. Liezel peppers Jason with questions, and he fills her in about the uncomfortable meeting with Antonin Mora, the explosion that brought down the U.N. building and killed Mora, Mora's miraculous resurrection from the blast, and most importantly to Liezel, Jason's relationship with Jill.

While admitting Jill's attractiveness, Jason covers himself nicely, explaining that they only knew each other for three days, and that nothing happened between them. Seemingly satisfied, Liezel relaxes.

After Jill's shift is over, they walk to the safe house, and Jason and Harper get reacquainted. Harper is casually dressed in a puffy white shirt with dangling draw strings where the top buttons would normally be--- ready to begin his shift at the café. Since Jason last saw him, he's let his formerly perfectly quaffed gray and black streaked hair grow long enough to tie it in a man bun. The worry lines in his forehead are more pronounced than before, and he's lost a lot of weight. After learning about their journey, Harper provides some discouraging information. He has been unable to contact anyone in America. He assumes everyone he knows is dead. However, he has maintained contact with his counterparts in Canada and Mexico, and he has been receiving bits and pieces of news about conditions in America. The news is not good. Major cities and military bases were leveled and will remain radioactive dead zones for hundreds of years. The Federal Government has ceased operating, and the few remaining state governments are struggling. 80% of the wealth in America evaporated with the destruction of the financial system. The oil refineries that were clustered in Texas and Louisiana were wiped-out, and oil is leaking heavily into the Gulf of Mexico. The only refinery still in operation is in North Dakota. Since almost all oil refineries were destroyed, farming and transportation came to a dead stop. America will be out of food soon. Food and medical aid are pouring in from other countries, but they languish in the few remaining seaports and airports due to the lack of appropriate vehicles and transportation fuel. Electronic components in e-vehicles and consumer devices were knocked-out by EMPs. Millions are starving to death every day. Bodies are piling-up and rotting because there are no resources to bury them. The lucky ones have fled to Canada and Mexico, straining the resources in those countries. Wealthier Americans that had foreign assets have fled to other countries around the world. Power plants are shutting down due to lack of spare parts and fuel. Even solar and wind systems are starting to fail. Steady rains have washed radioactive fallout from the skies, but now the contaminated rivers are carrying radiation into the coastal waters. Lawlessness reigns everywhere, and there are rumors of cannibalism. Millions are leaving America. No one is going in. Harper strongly urges his guests to abandon their journey.

After Harper paints this bleak picture, Jason lets out a sigh, grimaces, and rubs the back of his neck, trying to find some logic for continuing. He can't. Liezel reaches over and squeezes Jason's hand. "Honey," she says, "please listen to Mr. Harper. If we keep going, we'll end up in a radioactive pit of snakes. Joshua may not even be alive, and we could die trying to find him. We'd have to be crazy to continue. Please reconsider. We could stay here or return to Israel, or we could at least wait to see if conditions in America improve."

Jason is really struggling with the conflict between what his heart and mind are screaming at him. He looks up, trying to find an answer in the ceiling. "I don't know," he finally says. "I just have this strong feeling Joshua **is** alive, and I have to find him. On the other hand, I don't want to put you in danger. Let's sleep on it. Maybe things will be clearer in the morning."

Liezel latches onto his hand with both of hers, and she looks up at him with a tortured expression. "Jay, look what we've been through already. And this part of the trip was supposed to be the safe part. It's as if someone, or something, has been trying to stop us--- maybe even kill us. I'm sorry," she says, shaking her head as her forehead wrinkles up with worry. "I... I've had it. I can't go on. I just can't. As much as I love you, if you insist on going, you'll have to do it without me. Please, please say you'll stop." Emotionally exhausted, she drops her head against his chest, unable to look at his hurtful expression.

Jason drops his mouth open in shocking disbelief. After the miracle of finding each other, she's willing to abandon him. *'Where is the loyalty?'* he thinks. *'Maybe she doesn't love me as much as I thought.'* Liezel's thoughts are identical. For the first time since they found each other back in Israel, there's an insurmountable wedge between them. They're both tired and beat-up from the ordeals of the day, so they decide to re-visit the issue in the morning. Symbolic of the wall that's now dividing them, they go to bed, silently facing away from each other. Worry, fear, but mostly heartache engulf them until fatigue finally wins-out and they slowly close their eyes.

The morning doesn't bring a resolution to the dilemma. Jason gives it one more try. "Honey, please, please change your mind. I can't bear the thought of leaving you behind, but can't you see why I have to find Joshua?"

"Of course I do. I understand perfectly, but Harper's news is telling us that this is a suicide mission. Can't you understand why I can't go, and why I don't want you to go either?"

Frowning, they silently peer into each other's eyes, searching back and forth from one eye to the other, desperately hoping for a sign that the other will give-in. After several seconds, neither one does.

The atmosphere at breakfast is despondently quiet. Neither Jason nor Liezel can manage more than just a few bites. Jason hugs Jill and Harper and thanks them for their hospitality. They promise to take care of Liezel and help her get established in Strasbourg. He gives Liezel a sad teary kiss and holds her tightly, not wanting to let her go. Liezel responds likewise. The embrace lasts and lasts. So do the tears. They can't seem to let go because of the finality it might represent. Finally, they pull away from each other. Jason caresses her cheeks with his hands. They say "I love you" at the same time. Taking a deep breath, Jason sighs, "Alright then, I guess this is it. Once communication channels are established, I'll contact you." He pauses, hoping for a sign from Liezel that she's changed her mind. Not seeing it, he says, "I'll love you forever, Honey. Always remember that." Liezel can only manage a painful nod of agreement. After one final squeeze, Jason slowly turns and walks away, sadly looking back. "You'll take good care of her, won't you?" he pleads to Harper.

Harper nods, "Of course, Jason. May God go with you."

Liezel smears her tears across her face with her fingers, but new tears take their place. "Be safe, Jay. Come back to me."

Jason is so choked-up he can only manage a short nod. The door quietly closes. He walks down the sidewalk thinking that walking away from Liezel is the hardest thing he's ever done. His eyes well-up again. He stops. *'I can't do this,'* he says to himself. *'She's my everything. I have to go back.'* As he's turning around, he hears running footsteps. It's Liezel! She almost knocks him over when she crashes into him. Her hug never felt so good. She presses her head into his chest. He lays his head on top of hers and gently strokes the back of her head.

After a moment, Liezel pulls her head away and looks up at Jason and says in a half-angry, half-loving tone, "Damn you! Why do you have to be so stubborn?"

"Me?" Jason says with a relieved smile, "Look who's talking. But it doesn't matter. All I care about right now is that we're together."

Liezel responds. "I've never been so conflicted in all my life, but one thing I do know is that I couldn't let you go again. If anything were to happen to you, I just couldn't live with myself. If you insist on going, I need to be with you--- even if it means neither one of us makes it." Jason's earlier lump in his throat returns. He just puts his arm around her. Then they pivot towards the Israeli Consulate.

A half-hour later, they turn onto the Consulate's street. Ahead is a chaotic scene. Lights are flashing from the tops of fire trucks. Fire crews are hosing water into windows and on top of the roof of an old three-story building. People are standing around barricades in the street. Police cars and ambulances are there, too. Two people on stretchers are being loaded into one of the ambulances as another one speeds away with the siren blaring. Flames intermittently lick out from three windows on the top floor. Heavy black smoke pours out of the other windows and from the roof. Jason looks at the piece of paper with the Consulate's address on it. He starts counting houses from the corner. "Oh no!' he cries to Liezel. "It's the Consulate!" They quickly jog to one of the barricades. Just on the other side is a man with an oxygen mask being attended-to by a medic. His hair, face, and glasses are covered with soot, and his nostrils are black from breathing smoke. "Excuse me, sir," Jason yells. "Excuse me. Are you with the Consulate?" The man nods. "We're from Israel. You were supposed to be expecting us. My name is Johnson. We're trying to get to America."

The man nods back and removes the mask. He coughs a couple of times. "Yes Dr. Johnson. We've been expecting you. We had the travel certificates ready to load into your wrist comms, but I'm not sure they survived the fire. Try coming back tomorrow." He coughs again and returns his mask to his face. Discouraged, Jason and Liezel walk back to the safe house. Harper contacts his friend from the Consulate and arranges for someone to meet Jason there in the morning.

The next morning, Jason returns to the blackened building, leaving Liezel at the safe house with Jill. Harper leaves for work at the café. Like so many European homes, the Consulate is at least 300 years old with grand exterior stone carvings. Everything above the windows is charred. A faint stream of light grey smoke drifts upward from the roof. All the windows are broken, and the front door is open. A police car sits outside, along with a contractor's truck. Two men are boarding-up the windows. Jason moves one of the barricades aside and approaches the gendarme. The officer raises his hand as a signal for Jason to stop. He says something in French that Jason doesn't understand, but Jason gets the idea. He tries to communicate with the officer, but he's unsuccessful. Just then a fire department e-car pulls-up, and two men get out. One of them is the man he talked-to yesterday. His name is Jacob, and he and the fire department officer talk to the gendarme. Soon, Jacob motions Jason to come over, and the three men walk up the steps to the front door. The fire department officer holds a long metal poker and a flashlight. He carefully enters the building first. Twenty minutes later, they emerge disappointed. Without Embassy-issued travel certificates Jason and Liezel can't leave France.

This is welcomed news to Liezel's ears, and she sees another opportunity to make her case for terminating their journey. "Jay, I'm telling you, we keep running into roadblocks. Maybe it's Mora, maybe it isn't, but whatever it is they must be signs that we shouldn't be going back to America. Let's go back to the safe house... please."

Jason pauses as the gears in his head turn furiously. "No, Honey, I have an idea. We're going back to the train station." He looks down and starts operating his wrist comm while they walk. Jason almost runs into another pedestrian, but Liezel pulls him aside in time to avoid a collision.

Curiosity is killing Liezel, so she pumps Jason for information. "So, what's your idea, Jay?"

"I'm still trying to work it out in my head, Honey," he says. "You'll see. You'll see. We need to check the train schedule. Let's pick-up the pace a little." Jason's stride is longer than Liezel's, so she struggles to keep up.

"Can't we check the schedule with our wrist comms?"

"I just tried. I'm not getting anything. The train network must be down."

They don't talk much again because they're breathing harder. When they reach the station, Jason checks the schedule display. Then he grabs Liezel's hand and pulls her along as he jogs to the ticket kiosk.

"Where are we going, Jason?" Liezel asks, obviously frustrated.

"If we hurry, we can catch the PL Express to London, he replies."

"London?"

"Yes, London."

"But how's this going to work? We don't have the travel certificates."

"Trust me, Liez. I know the French."

They don't need to present the travel certificates yet, so the purchase at the kiosk is successful. "Got it," he says triumphantly. "The tickets are loaded-in. Let's go." He grabs her hand again and they walk swiftly to the gate area.

Liezel raises her eyebrows and gives him a 'I-hope-you-know-what-you're-doing' look. They arrive at the security checkpoint, and an officer asks to see their passport display on their wrist comms. The officer has a double chin, and he's wearing a uniform that's straining the shirt buttons above his belt. He appears to be of Middle Eastern descent. Dark beady eyes glare suspiciously over the reading glasses resting half-way down his nose. His mustache is very thin, almost like a pencil line just above his lips. He has a closely trimmed dark beard. "I see you're from Israel, and you're going to England," he says, frowning. "I'll need to see your travel certificates."

Jason takes a deep breath and pulls out two Krugerrands in his fist. "I think you'll find everything is in order, sir," as he slides them into the officer's hand. The officer looks at the coins, quickly closes his fist, and then squints back at Jason, boring into Jason's eyes with contempt. The officer says something in French into his wrist comm.

In a few seconds another officer shows-up. He is Securite Capitaine Koch, a fifty something short thin man with a dark go-tee and sideburns. They whisper back and forth. Then the Capitaine grabs Jason by the arm and says, "You both will have to come with me." They walk briskly into a small unadorned office labeled SECURITE. The room is dingy, and some of the yellow paint is peeling off the walls. One of the bulbs in the ceiling light is flickering, creating an irritating atmosphere.

Liezel looks annoyingly at her obviously embarrassed husband and shakes her head. "*This* was your plan?" she says.

The officer motions for them to have a seat on a bench near the door as he sits behind his desk. He removes his hat, revealing a totally bald head that makes his sideburns look like they belong on someone else's face. Silently glaring at them, he drums his fingers on the desk. The office is overly warm, and Jason and Liezel start to sweat.

Finally, the Capitaine clears his throat and says, "So, you are from Israel, and you tried illegally to leave France without the proper credentials. Of course, this is in direct violation of our requirements for Israeli travelers under our Sharia Law. This was a serious infraction, but you made it a larger crime when you tried to bribe a security officer. Very foolish. You have now subjected yourselves to a jail sentence."

Jason interrupts. "I'm so sorry, Capitaine, but..."

"Silence! You will get your chance to explain. I see that you are both Americans. So, what were you doing in Israel?"

"I was sent there by the American government to help Israel defend itself against the invasion. My wife went there to get away from Antonin Mora, who was persecuting her and her friends. Her friends were all murdered by Mora. You see we have a son..."

"Stop! Just answer the question. I am well aware, as is the whole world, of Israel's miraculous victory. I am also aware that the Islamic Counsel has declared that General Dayan is the 12th Imam. This declaration creates tremendous complications here for us. Did you know him?"

"Why, yes I did--- very well in fact. I worked directly under him."

The Capitaine squints at Jason. "So, you are complicit in killing millions of Muslims, Russians and Chinese."

"But we had no choice. They attacked *us*."

"Silence, monsieur." The Capitaine continues. "So, is he the 12th Imam?"

"I'm not qualified to say, sir, but I do know that he prevailed against impossible odds, and he utilized some supernatural forces that worked in his favor."

"So I understand. And it has not gone unnoticed that there haven't been any earthquakes or other natural disasters since Israel's victory. So, what are you doing in France?"

"We're just trying to get home to California. We have a son there, and I need to find him. I don't even know if he's alive."

"And why don't you have travel certificates?"

"They were lost in the fire at the Israeli Consulate."

"I see. But that is no excuse for bribing a security officer. That's a very serious crime. You should have requested replacement certificates."

"But we had no way of doing that. Besides, I'm sure you know that processing new certificates can take weeks--- weeks we don't have."

Deep in thought, the Capitaine looks at the ceiling, puckers his lips and drums the desk again. After a pause, he declares, "My grandfather was Jewish. He left the family here and immigrated to Israel many years ago to help Israel defend itself then. I never forgave him for abandoning me. He was later killed in a rocket attack." After another pause, he gets-up, puts his hat on, and unlocks the door to the train platforms. As he passes toward the other door, he briefly puts a hand on Jason's shoulder.

Jason and Liezel turn to each other with raised eyebrows. Jason watches the Capitaine until he's out of sight. Without another word, they dash through the door to the trains.

They quickly board the hyper-train to Paris. There are plenty of seats available, so they slide into one of them at the rear of the car. They slump down a little, trying to reduce their profile. When they realize they are only making themselves look suspicious, they sit up again. After an agonizingly long wait, the train starts moving. Finally, they sigh in relief and smile at each other. Liezel leans her head on Jason's shoulder and closes her eyes. Jason puts his hand on hers and closes his eyes, too. After an hour, the slowing of the train wakes them up. They're arriving in Paris. Passengers begin rising from their seats, gathering their belongings. As a large man passes, he bumps into Jason's shoulder. His pungent body odor causes Jason to turn away. The man looks down at Jason in distain and moves-on. Soon the car is clear of passengers except Jason and Liezel and a nervous looking woman at the front of the car. She's wearing sunglasses, a head scarf, and a dirty beige jacket. Jason takes note of the jacket, because the temperature in the car is too warm to warrant it.

After a brief stop-over, the car fills-up with passengers and continues on to Calais. Soon after departure, a droid comes down the aisle with snacks and drinks. Jason takes two yogurts, two bottles of water, and a package of assorted cheeses--- not the substantial meal he and Liezel were hoping for, but this is France. The droid continues down the aisle to another car. Just then the nervous woman jumps into the aisle and zips open her jacket. As she reaches inside, another man springs-up from a nearby seat

209

and slams into her. They both hit the floor and struggle with each other. The man succeeds in getting the woman in a Full-Nelson, thus immobilizing everything but her flailing legs. Jason leans into the aisle and sees what looks like a suicide vest inside the woman's jacket. Without thinking, Jason jumps into the aisle and pins her legs down. The man yells something in French to Jason, but Jason responds in English that he doesn't understand him. Then in English he quickly tells Jason to tap the face of the man's wrist comm as the man continues wrestling with the screaming woman. Jason complies. Within seconds, two men (obviously fellow agents of some kind) burst into the car from each direction. They pull-out weapons and point them at the woman, yelling something at her. The woman stops struggling, so Jason gets up. Suddenly she snaps her head back into her captor's nose, causing him to lose his grip. The woman gets a hand free, screams something, and then reaches for the inside of her jacket again. Almost simultaneously, a crisp "pop, pop" pulses through the car. The woman collapses with two laser holes in her forehead. Jason freezes for a moment, realizing how close he came to death. Still in an unstable daze, he plods back to his seat. Without acknowledging Liezel, he slowly sits down and stares at the seat in front of him.

Liezel shakes his arm. "Jay, what happened? I couldn't see."

Jason blinks as he comes out of his trance. He then recounts the rapid events. As he's finishing briefing Liezel, one of the agents approaches Jason. "Thank you for your help, monsieur, but that was both brave and foolish. You could have been killed."

"I guess I should have known better, but I didn't really think about it. I just reacted. Thank you for your quick thinking, officer. Was she really wearing a suicide vest?"

"It looks like it, but we have experts on the way to confirm."

Jason presses the agent. "So, what was she saying?"

"I couldn't understand everything--- something about Mora." Jason and Liezel quickly turn towards each other. A chill comes over them. Whether or not he's dead, it's now clear that his influence lives on. First it was Ivan. Then the speed boat that hit the tanker. Now this woman. Mora seems to be invisibly haunting them. Who or what else might be lurking ahead?

After a delay while the scene of the shooting is processed and the body is removed, the train continues its trip to the Chunnel and England. Upon arriving in London, they take an e-cab to the Israeli Embassy. When they arrive, they find vehicle barriers at the front gate and security guards in front and behind the gate. The travelers are questioned and searched. They're relieved when the guard says they're expected, and he motions them through.

Once inside, an assistant greets them and takes them to meet Ambassador Moshe Joppa. Joppa is in his mid-fifties and is dressed very casually--- khaki pants and a khaki shirt which is unbuttoned at the top. A large clump of gray hair curls out from his chest. He's half bald, with a short beard and hair like Albert Einstein's. Granny glasses complete the picture of someone that looks more like a reclusive professor than an ambassador. With an excited grin, he puts his pipe down, jumps up from behind his desk, and runs over to hug and kiss them--- Jason once and Liezel twice. He's obviously overjoyed to meet the famous travelers. Liezel is a little put-off by his tobacco-smelling breath and stained teeth.

"Welcome to England," Joppa says excitedly, with a thick Hebrew accent. "We weren't sure you would make it after your tanker was attacked. I understand you were thrown overboard in the explosion."

"Correct, Mr. Ambassador. Fortunately, we were rescued by a couple of fishermen. It's been a rough trip. On the train here there was also this suicide bomber that almost blew us up. Oh, and our travel certificates were lost in the Strasbourg Embassy fire--- a bunch of nastiness we certainly don't want to repeat. If it weren't for a compassionate security captain, we would still be in France and in jail. Anyway, here we are.

"Oh my. You *have* been through a lot. Well you're safe now, and please call me Moshe. So, what was this bomber all about? We hadn't heard about that."

"I'm not sure, but she was apparently one of Antonin Mora's fanatic remnants. I hoped most of them had been rounded-up by now, but obviously they haven't found all of them yet."

Liezel breaks-in. "Jason's being way too modest. He actually risked his own life to help subdue the woman."

"Well, you are even more heroic than we heard about from your amazing exploits in Israel--- a true miracle over there, yes?"

"Absolutely, Sir, er, Moshe."

Joppa continues. "It's amazing how God continues to keep his covenant with Israel. Perhaps now we will have truly lasting peace. But you must be tired. Come, sit," as he stretches his hand out towards a couple of comfortable-looking chairs. "Deborah," he says to his assistant, "some tea for our special guests, please."

Jason relates more stories of his and Liezel's experiences in Israel, and of their improbable reunion. Moshe brings the pair up to date on the situation in England. He informs them that their planned sea voyage to Canada has been canceled. In fact, all shipping in the Atlantic has ceased due to radioactive water draining from America that has spilled into the ocean. The Gulf stream has brought that water to the British Isles. Soon, England will be completely surrounded by radioactive water. The only way into Canada is by air. Aviation fuel is so scarce that the few passenger flights are booked for four months out, and they're outrageously expensive. Moshe has called-in a favor and has arranged for the pair to be on a less expensive cargo plane to Nova Scotia tomorrow morning. They'll have to get to Canada on their own.

It's the best Moshe could do. In the meantime, Moshe has reserved a hotel room for them a short walk from the embassy. An embassy e-car will pick them up in the morning and take them to the airport. The travelers express their gratitude. Moshe hugs Liezel two more times and has Deborah (Deh-**bor**-a) escort them to the hotel. They mention that they need to buy some clothes, so Deborah steers them to a shop on the way.

During the walk, Deborah shares some of her story. She's 35, married for eight years, no children. Her features remind Jason and Liezel of Anah back in Israel--- dark hair, bushy eyebrows, no make-up, but not nearly as attractive. She was very quiet during the meeting with Joppa, but now she won't shut up. She starts sharing personal information about her boring marriage and private details Jason and Liezel really don't want to hear about. Her voice is shrill and annoying--- very nasally. Her laugh is more of a snort. When she turns her head the right way, the sunlight illuminates barely noticeable dark peach fuzz above her upper lip.

The shopping trip is short and productive. Each of them selects two sets of clothes, jackets, extra socks, and underwear, plus hiking boots and backpacks.

When they enter the hotel lobby, Deborah suggests they have an end-of-the-day drink. Liezel's jealousy bone starts tingling again, but she goes along, because after what they've been through today, a drink might just hit the spot. They find a cocktail table in a dim corner of the hotel bar. Jason orders a beer, making sure it's not brewed in Strasbourg. The ladies order wine. Deborah shares some more stories about her life, particularly her career at the embassy. She's been there for ten years. Moshe's been there for six years. One evening after a long day, she said that she and Moshe went to a happy hour at this very hotel. He made a pass at her that she rejected, and she hinted that his wife might like to be aware of it. She received a raise the next day.

With a glass of wine in her, Deborah is actually quite entertaining, so they have another round. After Deborah has another glass ahead of them, Liezel notices that Deborah keeps giving both of them lingering touches on their arms when she laughs. A red flag goes up in Liezel's mind. Deborah's getting a little too familiar. When Deborah suggests another round, Liezel objects, politely saying that Deborah's husband must be expecting her, and that Jason and she need to get something to eat. Deborah grows more insistent. Finally, Jason has had enough. He stands up, leans toward her, and puts both hands on the table. In a stern voice he says, "Deborah, thank you for taking care of us and being so welcoming, but we are both very tired and hungry. It's really time to call it a night."

Deborah slumps down in her seat, obviously disappointed. She motions for the waitress to come over. "I've got the tab," Jason says calmly.

Deborah quietly stands up, veering to one side. "I'll see you in the morning," she glumly says, slurring her words a little. She walks away, bumping into a couple of chairs as she goes.

Liezel says to Jason, "Thank you, Honey. That was painful." They order some food, and then check-in.

The next morning, Deborah picks them up, and profusely apologizes for her behavior the night before. They drive to a remote terminal at the airport, check-in, and say good-bye to Deborah. The plane is huge and old, the type used for transporting heavy military equipment--- tanks and the like. It's full of cargo containers, so Jason and Liezel sit in the jump seats behind the pilots. There is one other passenger--- a thin, quiet man named Jack Potts who is also a pilot, and he's on his way home to Halifax . He straps-in on a small bench seat behind the cockpit bulkhead. The working pilots introduce themselves--- Russ and Howard. They're both in their early forties. They look like they haven't shaved or combed their hair in a couple of days. Their eyes have sort of a wild look about them. As the plane lumbers down the runway, Jason and Liezel peer past the pilots to see the end of the runway fast approaching. They get nervous because the plane is shaking and it's still on the ground. Liezel clutches Jason's arm. Potts is sound asleep. As the end of the runway disappears from their view, Liezel digs into Jason's skin with her fingernails, and she squeezes her eyes shut. Then the shaking stops. They're airborne. The two passengers breathe again.

"Don't worry, folks," Howard the co-pilot shouts back, grinning. "We have these close calls all the time. They keep overloading the cargo bay, squeezing every Unicoin out of this operation." The pilots give each other a high five and laugh. Then they break-out a bottle of scotch. "You folks want a snort?" Howard asks. Jason and Liezel look at each other in nervous disbelief. Before they can object, Howard says, "Don't worry about this, either. The plane's on A.I. We don't even have to land it." It's 9am, so the two passengers decline the beverage invitation. The pilots pass the bottle back and forth, laughing from time to time. An hour into the flight, Jason and Liezel don't notice, but the pilots have fallen asleep. Soon, Jason and Liezel drift-off, as well.

About a half hour from Halifax, Liezel is wakened by a jolting of the plane and a "beep, beep" sound coming from the instrument panel. A red light is also flashing. She blinks her eyes and looks around, trying to absorb what's happening. Realizing that something's wrong, she pokes Jason awake, and she then yells at the pilots. They don't respond. She quickly unbuckles herself and jumps between the pilot's seats. She yells again and shakes Russ awake. He blinks and stammers, still woozy from the booze. Finally, the emergency registers with him. He slaps Howard in the arm, and he wakes-up, too. "Howard, we've lost number four!" Russ says in a panic.

Howard peers out of the side window. "Yeah, it's smokin'!" he yells back. "Cut the fuel!"

"Check," says Russ. "We're dropping too fast. I'm taking it out of A.I. Get back in your seat, miss, and hold on. This is going to be rough."

Russ contacts the Halifax tower and requests an emergency landing. Five minutes out, the plane is under control, but it's shaking. There's no room for error--- they have to land on the first approach. The runway is in sight, but there's a small plane on it! Apparently, it lost power because it's not getting out of the way. At ten seconds to touchdown, two people bail out of the small plane and run away. Russ and Howard let out a primal scream together. The plane's wheels just clip the tail of the small plane, slightly jostling the big plane, but Russ manages to keep it on track. The plane hits the runway hard and bounces. Then it bounces again and tilts. Russ levels the plane quickly and it finally settles down. Russ engages the reverse thrusters. The plane swerves, almost veering off the runway. Russ and Howard both hit the foot brakes hard. The tires start smoking. As the other end of the runway approaches, the plane slowly comes to a stop. Fire trucks rush out and start spraying the smoking engine with foam. Both pilots and passengers slump back in their seats, motionless with relief. They have arrived in North America. Now the tough part begins.

CHAPTER FIFTEEN---A BROKEN AMERICA

After passing through customs, Jason and Liezel face the stark reality that they have no idea where to turn or what to do next. They have no friends or contacts here. They are alone. The high cost of the air fare has put them way over budget--- and they're not even in Canada yet. Although they still have a few Krugerrands in reserve, it's impossible to tell how long their money might last, given how expensive everything has become. They consider conserving their remaining financial resources by hitch hiking or jumping onto a freight train. Both options are fraught with risk. Then there's the problem of where to sleep at night. They grab a meager bite to eat, and later catch a bus into town. During the bus ride, Liezel strikes up a conversation with the elderly woman sitting behind them. Soon, the woman's husband joins-in. Within a few minutes, they and Liezel are best friends. Jason just sits back and marvels at Liezel's ability to make quick friends with almost anyone--- anyone but an attractive female showing interest in Jason, that is. The elderly couple are Ann and Dean Stocksdale from Winnipeg. They're here in Halifax visiting their daughter. Jason perks-up when he hears they're from Winnipeg, and he joins the conversation. He explains that he and Liezel are trying to get into northern California, and they are looking for any helpful advice on how to get there.

As luck would have it, Dean is a retired petroleum engineer, and he's very familiar with the rail systems in Western Canada and the U.S. He has an idea about how to get into Northern California without running into radioactive dead zones. They also have a grandson who works in the oil fields in North Dakota--- one of the few areas where life in America is somewhat normal. But first, he offers the same sort of depressing news about America that they've been hearing all along. Liezel's expression sours, but Jason is undeterred. Dean explains that there are chemical trains running from the port in Quebec into North Dakota. If they can catch one of those trains it should lead them to the oil fields--- an economic oasis in an otherwise bleak America. He's not sure how to proceed from there, except to advise dropping south and then going west to avoid the dead zone around Bremerton, Washington. Dean gives Jason his grandson's name and comm number, but he warns that they have not been able to get in touch with him in three weeks due to poor communication links in America. Finally, Dean suggests buying protein dense travel food while they're here or in Quebec, because everything gets more expensive the farther west one goes.

From the bus depot in Halifax, the intrepid travelers catch another bus to Quebec. For once, the trip is uneventful. The port is within walking distance of the Quebec bus depot, but it's getting dark, so they find a cheap hotel near the port. In the morning they purchase four jars of peanut butter, a box of protein bars, a box of crackers, six cans of tuna, four water bottles, a flashlight, and a multi-purpose camping tool. Their backpacks are now as heavy as they can comfortably support. Grabbing two more bottles of water, they head down to the port. The port is similar to the Israeli oil terminal, only much larger to accommodate other types of freighters and passenger ships. Gantries and cranes are everywhere. Several large driverless forklifts move some of the thousands of stacked cargo containers that blanket the area. Railroad tracks run through the docks parallel to the moored ships. Jason and Liezel scan the port from the small hill they're on, but they don't see anything that looks like chemical tanker cars. They decide to go down to the port and ask around.

The entire port is heavily fenced, with a guarded entrance a mile away. As they make their way along the fence toward the guard station, they see a couple of mechanics working on one of the forklifts. The mechanics can't provide any information, neither can the guard at the entrance, siting security protocols. Frustrated, they walk down the street to a small café near the tracks to have some breakfast and what may be their last cup of coffee for the foreseeable future. The place has an uninviting sterile appearance, with an ordering kiosk and a wall of small doors where they pick up their order. They find a table next to four older shabbily dressed unshaven men. The men's conversation suddenly ceases when Liezel shows up. Within five minutes, Liezel has them fully engaged in conversation with her. Jason just smiles and heads to the men's room. When he returns, Liezel tells him that the men meet here almost every morning, but they don't recall anything like a chemical train. However, two times a week an oil tanker train goes into the port. It typically leaves the next day, apparently to refill again from somewhere west. Luckily, one should be due in today. From Jason's bus conversation with the Stocksdales, the only operating oil fields in the West are in North Dakota and Western Canada. Either destination will get them closer to San Marita. They decide to hang around, which doesn't disappoint the old men. As the morning progresses, Liezel has them laughing, and she knows their life stories. They all went to high school together. Two are married to very understanding wives, one is divorced from a gold-digging American much younger than he, and one is a widower. They call their little group the "ROMEO" Club (Retired Old Men Eating Out).

After the third cup of coffee, Jason feels uncomfortably jittery, so he switches to complementary water. It's now after noon, and the ROMEOs have left. A few freight trains pass in and out, but still no tanker train. He asks Liezel, "So, do you think those guys know what they're talking about?"

"Probably not," Liezel replies, "but we have nothing to lose by waiting, do we?"

"I guess not. But I'm not getting another cup of coffee."

Another twenty minutes go by. The pair doesn't say much--- they just stare out the window. Jason starts thinking about a plan B. Just then, the café window starts vibrating. Soon, five attached locomotives rumble-by--- it's the tanker train. Fifteen minutes later, the caboose passes. The train is just barely crawling now, apparently navigating the spaghetti-like maze of tracks inside the port. Without warning, Jason jumps up and snatches his backpack. "Honey, we've got to go--- now!"

"What? Why now?" Liezel asks as she grabs her backpack, too. He grabs her by the arm and pulls her out of the café.

As they're running after the train, Jason replies, "We have to get on now while the train is slow. If we wait until it leaves tomorrow, it might be moving too fast."

"But the guard will spot us."

"Not if we hide in the caboose."

"But what if someone's in there?"

"I didn't see anyone. I'm guessing this type of train doesn't need a conductor. We'll just have to take that chance. Besides, I have a plan."

Liezel thinks, *'Great. Another plan. I hope it's better than the last one.'*

Fortunately, the train is hardly moving when they get to the caboose, so it's easy to get on to the rear platform. Jason peeks through the rear window. He was right--- the car is empty. The door is unlocked, so they quietly go in and lie on the floor under a bench. Soon, they pass the guard station, and Jason gives Liezel the thumbs-up. Suddenly, they hear a "click". A small door opens to a compartment at the front of the car, and a uniformed man emerges, obviously a railroad employee. He turns toward the front door of the car without noticing the two stowaways. Jason faces Liezel and holds his index finger up to his puckered lips. They hold their breath. The man then steps out onto the front platform and closes the door. He disappears from view, apparently leaving the train.

As the afternoon rolls-on, the train advances three cars at a time, presumably to discharge the oil into a storage tank. As dusk approaches, Jason and Liezel are quite hungry, so they enjoy a scrumptious feast of peanut butter and crackers. Jason crawls to the door where the man surprised them earlier in the day. It's a lavatory, and they take advantage of it. The interior of the car is sparse. There's a lumpy looking sofa, a water jug, a trash can, and a small table at one end of the bench they're under. There's also a small computer station and a split screen monitor at the table. A solar-operated air conditioning system hums in the background, along with the sound of air rushing through two registers. The oil transfer operation continues into the night. About ten o'clock, the empty train moves to a siding for the night. While the rail yard is generally well lit, the area around the caboose is fortunately in the shadows. The stowaways finally relax and move to the sofa. Liezel lays her head on Jason's chest and drifts off. Jason stays awake for a while and gently strokes Liezel's hair. The air conditioning system shuts off. Apparently, the back-up batteries have been drawn down. Despite the stressful and nearly fatal events of the past week, Jason feels an uplifting sense of gratefulness that he has such a wonderful woman sharing this adventure with him. Israel seems ten thousand miles away. San Marita seems even farther.

At dawn, the sleeping couple are jolted awake by a sudden movement of the train. They begin moving around and quickly feel the aches and stiffness from their makeshift sleeping arrangement. Jason's neck is particularly sore. He cautiously raises his head above the windowsill to see a yard jockey moving the caboose onto another siding. Then it comes to a rest. After a half hour, the caboose is jolted again as it's re-coupled to the train. The rear of the caboose is now the front. Soon they hear voices.

"Shh, I think someone's coming," Jason whispers. "Quick, let's hide in the lav." It's uncomfortably cramped in there. Jason sits on the seat while Liezel sits on his lap holding both backpacks. Liezel closes the door just in time. They hear the car door open, and someone walks-in. Then the man speaks something in French into his wrist comm. Five minutes later the car is jolted again. The train is underway--- destination unknown.

A half-hour into the trip, Jason's legs and butt are starting to ache. He squirms. Liezel tries to adjust her position, but it doesn't seem to help. After another half-hour he surrenders to the darkness, the weight, and the boredom. He begins drumming his fingers up and down Liezel's arms. She wiggles and softly slaps one of his hands. The movement causes a couple of the cans in one of the backpacks to clang together. They both freeze. After a minute they relax again, concluding that the noise of the train must have drowned-out the noise of the cans. Jason is really aching now, so he whispers, "Honey, my butt's killing me. Do you think you can stand up? Just squeeze the backpacks so the cans don't make any noise." She starts to rise but barely moves. She drops back down again. She leans forward more and tries again. This time Jason pushes her backside--- success. Jason lets out a quiet sigh of relief and begins rubbing his legs. Then he tries to stand. He shuffles his feet around and slowly rises. He's able to brace himself against the walls of the lav, but Liezel can only rest her head against the door. The train sways as it negotiates a long curve in the tracks, forcing Liezel to move one of her feet to brace herself. As she does so, some of the cans collide again. Seconds later, the door suddenly opens, causing her to fall-out onto the floor of the car. She lets out a short scream. Cans and peanut butter jars spill-out of the backpacks and roll across the floor.

"Ah-hah! I thought I heard something. Who are you, and what are you doing here?" a man angrily demands.

Liezel looks up from the floor, and in a soft innocent voice says, "Is this the ladies lav?"

Jason snickers but quickly sobers-up when the man points his weapon at Jason's head. The man puts his wrist comm to his mouth, but before he can speak, Jason pleads, "Wait. Please. Let me explain."

The man tells them to move to the bench. He sits on the sofa, crosses his legs, and listens to Jason's story, pointing his weapon at Jason the entire time. As the man learns of Jason's accomplishments in Israel, his attitude begins to soften, and he sympathizes with Jason's quest to find his son Joshua in San Marita. The man's name is Walter. When he takes his hat off, he reveals a half bald head with graying sides. His granny glasses and gray mustache make him look older than his fifty years. There's an air of sadness in his eyes and speech. After a few more interrogatories, he holsters his weapon, evidently convinced that the couple isn't a threat. He tells the stowaways that the train is headed back to North Dakota to take-on more oil. Great! It's just what Jason and Liezel hoped to hear.

"I sympathize with your situation," Walter explains, "but I'm still going to have to report you. I could lose my job if I don't."

Then Liezel tries persuading him by re-telling the harrowing events and near-death experiences the two of them have had just trying to get this far. She concludes by asking how they could get off the train in North Dakota without anyone knowing so he won't get in trouble. Walter frowns and rubs the back of his neck, obviously conflicted. He stares at the ceiling, deep in thought. Liezel nails the deal with her bright blue doe eyes. Walter takes a deep breath. He caves.

"Alright," he says, "the train's not going to stop until Williston, so I don't think anyone will know you're on board. It'll slow down enough for you to hop-out before we get into the yard. But you'll have to keep out of sight until then."

"Oh, thank you, Walter," Liezel beams as she jumps up and gives Walter a huge kiss on the cheek. He grins and turns red. Liezel continues, "We'll be no trouble, I promise. Do you want some peanut butter crackers?"

Walter shakes his head, "No thanks," while glaring at Jason with his cold beady eyes. While Jason is grateful for Walter's cooperation, he vows to keep his guard up. He's not sure Walter can be trusted.

The train slows down through Montreal and Toronto but doesn't stop. Jason and Liezel slide under the bench during those times. The three travelers share stories about their backgrounds during the three-day trip. Walter was born in Alberta but moved to Quebec when he joined the United Nations thirty years ago. Hence the dual language capability. He later moved to the U.N. headquarters in New York. Three months ago, his wife died after a long struggle with cancer. He's very bitter about it because all cancers were supposed to be curable. He decided to join the railroad because it meant being away from home--- too many memories there. The timing of the change of jobs was good, because he didn't want to move to Strasbourg when the U.N. headquarters moved there. Besides, had he not made the change he might have been killed when the U.N. headquarters exploded. His job is very boring. He usually reads on these long trips, but he's actually glad to have some company this time, especially someone as attractive as Liezel.

Between infrequent communications with various station operators along the route, he peppers Jason with questions about the great battle. Walter had read about some of these accounts, and about Israel's speedy recovery after the battle, but he appreciated the first-hand details. He complimented Jason on his key role, opining that he was obviously a key to Israel's success. Jason modestly explained that it really was a combination of the supernatural miracles and General Dayan's amazing leadership. Walter appeared fascinated and deep in thought. He continued peppering Jason about his role, but mostly about General Dayan,

"The Lion of Judah" as he came to be known. His focus on Dayan bordered on obsessive. Jason wondered why.

"So, Walter," Jason asks, "during your time with the U.N., did you ever meet Antonin Mora?"

Walter stiffens. He nervously clears his throat. "Yes I did, actually. I chaired one of his committees in New York. I heard he died in Israel in the battle."

"He did," Jason replies, "along with his assistant Madam Derofski. I can't say that I'm sorry either one of them are dead. There was something cold and disturbing about Derofski, and Mora was responsible for my parent's death."

"Really? How so?" Walter asks.

Jason tells the story of how Mora (when he was Mayor of Rome) sacrificed Jason's parents just because they were Jews.

"Sorry to hear that." Walter says. He appears to fumble for more sympathetic words but remains silent.

After an awkward pause, Jason asks, "So, what was your committee doing?"

"Oh, just some long-term planning. I really don't know how it turned-out." Then he quickly changes the subject. Jason prods some more, but Walter continues to be vague. Jason senses Walter is being purposefully evasive. Jason wonders what he's hiding. From then on, the mood in the caboose remained subdued, and Jason became even more guarded.

Eventually, Walter got around to Liezel. He was mesmerized as she told the story about her disappearance and retreat to the enclave in the hills of San Marita, and about her fleeing to safety in Israel where she was reunited with Jason. As Liezel talked, Jason's squinting eyes bored into Walter's face, trying to get a clue as to Walter's true intentions. She further told Walter about growing up on her father's ranch, and about the night she met

Jason at a country western dance club and tried unsuccessfully to teach him how to dance. "You're a lucky man, Jason," he said. Breaking his fixation on Walter, Jason agreed. He then turned to Liezel with a loving smile, and squeezed her hand.

On day two, the train approaches Winnipeg. Walter receives a communique that his schedule has changed. Instead of merely slowing down, the train will briefly stop in Winnipeg where he will be replaced.

"You'll have to get off here," Walter insists in a strict tone. "My replacement won't be as sympathetic to you as I have been. If he sees you, he'll report us all. Go to the back platform and jump off when I give you the signal."

"But how can we get to the oil fields?" Jason asks.

"I don't know," Walter replies, "and I really don't care. I've taken too much of a risk with you two already."

Now discouraged again, they thank Walter for his help and gather their belongings. Jason places a Krugerrand on the table, and they quickly exit the rear door. Soon, the train slows down, and Walter gives them the signal. They jump off, trying to hit the ground running. Jason trips and falls on his bad knee. He comes-up limping. Liezel falls hard and she stays down. Grimacing, she grabs her shin and exclaims, "Damn it. I think I twisted my ankle." Jason helps her away from the tracks and into the nearby woods where he eases her down against a large tree. He probes her ankle gently. Liezel cringes and cries, "Ouch!"

"Sorry, Honey," Jason says. "Okay, let's rest here for a bit while we figure out our next move. This really screws us up. Now we're stranded. Maybe that's what Walter wanted. Since he told us he once worked for Mora, I didn't trust him anymore, so we may be better off without him anyway. I wonder if he was really going to be replaced, or was he just trying to make things hard for us. I guess we'll never know for sure."

Jason leaves Liezel at the tree and limps out to the tracks again. The train is out of sight. He starts working his knee, and finds that the pain is starting to dissipate, so he decides to walk down the tracks to see what's ahead. Initially, he can't see anything but forest on each side. Soon, the tracks curve. The forest gives way, and he sees the rail yard and Winnipeg's skyline beyond. With Liezel's bad ankle, she's not going to make it into town. The day is drawing to a close as he starts walking back. After a few minutes he realizes he can't find where he started from. All the trees look the same. Then he yells, "Liezel...Liezel!" No reply. He tries his wrist comm--- no signal. He starts jogging but the knee pain returns, forcing him to slow down again. He yells again. Finally, he hears her yelling back, and he finds her. He immediately asks her to check her wrist comm--- no signal either. Jason doesn't understand why the comms worked in Quebec but not here. Without comms, their access to credit is blocked. All they have left to purchase anything with are the Krugerrands. It's getting dark now, so they decide to spend the night right there. After feasting on tuna fish and crackers, Jason removes the remaining cans from Liezel's backpack and makes a pillow out of it for her. He uses his backpack as a footrest to keep Liezel's ankle elevated. Then he sits back against a tree, knife in hand.

As the night progresses, the forest starts to talk--- crickets, frogs, and an irritating mosquito singing in Jason's ear. He slaps at it, only to cuff his own ear. The two make small talk, wondering if their life will ever be pleasant again. Later, the ground starts vibrating, and a rumbling noise interrupts the night. A train rolls-by, and it's a long one. The noise drowns-out the sounds of the forest. After twenty minutes, the caboose passes. Then it, too, disappears around the curve. Liezel finally falls asleep, but despite feeling drowsy, Jason is too worried to let himself go just yet.

The next morning, Jason is awakened by chirping birds and a beam of sunlight on his face. Instead of remaining in his sitting position, he's lying on the ground next to the tree. A little disoriented, he blinks and looks around. Liezel is gone! He jumps up and trots to the tracks. There's no sign of her in either direction. He yells her name. To his relief, she quickly replies. She's down the tracks about fifty yards at the edge of the forest. "Liez, what are you doing?"

"I'm gathering breakfast. Just look at these wonderful wild berries." As she heads back to him, she says, "Oh--- good news, I don't think my ankle is broken. It hurts, but I can limp around on it okay."

'What a trooper,' Jason says to himself, *'One in a million.'*

After filling-up with fresh berries, they agree that Liezel's ankle is too weak and sore for much walking. Therefore, Jason leaves her in the forest and heads down the tracks towards town to find transportation. This time he marks their location by stacking four rocks on top of each other at the edge of the railroad tracks.

Three hours go by, and Liezel is getting worried. Another train goes by. Then another. At the five-hour mark, she decides that something must have happened to him, so she starts hobbling down the tracks, leaving both backpacks behind. She gets about a hundred yards before the pain becomes unbearable. She drops to one knee, mad at herself for making things more difficult. Then she hears a whirring sound. Her heart leaps. It's Jason coming around the curve on an e-bike!

"Sorry I took so long, Honey," he says, "but there weren't a lot of choices. I finally found this e-bike on a used bike dealer's lot. Interestingly, the salesman's name was Roy Johnson, but we quickly figured-out we're not related. Anyway, after I told him our story, he was pretty sympathetic, so he gave me a break on the price. He even threw-in a box of protein bars as a part of the deal. Unfortunately, I had to cough-up the rest of our Krugerrands."

The bike's an electric three-wheeler with a solar panel above the riders. Solid state batteries keep the bike operating during low-light periods, but the bike can also be pedaled. The seats are overly worn, and it looks like it's been ridden hard and long. It must have served the previous owners well, because they affectionately wrote "Nellybelle" on the side.

Liezel looks-over the bike, dismayed. "So, *this* is supposed to get us all the way to California? It doesn't even look like it could get us into downtown Winnipeg."

Defending his purchase, Jason responds, "Don't worry, Honey, I know these bikes. They're simple--- hardly any moving parts. The batteries are new, and the tires are new and foam-filled, so we don't have to worry about either of them needing replacing. These things are really reliable... really."

Without access to money, the new plan is to get to the oil fields where they hope to find work to fund the rest of their journey. The quest to find Joshua will have to wait. These new obstacles only increase Liezel's doubt about the trip, but she **has** to stick with her husband. He's gotten them this far despite all the other roadblocks. Besides, it's too late to turn back now. Their only hope is to find work in the oil fields. She hops onto the passenger's seat behind Jason, and they head back to pick up the backpacks. On to North Dakota!

Fortunately, mild sunny weather is with them. It's a journey of almost 400 miles. Traveling ten hours per day, it should take three days, barring any problems. There's enough food to last, and then some. The problem is water. They filled-up their four bottles in the caboose, but between yesterday and today before they started the trip, they drank two already. Somehow, they'll need to beg, steal or take a chance on stream water.

Once they're on the other side of Winnipeg, traffic is thin. Other e-bikes and a few e-cars are on the road, so they're in good company. One e-car comes a little too close to them, blowing them sideways as it whizzes-by. Someone from the car lets out a wolf whistle. "I don't think that was for me, Honey," Jason jokes.

The larger hazards, however, are the A.I. trucks. They're big, fast, and noisy. Some of them tow as many as three trailers. They have proximity detectors that trigger the horns when they approach an object, but Jason still has to be quick to get to the side of the road in time.

Because they got a late start in the early afternoon yesterday, dusk forces them to look for a place to stop before they reach the border. The batteries are only half drawn down, but they will need them tomorrow until the sun hits the solar panels at a steep enough angle. Houses are sparsely spaced in this rural area, but they soon spot a small domed bungalow set back off the main road. There's a weathered-looking man with a full head of bright white hair sitting on the front porch in a rocking chair in front of a dimly lit window. He's smoking a pipe, and he has a shotgun laying across his lap. They decide to approach him.

"Howdy," Jason says, trying to set the man at ease by acting western-friendly.

The man tilts his head down to peer over a set of black thick-framed glasses, revealing a pair of white bushy eyebrows. He stops rocking, and he sits up in the chair. He puts his pipe down, and he slowly slides his hand over the trigger guard of the shotgun. "Evenin'," the man says in a soft gravelly voice. Jason tells him their story, especially the purpose of their travels. The man asks a few questions, and he appears to be satisfied that they pose no threat. His name is Frank. Initially stoic, he softens-up as the conversation progresses. "Word is that America's no place to be right now." Then his demeanor saddens. "My favorite nephew and his family somehow made it here from Ohio, but over the next two weeks they all died from radiation poisoning." He pauses to rub his eyes. "So if you insist on continuing, yer gonna need a lotta luck. Tell you what, I can't let you in, but you can pull 'round back and sleep on the rear porch if you want. I'll bring out some blankets, and you can fill yer bottles from the spigot out back. My wife just made a big pot a venison stew, so I'll bring you some after you're settled." Frank slowly struggles to get up. Then he shuffles to the front door. He opens it and yells, "Rose-Marie, we got company."

The travelers wake up just after dawn. Their hosts don't appear to be up yet, so They leave the folded-up the blankets on the porch and hit the road. Before doing so, Liezel grabs some pebbles from the driveway and arranges them to spell "thanks" on the porch floor. With a nourishing dinner inside them and a clear cool sky, the day goes pleasantly well. Thanks to an early start, they hit the border at noon. Strangely, the port of entry semi-fore lies broken on the ground, and there are no signs of any border agents. They pass-on through. Liezel pats Jason on the shoulder and says, "Welcome to America, Honey." They both smile. As they get farther inside America, they don't see any e-bikes, and not many e-cars. Heavy A.I. tanker trucks and semis rule the highway.

They pass field after field of decimated crops, stripped of all food value. All the towns appear to be vacant. Fortunately, Jason recalls the way to Williston from when his wrist comm was working, and the highway signs are ubiquitous enough to keep them on-track. They spend the night in an empty house outside one of the abandoned towns. Jason correctly thought that their chances of finding water were better in rural areas where solar powered wells are the norm, as opposed to cities where the electricity supply might be spotty. Although the lights in the house worked, Jason decided not to use them, fearing it might attract unwelcomed attention. He hid the e-bike out of sight. The following day passed like the day before. Their progress is slower than they predicted, because they needed to make more frequent stops to stretch their legs. Finding water was not a problem, and they still had enough food in their packs. However, they're running low on crackers.

The third day starts out much the same, but as they hit central North Dakota, they're stopped at a roadblock by armed men. The men tell the couple that they are militia who are there to protect crops and livestock from raiders. They're satisfied with Jason's explanation of their purpose, and they let the travelers through. Soon, they see healthy-looking crops and livestock--- all to support western North Dakota. As they reach the crest of a small rise in the highway, Jason stops the bike. They are awed by what they see--- thousands of drilling rigs cover the landscape like a forest. By one o'clock they begin encountering tents and mobile homes--- hundreds of them, maybe thousands. The pungent smell of oil fills the air. People and e-bikes are buzzing about. They hear music. Most of it offends their country music tastes. They sometimes have to slow down to avoid hitting A.I. trucks or other e-bikes. Supply trucks carrying pipes, pumps, and other equipment compete with the tankers for the road. Then they pass cluster after cluster of commercial buildings--- mostly bars, eateries, and stores of various sorts. The buildings are plain metal structures--- dust-covered with dirty windows. They were obviously hastily constructed, reflecting only the functional needs of a rapidly growing town. Several buildings have make-shift signs. There doesn't appear to be many women around, so Liezel understandably attracts quite a bit of attention. Finally, they enter the town of Williston at the heart of the Bakken Shale formation. They made it.

They pull beside a man on another e-bike and ask for directions to the oil company field offices. The man replies, "If yer lookin' fer a job, the Central Employment Office is right thar where that line o' men is." The man points a dark-stained finger to the next corner. Then he gives Liezel the once-over. Jason is starting to feel nervous with all the looks Liezel is getting. At the employment office, he parks their bike in a row of other e-bikes, and they get in line. An hour later they're forced to fill-out paper applications because comms aren't working. The other applicants have the same problem, and this causes a frustrating delay. When they finally talk to an interviewer, Jason happily discovers that his skill set is in great demand. Most applicants want jobs on the rigs or in the refinery, but there aren't many software engineers here.

Liezel is not quite so lucky. The only job available for her is for a part-time cleaning person, and there's a waiting list. The interviewer directs Jason to the Bakken Supply Co. where Jason hopes to be hired. Before Jason leaves, the interviewer asks him if he wants to register to vote in the special election. The Dakotas, Minnesota, Montana and Idaho are considering being annexed by Canada. Those states that approve the annexation will be provided with much needed central government structure, support, and a viable central monetary system. It sounds like a good idea, but Jason declines to register because he doesn't plan on being there on election day.

Buoyed with a new sense of hope, the pair exit the Office. As they approach their parking spot they freeze. Their e-bike is gone! Frantic, they ask the men in line, but no one noticed anything helpful. However, one man said he saw a man pedal an e-bike away instead of engaging the electric motor. Dejected, tired and angry, Jason and Liezel collapse on the front steps of the office. Jason sits with his elbows on his knees and buries his face in his hands. "Can't we ever catch a break?" Jason laments. "It's like a dark cloud that keeps following us at every turn. All these roadblocks can't be just coincidence." He pulls his hands away from his face and briefly looks up. "It can't be Mora. He's dead. Or is he? No, he **must** be dead--- he never showed-up again. Or is it Derofski?" He lowers his head into his hands again. "It's all my fault for dragging you into this. It's all my fault. I'm so sorry." Liezel is quiet. She looks up at the sky for help, trying to fight back tears. Then her head drops.

After a prolonged moment of silence, Liezel raises her head and looks at Jason's surrendered body. She takes a deep breath. "Look, Jas, yes we got screwed, but as long as we're still alive we can find a way. We'll just have to stay here longer than we planned. That's all. Then we can keep going. In the meantime, we focus on what's right in front of us. Now, let's see about that job."

Just when things are at rock bottom, a ray of hope appears at the Bakken Supply Company. The job interview goes very well, and Jason is hired on the spot. He starts tomorrow, and they'll give him a three-day advance on his pay in American dollars--- cash. At the Central Housing Office, they're disappointed to learn that the only housing available is a modular dormitory for Liezel. Jason is put on a waiting list for a men's dorm. Based on Jason's employment ticket, Liezel is accepted at the dorm, so at least she will enjoy a much-needed hot shower and a real bed. Jason, however, will have to report for work in the morning tired, stinky, and dirty.

After Liezel gets settled in her dorm, they find a police station to report the bike theft. The police don't offer much hope since most e-bikes are so similar and they change hands so often. As the day ends, they walk around, familiarizing themselves with their new community. Later, Liezel takes the blanket off her bed and spreads it under a tree outside her dorm. Since one of their backpacks was stored in the stolen bike, half of their food is gone. They share one of the two remaining cans of tuna and a couple of protein bars for dinner. A full moon pokes above the horizon in a cloudless sky. Despite all the negatives of the day, the pair concludes that they're in a better position now than they were the day before. Liezel gives Jason her blanket, and they kiss good night. Jason feels exposed under the tree, so he crawls under Liezel's modular dorm and wraps himself in the blanket.

Although Jason is worn-out, the bright moon keeps him awake. Then the noise starts. Without comm screens and other diversions, lonely men turn to gambling, drinking, and fighting. A couple of Liezel's dorm mates use their numerical advantage to make some extra money. The commotion settles down about 3 a.m., and Jason starts to drift off. Then the rain comes--- first a drizzle, then a downpour. Jason has unfortunately picked a low spot to bed-down. Soon his blanket is saturated with cold rainwater, and it seeps into his clothes. He rolls out of the blanket to a drier spot farther under the dorm. He begins shivering in the cool night air. There will be no sleep for him tonight.

Dawn doesn't come soon enough for Jason. Tired and wet, he rolls out from under the dorm and into the sunlight. He starts sneezing. After scraping the last of the peanut butter out of the jar, he throws the blanket over a tree limb to dry and he heads off to work.

His new boss is Jim Dennis. He's in his late sixties with receding white hair and a thin white mustache. He's been in the Bakken for twenty-five years. Starting as a transport coordinator, he eventually worked his way up to General Manager. When Jason shows up, Jim's jaw drops. "What in the world happened to you, Johnson? You look like you took a shower in a mud puddle. And you certainly don't look like the PhD engineer that I thought I was getting."

By now, Jason is sporting a one-week-old beard, and it's caked in mud. His clothes are muddy and wet, and he's sneezing. "Sorry, Mr. Dennis. I had to sleep outside last night, and I got caught in the rain. It was a terrible night. I didn't get any sleep, and I caught a cold. But I'm ready to start. Just point me in the right direction."

"Hold-on," Jim says. "I admire your dedication, but you can't work here looking like that. Tell you what, we've got a shower in the back, and I think there's a sweatshirt and jogging pants you can borrow. Go get cleaned-up, and I'll see you in a few minutes. Did you have anything to eat?"

"Not really, just some peanut butter--- but it was chunky style!" Jason manages a half-hearted smile. Jim smiles back.

Later, Jason emerges from the back looking like the world's most casual office dresser. A hot cup of coffee and a large corn bread muffin wait for him at his desk. The day goes well, and he's able to make an immediate contribution. At the end of the day, Jim gives

Jason three day's pay so he can get some clothes, food, and so he can pay for Liezel's dorm.

Since the Federal Reserve system was destroyed by the bombing, the monetary system in North Dakota is a hybrid of American paper money (that many people horded after the cashless wrist comm system was introduced), old coins, and Canadian money. Bartering is common. The oil, natural gas and gasoline from the region goes mainly to Canada in exchange for Canadian dollars, food, and consumables. Small amounts of fuel go to a few small towns in the U.S. that are still occupied.

After being paid, Jason picks Liezel up at her dorm and they head for one of the modest eateries in town. While they enjoy food that for once isn't peanut butter or tuna, Jason glances out of the window. "Liezel, is that man across the street who I think it is?"

Liezel jumps up from her seat. "It is! It's that guy Walter from the train. That lying bastard! He said he had to get off at Winnipeg. I'm going to get in his face and open up a can of woop-ass." She starts to step away, but Jason grabs her arm.

"Wait, Honey. Just let it go. There's nothing we can do about it now, and it might cause a scene. And I certainly don't want you to draw any more attention to yourself than you already have. Besides, there's something very dark about him. He and Mora may have known each other better than he let-on, so he may have some connections here that I'd rather not deal with. Anyway, jerks like him eventually get what they deserve. By the way, I have some good news--- my boss is letting me sleep in the office until a dorm spot opens-up. Jim's a great guy---very kind and trusting. We can also put our names on a waiting list for a couple's room. So it looks like things are going to work out here until we have enough money to get to California."

"That's fine for now, but how are we going to get to California?" Liezel asks.

"I don't know yet, Honey. E-bikes are pretty expensive here. We'll have to work here for quite a while to buy another one, or we'll have to figure-out another way."

The days became weeks. Liezel's ankle healed, and she finally got that part-time cleaning job. She also struck a deal with the dorm management company for cleaning the dorm in return for free rent. Between the two incomes, they're saving money as hoped. A couple's room became available, but they decided to pass on it, because if they took it, the higher rent would mean they wouldn't be able to save as much money for the rest of their journey. It was frustrating to be apart at night, but they managed a few romantic interludes in remote places now and then.

Life in Williston wasn't easy, and there wasn't a lot to do except work and drink. Women especially were on edge because they were greatly outnumbered by horny men. Early one morning, Liezel was just finishing her shower when she heard someone enter the shower room. A faint shadow drifted across the shower curtain. She called-out, "Sandy? Joyce?" but there was no response. The shadow disappeared. (Most of the other women in the dorm had already left for work, but two others were sleeping-in because they worked the night shift.) She assumed one of the women had briefly come in, but she was alarmed because she didn't get a reply. She pulled the curtain back to reach for her towel, but it wasn't there. Instead, it was lying on the floor. She cocked her head slightly to one side and frowned, wondering how it could have fallen from the hook. Now she was worried--- the horrifying attack by Ivan was still vivid in her memory. She picked the towel up, pressed it in front of her chest, and ran to the doorway of the shower room just in time to see the front door of the dorm slam shut. The slamming door woke the two sleeping women. As Liezel ran to the window, she heard a loud voice from outside cry, "Hey!" It was Jason. He was holding a cardboard tray, and he had a surprised look on his face. A small bag was on the ground along with two cups lying in a puddle of coffee. Jason's shirt and pants were wet. He was angrily looking at a man who had apparently tripped into Jason and had fallen.

"Jason!" Liezel yelled. "Stop him. He was snooping around in here. He scared the hell out of me!"

Jason tossed the tray aside and darted after the man who had just started to dash-off. Jason's football days came into play as he instinctively tackled the man hard. They crashed to the pavement, and Jason quickly put a full-Nelson on the man while hooking one of the man's legs with his. Fortunately, a cop was nearby, and he took the man into custody after Liezel explained what had happened. As the man looked back, Jason immediately recognized him. It was Walter--- grinning back at Jason. Walter then turned back to the cop, and they started chatting and laughing. Jason fumed, but realized he could do nothing more.

After a month and a half, Jason and Liesel had saved only 30% of the cost of a used e-bike, so they decided to find some other way to get to California. They put the word out that they're looking for a ride west. One of Jason's co-workers had a friend who knew a man who had a lucrative business of driving a tanker truck full of diesel fuel from the refinery in Williston to Port Orford, Oregon, so they contacted the man. He demanded $7,500 Canadian to take them. For an extra $1,500C he agreed to take them all the way to San Marita. Although it meant working another month to come up with the money, they took the deal.

The day of departure arrives. Jason can't thank Jim enough for his kindness and trust. Jim tries to persuade Jason to stay, warning him that some of these wildcat truck drivers are pretty rough. Then there's the unknown and potentially dangerous conditions waiting for them in California. Undeterred, Jason remains optimistic. With enough food in his backpack for 6 days, he says good-bye. He walks outside where Liezel is supposed to meet him, but she isn't there. He and Liezel need to meet the rig at the refinery at 7am sharp, and there's no time to waste. He nervously scans down the street toward Liezel's dorm. No sign of her. Now he panics. If they don't meet the rig on time, the driver said he's on a tight schedule so he'll have to leave without them. Jason can then kiss his deposit good-bye. It's not like Liezel to be late for anything, so Jason is also worried that something may have happened to her.

He turns up the street to see the rig at the refinery. It's exhaust billows into the air as the engine revs-up. Quickly, he turns back toward Liezel's dorm and races down the street. Bounding up the dorm steps, he throws the door open to see a crowd of women crouched on the floor of the dorm right in front of him. Someone is on the floor, and there are other women tending to her. Jason's heart stops for fear it's Liezel.

"Liezel!" he shouts, trying to catch his breath.

To his relief, Liezel pops her head up from the group. She's not the one on the floor. "Liez, are you okay?" Jason says.

"Jay, yes, I'm fine. Sandy, here, just collapsed, so I was giving her CPR. It looks like she's coming around now."

"I hate to sound uncaring, but we've got to get out of here NOW or we'll miss our ride!"

"Okay, okay. Just let her rest, then get her up when she feels like it," she says to the women.

Liezel grabs her backpack, and they charge up the street. Liezel starts to lag. "I'm going to run ahead," Jason says to her, and he takes-off. He's within 200 feet when the rig revs-up again and starts rolling. Jason screams and frantically waves his arms, but the rig keeps moving. As it picks-up speed, Jason sees he can't catch it, but he keeps running. Soon, he realizes his efforts are in vain, so he stops, completely out of breath. He drops his head in defeat. Then he turns to Liezel and waits for her. "Sorry, Liez," he says. "I can't catch it. We're screwed."-

"What do you mean? Why did you stop?" Liezel asks.

"Can't you see? He pulled away. He's gone."

"No he isn't. Look, he's just sitting there. Let's keep going!"

Jason spins around to see that the rig has indeed stopped. They start running again. They get closer and closer. Jason starts waving his hands again. Finally, they get to the door of the cab and almost collapse. Jason pounds on the door. After an agonizing couple of seconds, the door swings open to reveal an oaf of a man wearing a sheepish grin. "Johnson?" he asks. "I didn't think you was gonna make it. Lucky fer you this accident up here held me up. Hop on in."

The cab is dirty, dusty, and cramped. There's a long low crack in the windshield, partially hidden by a hula dancer bobble-head. There's also a picture of a hussy clipped to the visor above the driver's head. The driver's name is "Bark" Dorman, a former lumberjack. He weighs over 350 pounds, has scraggly shoulder length hair, and a foot-long beard with tobacco drool on it. His plaid shirt with torn-off sleeves exposes an ugly collection of tattoos of skeletons, swords, and more hussies. To make matters worse, he smells like he hasn't taken a shower in 4 days. His breath is equally rank--- a combination of tobacco and whiskey. Liezel's jaw drops as she takes-in this disgusting scene. She glares back at Jason with a *'This-is-the-best-you-can-do?'* look. Jason just shrugs his shoulders. What other choice do they have. Bark's grin turns to one of embarrassment as he quickly brushes his hand over the seats to sweep some food packaging onto the floor. Gritting her teeth, Liezel sweeps her hand over the seat, as well, to brush-off the remaining crumbs. As she does so, she realizes too late that she has run across a small smear of unidentifiable liquid. She looks at her open hand, wrinkles her nose, and sits down. Then Jason gets in, and they head out. A moment later, she affectionately puts her hand on Jason's knee and subtly wipes the liquid off. Not realizing what she just did, Jason glances at her and grins. She returns the grin.

Normally, Liezel would be more turned-off by the filthy cab, but the things she's been through over the last few months have somewhat desensitized her. Dorman, however, is another issue. Whenever they swerve or hit a bump, Dorman's sweaty arm brushes against Liezel, causing her to cringe. On those occasions, Bark just smiles at her, exposing the few yellow tobacco-stained teeth that he has left. On several occasions, his leg drifts over and touches Liezel's. She wishes Jason had taken more time to find a more pleasant way to make the trip. She wonders, *'How am I ever going to survive this trip with this disgusting oaf?'*

As they approach the edge of town, Jason looks out of the window and sees Walter sitting on an e-bike. Walter looks up at Jason with a sly smile as the truck goes by. The paint on the bike has been scratched-off where the name Nellybelle used to be. Jason gives Walter the one-finger salute.

The two passengers are excited for being on the last leg of a long difficult journey. At the same time, they're apprehensive about what they'll find, or won't find, when they get to San Marita. Liezel still has misgivings and wishes they would have stayed in Israel. But the point of no return was passed a long time ago in England, and she made the decision to be loyal to her husband regardless of the consequences.

No one says much for the first hour. Jason asks Dorman a few questions about himself and the nature of his business. He's been in Williston for ten years. He's never been married. (What a surprise.) He was a rigger at first, but he tired easily because he was too big for the job. When A.I. trucks took over the transportation of fuels, he rode in one until the transport companies gained confidence in them. Then on one trip to Oregon, he got wind of complaints that several fishermen in Port Orford weren't getting all the diesel they needed for their boats, so he bought an old pre-A.I. truck and started the business. It's been a gold mine for him. Liezel wonders where his money goes---certainly not for clothes or personal hygiene items.

They make good time the first day until they hit the mountains. Dorman pulls the rig over for a food and relief break and to tap some of the load to re-fill the truck's fuel tanks. Liezel pleads with Jason to switch places, which he does. As the truck climbs, the air gets colder. The afternoon wanes, so Dorman pulls off the highway to a small abandoned town for the night. After a backpack dinner, he warns the two passengers not to sleep in an abandoned house. The faint unpleasant odor they smell throughout the town is from decaying bodies in the homes. He withdraws to the cab bed, and he directs them to an empty hardware store. "Hold on," he says. He reaches into the sleeper cab and pulls-out two blankets. "Here, y'all might need these," he says. In their haste to get out of Williston, they overlooked their need for blankets. Before they could say "thanks" he retreats back into the cab and shuts the door. The two passengers are left outside looking at each other with mouths open, surprised and speechless. They see Dorman in a brand-new light.

The next day the rig makes it over the Continental Divide. Now it's downhill to the coast. After the early afternoon break, Dorman's breath smells of tobacco and whiskey, and he's more talkative. He pulls-out a bottle and asks Jason and Liezel if they want a swig. Liezel looks at the drool on the mouth of the bottle and gags a little. They politely decline. As his sipping continues, Dorman gets more boisterous and starts singing country western songs. Liezel recognizes one of them and starts singing along. Jason rolls his eyes. Dorman gets carried away going down the mountains. The rig speeds-up and it swerves onto the shoulder. He catches it just before it hits the guard rail. They're at the top of a 200-foot cliff. "Bark, slow down!" Jason screams.

"Whoa, that was a close 'un, heh, heh," Dorman nervously chuckles, trying to give the impression that he was in control the whole time. The incident seems to sober him up, and he puts the bottle away.

As the second day comes to an end they roll into another abandoned town and park at the local high school. Jason and Liezel decide to check-out the showers in the gym. They discover an open wall of shower heads and soap dispensers. Thanks to solar-powered pumps and water heaters, the showers are operational. There's even some liquid soap in the wall dispensers. They quickly tear-off their clothes like they're inundated with fleas. Jumping into the showers, they let the steamy water cascade down their heads and backs. A hot shower never felt so good. They turn to each other and smile, water cascading down their faces. They chuckle. Then without a word, Jason walks over to Liezel. They embrace and kiss under the warm waterfall. He lovingly runs his hands over Liezel's smooth soapy back. Passions rise.

Suddenly, the romantic moment is crushed by Dorman's obnoxious voice singing from the set of showers on the other side of the wall. Liezel instinctively ducks behind Jason. They quietly fumble around, not knowing what to do. They forgot about towels, and they don't want to put their clothes on over their wet bodies. Just then, Dorman waddles around the corner into view, his large belly draping over an overly used towel. He's wearing water-proof ear buds, and an old micro-player is dangling from his thick neck. Liesel lets out a scream, startling Dorman. She ducks behind Jason again as he covers himself with his hands. "Oh, sorry!" Dorman says, turning sideways and covering his eyes. "Sorry, I didn't know y'all was here," he apologizes. "I'll leave ya to whatever y'all was doin'." He slowly backs away and disappears around the corner. Jason and Liezel hurriedly rinse-off. With no towels around, they squat awkwardly under the air dryers, giggling.

On the morning of the third day, the truck is running, and the passenger door is open when Jason and Liezel emerge from the school. Bark is wearing a big Cheshire cat grin as they get in. Jason looks up and says, "So, what are **you** grinning at?"

Still smiling, Bark says, "Oh, nothin'. Jest wondrin' how yer night went."

Since Liezel knows that Bark showered last night, she volunteers to sit in the middle again, because it's more comfortable for Jason at shotgun. The two passengers are in good spirits--- they're only a day and a half from San Marita. As the rig gets closer to the coast, the scenery changes from snow-capped mountains and pine trees to glassy lakes, beautiful rivers, and vast stretches of green grass and dense forests. It's as if World War III never happened, except for the tents.

The lakes and rivers are lined with brightly colored tents along the shorelines, crammed together several rows deep like oversized gumdrops on a plate. Most appear abandoned, but an occasional smoking campfire indicates that some inhabitants are still alive. As the rig passes these areas, the smell of death drifts through the cab. Bark says that by now all the lakes and rivers have been fished-out, and soon none of these people will survive. He points to a bear that's dragging a dead body out of one of the tents.

As they reach the outskirts of Port Orford, they pass a few scattered tents. A pick-up truck is parked next to one of the tents, and two men are loading bodies into the bed. The town of Port Orford is idyllic--- spectacular cliffs, tree-lined streets, and a pristine beach. Its peak population was two thousand before the War, but half the residents left or died from inadequate medical care and starvation. The fishing industry has kept the town alive, but it may only be a matter of time before the radiation that's been draining into the ocean from Bremerton drifts down to Port Orford. Other coastal towns farther north have already been affected.

There are two small marinas here, and Dorman delivers the diesel to both. One of the marina managers tells him that they probably won't need more fuel until much later, because some of the boats have decided to work farther south, away from the advancing radioactive waters. Dorman says there's one motel in town, and the last time he was here it was still in business. It's not fancy, but it overlooks the ocean, and it might be the last chance for his two passengers to get a good night's sleep in a real bed with clean fresh sheets. To Jason and Liezel, it sounds too inviting to resist, and since they don't want to hit San Marita at night, they decide to take Bark's suggestion. As they pull away from the marina, Bark slides his hand over Liezel's knee. She instinctively jerks her leg away and scowls silently at him. "Oh, sorry, Sugar," Bark says. "I was goin' fer the gear shift." Jason was looking away at the time, but he turns when he hears Dorman's comment. He frowns quizzically at Liezel, but he doesn't say anything. Liezel frowns back at him with an I'm-not-sure-what-just-happened look and shrugs her shoulders.

The Ocean View Motel is indeed still in business. There's a small truck and an e-car parked in front of two of the rooms, indicating that there are lots of vacancies. Dorman parks the rig near the road, and the three check-in. Feeling rather jubilant that their journey is almost over, Jason treats Dorman to a hot appreciation dinner at the Ocean View Café next to the motel. Jason and Liezel have two of the coldest beers of their lives while Dorman has four. They all head back to the motel feeling quite mellow. Later that night, Jason and Liezel enjoy a romantic shower, picking-up where they left-off when Dorman interrupted them at the high school. It's the last shower they will get for quite a while.

The following morning Jason and Liezel walk out of their room into the bright sunlight. It's a cool morning, but the sun warms them up quickly. None of the three are hungry yet, and they're anxious to get on the road. For the two passengers, the end of a long tortuous journey is only five hours away. Dorman has paid his motel bill, and the truck is running. Jason gives Liezel his backpack, and he tells her to get into the truck while he settles-up in the office. Liezel is a little hesitant, remembering what happened yesterday, but she gives Dorman the benefit of the doubt about accidentally touching her knee. She crawls into the cab but leaves the door open.

Jason is watching the desk clerk count out his change when he hears an engine rev. He turns around in time to see the rig pulling out. He bolts out of the office, and races across the parking lot giving frantic chase to his kidnapped wife. All he sees is the rear of the tanker and an open door on the cab. Then Liezel's hand thrusts out, trying to grab the door. Jason hears her scream as her hand is yanked back into the cab.

Inside the cab, Dorman's sweaty arm is wrapped tightly around Liezel's neck in a choke hold. The back of her head is pressed awkwardly against his chest. She tugs at his arm, trying in vain to break free. He's just to big and strong. She blindly reaches up, clawing at Dorman's scraggly hair. When she's finally able to grab a handful of it, she yanks down as hard as she can. His head jerks down and he yells in pain, "Bitch!" Then he tightens his grip on her neck, and he pulls her chin up as high as it will go. "Leh go or I'll kill ya right here!" Liezel's eyes begin to blur. She can't breathe. She feels faint. Then she gets an idea--- she lets go and pretends to faint. In response, Dorman's grip relaxes a little. Seizing the opportunity, she quickly spins around and punches his nose with the heel of her hand as fast and hard as she can. Caught by surprise, his head bounces back, and he screams. Blood immediately starts running from his nose, and he involuntarily reaches for it. Now Liezel is free. She grabs the wheel with both hands and yanks it. The truck veers sharply to the right. It hits an abandoned car, jack-knifes, and crashes through the guardrail. The truck and the tanker tip over and slam onto the pavement. Glass flies everywhere. The truck skids to a stop, the front half of the cab hanging over the edge of a steep cliff. The tires continue to spin.

Moments before, Jason runs after the rig as fast as he can, but after sitting all day and night for the last few days, his legs are weak, and they soon give out. Running turns into out-of-breath jogging as he sees the tanker disappear around a bend in the road. He collapses to his knees and lets out an agonizing scream, "Liezel...Liezel!" He falls over onto the pavement, crying. He can't believe that after all this time and tribulation, and with only five hours away from their destination, she's gone. Then suddenly, the sound of a loud metal to metal collision shatters the quiet morning air. Immediately afterwards, there's another crash and the sound of scraping metal. Then there's another crash. He perks-up. Mustering the strength he thought had left him, he stumbles to his feet and starts jogging down the road again. As he rounds the curve, he first sees the tanker lying on its side across the entire road. Then the cab comes into view. It has broken through the railing on the side of a steep embankment. The front tires are dangling over the edge. The passenger door on the cab has been torn-off, and Liezel is running toward him.

Elated, Jason thrusts his arms toward her. Crying, she does likewise. They crash into each other and squeeze each other like they would die if they ever let go. Liezel rests her head on Jason's chest. Jason rests his head on her head. There's no need to speak. They just stand there, breathing heavily with their eyes shut. Then Jason looks up, and a chill envelops him. Dorman is limping toward them. Blood is running from his nose and dripping from his mustache. He's muttering something and pointing a weapon at the pair. Instinctively, Jason grabs Liezel's hand and with new-found strength in his legs they begin running in a zig-zag pattern back towards the motel. Bullets whiz-by and ping across the pavement. As they round the curve, Jason looks back. There's no sign of Dorman. They burst through the motel office door, stumble, and fall onto the floor. Totally out of breath, he manages the words, "Police...call...police!" to the shocked office clerk. He then rolls onto his back, arms stretched-out.

"Jason!" Liezel yells, "you're bleeding!"

Jason jerks his head up and starts frantically feeling around his torso. His hand quickly runs across a wet spot on his side. He glances at his glistening red hand, then turns his attention to his side. His white tee shirt has a small red stain. Liezel slowly pulls his shirt up to reveal a superficial laceration. "It doesn't look too bad, Honey. It's bleeding a bit, but it doesn't look too deep. I think I can just clean it and put a thick bandage on it, if they have something here."

"I guess one of Dorman's bullets hit me after all. I just didn't feel it."

When the police arrive, Jason and Liezel are sitting on a small couch in the motel office, sipping some water and trying to stop their hearts from pounding. Liezel has placed a bandage on Jason's wound. She tells the officers their story. As she finishes, another cop enters the office and reports that he couldn't find anyone at the scene of the crash. Jason and Liezel give each other a worried look. He's out there somewhere.

Their worries about Dorman quickly fade as they realize their plans have hit a brick wall once again. "Liez," Jason quietly says, "I can't believe this. We're stuck once again. The roadblocks we keep hitting have got to be more than just bad luck. I'm almost convinced that something or someone doesn't want us to get home. We're so close, but I don't know how we're going to get there now. Our money is gone. It's way too far to walk, and dangerous, too, especially with Dorman still out there." He falls back into the couch, tilts his head back and squeezes his eyes shut. As he takes a deep breath and sighs. There's nothing more to say, so they just sit there in dejected silence.

Then Liezel seizes the opportunity and says, "Jay, Honey, maybe we should reconsider going all the way to San Marita. Port Orford is a beautiful little town. We could stay here and put down some roots. We could find Joshua later and bring him back here to live."

"I wouldn't count on it, Mam," one of the officers says. "Almost everyone here depends on the fishing industry in one way or another. When the radioactive waters drift down here, this town will be a ghost town. Most people have already left. And did I hear you say you want to go to San Marita?"

"Yes, officer," Jason says. "That's our home, and we're trying to find my son."

"Well, I don't know where you came from, but you should have stayed there. Last I heard, San Marita is a food-starved war zone--- gangs of cannibals fighting each other. I hate to tell you this, but you need to be realistic. It would be a miracle if your son is still alive--- unless he joined one of the gangs, that is. And that would only be temporary. If I were you, I'd head to Canada. At least there's an active government there and a way to survive. That's where I'm going after this town shuts-down."

Thwarted once again, the travelers lean forward and bury their heads in her hands. As hard as they try not to, their eyes start watering. Suddenly, Jason stiffens. His eyes widen and a blank stare appears. Throughout their arduous journey and despite all the life-threatening obstacles that periodically discouraged him, he found ways to keep going. Now he realizes that hope of finding Joshua is truly gone. Worry turns to fear as he realizes that since they are without resources their own survival is now in doubt. As the officers leave, the door symbolically slams shut on Jason and Liezel's last hope. Then one of the officers unexpectedly returns. Curious, Jason and Liezel look up. "Listen," the officer says, "I still strongly advise against it, but if you really want to get to San Marita, I have an idea. There's a truck that delivers fresh fish to a couple of towns south of here. Maybe the dispatcher will let you hitch a ride. I'm not sure exactly where it goes or when it leaves, but you could check it out." With a glimmer of hope, they blot the corners of their watery eyes and thank the officer.

As the officer starts to leave again he turns back and says, "Do you have any weapons?"

Jason subtly shakes his head 'no'. The officer frowns, takes a deep breath, and continues on.

"Well, Honey," Jason says, "what do you think? Shall we at least check it out?"

"I suppose so, but I think Canada sounds like our best option."

"But you have to understand that after coming this far I can't just abandon Joshua. You do understand, right?"

"I know, Honey, I know, but I'm really scared. Fighting the elements is one thing, but being eaten by cannibals is not the way I want to go."

"Yeah, me either. Tell you what--- if we can't get home on this fish truck, then we'll head for Canada. I don't know how we'll get there either, but at least it sounds more promising, and we might be able to catch a ride with other people heading there. Okay?"

Reluctantly, Liezel nods her head and says, "Okay."

Walking down to the marina, they find an A.I. refrigerated truck being loaded with a fresh catch. They learn from the dispatcher that the truck will head south and make three stops, none of which is San Marita. He says he's heard that San Marita is almost abandoned and still very dangerous. He advises not going there. Anyway, company policy doesn't allow anyone to hitch a ride on the truck--- too much liability. Fresh doubts creep into Jason's and Liezel's minds, especially Liezel's. But to Jason, the desire to find Joshua trumps all discouragements. He tells the dispatcher his frustrating story, trying to persuade him to make an exception. Jason points out that the lawyers that formulated the no-ride policy are probably long gone anyway. This is a new world now, and everyone is struggling to survive by any means possible. The dispatcher's eyes start to reveal some sympathy. He looks at Liezel's doe eyes and finally relents.

The closest stop is still thirty miles from San Marita, but at one point the route will bring them within five miles of Liezel's father's old ranch. Jason tries to persuade the dispatcher to extend the trip to San Marita, but it can't deviate from the commitments that have already been made. The dispatcher explains that the truck is pre-programmed, and it will shut down if Jason takes control and deviates from the planned route. Although the truck can't deviate from its route, Jason guesses that he might be able to temporarily stop the truck, allowing them to get out. They decide to try to make it to the ranch first. A half-hour later they are on their way.

The truck passes the motel, and it then rounds the curve where the tanker crashed. Jason and Liezel peer nervously from side to side for any signs of Dorman. The truck slows down as it maneuvers around the tanker wreckage. No doubt that's where the tanker will remain. As the fish truck slowly accelerates after it passes the wreckage, it lurches slightly--- probably over some debris. Jason checks the rearview mirrors, but he sees nothing unusual. The duo trade sips from a cold birch beer, and they settle-in. Although there's no driving for him to do, Jason sits in the driver's seat, just checking the gauges and making sure the A.I. system is working properly. He stays alert in case he needs to intervene. He pumps the brakes to see what the truck's reaction is. No problems--- the truck slows down, and then resumes its speed when he releases the brakes. He thinks his plan will work. They're alone on the highway now, traveling along the coast. The ocean view is spectacular. Sunlight dances off the choppy waves like hundreds of small lights flickering in the water. Small rocky islands whitewashed with sea gull leavings rise through the endless water. The view is interrupted from time to time by an occasional green hill as the road meanders inland to avoid the steep cliffs. "Isn't this beautiful?" Liezel remarks.

Jason turns and gazes directly at her. "It sure is, Honey," he says softly. Flattered, she looks back and smiles. She leans back, closes her eyes, and takes a deep breath. For the first time on their long arduous trip, she's relaxed. Finally, the end of their journey is within reach. Not fully trusting the A.I. system yet, Jason keeps his eyes open. Suddenly, he catches movement in the rearview mirror. He blinks a few times and waits. Leaning forward and squinting into the mirror, he sees it again--- strands of long brown hair blowing in the wind. Then it disappears. Jason gasps. "Dorman!" he mumbles. "Liezel, wake up! It's Dorman!"

"What?" she says. "Dorman? Where?"

"I don't believe it. He's on the back bumper of the truck!" Jason replies. "He must have jumped-on when we went around the tanker."

"Oh, my God!" Liezel says in a panic. "Are you sure it's him?"

"I didn't see his face. All I could see is hair, but it sure looks like his."

"So, what'll we do?"

"I don't know. If I take the wheel and try to shake him off, the truck might think it's deviating from the route, and shut itself down. Maybe if I bring the truck to a full stop he'll step off and try to get into the cab. When he does, we'll just take-off and leave him… No, that won't work. He'll just hop back on."

"Maybe he'll get tired of holding on, and he'll just drop-off," Liezel suggests.

"Maybe," Jason replies. "As long as the doors are locked, and the truck keeps moving, I don't think he can do anything. Maybe he **will** get tired."

Twenty minutes go by. Then Jason gets an idea. "Hey, Honey, do you remember that big rig we pulled-out in front of back at the marina?"

"Yeah, what of it?"

"I'm going to slow our truck down so it can catch-up."

"So, what happens then?"

"You'll see."

Before long, the big rig pulls into view. Jason keeps pumping the brakes to bring it closer. It, too, is A.I. controlled without a driver. When they hit a stretch of long straight road, the rig moves across the dotted line to pass. Jason patiently waits. When the time is right, he jerks the wheel, swerving the truck into the rig's lane. "Hold-on, Honey!" Jason yells. He immediately slams on the brakes, causing the rig to crash into the rear of the truck. The impact throws Jason and Liezel back into their seats, their heads banging against the head rests. The air bags deploy with a sudden bang, sending white vapor into the cab. Both vehicles automatically come to a screeching halt. The truck's engine shuts-off. "Are you okay, Honey?" Jason asks, coughing and waving his hand in front of his face to try to dissipate the air bag vapor.

"Yeah, I'm fine. Did it work?"

"I don't know, yet. Let me check. Lock the door behind me."

Jason cautiously opens his door, and he slowly makes his way to the rear of the truck. By the time he reaches the rear corner his heart is pounding. He hesitates. Then he apprehensively peeks around the corner. Suddenly, a large hand thrusts-out and squeezes Jason's neck in a vice-like choke hold. He gags and grabs Dorman's hand, trying futilely to pull the hand loose. After a brief struggle, the hand grows limp and releases its grip. Dorman's upper body flops to the side, pinned between the back of the truck and the front of the big rig. Thick streams of blood run onto the pavement. With a sigh of relief, Jason returns to the truck cab. "Dorman won't be bothering us anymore," Jason quietly says to Liezel as he rubs his neck.

"Are you sure, Jay?"

"I'm sure, Honey."

Liezel sighs in relief. "So, what now?" she asks. "How can we get the truck going again?"

Jason thinks out loud. "Okay, the truck's off its route, so it shut down. Maybe if we get it back on route it will start-up again. Here, get behind the wheel. I'm going to push it. When I do, steer it back into the right lane." Jason has a tough time getting the truck moving, so he hops-up on top of Dorman's lifeless body. With his back against the rear of the truck, and with his feet against the big rig's grill, he slowly pushes the truck forward. Dorman's body suddenly slips down to the pavement, surprising Jason. He lands on Dorman's lifeless head. Then he rolls-off and continues pushing the truck with his hands. Suddenly, the big rig's engine fires-up, and it starts rolling towards Jason. Recognizing the danger, he races back into the truck's cab and helps Liezel turn the wheel. The big rig hits the truck, bumping it into the right lane. One more bump and the truck is clear. The big rig rumbles-by. The truck is back into position, but the engine is discouragingly silent. Jason hops-out and starts pushing the truck again. "Liezel," he yells, "is there a start button on the dash somewhere?"

"Yeah, I see it." Crossing her fingers and mumbling a quick prayer, she pushes it. The engine growls. It starts! Jason hops back into the truck and shouts, "San Marita, here we come!"

CHAPTER SIXTEEN--- HOME AT LAST

The rest of the trip is fortunately uneventful, but Jason wonders when the other shoe will drop. Surely, Dorman couldn't have been one of Mora's men--- he was too rough around the edges and isolated from Mora's influence. Or was he. But it doesn't matter anymore. His bloody corpse is no longer a threat. They soon cross the California border. While the truck is partially unloaded at the town of Yreka, Jason talks to a man about the situation there and in San Marita. Yreka has about thirty people left from a peak of eighty thousand. They're all thin and tired looking. The man has a nasty cough. The remaining residents are surviving on fish, potatoes, nuts and fruit trees. They'll put boxes of produce on the truck when it makes its return run in exchange for the fish they're taking now. Jason inquires about Joshua and Kathy. The man says no one came here recently, and he doesn't know a boy named Joshua. He hasn't heard anything about San Marita in a month, but the last news was that it had turned into a dangerous place with few people left. Jason's heart sinks as this news only confirms all the other reports about America and San Marita. As the hope of finding Joshua starts to fade, Jason laments his decision to leave Israel, putting the woman he loves in danger. But there's no going back now.

The truck resumes its journey. An hour later, they reach the targeted spot where Jason slows the truck to a near stop. When he releases the brakes, they quickly jump-off as the truck begins moving again. They walk briskly, encountering no one else on the road. What they do see is disillusioning--- crops stripped of all food value; rotting carcasses of butchered cattle. A gentle breeze blows the carcass stench into their path. Then there is the occasional human remains--- perhaps victims of fights for food. An hour and a half into their journey they reach Liezel's father's old ranch at the edge of San Marita.

They start down the long gravel driveway to the ranch house as the sun is setting. Liezel tugs on Jason's arm, stopping him. "Wait a minute, Honey," she says. "I just want to take-in this scene for a minute." Split rail fencing line both sides of the driveway. There's a tight row of tall eucalyptus trees in front of the fence on the left. The house and the hills behind it are in the sun's shadow. The last of the sun's light has created a spectacular bright orange ceiling on a thin blanket of clouds above the hills. With the exception of the weeds in and along the driveway, everything looks like Liezel fondly remembers it. As they move forward again, they notice a dim light peeking out through the curtains in one of the bedroom windows. They step onto the wooden-floored front porch and try the doorknob. It's locked. They peek through the lit bedroom window, but they can't see anything. Then they knock, softly at first, trying not to scare anyone inside. No response. They knock louder, then return to the front door and knock loudly, raising their voices at the same time. When they stop, the only thing they hear are a few crickets. Jason picks up a rock and smashes a glass pane in the door. Instantly, an alarm starts screeching. Startled, they jump back and wait. Seeing no response, he reaches in and unlocks the door. As the door opens, a foul smell almost knocks them over. Jason shuts the door immediately, and they remain on the porch. Afraid the alarm will attract unwanted attention, Liezel runs around to the side of the house and throws the main circuit breaker from the solar battery station. The alarm dies down and stops.

"I'm not going in there, Jay," Liezel emphatically states. "Let's try the stable." Jason agrees. On their way to the stable, they see the remains of a cow about fifty yards to the right. A group of cackling vultures are hopping around and inside it. The atmosphere in the stable is musty, but at least is doesn't smell like death. While there's still a little light left, they climb the stairs into the hay loft.

They spread some hay down for bedding, then lean against the surrounding bales. Jason reaches into his backpack for some apples and peanut butter. Their food supply is dwindling. They will need to find food soon. The evening turns cool, so they huddle together and fall asleep.

The sound of chirping birds wakes them up the next morning. Liezel starts down the stairs first, but her face runs into a large spider web that formed during the night. She screams and starts flailing away at her face and hair. Jason starts to chuckle, but, seeing how distressed she is, he quickly jumps to her aid. "Sorry, Liez," he says. "Here, step back. I'll go first."

The morning air is fresh and devoid of any smells of civilization. Two black vultures soar above the road at the end of the driveway. Liezel leads Jason around the stable toward a pond. As the pond comes into view, she thrusts her arm in front of Jason's chest and stops. "Look," she whispers. "It's a horse. Wait, I know him. It's Tanner!" Alarmed, the horse lifts his head from the pond where he was drinking. He starts to bolt away, but Liezel calls his name. He stops and cocks his head. She calls him again, and he trots over to her, whinnying and nodding his head up and down. Although he's dusty and muddy, he's a beautiful buckskin with a dark brown mane and tail. Liezel wraps her arms around his neck and presses her cheek against his. Then she begins stroking his face and neck. He's definitely glad to see her. When the reunion seems to run its course, Tanner pulls away and walks back into the stable. Jason and Liezel follow him to a large wooden bin. Tanner kicks at the bin. Liezel gets excited and runs over to it. She opens the lid to find a steel barrel with another lid on it. She lifts the lid and shouts to Jason, "Honey, it's oats!" She barely gets the words out when Tanner nudges her aside and dives into it, licking and crunching. Jason finds a bucket and runs over to the bin. He and Tanner fight for position, but Jason comes up with a full bucket. Liezel lets Tanner have his fill, but she shuts the bin before the horse hurts himself by over-eating. Jason gives Tanner one of his precious apples as he rubs the horse's neck.

Jason and Liezel decide to eat some of the oats before they head into town. The oats are crunchy but almost tasteless. They follow the oats with an apple. Jason leaves Liezel and Tanner in the stable, while he returns to the house. Holding his breath, Jason goes in. He comes out with two jars. They fill them with oats and put the jars in their backpacks. They fill their empty water bottles from a spigot on the side of the house and then head to town. They're not sure what they'll find when they get there, but at least they can come back to the stable if necessary.

San Marita is eerily quiet. They decide to go up a hill into the woods to scout out the town from a position of safety. Suddenly they hear the sound of rustling leaves ahead. A small deer darts-off deeper into the woods. Then almost immediately they hear the muffled "pop," from a laser rifle. The deer drops to the ground with a thud. When they hear the crunching sound of footsteps, they duck behind a large tree. A man shows up and bends over the deer. He nudges its head with the tip of his rifle to make sure it's dead. Liezel gasps and whispers to Jason, "Jay, I know that man. It's my friend Sue's husband Rob. Remember him?"

"Right, Rob Tyber," Jason whispers back. "Hey Rob!" Jason shouts. "Over here. It's Jason and Liezel Johnson." They step out from behind the tree. Rob pivots in their direction and points his rifle at them. When he recognizes them, he lowers it, and he smiles.

"Hey, you two," he whispers. "Liezel, I thought you were dead. Where have you been?"

"Israel mostly," Liezel replies. "We just got back yesterday." The three approach each other and they hug.

"Shh," Rob says quietly, "If anyone hears us, we could be in big trouble. I almost didn't recognize you with that beard."

"Yeah, there weren't a lot of opportunities to shave along the way," Jason replies.

Jason and Liezel tell Rob their amazing story. Then Rob describes the events in San Marita: after the bombing, everyone was scared. Looting and hoarding began almost immediately. Soon, most residents left town. Those with weapons took over and grabbed whatever they wanted, including women and girls. Police officers either joined the gangs or were killed. As the weeks dragged on, gun fights and murders increased in frequency as food resources dried-up. Lakes and ponds were fished-out. The wild game that was in the area either ran away or were killed. Liezel and Jason nod in affirmation when Rob describes the stripped crops, butchered farm animals and unburied human corpses. There was plenty of water from the solar wells, but water wasn't enough by itself. People started dying of starvation. Some cannibalism occurred. He and Sue were fortunate. Their house had an old hidden fall-out shelter left over from the nineteen fifties that they had stocked with several months of survival food. They kept a low profile for fear someone might figure out they had food and would try to take it by force. Over time, the town's ammunition ran out, so some of the game returned. Rob and Sue had plenty of food, so Rob was able to conserve his ammo. Wrist comms and money are useless because there's nothing to buy, and the banking system had collapsed. There aren't any communications, government services or fuel. No one has come into the town in a month. Rob isn't sure how many people are left, but they don't have contact with them. Jason asks about Joshua and Kathy, but Rob can't provide any information. The future is bleak, but Rob hopes that there won't be much competition for the returning game or for the remnants of crops and fruit trees. By trying to live more off the land, their storage food might last until the next crops volunteer. If that scenario doesn't come to pass, they don't know what they'll do. He'll save two rounds of ammo for themselves.

This discouraging picture confirms what the travelers have been hearing all along, only this time the news is from a first-hand source, and it crushes Jason. He now realizes that the chance of finding Joshua alive is almost nil. His lips quiver as he fights-back the tears. Liezel feels what he's going through, so she rubs his back to try to comfort him. "Have hope, Honey," she says. "We don't know anything about Joshua for sure. We haven't even started looking, yet. I'll help you look tomorrow."

Rob invites the pair to his house. Fortunately, the way to Rob's house allows them to stay mostly out of sight. On the way, they see the remains of two clothed bodies on the sidewalk being pecked at by squawking vultures.

Rob will wait until after dark to gut and butcher the deer. Then he'll bury the remains to hide the evidence. Thanks to the solar battery system, their freezer will keep the meat for a long time. They sneak into the house from the rear, leaving the unkept front yard looking like no one lives there. Liezel and Rob's wife Sue have a nice reunion, and Liezel tells her their story. They all enjoy a cold glass of water and are grateful they have someone they know to talk to.

Jason describes what they know and have seen on their journey here. The only hope he gives their hosts is that since several northern states will probably vote to be annexed by Canada, perhaps Oregon, Eastern Washington, and northern California might do the same. With any luck, law and order, governance, and the distribution of food and goods might return to the area.

Thinking again about the slim chance of finding Joshua, Jason breaks down and drops his head. "I'm sorry, Honey," he laments to Liezel. "I'm sorry things are so much worse than I thought they'd be. I should've listened to you. We should have stayed in Israel. I'm so sorry."

Liezel caresses Jason's neck, and kisses him on the head. "Come on, Honey. I'm not blaming you. Initially, you know I didn't want to, but I agreed to come, and I'd do it again just to be together. Josh may still be around somewhere, so let's not jump to conclusions just yet, okay?"

Jason nods his head in agreement. "Okay, Liez. Thanks for not saying "I told you so." You're the best."

Late the following morning, the hosts serve a simple breakfast of dried fruit and cereal with rehydrated powdered milk. Jason's plans for the day are to check Kathy's house, then they'll proceed to the condo. If they strike-out there, and there's still time, they'll try to get into Jason's office at the plant. Rob re-emphasizes the importance of staying out of sight as much as possible. With water bottles and dried apples in Jason's backpack, they head out.

They stick to the woods as much as possible. But when Kathy's street comes into view, they have to take a chance in the open. The street is deserted except for a few tumble weeds. The yards are overgrown, and there's a familiar pungent odor of rotting flesh in the air. They scoot along the easements behind the domed houses until they reach Kathy's rear door. It's locked. Jason peeks through the kitchen window, but there's no sign of anyone. The rear bedroom window curtains are shut, preventing any visibility into the interior. They cautiously sneak around to the front of the house. The screen door is hanging to the side from the bottom hinge, and the front door is ajar. As he goes in, Jason tells Liezel to crouch down around the side of the house. The acrid smell makes him cough, so he covers his mouth and nose with his shirt sleeve. There's nothing remarkable in the kitchen or the front bedroom except some trash on the floor. The door to Joshua's rear bedroom is half-open. Flies are buzzing around. Jason's heart is pounding as he fears the worst. He slowly pushes the door open. He coughs again. Lying on the bed is the caved-in remains of a very large man, smothered in flies. Jason bolts out of the house. When he's back on front the walkway, he bends over and heaves. Hands on his knees, he spits a couple of times and

261

wipes his lips. When Liezel rushes over, he turns to her and simply says, "He's not in there." He spits again.

Liezel puts her hand on the back of his neck, trying to comfort him. "Whew! she exclaims, holding her nose. "I can smell it from here. Dead body?"

"You don't want to know. It was the most disgusting thing I ever saw."

"Just rest a minute, Honey. Here's some water. Well, if Josh isn't in there, then it means he could still be alive somewhere else. Maybe he's at our condo. Are you okay to go now?"

Jason nods his head yes, but Liezel can tell by his tortured expression that he's more discouraged than ever. Kathy's house was the place where they had the best hope of finding Joshua. They duck back into the woods again. A half-hour later they reach a spot that overlooks the dead end of a street that leads straight to the town square and their condo. A piece of trash tumbles across the street in the breeze, and it joins others that are snagged in a bush. Fifteen years ago, the square was redeveloped to look like a town square from the 1940's. A gazebo sits in the middle of an overgrown beige lawn with pink and white oleanders and azaleas ringing its perimeter. A small group of pigeons survey the square from the top of the gazebo. Jacaranda trees and California oaks dot the square, providing shade for the many benches. A large ornate clock with a face of Roman numerals stands on a tall equally ornate post at one end of the square. Dead flowers and water-starved plantings surround its base. The three-story shops and offices on the outside of the square have exterior facades that reflect the 40's as well. Except for the ground floor windows that have all been broken-out, the scene is nostalgic.

Before they proceed, they decide to eat their apples and enjoy the peaceful view. Jason turns to Liezel and says, "Honey, doesn't it boggle your mind to think that just a few months ago, this was a wonderful little town right out of a child's story book? Now it's a scary ghost town, full of dangers and the stench of death. I have this horrible feeling that if America doesn't recover soon, it never will. Then it won't matter if we find Joshua or not."

The condo building is one of many that sit behind the buildings on the square. It's a high-end five-story structure whose units were priced to reflect the desirable views of the square and the mountains in the distance. Jason and Liezel are excited to finally lay eyes on their home, but at the same time they're sad to see the deteriorated condition of the area. Their eyes sweep apprehensively back and forth over the square for several minutes. Seeing no sign of trouble, they move cautiously down the tree-covered slope and onto the street below.

Trying to expose themselves as little as possible, they creep along next to the buildings on the shadowed side of the street. As they reach the perimeter street of the square, the pigeons suddenly fly away as if they were spooked by something. The pair freezes and crouches down at the corner of a building. Then they hear the faint whirr of an e-bike. The sound gets louder until it whizzes by right in front of them. A man they don't recognize is on it, and he doesn't see them. The bike is almost out of sight when it sharply veers and jumps the curb onto the lawn. From out of nowhere, two long-haired bearded men suddenly race toward the bike. The bike bogs-down in the tall grass and weeds, and the men catch-up to it. Jason and Liezel don't see any more of the confrontation, because they quickly back away out of sight. Then they scoot behind the building and run to the next block. Now they know for sure that there are others still in town---others that need to be avoided.

They circle around on other streets that eventually bring them to their condo building. The glass panels from the front doors lie shattered in the foyer. Jason pulls-out his knife, and he moves slowly forward. Liezel is right behind him, holding on to his belt. They decide not to try the elevator, thinking that its noise might draw attention to their presence. As they quietly creep up the stairs, they find a large pool of smeared blood on one of the landings along with bloody handprints on the walls and the railings. Bags and empty cans are strewn about. They briefly consider turning back but decide to press-on. When they reach their floor, Jason slowly opens the door to the hallway. He doesn't see or hear anything, so they quietly walk down the hallway. Liezel inadvertently lets the stairway door close noisily behind them. Shrugging their shoulders and grimacing at their mistake, they freeze. When there isn't any reaction to the slamming door, they proceed. They reach the door to their home and discover that the doorknob and backing plate are lying on the hallway floor. His knife poised for trouble, Jason slowly nudges the door open. Both he and Liezel gag and cover their mouths at the now-familiar odor of death. Jason walks briskly to the balcony door and slides it open. He and Liezel stick their heads out and gulp in the fresh air. Jason surveys the ground below, then tells Liezel to lie down on the balcony floor while he quickly checks-out the interior. On the way to the kitchen, he looks into the bedroom through the open door to see the rotting remains of a man and women embracing on the bed. The body of a small child lies between them. The cupboard doors are open. The shelves are bare. There's nothing edible in the refrigerator. Trash and containers cover the counter tops. Moldy debris sits in the sink where cockroaches scurry around when Jason approaches. Jason mumbles to himself, *"I guess when we're all gone, you guys will rule the earth, won't you?"* He sadly motions to Liezel to follow him out. There's nothing here for them.

After checking Kathy's brother's house and finding nothing, Jason loses all hope. He breaks-down and drops his head on Liezel's shoulder. "That's it. Things are so much worse than I thought they'd be. I'm done. I've got to face the fact that Joshua's gone. There's nothing for us here. Maybe we can make it back to North Dakota somehow."

"Maybe," Liezel says, "but we still have your office to check-out."

Jason runs his fingers across his eyes, trying to wipe the discouragement away. "Yeah, we can try, but he wouldn't have been able to get in there. It's too secure. Anyway, thanks for not saying 'I told you so.' And just for the record, I couldn't have kept going without you. You have this amazing inner strength, and you seem to know just what to say at the right time."

"It must be the cowgirl in me, I suppose," she replies. "But you have to know that you're my rock, as well. I guess we just make a good team."

Jason's plant and office aren't far, and they make it there without incident. The perimeter security system is still intact, so he thinks it should be safe inside. The pupil scanner recognizes him, and it grants access. The grounds are deserted. Hundreds of pieces of trash have stuck themselves to the security fence, and weeds pop out of the cracks in the pavement. Another eye scanner unlocks the door to Jason's building, and they go in. Expecting more of the repulsive smell of death, they're pleasantly surprised when there isn't any. When they open the door to Jason's office, they find everything is as he left it, although a little dustier. Figuring that any unsavory characters would not be able to enter the facility, and noting that there wasn't any evidence of forced entry, Jason decides to take a chance. He goes back into the hallway and yells, "Hello. Anyone here?" in each direction. Silence. He calls out again, only louder. After more disappointing silence, he says, "Come on, Honey. Let's check-out the cafeteria and the lab."

The cafeteria is dark and empty, and it smells of soapy water and garbage. There's a light on in the kitchen, so they go in. The only sound is the humming of the refrigerators and freezers. Dirty dishes soak in grey water in one of the sinks. Just in case, Jason opens a refrigerator door. "Honey," Jason says excitedly, "there's food in here! Quick, check the freezers."

"There's more in here!" Liezel says.

Jason checks one of the stoves. "It's still warm!" he says. "Someone's here."

Suddenly, a voice from behind startles them. "Stop right there!"

Jason and Liezel cautiously spin around to see a laser pistol pointed at them. "Don't shoot!" Jason says. "I'm Jason Johnson. I used to work here."

The man lowers his weapon and smiles. "Jason, it's me, Bill Lucot. You probably didn't recognize me with this stupid beard."

"Bill. Of course. Boy are we glad to see you!" They vigorously shake hands and hug. They're all beaming with excitement at discovering another friendly face.

"Liezel, Bill is our Lab Director. You remember my wife Liezel, don't you?"

"Of course. We only met once, but I remember you very well. How are you?"

"Well, a few pounds lighter and in need of a shower, but just fine thanks."

Jason brings Bill up to date on the situation in the world. Bill echoes Rob's thinking that they should have stayed in Israel or Europe, or even Canada. Jason looks at Liezel and says if they don't find Joshua, they should probably try to make it to one of the states that are being annexed by Canada, or even North Dakota. At least there he knows he can get a good job. Liezel agrees.

Then Bill shares his story. When all hell broke loose, he was taking a nap in his office. (He had just put in an all-nighter to meet a report deadline.) His door was shut, so he didn't hear everyone leaving. When he woke up, he saw the panic in the streets, and he checked his comm for the news. Since there wasn't anyone to go home to, and since his parents had both passed, he decided to secure all sensitive information at the facility in case of an invasion. During this time, he discovered that he was the only one left in the plant. By the time he finished his tasks, it was dark, and the looting and gunfire had started, so he just hunkered down. As the days passed, he concluded that the plant was the safest place to be, and there was plenty of food in the cafeteria. To make the food last, he transferred as much as possible from the refrigerators into the freezers. He concentrated on eating the earliest expiring foods first. When the comms went down, he felt blinded, but he had faith that state and local governments would restore the situation. However, as time went on, his patience deteriorated with each passing day. Then he just gave up hoping, and he went into a pure survival mode. Occasionally he would see one or two people roaming about beyond the fence. He didn't know if he could trust them, so he never revealed himself. To pass the time, he started working in the lab to restore communications with the outside world. He was unsuccessful.

"Hey," Jason breaks-in, "I just restored Israel's comm system. With your help, maybe we could do that here! Let's see what you've done so far."

"Wait a minute, Jay," Liezel says, "we haven't finished our main task--- to find Joshua, remember?"

"Of course I do. But I don't have any idea where to look next. Do you?"

She stops to think a minute. "Actually, I do. Come on. If we don't find Joshua there, then we'll head for Canada if you still want to."

Bill gives them a can of fruit and a half-full jar of peanut butter from the pantry. They refill their water bottles, and they leave. On their way out of town, they pass more abandoned buildings and homes, many with broken-out windows. They're about to turn a corner when they hear voices and squawking. Jason kneels-down and peeks around the corner. A man and a woman are bent over a small cage--- possibly a raccoon trap--- and there's a very upset vulture inside, frustratingly trying to flap its wings in a futile attempt to escape. Not knowing if the two trappers can be trusted, they take another route.

CHAPTER SEVENTEEN---THE FINAL CONFRONTATION

The tranquil existence at the New Judah is suddenly interrupted. Joshua and Sherri are walking down the hill with a bucket of tomatoes, soybeans and fresh berries when Sherri spots two people on the road below. She grabs Joshua by the arm and points. "Look, Josh, on the road--- two people, and they're stopping at the gate!" They immediately duck behind some bushes and nervously watch the intruders.

"Oh, no," says Josh "they're coming up here! Hurry, we've got to get back!" Trying not to be seen, they crouch down and scurry down the path to the cabin. Joshua grabs a couple of pitchforks, and they hustle inside the house. They warn Kathy, and she retreats to her bedroom, unable to face another conflict. Joshua and Sherri post themselves near the door, pitchforks ready. They wait. Before long they hear voices talking about the solar oven. The pitchforks are getting slippery under the youngsters' sweaty hands. A silhouette appears outside the front window. Josh and Sherri duck out of the intruder's line of sight.

Then there's a knock on the door. A man's voice says, "Hello. Is anyone there? We mean you no harm."

Wide-eyed, Joshua shouts back in disbelief, "Dad?"

Jason can barely contain himself. "Josh, is that you?"

Joshua drops the pitchfork. He nervously fumbles to unlock the door and yanks it open. Jason's bedraggled and unshaven appearance cause him pause for a brief moment, then he rushes to his Dad's arms. "Dad, it's really you! I knew you'd come back. I just knew it!"

"Thank God you're alive, Son. Thank God." He kisses Joshua on the head again and again. Everyone tears-up at the sight of the surprising happy reunion. Kathy comes out of her bedroom. Her heart skips a beat at the sight of her ex-husband.

All this time, Liezel is standing behind Jason, so no one sees her until she says, "Hey, remember me?"

"Liezel!" Josh shouts, "Oh my God, I thought you were dead!" Joshua wraps his arm around her as she joins the hug-fest. Sherri and Kathy join-in as well. After the excitement wanes a bit, the new arrivals enter the house. Jason and Joshua remain glued together, beaming with joy. Finally, they all sit down and tell their stories. It takes almost two hours because they keep peppering each other with questions. Jason is amazed and proud of what his son has accomplished. Liezel is likewise impressed. When the three residents of New Judah learn of the extent of the bombing and of all the supernatural events during the great battle, they are both amazed and at the same time disheartened at the state of things in America. All agree that it will take even more miracles to restore America or even bring hope for their long-term survival. Never having met Jason or Liezel before, Sherri remains silent. Kathy looks at Jason adoringly, but she also sadly realizes that with Liezel back in the picture, there is no chance for a reconciliation with him.

Then Joshua asks his dad how he knew the enclave was here. Liezel jumps-in, "Actually, I knew it was here. This was my home after I disappeared."

"Home! Weren't you kidnapped?" Josh asks.

"No, no, I came up here on my own. When your dad was away on business, a good friend of mine from work brought me up here to check things out. She wanted me to join this group of people who were trying to expose Antonin Mora. Mora knew about the group and wanted them silenced, so they hid up here. I don't know who

270

built this place originally, but it served our purpose. Anyway, one day while we were at work my friend was dragged away by Mora's goons and shot. I knew they would be coming for me next, so I ran up here to hide."

"But why didn't you tell Dad? Everyone thought you were dead."

"I had to act quickly. He was out-of-town, and I was afraid Mora's goons would monitor my wrist comm, so I left it at home, hoping that everyone would think I ran away. I didn't want to openly communicate with him, because that would put him in danger--- maybe even you and Kathy, too. I didn't want to leave a note either, fearing someone would find it before your dad got home. Of course, I didn't want him to worry, so I gave my friend Belinda a note to give him as she was moving out of town. I don't know what happened, but your dad never got the note. Unfortunately, I had no way of knowing that."

"Wait a minute," Josh says," I remember your friend. Mom and I ran into her on the way to your condo. I remember her giving an envelope to Mom to give to Dad. Was that your letter?"

All heads turn towards Kathy. Horrified and embarrassed at being discovered, she shouts, "Alright, alright, it was me. I'm sorry. I'm sorry." She jumps-up and runs into her room, slamming the door behind her. Everyone is stunned--- especially Jason. He shakes his head in disbelief.

Looking at Liezel, he says, "How could she let me be tortured like this all this time, wondering what happened to you? She's got to pay for this." Kathy stays in her room for the rest of the day.

The next morning, Jason emerges from the "rat" room while Liezel lies awake but with closed eyes, trying to get a little more rest. Joshua greets his dad, and after some brief morning chatter Joshua casually mentions the previous inhabitants of the "rat" room. Their conversation is interrupted by Liezel bounding out of the room, screaming. Jason and Joshua share a chuckle. "Don't

worry, Liezel," Josh says smiling. "They're long gone by now."
Liezel gives Joshua a playful slap on the head. During breakfast,
Jason describes his plan to get with Bill Lucot to try to re-establish
communications with the outside world. If they're successful, it
could facilitate the restoration and long-term survival of San
Marita.

Kathy stayed in her room until mid-afternoon. When she finally
emerged, no one spoke to her. They just glared. She fixed herself
supper and took it back to her room. Jason and Liezel used all
their strength to keep themselves from raking Kathy over the
coals.

For several days, Jason leaves for the plant in the morning and
returns at dusk. Then one day he comes home around noon,
dejection written on his face. "We've tried everything," he
announces, "but nothing has worked. I tried to do what we did in
Israel, but it's just not the same. Bill said he'll keep working, but
I'm done. I need to do my part around here anyway." He falls onto
a stuffed chair. Liezel kneels beside him and places a reassuring
hand on his forearm. Then she brings him a glass of water. A
somber silence falls over the room as everyone's hopes for a
foreseeable recovery are crushed. Kathy is especially
disheartened, because without communications, the day of
restoration will be delayed or not come at all, and she will feel
more and more like she doesn't belong here.

Joshua tries to lift everyone's spirits by pointing out how
fortunate they are to have shelter, water, and food. As he's giving
his pep talk, Sherri hears a faint buzzing sound at the window
behind her. When she turns around to see what's causing it, she
jumps off the sofa and screams. Dozens of flies have landed on
the lower part of the exterior windowsill. Within seconds
hundreds more arrive, nearly blocking the sunlight from coming-
through. Then they start to trickle into the cabin. Everyone backs
away from the window at the creepy sight. Sherri covers her

mouth and gasps. The flies attack her, getting snagged in her hair, and crawling over her cheeks and her tightly clenched eyes. They bombard her relentlessly. One goes up her nose. She screams and swats at it. Then two more land on her lower lip. She feels the irritating scratching of their prickly legs. She shakes her head, waving her hands frantically in front of her face. She spits the flies off her lips. Four more take their place. Unable to thwart the attack, she falls to the floor, clawing at her hair and face in vain. Joshua rushes down to help her fight off the pests.

As quickly and mysteriously as they came, the flies disappear. Then Joshua rises and looks out of the window and shouts, "Hey, Dad, look. There's a woman out there!" The rest of the group scramble to the window. The interloper looks scary. One half of her face is heavily scarred, like she's been in a fire. Her eye on that side is fused shut and drooping. Half her dull jet-black hair has been burned-off. She's wearing a soot-covered gray jump suit that's been burned-off at the shoulder. Her arm is fire-scarred. She just stands there, waiting. A dark cloud moves-in to block the sun.

Jason stares in disbelief, then he utters a name that send chills up his and Liezel's spines. "Derofski! How in the world did she find us?"

"Derofski?" Joshua asks. "Who's that?"

"She's the one person in the world you hope you'll never see. Everyone stay here. I'm going to see what she wants."

While Jason slowly walks out to meet the nemesis he thought was dead, Liezel explains to the other three that, although she personally never met Madam Derofski, Jason told her how dark and mysterious she was. She was Antonin Mora's assistant, but she seemed to really be the one in control. Along with Mora, she was buried when the Jerusalem Temple slid into a fiery crevasse at the end of the great battle for Israel. There was no way she could have survived. Jason personally confirmed her demise, or so he thought.

"Dr. Johnson," Derofski begins, "your determination and resourcefulness impress me. We tried to stop you several times, but you managed to survive. However, I am even more impressed with your son Joshua."

"What do you want, Derofski?" Jason says, anger welling up inside him. "And you leave my son out of this! Why aren't you dead, anyway?"

"Hah," she replies, "I'm resourceful as well. Over the centuries, men have tried to do me in, but I was immune to their attempts. I'm sure you're wondering if Antonin Mora is alive, too. He is not. He outlived his usefulness to me, but I still have my followers. We are reconstituting as we speak, and I will be joining them shortly. As to what I want--- I want your son."

"Well you can't have him," Jason fires back emphatically. He drops one foot behind the other and raises his clenched fists.

Derofski continues, "Unfortunately, you can't stop me. I think you know what I can do. If your family doesn't come out here, they'll all die."

Deep inside, Jason fears how powerful Derofski really is. Not wanting to take any chances, he motions the three inside to join him. "Now that's very wise, Dr. Johnson," Derofski says. "I want Joshua for sure, but I invite any of you to come with me, as well. I promise those who do will thrive. You'll never be hungry again. You'll have anything you want, and you'll be safe."

"Count me out," Jason fires back, grabbing Joshua with both hands, and protectively pulling him back. "I'll *never* go with you. You're not only evil. You're mad."

"Count me out, too," Liezel says as she grits her teeth and wraps her arm tightly around Jason's elbow.

"Same here," Josh chimes-in. "I'm staying with my dad."

"Count me out, too," Sherrie says as she grabs Joshua's arm. They all scowl, fearful but defiant.

Kathy emerges from her self-imposed isolation, but she stays in the background and doesn't say anything. Everyone turns towards her, waiting for her to reject Derofski.

"Mom?" Joshua says. "Mom, what are you waiting for? Tell her you're not going with her."

Instead, Kathy walks toward the threatening intruder and announces, "I'm tired of struggling. We're just kidding ourselves, here. America is dead, and it's never coming back. We're just marking time until we die. You all have someone, but there's nothing here for me. Madam Derofski, I'm coming with you. The rest of you are stupid if you don't join her, too."

Joshua screams, "No, Mom, don't do it! Please don't go!"

Derofski smiles as Kathy stands defiantly next to her. "Smart choice, Kathy. I knew you couldn't resist. By the way, you don't need to call me Madam. My first name is Eve. Joshua, come here and let me look at you." Frightened, Josh looks at his Dad, desperately hoping for protection. Feeling embarrassed and defeated, Jason nods to his son to cooperate. Disappointed at his father, Josh reluctantly steps forward. Derofski reaches under Josh's chin and tilts his head up. "I can see you want to be with your mother, don't you, Joshua? I also see you are on the fence spiritually. Good. You are young and moldable. Just what I need. You will give me many decades of service. You will join me and be the new Antonin Mora, but you can do so only by exercising your free will. So now I will give you that choice." With lightning speed, Derofski darts over to Sherri. She grabs her hair from behind and pulls her head back. At the same time, she puts a large knife to Sherri's throat. Glaring at Joshua with a fiendish smile she says, "Either join me or watch your girlfriend die!"

Joshua is in anguish. He looks at his dad for help. Then he looks at Sherri who is now sobbing uncontrollably. She can't find any words. She squints her eyes shut, waiting for the worst. Joshua looks back at his dad again. Jason's helpless expression says volumes. "Sorry, Son," he says, "It looks like this decision is yours and yours alone to make. I don't trust this evil woman one bit. Neither should you, but I understand how powerful love can be, especially at your age. Before you decide, I want you to know that I love you so much that we risked our lives to find you. But if you don't go, I believe her when she says we'll all die." Then Jason straightens-up and says, "Derofski…"

"That's *Madam* Derofski, Dr. Johnson."

"*Madam* Derofski, I will be ten times more useful to you than Joshua. Take me instead."

"Nooo!" Liezel and Joshua scream in unison. "You can't!" Liezel drops to her knees and clutches Jason's legs so tightly he almost falls over.

Derofski presses the knife into Sherri's throat, but she doesn't draw blood just yet. "Forget it. It has to be Joshua. So, what'll it be, Joshua? Don't you want to join your mother? I need an answer now… or else!"

Joshua drops to his knees and buries his head in his hands, sobbing. "That's not fair. I can't decide. I just can't!" He looks up at his father, begging for help. "Dad, do something. *Do* something… please!"

Jason is paralyzed. "Very well," Derofski says. Her grip on the knife tightens, and she pulls Sherri's head back farther. Suddenly from behind, Cat leaps into the scene and pounces on Derofski, driving her fangs deeply into the right side of Derofski's neck. Blood squirts out instantly as the jugular erupts. The lion's claws rip into Derofski's back and the arm that's holding the knife. The attack knocks Derofski and Sherri into Kathy. As they all hit the ground, the knife accidentally drives into Kathy's chest, piercing her heart. She briefly coughs, then she goes limp. Sherri rolls free and covers her head with her hands, still sobbing. Derofski squirms on the ground, trying to free herself from Cat's grip. As a pool of blood spreads out on the ground from Derofski's neck, her flailing gets weaker. Finally, the knife drops to the ground. With her terrified eyes frozen open, her body gives up.

"Mom!" Joshua cries. He drops beside her and buries his head in her neck, crying uncontrollably. Jason drops down on one knee and lays a sympathetic hand on his son's shoulder. His eyes tear-up. Sherri stumbles to her feet. As Cat rubs her bloody face against Sherri's pant leg, Sherri reaches down with a trembling hand and strokes Cat's neck. Still crying, Joshua pivots into his father's chest. Liezel and Sherri join-in. The sun breaks-through the dark cloud that once accompanied Derofski. The horrific ordeal is over.

Later, Joshua and Jason bury the bodies. Joshua puts a stick cross above Kathy's grave, and they all gather around. Liezel says a kind prayer over her. At the end of the prayer, Joshua kneels next to Kathy's grave and puts a hand on top of the dirt mound. He sobs and wipes his nose with his sleeve. Jason's eyes water, as well. Although he and Kathy were divorced, he loved her once and is saddened by her tragic death. He kneels beside Joshua and lays a gentle hand on his shoulder.

Derofski's grave goes unmarked--- just a mound of loose dirt. The four survivors start to head back into the cabin when they notice a small black snake slithering onto the top of Derofski's grave. They all back away quickly but relax when they realize the snake appears harmless. Then Joshua asks, "Dad, is Derofski going to stay dead?

"I don't know, Josh. I certainly hope so. But like I said before, I thought she died on two other occasions, yet she came back. You know, when she said her name was Eve, it jogged my memory.

When we met with her and Mora in Strasbourg, I noticed the name plate on her desk said 'Madam Eve L. Derofski'. Eve L.--- evil, get it?"

"You mean you think she was Satan? But she said she was immune to death."

"Yes, I heard her say that, too, Son. Maybe she was just a demon of some sort. I really don't know what to make of it."

Liezel speaks-up. "True, she said she was immune to attempts by men. Cat is not a man. So maybe she really is dead and won't come back. Let's hope so anyway. The good news for you, Jason, is that we now know that Mora is really dead."

"Yeah," Jason replies, "thank God for that. My only regret is that I didn't get to do him in myself."

"Jay, it's over. Please, please just get him out of your head. We've got a lot of more important things to focus on. Don't spoil your life--- our lives--- by letting him reach you from hell."

"You're right, of course, Honey. I'll try--- with your help." He gives Liezel a gentle one-arm hug and kisses her forehead.

The scene is interrupted by the distant noise of heavy engines down on the road. They peer through the trees to see men and equipment at the crevasse. "What are they doing, Dad?" Josh asks.

Jason hesitates, trying to figure it out. "I'm not sure. Wait--- it looks like they're going to build a bridge over the crevasse. That means vehicles will be coming here from the outside--- maybe food and supplies!" Just then, they hear a long-forgotten musical tone coming from Jason's wrist comm. Puzzled, he lifts his hand and taps the screen.

"Jason? It's Bill. Are you there?"

Full of excitement, Jason exclaims, "Hey everyone. It's Bill from the lab. He's got the comm system working! Bill, congratulations. I thought we reached a dead end. How'd you do it?"

"I have no idea. I didn't do anything. I was just putting some of the equipment away when I saw my comm light-up, so I gave you a call. And another thing--- the big screen is working, too. I'm getting a broadcast from Canada. There's an Israeli General announcing that a peace agreement has been signed between the Muslims and Israel, and that all jihadist groups have disbanded. The split screen shows Israeli soldiers and Arabs shaking hands, smiling and hugging. I never thought I'd see the day!"

"I don't believe it! Hey, Bill, what's the speakers name?"

"I don't know, but they just referred to him as the Lion of Judah."

"It's Dayan! Of course, who else would it be? Funny, we have our own lion of Judah here, too--- New Judah, that is, and she just saved our lives. More good news, Bill, a construction crew is building a bridge over the crevasse here. Hopefully, that means trucks could be coming with food and supplies! What a turn of events, huh?"

"Amazing," Bill replies. "I don't know what's happening here, but for the first time since the bombing I'm actually hopeful. We should all say our prayers tonight, for sure."

Jason, Liezel, Joshua and Sherri walk to the top of the hill to get a better view of the construction at the crevasse. Jason and Liezel put their arms around each other. The two youngsters stand in front of them, holding hands. Cat follows and sits down at Sherri's side, licking her paws and rubbing the red stains off her face. Jason reflects on all the events of the last few months--- his near-death experiences, finding Liezel, the miracles in the battle for Israel, the huge obstacles on their trip here, finding Joshua when it appeared hopeless, and now world peace seems to be finally at hand. What a turn of events. There have been so many miraculous interventions in the last few months, he wonders if a divine hand was involved. He also wonders if Dayan is indeed the 12th Imam, or is he someone else. And are the God of Israel and Allah one in the same? Could the answers be in the unopened envelope that Dayan left for Jason--- the envelope that was left behind on the oil tanker in the Mediterranean? He may never know. He puts his other arm around Joshua and pulls him to his side. Jason looks up to the sky and sighs. "You know," he says, "by all rights none of us should be here now. Yet here we are. I kept wondering why that is. Too much has happened to believe it's luck or coincidence, or even our own abilities. So I've come to believe that it's our amazing God that has smiled on us and pulled us through."

"I think your right, Jay," Liezel says. "Certainly we've done nothing to deserve it."

"I think you're right, too, Dad," Joshua adds.

"I *know* you're right," Sherri pipes-in. "We could've died here, too, you know, but we found this place and all the food that was just waiting for us. And now it looks like the outside world is reaching out to us. How can this be anything but God's grace." They all smile and gently nod.

Soon, a tractor-trailer pulls-up behind the construction team. It has a large red maple leaf emblem on the side. On the opposite side of the crevasse, a small group of disheveled-looking people from San Marita gather to watch the construction. Among the group of observers are two elderly men with long gray beards. Suddenly, Joshua points down to the road. "Look, Dad, I think those two men down there are waving at us."

Jason and Liezel look down and do double-takes, straining to bring the men into better focus. Then they look at each other. "Jay, is that who I think it is?"

"Could be, Honey. At this point it wouldn't surprise me." Smiling, they wave back.

A gentle breeze parts the clouds, allowing the sun's rays to beam down on the town. While the residents of New Judah contemplate the uplifting scene on the road below, unbeknownst to them something strange is happening at the gravesite. A smoky reddish vapor starts rising from Derofski's dirt mound, causing the snake to scurry away into the brush. As the vapor continues to rise, the mound of dirt slowly collapses, leaving a cavity where Derofski was buried. The vapor starts spinning, forming a six-foot long red dust devil. It slowly rises above the grave and hovers there. A chill comes over Jason as he senses the presence behind him. Wondering what could be causing this eerie feeling, he slowly turns around. The supernatural sight startles him. Then the apparition suddenly darts away into the clouds.

THE END

ABOUT THE AUTHOR

John Berry is a retired former Vice President of a national engineering and construction company. He holds a Bachelor's degree in Mechanical Engineering from Case-Western Reserve University where he excelled in football and track. He was even a free agent with the New York Giants. Mr. Berry also holds an MBA from California Lutheran University. This book was inspired by a discussion he and his daughter Kathy had about the end times and the battle of Armageddon. He is a new writer, so just for fun he named most of the characters after family and friends. He lives with his wife Marita on a tributary to the Chesapeake Bay in Maryland. His activities include Christian counseling, community volunteering, gardening, boating, weight-lifting, and (along with Marita) watching his active three year old granddaughter Harper during the day.

THANK YOU

Thank you for reading my book. I enjoyed writing it, and I hope you enjoyed reading it. If you did, please do me a favor and find my book on Amazon books and write a review. The feedback will help me be a better writer, and the review will help increase the book's visibility in the crowded ebook space.

Thanks again,

John Berry